THE DYING OF THE LIGHT: BOOK ONE

JASON KRISTOPHER

grey gecko press

Text ©2011 Jason Kristopher
Design ©2025 by Grey Gecko Press

Published by Grey Gecko Press (http://www.greygeckopress.com)

Published in the United States of America.
Printed in the USA, the United Kingdom, and Australia.

Library of Congress Cataloging-in-Publication Data

The dying of the light: end / Jason Kristopher
Library of Congress Control Number   2011940749
ISBN   9781945760396

Third Edition

*To my family and friends
who always believed*

*And most especially
to my nonnie Margie
who was always my biggest fan*

Characters of Note

MILITARY PERSONNEL

Col. George Maxwell, AEGIS CO   Army Ranger
Cmdr. Frank Anderson, AEGIS XO   Navy SEAL

First Team

ALPHA SQUAD

Maj. Kimberly Barnes, CO   Army Special Forces
David Blake, XO
Gunnery Sgt. Dalton Gaines   US Marine Corps MSOR
Cpt. Tom Reynolds   USAF 1st Spec Ops Wing
Sgt. Rachel Eaton   Special Forces
Cpt. Angelo Martinez   Ranger

BRAVO SQUAD

Lt. Jake Powell   SEAL
P. Off. 2nd Class Edward Ames   SEAL
Sgt. Desmond Jones   Ranger
Sgt. Victor Roberts   USMC MSOR
Sgt. Arkady Ivanovich   Special Forces

Second Team

CHARLIE SQUAD

Maj. Shawn Carver, CO   Special Forces
Cpt. Lawrence Greer, XO   Special Forces
Lt. Manuel Ramos   USAF 1st Spec Ops Wing

DELTA SQUAD

Cpt. Janet Turner   USAF 1st Spec Ops Wing

Characters of Note

Third Team

ECHO SQUAD

Maj. Terrance James, CO   USMC MSOR

FOXTROT SQUAD

Corps. 1st Cl. Lucia Santos, XO   USN

Fourth Team

GOLF SQUAD

Lt. Malcolm Dagger, CO   USMC MSOR

HOTEL SQUAD

Sgt. Gordon Tremaine, XO   Ranger

Eighth Team

MIKE SQUAD

Lt. Adrian Masters, CO   SEAL

NON-MILITARY PERSONNEL

Dr. Mary Adamsdóttir   Head of Research, AEGIS
Rebecca Campbell   fiancée of David Blake
Eric Campbell   adopted son of David Blake
Morena Forrest   survivor of Laramie, WY
Michael Forrest   survivor of Laramie, WY
Henry Gardner   AEGIS Government Liaison
Harry Stafford   survivor, Wash. Territory

Acronyms

AEGIS	Advanced Experimental Genetics Intelligence Service
ACU	Army Combat Uniform, standard US Army uniform
CDC	Centers for Disease Control and Prevention
CO	Commanding officer of a unit or group
DARPA	Defense Advanced Research Projects Agency
ICV	Infantry Combat Vehicle
IED	Improvised Explosive Device
OSS	Office of Strategic Services (precursor to CIA)
REAPR	Real-time Enemy Assessors and Physiology Readers
USAMRIID	United States Army Medical Research Institute for Infectious Diseases
XO	Executive officer, second in command of a unit/group

prion (noun): a protein particle that is believed to be the cause of brain diseases such as BSE, scrapie, and Creutzfeldt-Jakob disease. Prions are not visible microscopically, contain no nucleic acid, and are highly resistant to destruction.

— *Oxford English Dictionary*

... much more science is needed. There are many things we don't understand, and the whole science of how prions propagate and cross species barriers is developing as we speak.

— Dr. Neil Cashman, University of Toronto's Center for Research in Neurodegenerative Diseases

We were amazed at how efficiently they spread.

— Adriano Aguzzi, of the Swiss Federal Institute of Technology in Zurich

The bottom line is, if we don't tightly control these diseases, we're going to regret it big time.

—Dr. Pierluigi Gambetti, director of the National Prion Disease Pathology Surveillance Center

PROLOGUE

FALL CREEK, COLORADO
1 YEAR AGO

I DIDN'T SEE REBECCA DIE the second time.

Or the first, for that matter.

I knew that I didn't want to be out on the street right now. Not this close to nightfall. *Night is* their *time.* I realized I was whispering to myself. If I kept this up, I was going to go as bat-shit crazy as old man Feldon had been even before it all hit the fan.

He only ended up ranting and raving in the street, not eating people. He got off easy.

The waning Colorado sunlight fell across the street below me, and I could see more than a few of the bastards milling around, looking for a meal. I hid behind the roof sign for the small grocery store, my rifle across my back and my pistol in hand.

As I looked across the street, I could see my goal: Monty's Sports & Outdoors. Ten rounds in the pistol and a few in the rifle wasn't going to do it. I needed some more ammo if I was going to survive getting out of here. Unfortunately, there were about thirty walking death machines separating me from my next step on the road to Splitsville.

I sighed and checked my pistol's magazine once more, shifting the weight of the rifle. *Maybe if I move down the street I can find a quieter place to cross over.*

Suddenly, my eye caught on one of them wearing a sundress and standing apart from the others. Despite the rips and tears in the dress, I could see the pattern of flowers and pale yellow fabric.

My vision tracked upwards, catching other details, like the silver watch and the simple necklace, framed by the long blonde hair, the bite and claw marks evident on her shoulder and upper arm. I knew what I would see as I raised my gaze to the thing's face, and as much as I hoped I was wrong in those few seconds, I wasn't.

It was Rebecca, my fiancée.

It had taken me most of two days. I'd grabbed the only guns I had in the house and went out looking. When she wasn't waiting at the house like I'd asked, I'd headed back there each night when my search yielded nothing. I couldn't leave without knowing—not guessing, but knowing for certain—that she was either dead or . . . something else.

A part of me hadn't wanted to find her, had hoped that she was still beautiful, still laughing, still so vibrantly alive somewhere . . . else. But now, that hope was gone. I'd found her.

Or rather, what was left of her. Though her face was slack-jawed and vacant, the beauty was still there and I had to look away. Dammit, why hadn't she listened? I hadn't found Eric anywhere, but now it was too much to hope that her young son had made it out of the house alive.

I'll admit I sort of lost it then. I fell back to the roof and cried. I don't know how long it was before I pulled myself together, but it was a while.

It's time. Shit or get off the pot, Dave. Fish or cut bait.

I looked back over the edge of the roof, and sure enough, all of them were still there. Glancing to the side, I measured the distance to the next roof, and knew that I could make it.

I holstered the pistol and drew the rifle off my shoulder, sighting on what used to be my fiancée and taking a deep breath. I offered a silent prayer, and then, as I squeezed the trigger, I closed my eyes.

It was the only thing I could do for her now.

CHAPTER ONE

WASHINGTON TERRITORY, 1872

IT'S LATE IN THE YEAR, and the cold seeps into the very bones of the soldiers who have been sent to this backwater of the country, searching for a tribe of Indians said to be massacring—and sometimes *eating*—settlers, hunters and miners.

Newspapers back home call these reports about savage cannibals and murderous creatures " . . .nothing but the deranged ravings of madmen and fools." Unfortunately, the uproar causes President Grant to order the Army to investigate. The Army assigns Captain William Trace of Kentucky to "find out just what the hell's going on up there," in the words of the president himself.

Captain Trace uses local scouts and hunters to find the camps and mining outposts that have been attacked, but rather than evidence of Indians, he discovers only nightmares. Buildings burnt and collapsed, torn down from the outside. Broken and bloody remnants of the camps are strewn about like so much garbage, many of them with teeth marks in the skeletons. *Human* teeth marks, his medics tell him.

The detachment comes upon a site with some buildings still smoldering in the chill of the early morning. They find fresher bodies, only hours old, and several soldiers vomit, overwhelmed by the carnage. As a small squad investigates an out-building, they are attacked and wounded by "a creature from the depths of hell."

The soldiers' combined fire manages to destroy the thing, but it's only after the smoke clears that they realize that it is, or at some point *was*, a human being. The medic moves among the soldiers, treating the bites and other wounds. He assures them that they will heal and prescribes each a healthy dose of whiskey from his stores . . . for the shakes, of course. The rest of the detachment clears the town, burning what little remains and setting up camp while their captain and his advisers determine their next destination.

Several hours later, during a check on his men, Captain Trace realizes something more is going on and summons the company medic. The wounded men are violently ill, shaking, trembling, turning pale and lapsing into an unconsciousness from which he cannot awaken them.

Captain Trace immediately orders a wagon to transport the wounded soldiers to the closest Army base, Fort Vancouver. He provides the wounded soldiers and their drivers with water, rations and extra horses from the detachment's stores, knowing it will take three days to get there. He orders the drivers to take alternate shifts and to rotate out the tired horses as needed.

Captain Trace and his men are en route to the final site, with Fort Vancouver a day's ride to the southwest, when a forward scout rides back and informs his sergeant of something he's found. Trace and his trusted sergeant investigate, fearing the worst. Their fears are confirmed when they discover a wagon almost painted in blood and snapped harness—and no men or horses.

After conferring with his medic, Trace realizes this is not the simple mission he thought. Something darker is at work here. He orders his men to search the surrounding areas in groups no smaller than five soldiers, and any wounded men are to be captured, if possible, or shot until dead if they pose a threat.

A day later, several squadleaders report sighting and destroying creatures similar to the one that attacked them the week before—but these are wearing the tattered remains of US Army uniforms. In order to maintain discipline, Captain Trace informs the men that the wounded soldiers are sick and pose a serious health risk.

As they have no advanced medical facilities nearby, he orders them to shoot any such soldiers on sight. Though rattled, his men follow him to the last attack site.

There, they find a small boy of no more than twelve, frightened and filthy, hiding in the basement of the saloon. Although unmarked with bites or other wounds, he acts crazy, as though his mind is gone. Trace and his men complete the destruction and burning of the town, and they take the boy back to Fort Vancouver with them.

Once he calms down, Captain Trace finds a suitable home for the youngster with a local woman who has lost her family to Indians. Captain Trace knows that he will be in good hands, and thinks no more on it.

Rumors fly for months at what caused the Army to burn village after village, and those brave enough to venture out find only blackened remains, with no clues to the story.

Early the next year, President Grant orders the Department of the Army to create a special investigative unit to investigate incidents such as the Washington Territory attacks. Unit 73 responds to only nine outbreaks nationwide over the next thirty years, all involving minimal casualties.

Most of these incidents are in northern states, and Unit 73's scientists theorize that while some infections are neutralized completely, there are other specimens still out there, frozen in high mountain passes or even stuck in box canyons.

The researchers inform their commanders that it is very likely more incursions will happen, but there's no way to tell when or where.

As expected, this does not fill their commanders or the president with joy.

Work continues as medical science improves, with the men and women of Unit 73 trying to discover the source of and cure for the contagion that causes people to turn on their fellows. Unfortunately, the lack of incidents leaves few samples to work with, so progress is slow and halting.

In some of those few outbreaks, survivors are found, but inevitably turn due to having been bitten, except in one unique case.

WASHINGTON TERRITORY, 1931

Harry Stafford is a resident of a small hunting camp in northern Washington, and has been described by those who know him as a reclusive, ornery old goat that would shoot you soon as look at you. Though they don't much care for him, the others in the camp tolerate his rantings, as he is the best hunter and trapper among them.

Stafford often rambles about having been attacked by crazies and cannibals when young, only just escaping with his life when the Army rescued him. No one believes him, putting his ravings down to that of an old man suffering from senility. But when he comes stumbling into town from the hunting camp, crazy-eyed and covered in blood that isn't his, gibbering about monsters . . . well, things start to change.

The townsfolk figure ol' Harry Stafford's finally lost it completely and done someone in. They lock him away, and the sheriff and his two deputies head out to the camp to check on everyone else.

There, they find that the main hunting lodge has burned nearly to the ground, and is still smoking, with the remnants of thirteen charred bodies inside.

Nearby, they find a bloody trenching tool. The sherriff charges Stafford with the murders of the residents of the camp, and the bloody trenching tool is entered into evidence.

Before the trial of Stafford begins, the old man and all the evidence related to his alleged crime are taken into custody by men identified on paper only as federal agents Johnson and Smith. It turns out they work for Unit 73 and return with Harry, the trenching tool, and the remains of the dead to their base at Fort Lewis.

The agents question Stafford and gradually piece together his story. A walker—named after the lieutenant who helped discover them—had come out of the dense forest and attacked and bitten one of the hunters from the camp while he was checking his traps.

During the fight with the walker, the hunter accidentally decapitated it and made his escape, but he was mortally wounded. He barely made it back to the camp to tell Stafford what had happened.

Stafford tried to dispose of the hunter's body after he expired. After all, sixty years before, he'd hidden in a saloon's basement as the only people he had ever known were killed and eaten. He knew what was going to happen.

But while he was trying to burn the body, he was caught and tied up by the other hunters, and then, by the time he'd managed to work himself free again, it was too late: the rest of the hunters had been infected.

He stalked them one by one, taking them down with his well-honed stealth and speed. When only two were left, he dragged the rest of the bodies into the main hunting lodge as bait. It worked. They followed him, then he ran around and chained the door shut with them still inside, setting fire to the building.

Throughout his interrogation, Stafford claims that he hasn't killed anyone but the monsters that would have killed him. Intensive analysis is conducted by Unit 73 personnel, who determine that there is evidence of human teeth marks on each of the thirteen bodies as well as other indicators of walker activity.

This evidence lends support to Stafford's claim of mass walker infection. Years later, analysis of samples from the blood remaining on the trenching tool would test positive for the "zombie" prion, further exonerating the old man.

The agents eventually realize that the walker that had attacked the camp must have been some unfortunate soul who was either a remnant of the original Washington Territory attacks, or someone attacked by one of the wounded soldiers nearly sixty years before.

It is later determined that the only way this could have happened would have been if the walker had been trapped in one of the blizzards and frozen, only to have thawed out and been just as deadly decades later.

The agents give Harry a nice, quiet place to live in the country, far from anyone else and with every conceivable need provided. They check up on him just over a month after his release and find that he has hanged himself.

His suicide note is short and to the point: "I can't live with this anymore. I can still hear the screams."

POLAND, 1942
BELZEC EXTERMINATION CAMP

Unit 73 is made a part of the Office of Strategic Services when it is determined that walker attacks have been occurring not only on US soil, but also overseas, with reports coming in from posts and Army units throughout World War One and the early days of World War Two.

Agents from Unit 73 drop behind enemy lines in southeastern Poland to investigate rumors that Joseph Mengele has begun experimentation with walkers. The agents investigate a subsidiary camp near Belzec and discover the truth is even more horrifying than they were expecting.

Not only are the Nazis engaged in research on walkers, they are also *manufacturing* them, and at a rate that is staggering to behold. Unit 73 confirms that the SS *Oberführer* in command of the camp is attempting to create some sort of biological weapon to be dropped on targets from the air.

During their infiltration, the agents count more than five thousand active walkers in pens at the smaller camp, and discover the source of the new ones: the Jewish, Romani and Polish prisoners from the main Belzec camp. Even worse, the prisoners know what is happening, and are powerless to stop their deaths and eventual rebirths.

As the agents acquire intelligence, it is delivered to Unit 73. In cooperation with soon-to-be Supreme Commander (Allied Expeditionary Force) General Dwight D. Eisenhower, they destroy the camp, its walkers, and all the Nazis stationed and working there.

Operatives manage to collect some evidence of mass infection of prisoners of war, but the war soon ends, and due to their nature, the incidents are quietly covered up and never brought to light.

In 1963, the newly-created Defense Advanced Research Projects Agency (DARPA) takes over funding of Unit 73, renaming it the Advanced Experimental Genetics Intelligence Service (AEGIS).

AEGIS' primary mission is codified and standardized. The two main purposes of the unit become containment and investigation.

First, to contain and eliminate any and all walker incursions through the United States and its territories, including the manufacture of cover stories to prevent worldwide chaos.

This is accomplished through the use of military personnel under strict security and need-to-know access—Special Operations groups who are simply told that the victims are dangerously sick and the illness is incurable.

Second, to determine the source of the infection and find a cure.

ARIZONA, 1986

She takes a quick break from her work and leans against a corner of the barn, sweating through her thin shirt as the bright Arizona summer sun pours down on her. Even for Arizona it's hot, and it isn't normally this bad so close to sundown. A sudden strong breeze brings her upright, and she lifts her chin into the wind, sending her long red hair streaming out behind her.

A child's laughter captures her attention, and she smiles as she looks over at her little brother, Johnny, playing in the front yard in the sprinkler. She wants to join him, but her father will tan her hide if she shirks her chores, so she turns back to the task of mucking out the horse's stalls. Even at thirteen, she has a strong work ethic and knows her responsibilities.

Her favorite, a mountain of a horse named Jack, whickers from the next stall and she smiles at him, extending a treat for him to munch on. She loves his chestnut brown coloring, and rides him every chance she can, which isn't much these days, what with school and chores and homework.

As she finishes clearing the stall, she hears her mother call her and her brother inside for dinner, and puts back her tools, making sure the barn door is closed and secured. She can smell the delicious aromas of the food, and her stomach rumbles as she realizes just how hungry she is.

She turns off the hose as she passes the corner of the house, causing little Johnny to set up a wail that is probably heard miles away. She just rolls her eyes and pushes him inside to wash up. Her father comes in just behind her through the screen door and starts to head for the table, but is stopped short by his wife.

"Johnathan Michael Barnes, you know better! Get over here and wash your hands," she says. "And take off those dirty boots!"

John Barnes laughs as he picks up his wife in a huge bear hug and swings her around. "Ellen, one of these days I'm going to eat with dirty hands, and I'll survive just to spite you."

Kimberly looks at her parents laughing, the love they feel for each other clear in their eyes and smiles and little touches. Being a normal young teenage girl, she is concerned with such things, and sighs with hope that she will find that sort of love someday.

Her reverie is broken by the sharp pinch Johnny gives her as he sits down at the table, having run some water over his hands—his version of washing up. She jumps and smacks him on the back of his head, causing a fight, which is quickly broken up by their mother. Having washed up and taken off his dirty boots, her father sits down at the table and leads them in saying grace.

"Lord, we thank you for blessing our table with this bounty. In your name, we pray. Amen." He smiles as he looks around at his family. "Now, let's eat!"

The evening air is warm and heavy, and her mother allows them to sleep on the screened-in front porch.

She lies on her pallet, her long legs sticking out from the too-small blankets, and looks up at the stars through the screens. The night wind blows, taking much of the day's heat away and leaving her goose-bumped and shivering, but she doesn't mind one bit. She prefers to sleep outside when she can get away with it.

Sometime later, she starts awake. Something feels wrong, and she lies there for a few minutes trying to figure out just what it is that has awakened her, listening for even the smallest sound.

Suddenly, she knows: there is no noise at all. No crickets, no owls, none of the normal country night-noises that bother city-folk so. Not even any soft snorts or whickers from the horses in the stable. She glances at Johnny, snoring in his rolled-up blankets, and decides to leave him be. No reason to wake him, yet. It's probably nothing, anyway.

She crawls out of her blankets, the cool midnight air pebbling her skin, and creeps to the edge of the porch, peering out at the night. Nothing is moving except for a few branches of the trees, and yet she still feels a sense of wrongness that chills her more than any breeze. Just as she is about to go inside to wake her father, she hears a horse cry out from the barn, followed by the oddest moaning sound she's ever heard.

That's Jack! What's wrong with him? The horse's screams gets louder and she can hear him kicking against the walls of his stall, mad with fear.

Panic sets in. Kimberly finds herself running around the side of the house towards the barn, and is startled as the back porch light comes on and her parents run out of the house, stopping on the back steps. Her father holds his shotgun. Seeing her there, he points back to the house. "Get your butt back in there, Kim, and see to your brother, too," he yells.

She is obeying before she realizes it, running back the way she came as her father heads toward the barn. Kim grabs her brother from his sound sleep on the front porch and carries him into the house. As she comes into the front room, there is a loud boom and then another from the backyard as her daddy fires his shotgun. She can hear a loud crack from the barn. She stops in the middle of the room, staring out of the back door. Johnny wakes up and tries to pull away, and she holds him tightly.

Suddenly her mother screams from the back porch steps, and she hears that moan again as another shotgun blast goes off, closer than the others. She holds Johnny tightly to her chest as her father yells, and she sees *something* attacking him.

He struggles with whatever it is, yelling to her mother, "Ellen, get the kids out of here! Go now before . . ." Whatever he is about to say is cut off as the struggle with the creature causes her father's finger to slip on the trigger. Another loud boom, and her mother falls backwards into the kitchen, her screams cut off and her chest a mass of blood, ruined skin, and bone.

"God, no!" shouts her father, stunned into stillness by Ellen's death. "No, no, no . . ."

He doesn't see the rotting arms reaching for him, only coming back to the moment as the walker takes a large bite out of his forearm. He yells and curses, and with a mighty shove knocks the creature back, chambering and firing his last shell point blank into its face, blowing its head to pieces.

Kimberly sinks to the floor, her brother now screaming in her arms, his face hidden against her body. Her father, cursing and holding his arm, comes in through what is left of the back door and kneels next to his wife. He moans and cries as he cradles her in his good arm and begins to rock back and forth. In a daze, Kim sets her brother down. He clings to her legs as she walks to the kitchen's wall-mounted phone and dials 911.

"911, what is your emergency?"

"Mom . . . mom's dead and my daddy's hurt. Come quick."

"What's your address? Hello? Hello?" Kimberly can't seem to put any more words together and drops the receiver. She goes back into the living room and sits down on the couch. Johnny crawls up next to her and she wraps an arm around him, staring across the room at the wall.

She doesn't notice the flashing lights appearing outside, or the men knocking on the door. There are people who come to look at her daddy's arm, and she can just barely see them pull him away from her mother through the doorway. Men and women both come into the living room and try to talk to her, but she can't answer them, as if she doesn't remember how to talk, and Johnny is silent and still, his tears leaving stains on his cheeks. One woman sits down on her mother's rocking chair.

"I'll stay with you, dear," she says, reaching out and patting Kim's arm.

Eventually, Kim looks up when she hears a neighing horse outside. *At least Jack's ok. I still have Jack, and Johnny, and Daddy.* The lady sitting nearby notices her perk up, and, desperate to reach the girl, decides to try one last gambit.

"I tell you what, I'll go find out what's going on with your horse, ok? I'll be right back. You'll be here when I come back, won't you?"

Kim looks at her for the first time and nods. Once the older woman is gone, though, she hears whispers from the kitchen, and creeps closer, trying to hear what is being said.

"They're coming, Adam."

Another man sighs. "I know, Bill, but you know what'll happen when they get here. Damn feds. And what about the girl and her brother? What happens to them?"

"They'll take them and make sure they're looked after. Come on, Adam, we can't fight them on this."

"I know, I know, dammit! I just hate to see this. John and Ellen are—were—good people. They don't deserve this."

Kimberly doesn't hear Bill's reply as she backs away from the door, motioning to her brother to be quiet. He nods and follows her as she moves out to the front porch, away from the men inside, closing the door and moving around the side of the house.

Suddenly she crouches, pulling her brother down with her as the beam of a flashlight plays over the side of the house, then away.

She sees the deputies checking the yard, house and barn, and waits until they finish. She sees the nice lady walking back to the house as the men move out to search the surrounding land, and realizes that now is her chance. Kimberly and her brother sneak into the barn and into Jack's stall. She whispers to the big horse as he greets her, his soft nose brushing her shoulder.

She knows that she can't let those people, whoever they are, take her and her brother anywhere. Working with quick and practiced ease, she saddles and bridles the big horse, hoisting her brother up to grab the saddle horn as she climbs up behind him. Making sure they aren't being watched is tougher, but she manages to ride Jack out of the barn and almost to the edge of one of the fields before she hears the shouting start.

They realized I'm gone. The nice lady wants us back.

"Hyah!" she cries, digging in her heels, and sends the big horse flying through the night and into the field.

She doesn't know where she's going at first, but, as they gallop on, she realizes she's headed for her best friend Angela's farm nearby.

Maybe we can hide there. At least I know they won't turn us in.

There's a loud whirring from behind her. Some kind of chopping noise. She doesn't know what it is at first. As lights appear in the air behind her, she realizes it must be a helicopter, and judging from the way its searchlights are coming closer, they must be on her trail. Urging the big stallion to even greater speed, she and Johnny lay low against the horse's neck.

Suddenly the noise is right above her, then beyond her, and then the helicopter drops smoothly out of the air and lands just ahead of them, a large spotlight blinding her. Jack stops and rears at the sudden noise and light, throwing her and her brother from his back. They land rough. Johnny cries out as he comes down hard on his arm, breaking it with a sharp crack. Kim's fall is just as painful, her head slamming back into the dirt.

She tries to get up and to calm the horse, but her vision swims and she falls back down, barely able to focus on the men running towards her from the helicopter. One of them kneels down beside her, reaching out a hand, but she screams and flinches back, afraid he is attacking her as the creature attacked her father. He nods at someone or something behind her and suddenly she feels a sharp sting at the back of her neck, and notices the man looking at her intently.

He seems so sad, she thinks as she passes out.

PANAMA, 1988

Petty Officer First Class Anderson looks through his binoculars at the drug camp in the jungle clearing, wondering just what the hell happened to this place. No drug camp is ever what anyone would call 'nice', but this one looks like it's been hit by an army.

A different kind of army. The midges and mosquitoes are active in the late-morning heat, and the humidity is stifling, sweat pouring from all of the operators in streams. The cursing is fluent but very, very quiet. Bullet holes riddle most of the buildings and he sees smears of blood across many of the walls. Several fires burn, further adding to the chaos and causing even more damage.

At least one of the shacks is engulfed in flames, the harsh chemicals and shoddy construction materials feeding the fire that sends midnight-black smoke billowing into the sky. Through the binoculars he sees a few survivors of whatever has happened, just standing around almost motionless.

They're hurt, judging from the blood on their clothes and the few injuries that he can see, but why are they just standing around rather than evacuating? No shouts, no voices, no noise . . . not even any of the ever-present birds or insects.

Weird. Very weird, indeed.

He touches his throat mike, whispering. "No sign of hostiles. Estimate seven to ten friendlies. Structural damage, blood . . . it's nasty down there, sir."

A voice in his ear. "Roger. Take position for overwatch. Alpha, east. Bravo, with me."

The SEAL team breaks from cover at the base of the hill Anderson has scouted, moving to their assigned attack vectors. He slings his binos back into his pack and crawls forward to the next rise in the terrain, 500 yards from the clearing.

He climbs a huge *corotu* tree and takes up a position on one of the massive branches, his long-barreled, camo-painted Mk11 sniper rifle resting ahead of him. He glances through the scope, but doesn't see any movement or even the friendlies he thought he'd spotted earlier.

Where the hell did they go?

There is a burst of gunfire to the east of the camp, and a crackle of static over the headset, as well as a moan.

"Alpha team engaged. Repeat, Alpha engaged. Hostiles are unarmed," the team leader says, breaking off amid another rattle of gunfire. "They're attacking hand-to-hand. Holy fuck! One of them just *bit* Sparks!"

Anderson can hear the moans now without his headset. It's a sound that runs a shiver of fear up his back. Like nothing he's heard before, it's full of menace and death. He fights down the urge to bolt and looks through the rifle's scope again.

"Overwatch, no shot on hostiles. Repeat, no shot on . . ." he says, pausing as he watches two of the six-man Alpha team back out of the jungle into the small clearing of the camp, firing as they retreat.

One of them is obviously wounded and hangs on the other, one arm over his squadmate's shoulder, firing a pistol again and again at whatever he sees under the dense canopy.

"I see you, Alpha," Anderson says, focusing on one of the shapes moving towards his fellow operators in the clearing through the dark jungle. "L-T, they are headed west toward your position."

Suddenly, one of the shadows breaks out of the darkness into the cloudy daylight. "Targets appear as friendlies! Engaging hostile targets."

He aims and kills the first target with one well-placed shot to the temple. Alpha leader keeps firing into the jungle, and Anderson sees more appear, following the one he's just killed, moving out of the jungle.

More gunfire, this time from the west, and Bravo team emerges, the lieutenant falling back last as his men retreat, firing into the jungle. More shadowed figures move towards that squad as well, and Anderson can see they are going to get cut off and surrounded.

Through the high-powered scope of his rifle, he makes out more detail on the hostiles, now. Dressed in rags and tatters of clothes, these people aren't alive. *They can't be. Not with those wounds.*

The next one he shoots has one arm missing, the flesh of the shoulder hanging in strips, the limb torn off. All of those he sees are covered in wounds and blood, and should not be standing, much less attacking.

Well. I can fix that.

As he begins taking them out one by one, he hears the lieutenant on the radio. "Fall back to the central shack. We'll take these bastards out there. MacMillan," he says, and Anderson sees him gesture towards the tall, lanky second scout of the team. "make your way around to Anderson and give us some support."

He can see MacMillan's head turn his way, and flashes the scope of his rifle in a quick signal to the other man, who nods, crouches, and disappears.

Damn, that man makes me nervous. No one should be able to disappear like that. Even I'm not that good.

The others fall back into guard positions around the outside of the door to the central shack, firing quick bursts at the walkers. The lieutenant opens the shack door, looking for cover, only to be met by a crowd of grasping, tearing walkers. There is a short scream as he is torn apart in the doorway, and then the things pile out of the shack, falling on the other SEALs from behind.

Anderson freezes for a moment, and then, with regret, realizes what he has to do. He begins ending his former teammates' horror as they are attacked. One shot, one kill.

As he sights in on the last of his men, the SEAL gives him a thumbs-up and drops a grenade from his hand. Anderson turns away as the explosion takes out the shack and the things attacking and feasting on his team.

Must've had something nasty in there.

Another shack explodes. The detonation from this one is even larger, showering the surrounding jungle with scraps of debris and more than a few of those things.

As he turns back, he sees several other nightmares making their way toward his position, drawn by the sound of his gunfire. He laughs as he takes down his thirty-fifth kill, but he sees more of them still coming from other shacks and through the trees.

A sudden noise from the base of his tree makes him spin around on the branch and fire his pistol without even realizing that he's drawn it. The bullet caroms off some buried obstruction and zings out into the distance.

A shaky voice issues from around the trunk. "Stop! It's me, boyo," says Hamish, poking his head around the tree, only coming out when he sees it is safe. Bloody and filthy and clutching a bandage to one forearm, the Scot looks wide-eyed at Anderson who swears profusely.

"Sorry, Hamish," he says. "They're headed our way. What's with the arm?"

"One of the fuckers bit me," he replies. "The others?"

Anderson shakes his head in mute reply, and MacMillan curses. "Good thing I've got the radio," he says, suiting actions to words and twisting a dial on his mike. "Papa Bear, this is Rabbit Four. We are di di mau with two SEALs to LZ X-ray."

The reply is fast. "Roger, Rabbit Four. E-and-e to LZ X-ray, pickup at 1330 Zulu."

"Roger, Papa Bear. Out here." MacMillan looks at Anderson, who climbs out of the tree and readies himself for travel. "Let's get out of here, Frank. It's gonna be a long walk."

"Damn straight." They both stiffen as a moan drifts their way from somewhere close. They glance at each other and then hike up their packs and disappear into the foliage.

Over the next twenty years, AEGIS contains and eliminates twenty-seven separate incursions within the United States.

Through secret dialogues, other countries share scientific advancement with the goal of finding a cure, somehow, somewhere.

A few of the finest minds on the planet are brought in to consult, and given a plausible cover story. Almost none question the necessity, believing that the Army is just being well prepared. Special operations units are called in when necessary, and only told the most basic need-to-know information.

The situation appears to be manageable, at least for the moment, and although attacks become slightly more frequent, there is nothing to indicate that a massive escalation of military force would be in order.

Chapter Two

FALL CREEK, COLORADO
1 YEAR AGO

MONTY'S SPORTS & OUTDOORS WAS exactly what you would expect from a small-town outfitter. It wasn't huge, but Monty could get almost anything for his customers, even if he had to drive to Denver occasionally to pick it up. He carried mostly ammunition and some hunting rifles, tents and other camping gear, and the standard sports equipment. There was a musty scent to the air every time you walked in the store, and it was never clear if it was from the dust or merely the age of the shop.

Montgomery James Gordonsson, Junior was a huge bear of a man, standing head and shoulders above even the tallest of Fall Creek's citizens. Since he was so intimidating in size and appearance, most people found themselves hard-pressed to talk to Monty initially, but they soon discovered that he had a thoughtful and caring intelligence combined with an easy humor and wit.

At least, that was true before Fall Creek turned into Hell. I stared across the street at the dark and still store. *I hope he's still alive.* I'd come down from the roof, but my new hiding place in the bushes seemed more exposed each moment.

The problem was that this was the only scrap of cover in sight. I didn't see any movement inside the store, but that meant nothing, since I could barely see inside anyway. The movement I was more concerned with was that of the walkers on the street between me and my destination.

There were only five of them, and none of them were within more than fifty yards or so. I should be able to make it to the alley across the way if I was careful and quiet.

There's no point trying the front door. Monty would've made sure to lock up.

I took a deep breath and darted out of the bushes in a low crouch, one hand keeping my boots from falling off my shoulder and my sock feet making no noise on the pavement.

I made it. I couldn't believe my luck, but I didn't stop to revel in it. Once I was halfway down the alley and out of sight—and hopefully hearing—of the main street, I slipped my boots from around my neck and put them back on. I pulled the Springfield out of its holster and looked around the corner of the shopping center.

The service area behind the strip appeared to be deserted, but I'd already discovered in the last two days that looks could be deceiving. These things made almost no noise until they spotted some food, and then . . . well, they could be *loud.*

I spotted a loose piece of concrete nearby and judged the distance carefully as I threw it down the alleyway. It made just enough noise on the concrete paving to suit me, and nothing responded, so I figured I was probably safe.

I found the rear door to Monty's easily enough, and tried the knob. To my surprise, it turned, and I wondered if Monty had simply left, not caring about the contents of the store. *Unlikely. He practically lives here. Something's not right.* I turned the knob once more, standing just behind the door as I pulled it open.

Suddenly the door was thrust open fully, and I ducked as a wooden baseball bat flew over my head to carom off the open door. It's funny the things that stand out when you're in a situation like that. I clearly remember the grain of the wood as it passed by my eyes with only inches to spare, and the dull *bong* sound as it hit the metal door.

I also remember looking up into Monty's eyes as he recovered and started to swing again, only to pause for a moment as he recognized me, and I took advantage of that interruption to stand with my hands to one side in a peaceful gesture, the .40 caliber pistol in my hand notwithstanding.

"Son, you're liable to get blown away or killed doing some damn fool thing like that," he huffed. He looked both ways down the alley, and then pulled me inside with no more effort than shifting a heavy shopping bag between hands. He shut and locked the door behind us, then turned to give me a once-over under the bright light of one of his camping lanterns.

"Those things can hear like nothing I've ever seen. I was bringing in the last of the supplies I had stored out back when I heard you coming. I only realized I forgot to lock the door when you tried to open it."

I grinned at the big man and was relieved to see an answering grin in return, albeit a pained one. "You okay? It's a mess out there."

"I'm okay, David. More or less." He gestured to a bandage on his arm near the wrist and shook his head. "Some wackjob tried to bite me, of all things. I only told him I didn't have any more ammo, and he just flew off the handle. I had to shove him out of the store. That's when I locked up."

He jerked his head in the direction of the front of the store, and through the stockroom entrance I could see the rolling metal grate that he had locked in place.

Guess it's a good thing I didn't try the front door.

"What about you?" he asked.

"I'm fine, but I'm getting outta this place, Monty. There's nothing left for me here now. I was hoping to find some supplies here. You said you're out of ammo?"

"No, not really. Just didn't like the look of the guy, ya know? Told him all I had was already sold, but you're welcome to whatever you need. I know you're good for it once this crap is all over with. What about the missus and your boy?" He began rummaging around in a stack of boxes, finally pulling out a large black duffel bag and tossing it to me. When I just let it hit the floor, he glanced over. "What's wrong?"

"She ... I ..." I couldn't seem to speak. My tongue wouldn't form the words, and he caught me looking toward the street. The pain I felt must've been evident, and Monty had always been an observant guy.

"Shit. That's fucked up."

I'd lived in Fall Creek nearly all my life and I'd never heard this affable man utter a single word even close to profanity. *Everything really is going to hell, then.* I simply nodded, and Monty growled deep in his throat. "Well, if you're getting out, then I'll see to it you have what you need. Follow me."

I followed him to his office, where he opened the huge safe that dominated one wall and took a small box from a stack inside. He motioned for me to hand him the pistol and I did so. The gun was dwarfed in his huge hands, but he fitted the suppressor from the box onto the end of the gun and handed it back.

"That's a little something from me to you that don't nobody need to know about, kid." He looked me dead in the eye with a grim expression.

"Got it. Thanks, Monty. Listen, you want to come with me? I could use you in a fight."

He chuckled and shook his head, the motion shaking his whole body. "Nah, I'm no good at that sort of thing, David. Besides, I'm kinda tired. Think I might lie down here when you're done and get some rest. I figure I'm safe enough inside here for a couple more days, anyway."

With all the camping supplies, ammo and MREs you could ever need. He'll be fine. "I'll just grab a few things and be on my way. And I'll be back before you know it when I find help."

He smiled and eased back into the enormous office chair that somehow managed to cradle his bulk, scratching absently at the bandaged wound on his arm. "Sure thing, David. Sure thing. Just gonna rest here awhile."

The twenty-third zombie I killed was what had once been a little girl. She spotted me crossing a side street. By this time night was falling and she came at me out of the little backyard of what I presumed was her house. No more than four or five years old, she was dressed in the dirty and stained tatters of a pink dress, her hair still in pigtails.

The moan she issued at me was anything but childlike, and she was light as a feather as she attacked me out of nowhere, biting and clawing. Her small teeth wouldn't be able to break through my pants or jacket, but that didn't mean I wanted her crawling on me. Childlike or not, she was deadly.

She moved faster than any of the others I'd seen, and was on me almost before I could react. She clung to my leg, trying her best to make a meal of my thigh, and, as I tried to pry her off, I stumbled, falling back against the picket fence surrounding the small yard.

The fence had seen better days. It broke into splinters as I fell against it. I screamed as a huge piece of jagged wood pierced my arm. My balance gone, the girl swarmed over me as I landed hard on my back, and it took every ounce of will I had to fight through the pain from my arm and keep her from biting me as she snarled and spit, saliva and blood flying everywhere.

Suddenly, I saw my opening, and, grabbing her leg with my good arm, I swung her away from me into the stone wall of the house next door at full force. She hit with a sickening crunch and slid to the sidewalk, the creepy moans and gnashing of teeth silenced for good now. I groaned as the pain from my arm hit me again, and struggling to my feet, I gritted my teeth and swallowed hard as I gripped the spike of wood, took a deep breath, and pulled it out fast. I gasped as blood welled up from the wound, thick and black in the near-dark night.

Taking off my belt, I wrapped it around my bicep above the wound and cinched it tight, cutting off the blood flow. I'd have to do a more thorough job of cleaning and washing it later, when I had time, but for now all I could do was get moving again.

My scream had no doubt drawn the attention of every walker within a mile or more. As I retrieved my pack from where it had fallen, I tried to resist that bastard inner voice that told me I was a monster for killing a little girl, even though I would have been food if I'd given her even a ghost of a chance.

You're a jackass, the voice reminded me. *You should've checked that yard before crossing the street, asshole.*

My inner voice was not nice. Not anymore. Not after two days in this place.

This time, I checked the yard carefully before entering my little house on Roland Avenue. Not seeing any horror-film nightmares, I moved quietly to the porch and knelt down, covering the darkened interior with the pistol held in my good hand. I knocked softly on the frame of what had once been the front door. Shattered and twisted, it hung off of the hinges, glass covering the entryway floor. As it had for the last two days, only quiet stillness answered me.

No moans, no shuffling of dead feet. The house was empty. Even so, the events of the last two days had rapidly instilled new survival traits in my psyche, and I searched the shadows warily as I moved into the entrance hall.

I listened for long minutes at the base of the stairs, waiting to hear any noise at all. I realized after sitting there for fifteen minutes that I wasn't just listening anymore. I was avoiding going upstairs. Upstairs were the bedrooms. Upstairs I was certain, on some level, that I would find Eric. Or what was left of Eric. Even though I'd searched for him before, I had to do it again. To take one last chance of finding him alive.

Chance failed me, again. Upstairs, downstairs, the basement . . . all were empty. Eric was gone. There was no way for me to know if he was a zombie, had simply run off, or was hiding somewhere. I had been tempting fate running around looking for them. It was only pure luck that had so far kept me from getting killed, just like Rebecca. At the thought of what I'd done to her, I closed my eyes and took several deep breaths. Just because something was necessary and right didn't make it easy.

There was a part of me—a large part—that wanted to go out there into the night, searching for the kid, regardless of my chances of making it out alive. It was the right thing to do, danger or no danger. But the odds were almost nil that he was still the boy I remembered. And I had to get out of this town somehow.

It was then that I made the hardest choice I've ever made, even though it was clear what I had to do: I abandoned him, knowing full well that it would mean his death, if he wasn't dead already.

He's probably still alive, asshole. Hiding somewhere, waiting for you to come rescue him, Dad.

Like I said, not a nice voice.

Mentally cataloguing the few possessions I wanted to take with me, I calmly and quickly began stuffing them into another duffel bag I grabbed out of the closet. Without thinking, I used my injured arm, and bit my lip to keep from crying out again.

First things first, dumbass.

I moved into the upstairs bathroom and grabbed the first-aid kit, closing both doors into the room as well as pulling the window shade before turning on the lights. I wasn't sure that zombies were attracted to light, but there wasn't any sense in taking unnecessary chances. I'd seen enough horror movies and killed enough of them in the last two nights to know that 'better safe than sorry' was always the way to go.

Fortunately the electricity's still on. And the water. I turned on the taps and unwrapped the belt, wincing at the fresh flow of blood from the wound, but thankful that the spike had gone all the way through. I was sure there would be splinters, but right now all I could do was stop the bleeding.

Dropping the now-shredded T-shirt on the floor, I examined the hole in my arm and saw it wasn't as bad as I'd thought. The splinter wasn't that big, though the blood was still flowing freely.

Thanks, Dad. I opened the well-stocked first aid kit. As a Marine, he had always insisted on keeping an over-sized kit somewhere in the house, and I was very glad I'd learned that particular lesson.

I paged through the simple and well-illustrated field manual in the kit, and followed the directions.

I was amazed at the relative lack of pain as the coagulant powder stopped the bleeding, and I wrapped gauze around my arm after applying a bandage pad. I looked in the mirror when I'd finished.

Well, it ain't pretty, but it'll have to do. Hopefully I can make it to a hospital or something when I get to Lakewood.

Popping some painkillers, I repacked the kit, turned off the light and moved back into the bedroom. After putting on a warmer long-sleeve shirt, I picked up the bag once more, this time with my uninjured arm. Now that I'd at least bandaged the arm, the pain had started to fade a bit.

Extra shoes. Extra batteries. Extra clothes and a jacket. Water bottles. The bag was stuffed and bulging by the time I was through, but I didn't have to carry it very far.

I dropped it next to the bag Monty had given me, and I looked around at the kitchen just once as I paused by the back door, checking the path to the garage fifteen feet away. It was a cozy little house, but there was nothing left for me here now.

I made it to the garage and inside, the door shut and the light on, pistol at the ready. No movement, no noise. The camp stove under the workbench and the sleeping bag from the rafters overhead went into the back of my black 1988 Ford Bronco along with the duffels. I climbed behind the wheel and paused for a moment.

This beast was going to draw every one of the monsters for three blocks or more when I started it up. No V8 engine I ever heard ran quiet. Nothing for it, though. Once I was moving, I could just run down any of the bastards between here and I-70. Few things could stop an old-school Bronco once it was at speed, and the over-sized winter tires would keep the big vehicle on the road. And it was a hell of a lot better than walking.

I was as ready as I would ever be.

The first roar of the engine overwhelmed the noise of the big garage door going up, and I rocketed out, the tall radio mast barely clearing the door, even tied back as it was. I didn't see the first zombie I hit, but bits and brains flew over the windshield as I smashed into it somewhere around the sidewalk and turned out into the street.

I tried to remember the clearest path from my house to the interstate, given all the abandoned cars and other obstructions on the roads. I'd almost made it to the intersection of Roland and Main, where I was tempted to turn, when I heard a helicopter overhead.

What the hell is a chopper doing in Fall Creek? I wondered as I slowed and checked for zombies, then stopped and stuck my head out the window.

The moonlight glinted off the side of a Black Hawk as it banked low over the ten or fifteen old buildings the visitor's bureau referred to as "Historic Downtown Fall Creek."

Army insignia were visible on the side of the craft as it headed in the general direction of the town hall, and I assumed it would be landing in the main square.

That's my ticket out. I rolled the window back up and sped that way. Just like that, all my plans had changed. *I just have to get there. Somehow. Through a hundred or more zombies that all want to have me for a late supper.*

I stopped about half a mile away from downtown, ensuring the coast was clear before parking next to an alley fire escape. I got out and grabbed the duffel with all my clothes, some food, and ammo.

I wouldn't need the camp stove or sleeping bag. If it turned out these guys were no good, I could always come back here and head back for the interstate.

The duffel went on my back, along with the rifle. Pistol in its holster, I climbed onto the roof of the Bronco and grabbed the fire escape ladder just as I saw the first zombie come around the corner, drawn by the rumble of the big V8. Timing was everything, I guess.

I moved across the roofs of the downtown shopping district quietly and quickly. Fortunately, there were only minor gaps between them, and I lucked out in finding a loose board from one of the signs that I could extend across the larger spaces. Taking it with me each time, I was able to make my way toward the main square.

I dropped and crawled to the edge of the building near the main square, then slowly peeked over the edge. It seemed like a standard Army camp, at least from what I'd seen in movies.

There were a couple temporary helipads chalked onto the asphalt, and some tents set up, their sides rolled up to provide ventilation to the scientists working beneath them.

I could see a few random flashes of gunfire from the barricades they had set up. The zombies were being drawn by the noise of all the personnel, but were coming to the barricades in dribs and drabs, a few at a time.

I was done with Fall Creek now. I'd seen and done things in the last few hours that I had never thought possible, and I moved back, taking the first fire escape down to the nearest alley, crouching around the corner in the few shadows that were left as the sun began to rise. I hoped that these Army guys would be able to get me out of here.

Beyond the makeshift barricades—a few cars pushed together here and there, and a city bus blocking one street—there were at least two choppers, their blades turning as the Army personnel raced back and forth around their fortifications.

The problem was that I had no idea what sort of story they'd been told about what was going on here. Could've been anything, and they'd already seen several of their men go down. What was odd were the scientists they had with them. Obviously not military, they carried themselves differently, and flinched every time a gun went off.

At least there's none at this barricade for the moment. I could count about thirty or forty lying on the ground in front of it, though. The night hadn't been completely kind to these guys.

And here came another patrol, within a couple hundred yards of me. I took a deep breath and checked for walkers.

None spotted, I lowered my duffel to the ground, and holstered my pistol. Holding the rifle by one hand, I cupped the other and shouted around the corner.

"Don't shoot, I'm not infected," I began and jerked back as a fusillade of bullets struck chips off the edge of the building.

Genius, Blake. Pure fucking genius. Why don't you just fire your rifle in the air to calm them down, now?

From around the side of the building I heard a gruff voice. "God dammit Jenkins, cease fire! Who gave you an order to shoot, you dipshit?"

"Well, sir—"

"Shaddup, asshole, it was a rhetorical question."

I chuckled. Definitely not an officer, that one.

"All you other assholes will hold fire until I give you a direct order, clear?"

A chorus of sheepish voices answered. "Clear, sir!"

"Good. You, behind the corner there. If you're human, you'll come out with your hands over your head, and slowly, or you will by-god die where you stand. You get me?"

I grinned again. *This guy's been watching too much* Full Metal Jacket. "Yes, sir! Hands over my head and slowly, sir!"

I extended the rifle into view around the corner, keeping it pointed *away* from the squad, and lowered it to the ground. I held my hands up and inched around the corner, folding them atop my head as I walked forward, swallowing hard at the sight of no less than 10 M16's pointed straight at my face.

I was about twenty yards away when the man spoke up again. "All right, that's far enough. Turn around." I did so, barely moving. "You been bitten or otherwise wounded, son?"

"Yes, sir." I closed my eyes as the rifles rose once more to the shoulders of the young soldiers in front of me, and I prayed that they wouldn't fire as I yelled. "*Not bitten!* I got a piece of fence through my arm, sir, but I wasn't bitten."

"Take off your shirt. Slowly."

Very carefully—and not just because my arm was throbbing by this point after holding it over my head for so long—I removed my jacket and shirt. "Went all the way through, sir." I pointed out the entry and exit wounds, but he just looked at me.

"Well, if you're lying, you're dying, as they say. In any case, you're a damn sight smarter than some of these jackasses I've got here," he said, jerking a thumb in one grunt's direction as he rolled his eyes. From the anger I saw on his face, I guessed that was Jenkins.

"All right, son, get over to the medic and get checked out," he said. "They'll let you—"

I interrupted him by fainting as I moved forward, the stress of the past two days—three now, as I noticed the sun coming up—finally catching up with the blood I'd lost. I noticed his name stitched on his uniform as I reached out for him, though.

It can be funny what goes through your mind as you're passing out from stress and fear and blood loss. For me, it was a completely useless observation.

I've never met anyone named Maxwell before.

The massacre at Fall Creek changed everything.

With nearly 1,500 people dead, the cover-up was the most massive in AEGIS history. Along with all the civilians killed, the loss of the state troopers, national guard and soldiers in that action caused those in the know in the government to listen to what their military advisors had been telling them for years: that a corps of specially-trained and conditioned fighting men and women was needed specifically for these sorts of operations.

A classified Executive Order was issued establishing a secret Combined Joint Special Operations Task Force, reporting only to the Secretary of Defense and the president. Containing elements of all four military branches, no expense was spared in the outfitting of these teams, their budgets so deeply buried by experts in red tape and secrecy that not even Congress could find them.

An experimental team was formed—a prototype for those that would come after—and began training in the new expanded AEGIS facilities at Fort Carson, Colorado.

Chapter Three

FORT CARSON, COLORADO
PRESENT DAY

"ATTEN-TION!" THE SHOUTED ORDER WAS followed by the sound of many pairs of combat boots coming together in perfect synchronization. I squared my shoulders, took a very deep breath, and opened the door. The very tall, very loud soldier commanding this group made his way over to me. He looked me up and down like a prize fish and shouted once more as I managed to collect my wits and close my mouth.

"Parade rest!" As one unit, the team shifted to the more relaxed stance, and I straightened to some semblance of attention. I did not insult this man or the other soldiers by saluting, however. I knew that much.

"Blake, isn't it?" the soldier asked, his voice lowered to what seemed to pass for conversational volume for him. I could tell that he wasn't thrilled with my presence. For that matter, neither was I. He was greying at the temples, well over six feet tall, and built like Mr. Universe. I swallowed hard and introduced myself.

"Yes, sir. David Blake, reporting as ordered. I wasn't told who I was to report to specifically, sir." I lowered my voice to prevent accidental overhearing. "Is this . . . is this AEGIS, sir?"

He looked at me again, and I could tell he was mentally sizing me up, wondering if I was worth giving a damn about. I hoped that he thought so, or my stint with this group was going to be even harder—and quite possibly much, much shorter—than I thought.

Never make an enemy your first day, kiddo, I remembered my father saying. Suddenly, the soldier stuck out his hand and smiled.

"Colonel Maxwell, at your service. Welcome to Fort Carson. Glad you could join us."

Relieved, I smiled back and shook his hand. "I know I'm late, Colonel. I don't have any excuses. I'm simply not used to military bases just yet and I got a bit turned around."

The colonel snorted. "You will be." He looked thoughtful. "You know, you may not remember this, but we met once."

I frantically racked my brain trying to remember where I might have met the man. He smiled as the memory finally came to me and my eyes widened. There was only one other time I'd met anyone from the military as anything other than a lab-rat for Army doctors and psychiatrists. It had been just over a year since that morning, but I could still see the steel-and-rubber construction of the man who had so casually stopped his squad of soldiers from shooting me dead where I stood.

"Yes, sir," I said. "I meant to find you, after, but they wouldn't let me talk to anyone, sir. I was sequestered for four months. I can only assume that you got me to the medic, sir?"

He nodded. "Yeah, I ordered the squad to carry you. You remember Jenkins?" I laughed and smiled as the colonel continued. "That was that boy's last mission."

My face fell, and the colonel shook his head, grinning. "Nah, he's fine, but I think the sight of them nasties made him want to crawl back to his mamma's skirts. He's pushin' paper somewhere in Greenland now, last I heard."

I smiled in a rictus grin. "Well, sir, you and I both know what that sort of experience will do to a man. I'm just glad that they recognized talent when they saw it," I said, nodding to the silver birds on his collar.

Maxwell snorted again. "Even a blind squirrel finds a nut once in a while. Still, we lost some good people that day." The colonel's gaze went distant as he thought back, then cleared as he came back to the present. "So they tell me you're going to be a consultant."

"Yes, sir. General Morrison thought it best when he offered me the spot on the team, since I didn't have the training that your soldiers have. Still, he wanted me to go through all the new training alongside them, so that I can be ready for the field."

"That's a big responsibility, son. And not a little hard work. Top-of-the-line soldiers fail in training like this all the time. You're gonna be hating life pretty soon."

"I know, sir," I said, looking down for a moment, thinking about the past. When I looked back up, I thought I saw a flash of concern in the colonel's eyes. "But I'm game." I hoped he couldn't see the real reason that I was up for this mission—that I had nowhere else to go.

He looked at me, gauging me again, and then he cleared his throat and jerked a thumb over his shoulder.

"Take the last chair, Blake," he said.

"Yes, sir," I said, and moved to my appointed position, dropping my gear bag and attempting to match the pose of the soldiers, none of whom had even glanced my way. I counted eleven soldiers in the room, not including the colonel, who moved back to the front.

Looks like I'm lucky number twelve.

"Take your seats." A shuffle of movement, and we all sat down, alert and ready for whatever was to come. The colonel took a remote from his pocket and activated the projection system of the briefing room. The lights dimmed, and the screen at the front of the room lit up with a logo that I would come to know well: the AEGIS shield, with the crossed machete and M1 Garand and a castle turret behind.

"You have been selected for positions in a covert ops unit, code-named AEGIS. You all come from various units and services. We've got SEALs, Marine Force Recon, Airborne, Delta Force, Air Force Pararescue, Rangers and Green Berets. Warrant officers, sergeants, chiefs, and grunts. You all have one thing in common: you are the best at what you do. But let me tell you right now, nothing you have been through has adequately prepared you for this assignment.

"This will be a unique assignment for all of you. As you may have noticed, it's not just every branch represented here. You're also a mixed-gender team. We need the absolute best, and we cannot afford to ignore quality talent simply because their plumbing is on the inside. This is the one and only time I will say this, so listen up: I expect each and every member of this team to work with the others without regard to their sex. Hooah?"

"Hooah!" shouted the operators.

This was going to take some getting used to.

"AEGIS—known as the Advanced Experimental Genetics Intelligence Service—and its members are the front-line defense against the most fearsome enemy that our country, indeed our world, has ever known," continued Maxwell.

I shuddered as the colonel spoke, recalling why I was there and what I had seen. *I can't believe I volunteered for this.* It felt like a refrain that I was going to be repeating over and over in the weeks and years ahead.

"What I'm about to show you is classified above Top Secret." Maxwell paused to reinforce the seriousness of his statement. "Let me be absolutely clear: if there is any evidence that you have shared what you learn here today with anyone, you will disappear. Permanently." He stood back, crossing his arms over his chest. "There will be *zero* leaks in my unit.

"If any of you have a problem with that, leave now, and I'll personally put in your transfer back to your former unit." I glanced at the others, and none of them moved so much as a muscle. The colonel grunted in approval and nodded.

"Very well. The briefing materials on your desk will provide you with additional detail, and you'll be meeting someone in a moment who can answer any detailed questions you have, but what we're dealing with here can be summed up in one word. Officially, they're known as walkers. Unofficially, you know them better as zombies."

A cough from the other side of the room snapped Maxwell's head around. "This ain't a video game, and it ain't a movie. This is as real as it gets, soldier." He pressed a button on the remote, and the screen showed a photo of a nightmare: a long-distance shot of three walkers attacking some hapless soul, another in the background chewing on the arm it had just ripped from the man's body.

It was far too real a photo. Too detailed and visceral to be a fake. I swallowed and looked away, only to see the faces of those soldiers around me barely flinch. These hardened career military men and women weren't used to this sort of thing but they'd been in the shit, as they say, and it must've helped them get through it.

If they can do it, then so can I. Maxwell said this was going to be tough . . . I might as well start getting used to it now.

I noticed one of the female soldiers at the back, a tall redhead with long hair and the most intense green eyes I'd ever seen. She looked angry. I wondered why. What was it in her past or her psychological makeup that pissed her off about walkers? It was more than a little nerve-wracking that she didn't look surprised, not even a little. As if horror movies coming to life were just another day for her.

Spooky.

Maxwell continued with more gruesome pictures. "These were taken just prior to the decision to train our own AEGIS forces." He paused, pointing to a small town map now displayed by the projector. "This was what Fall Creek, Colorado—not even a hundred and twenty-five miles from here—looked like before the walkers got to it."

A few images went by of a pleasant mountain town, obviously culled from some sort of tourist publication. Maxwell pressed another button, and a video started playing. "This is what it looked like when it was all over."

The devastation was tremendous. The soldiers watched as the video shot from a helicopter played out on the screen. Burning buildings, bodies littering the streets, blood absolutely everywhere. Military vehicles surrounding the city as the picture zoomed out to an overview of the small town. Nothing moved, except the flames. No noise, except the occasional crash as a burning wall fell in.

Silence reigned in Fall Creek.

A part of me hated myself for not watching. *Of all people, I should watch this. They deserve that much.* But I couldn't bring myself to see it again. Not now. Maybe not ever. I took in the view of the Rockies out of the briefing room window, and thought about those I had known for so long and would never see again.

Even the deep blue of the Colorado skies couldn't soothe my anguish this time, and I realized I was looking in the direction of what had once been my home town. I sighed and turned back to the video.

The true horror was revealed as the helicopter landed in the park near the town hall. Some of the bodies were whole and appeared to be mostly unharmed. Most weren't. Covered in bite marks and with gore everywhere, these few were all that remained after the town tore itself apart. For most of the victims, this was the literal truth.

As I closed my eyes, remembering the sounds and the panic of those days, I heard a clatter as one of the men on the other side of the room exploded out of his desk and ran to the garbage can near the door, vomiting. I sympathized with him, but I found myself growing cold, almost numb. I stared at the wall and was only somewhat conscious of the soldiers all turning toward me minutes later as the colonel paused the video.

I glanced around at the soldiers looking at me, wondering what was going on, and noticed the video again. There I was, freeze-framed for all eternity as I walked toward a squad of soldiers, my rifle on the ground behind me, my arms raised and hands folded atop my head. I jumped as Maxwell broke the silence.

"Mr. Blake here was the only survivor of the massacre. Fall Creek was once home to nearly fifteen hundred men, women and children. Now, it's empty. Nothing lives there, and the whole area has been quarantined by us for the foreseeable future due to a 'toxic spill.' This was followed by an unfortunate fire that raged out of control and destroyed the town completely."

Colonel Maxwell realized that most of his team was staring at me, and gave me another look—this time one of pity—as he shouted, "Eyes front!

"When the town first fell off the grid and someone from outside finally noticed, several state troopers were sent in to investigate. We found their bodies and vehicles near the town hall. They had no idea what they were walking into, and were clearly outmatched and overwhelmed. When they didn't report back, their commander talked to the governor, who dispatched the Colorado Army National Guard's 157th Infantry out of Denver.

"You have all been chosen because you are the best at what you do. So were these guys." The colonel stepped to one side as he started another video. This one was from a helmet camera. I noticed that some of the soldiers—*operators, not soldiers*—began taking notes and talking in quiet whispers, critiquing the performance and methods of the unit on the screen. I was impressed that they would be able to focus after what they had just seen, and resolved to train myself to be just as good.

"We believe that the initial infection was spread by a bitten hunter returning to town," Maxwell continued. I turned back to the screen, as hard as it was. I had a general idea of what had happened to start the whole thing, but I hadn't been filled in on any detail. At the time, I hadn't cared to learn and wanted merely to put it behind me. Now, things were different.

"After it was all over, we had search teams scouring the mountains for weeks as far out as twenty miles, but we only found three of the bastards outside the city. They'd probably gone after animals or fleeing people. Where we realized the real magnitude of what we were up against, and just how unprepared we were, was when we discovered this video, taken sometime after the National Guard arrived in the town, likely during the second day."

On the screen, a small squad of soldiers walked through the afternoon light and moved into a small cafe. I realized I was looking at the same squad I'd seen from the roof across the street, and knew what was coming next. As usual, blood and broken bodies were everywhere, and the soldiers were taking their time carefully clearing the way as they moved forward. I saw a flyer posted on the glass by the entrance announcing Friday's high school football game against neighboring Ranger Canyon. A game that would never be played. *Go Ravens.*

Suddenly everyone jumped as a zombie came moaning through the kitchen door.

"Halt! Freeze or we will open fire," yelled one of the soldiers.

When the moaning just continued, the unit suited actions to words and fired. I shook my head as I watched the well-trained but ignorant men aim for and hit the zombie's chests and legs, which didn't even slow them down. More moans were heard from around a corner and two more walkers shambled towards the team. The sound of breaking glass from the front of the restaurant caused the camera to swing around, showing another walker moving in.

The squad fell apart and was overcome within moments, one of them running screaming out into the street, clutching an arm that had been bitten and mangled beyond repair. The camera fell to the ground as the soldier's helmet came off, sparing us the view—though not the sounds—of his squad being torn apart by the walkers left inside.

What the camera's unfeeling lens didn't spare us was the view out the front of the restaurant, and we watched as the wounded soldier called for help on his radio, not realizing he was also calling every remaining walker in the area straight towards him. I turned away. I knew what was coming.

There was the sound of a suppressed pistol shot, then another, and two loud thuds followed by the panicking soldier's voice. "Oh, thank God. You're not one of them, are you? Help me, I've been bitten . . ."

Another voice answered. "I know. I'm sorry." Another shot and a final thud. The video went silent as Maxwell paused it once more.

I knew what I would see when I turned back, and there it was: a dozen pairs of eyes, all staring straight at me, most in anger or loathing, a few ambivalent, which was scarier.

Only Maxwell's showed any sign of compassion.

It was my voice on the video. My apology to the soldier. My likeness on the screen holding a pistol, staring down at the body of the soldier I'd just killed.

I looked down for a moment then raised my eyes once more and met their glares with neither confidence nor pride, but acceptance. "I did what I had to do. I'd seen it before. He was bitten, and he was going to turn. *There is no cure.* It's as simple as that." I paused. "And I'd do the same for anyone."

The accusing, angry looks changed to reluctant understanding as they looked back at the screen, and at Maxwell, who resumed playback. I watched as the past version of myself scanned for more walkers, then took a knee next to the now-peaceful soldier. On the screen, I bowed my head.

I'm not a particularly religious man, but sometimes, what's right is right.

> May the road rise up to meet you.
> May the wind be always at your back.
> May the sun shine warm upon your face
> and may the rains fall soft upon your fields.
> And until we meet again,
> may God hold you in the hollow of His hand.

I murmured these words along with the video, then watched as I strode into the restaurant, pistol at the ready, out of the camera's view. Several more of the shots, and the view swung around to show me in extreme close-up as I looked straight into the camera.

I had no idea when it had happened that I might be watching the video later. In fact, I had been almost certain that I was going to be dead in hours, if not minutes. Watching myself in that video, I experienced a very strong sense of déjà vu.

"What I did, I did because there was no other choice. I hope that you can understand that."

The video went dark, the colonel turned off the projector, and the room's overhead lighting coming back on automatically.

Maxwell spoke again. "Those guardsmen had no idea what they were walking into. No one had briefed them on walkers, or how to take them down. No one knew that that was what they would be facing. When their squads didn't return, the Guard cordoned off the town and called the Army, which is where AEGIS comes in.

"When we arrived, we found more than six hundred active walkers in a small town that had once held well over twice that number of uninfected people. Walkers ranging in estimated age from four to eighty-five. Most of those who weren't killed or turned by the others died through accidental trauma or self-inflicted wounds when they realized there was nowhere for them to go.

"We lost nearly two full teams of operators cleaning up the town, many of whom were bitten, subsequently turned, and then attacked their own squads and fellows. Our operators for that mission were briefed with everything we could tell them. They knew to go for head-shots and to stay quiet. And they still died. Even with some knowledge of what's going on, things can get hairy. You've all seen it.

"*What Blake did was necessary.* He survived, despite every conceivable likelihood that he would end up as one of them. We *know* that bitten people turn into zombies. There is no cure, and there is no stopping or delaying it. There is merely an excruciating death and the knowledge that you will turn on your friends, your family and your neighbors.

"What you've all got on the desk in front of you is the sum total of what we know right now about the walkers. How to kill them, how to destroy the corpses, what to do and what not to do." He picked up one of the thick binders.

"This has been compiled over the last hundred thirty years, and is invaluable. Mr. Blake has volunteered to teach us what he knows to add to this, and how to deal with these things on a more personal level. We've never before had the chance to learn from a civilian survivor. He offers us a unique perspective and *you will all pay attention to what he teaches you.*

"Now, I've got someone I'd like you to meet. AEGIS isn't just about killing zombies. An equally important part of our mission is to find out how to stop them from being created in the first place, as well as give us new tech to fight them and/or protect us better. We have a group of scientists working hard on that, and I'd like you to meet their head researcher, Dr. Mary Adamsdóttir."

We took our cue from Maxwell and took our feet as he stood and extended a hand towards the tall and skinny woman that stood up and moved to the lectern.

"Thank you, Colonel," she said, taking up the remote and plunging us into darkness again. "Please, take your seats. This, ladies and gentlemen, is our enemy."

A complicated medical drawing appeared on the screen, and I knew I wasn't the only one left wondering what I was looking at.

"On the left, you see a normal protein. On the right, a 'misfolded' protein, called a prion," she said. "It can't be seen with a microscope. It's not a virus, but it does lead to bovine spongiform encephalopathy, Creutzfeldt-Jakob Disease . . ."

"Bovine spongi-what?" asked a soldier in the back.

Dr. Adamsdóttir turned and looked out at the soldiers. "Bovine spongiform encephalopathy." Seeing the blank stares on all of the faces looking at her, she chuckled and took off her glasses. "Sorry. I sometimes forget that not everyone I talk to is a geneticist or biological environmentalist, or . . . never mind. To answer your question, BSE is more commonly known as 'Mad Cow' disease."

The comprehension was instant. "Thanks, doc," said the soldier, and Mary turned back to the screen.

"BSE—Mad Cow—and CJD are just two variants of the several diseases that we've linked to these prions. You all know how easy it is to catch Mad Cow—all you have to do is eat the infected beef."

"I thought zombies—sorry, *walkers*—were caused by a virus or something," I said, looking on with interest. "If prions are spread by eating infected meat, wouldn't someone have to eat a walker to become one themselves?"

"Normally, yes, but this infection is like nothing we've ever seen before." She hit a button on the remote, and the screen displayed a new slide—this one of the rapid deterioration of cells.

"This shows the speed at which this prion causes reanimation. You can see with the marked samples that normal function ceases around eight to twelve hours after infection, with complete reanimation occurring in roughly double that, sixteen to twenty-four."

The lights came back up, and she began pacing the stage. "There are many, many things we don't know about this prion. Hell, prions weren't even theorized until the early 80s. At that point, we were still trying to isolate the virus that caused the spread, never realizing it wasn't a virus at all."

"So where does it come from?" asked another soldier.

The doctor threw up her hands and shrugged. "Your guess is as good as mine. We've been working on it for nearly twenty-five years and have only recently figured out the specifics of *what* it does. We still don't know where it comes from. We'll never know, at least not conclusively, where it originated, but in the end it makes no difference. It's here now, and isn't going anywhere.

"The process goes like this: A victim is bitten and the prions enter the bloodstream. From there the prion attaches itself to a certain molecule in the bloodstream, eventually making its way to the pre-frontal cortex where it replicates itself in extraordinary numbers, using just about every bit of biomass it can find there.

"This leads to a very painful death, of a sort. The prion changes the chemistry of the brain to such a large degree that regular body functions—breathing, for example—cease completely. The victim then expires, re-animating approximately eight to twelve hours after death. The reanimation occurs due to the new electrical signals being sent by the brain after death."

"But if the brain's dead, doctor—"

"We don't know. It's as simple as that. Using a captured specimen, we've documented electrical signals coming from the brain to the rest of the body, which explains how they can walk and move around, even that moan that they have.

"Whether this is a result of the mass of proteins in the pre-frontal lobe simply sparking a random electrical current, or something more sophisticated, there's no way of telling, yet. At least, if there's a pattern indicating a more advanced cause, we haven't found it."

"So, do they eat?"

"Yes and no. They have no need for sustenance, being dead. We have theorized at this point that the reason they attack humans is simply to spread the prions to another victim. There's a flaw in the code somewhere, though, because they don't stop biting, which is why they 'eat' normal uninfected organisms."

"But that would indicate . . . holy shit," I said, sitting back in my chair. "Holy shit."

"Exactly, Mr. Blake."

"Clue in the rest of us, will ya, doc?" asked someone in the crowd.

"What Mr. Blake is referring to is that if the prions—collectively or individually—are forcing the victims to seek out new hosts, it indicates a level of sophistication that is very, very rare and has only been found in a few parasites and viruses. There's a fungus in South America that does something similar with ants, but those are *ants*. This, though . . ." She shuddered. "It means that the damn things are very, very dangerous, Colonel."

"Holy shit," someone else said.

"Exactly."

I saw the mood in the room growing dark, and realized that this battle might be over before it was begun if these folks thought they had nothing to hope for.

"That's why shooting them in the head always works. And why their blood is so infectious," I said. "So, we keep our distance with our rifles and break out the flame-throwers for cleanup. These bastards won't know what hit them. I'm assuming fire will destroy these prions as well as anything else?"

"Yes, of course. Obviously, it's best to destroy corpses in a sealed environment, just in case, but a flamethrower should work just as well. It's not just the blood, though," Adamsdóttir said. "It's any bodily fluid."

"Okay, so no kissing them. I think we can handle that, doc," I said.

There was a general round of somewhat nervous laughter, and Maxwell stood up. "Thanks again, Doctor. I'll make sure that we get these yahoos over to you for medical processing before the end of the day." He turned back to us as Mary took her seat once more.

"That's it, folks. You know what we're facing, and you know the basics of how to kill it. Now, take your materials, get some chow, then study. Training starts tomorrow at 0600 hours." He straightened to attention. "Dismissed!"

It was chow time in the mess hall, and I was impressed by the quality of the food, as well as the relatively quiet atmosphere. It was not at all what I had expected. Hardly surprising, given that most of what

I knew of the Army was from movies and television. Undoubtedly, this new military life was going to take some getting used to.

As I left the line, I looked for a place to sit, and as I moved through the tables, one of the soldiers from the briefing called out, motioning for me to take a seat at her table with a few others from the team.

"Welcome to 1st Team," said the brunette at one end of the table. "Well, half of it, anyway."

I hesitated for a moment, and then joined them. I knew they wanted to ask me questions, but I left it to them to decide who was going to go first.

"Sergeant Eaton, Charlie Company, 3rd Rangers," the woman said, by way of introduction. "That is you on the video, isn't it, sir?"

I nodded. "Yes, that's me, and you don't need to call me sir, Sergeant. I'm not military."

She looked surprised. "You're not? Well, that answers my second question."

"No, go ahead. What were you going to ask?"

"I was just wondering where you had trained, sir, or at least what branch you served in."

"No training. Just hunting and target shooting with friends, and not very much of that."

"Then why go back out, sir? Why *volunteer* for this?"

I put down the fork I'd been holding in midair, my food undisturbed, and thought for a moment. A part of me wanted to say, *"Because the bastards took my fiancée and her son,"* but I wasn't ready to talk about that. "This is something I know about . . . that I seem to be good at . . . that I can do to save lives. I can't turn my back on that any more than any of the rest of you can." I saw more than one person at the table turn thoughtful.

I sighed. "Besides, what else was I going to do? Sit on a farm somewhere, never talking to anyone? You can't exactly chat with Joe down the street about this stuff. The Army gave me a choice: live in a gilded cage or do something about it. To me, that wasn't a choice at all.

"And don't call me sir," I said to break the tension. Eaton smiled and appeared to want to ask another question, but was interrupted.

"All right, you've had your turn, Eaton," said another soldier at her end of the table, a well-built though greying man with an easy smile and blue-grey eyes. I had noticed him at the briefing earlier, sitting near Colonel Maxwell. "Commander Anderson, SEAL Team Four, Mr. Blake. This may seem like a harsh question, sir, but how many did you have to put down?"

I looked at the commander and sighed, putting down my fork again. This wasn't going to be easy. He caught my eye as I looked around at the others, and gave me a slight nod. *He knows what this is like. He wants to get it out of the way so we can move past it.* I had the feeling that Anderson and I were going to get along well.

"Well, sir, I would say I don't have an exact number for you, but you all know that would be a lie." There was general agreement from around the table, as I had expected.

"I remember the face of every one of the twenty-seven walkers I killed during those two days in Hell," I said, pausing for a moment. "Even the children."

A soft whistle drew my attention to the other end of the table, where the redhead I had noticed earlier sat. She coughed as heads turned her way, most of them grinning at her. I noticed BARNES stenciled on her uniform. Now I had a name to work with, at least.

"Children?" she asked.

I found it hard to look at her—at any of them—as I answered. "Yes, children. There weren't many, just three. Three was enough, though."

Though the mood was somber for a while, it didn't last. SpecOps operators know as much about psychology as any soldier, and they turned the conversation to lighter topics soon enough.

That was when my friendship began with those soldiers drawn from such varying backgrounds. We hadn't been truly tested yet as a unit, and we would need to get to know each other much, much better, but we all knew now what we were going to be getting into, and that brought us together somewhat.

We might not be able to talk about what we were doing with anyone else, but at least we knew that we weren't alone, and that just might be enough.

Chapter Four

FORT CARSON, COLORADO

IN THE WEEKS AND MONTHS afterward, I grew stronger and more disciplined. I trained with First Team's Alpha squad, and those were some of the hardest days I have ever had, physically. There were many times that I regretted my decision to join AEGIS, and several times I considered resigning, despite knowing that I would have regretted it forever. Besides, what choice did I have? After all, they weren't just going to let the only living zombie survivor walk around without a care in the world.

Most of the others weren't even slightly fazed by the physical part of the training, all being Operators, but for me it was as if I'd thrown myself into some sort of crucible. None of my experiences could have prepared me for the truth of real training. Hell, the most exercise I had gotten to this point was climbing the stairs in my house after a long day at the bookstore where I'd worked in my old life.

Still, with the encouragement and help of the others in my squad, I held on, and at the end of the intense twelve-week 'zombie boot camp,' I looked and felt better than I ever had.

I could keep up with my squad, was showing great proficiency in sharpshooter drills and even learned the language of the military. I was spared none of the training, and found toward the end that I had come to enjoy it, using my pain and stress to help me push past the demons in my past and learn once more to hope for the future.

I'd known I wasn't going to be a military man from a young age, so when Maxwell approached me about accepting a commission,

I naturally declined. I told him I was happy to stay on as a consultant, and go through all the training the rest did, but I wanted to remain a civilian.

I had many reasons, not the least of which was wanting to be able to come and go as I pleased—not that I planned to go anywhere. It also seemed to me that it would be something of a slap in the face to the men and women I worked with. After all, why should I get something after 12 weeks that they'd worked years to earn?

Though surprised at first, and annoyed at the extra paperwork it would generate, Maxwell eventually acquiesced and left me alone about it. None of my squadmates ever brought it up, so I assumed Maxwell hadn't mentioned it.

On some afternoons, I instructed both squads of 1st Team in what I had learned during those two days in Fall Creek. Many of the standard tactics and procedures these fine soldiers had learned couldn't help them now, and some bad habits had to be unlearned.

At my urging, Colonel Maxwell ordered that everyone be fitted for new Army Combat Uniforms (ACU), much tighter and more form-fitting than the previous ones. I explained that anything loose or baggy could be used by a walker to grab and ensnare an unwary hunter.

It was during this period of difficult training that I learned to depend on my squad, who helped me through the roughest part. Barnes especially was helpful, and we grew closer as the weeks and months wore on. She was taking to her tentative position as squad-leader well, and whenever I faltered, she seemed to be there to lend a hand.

With her ready smile and an encouraging word here and there, I began to rely on her strength, and lent her mine when she needed it, though she never asked. She was strong, confident and independent, the soldier's soldier.

Over time, we gradually became good friends. She made an excellent leader, and we all expected her to be granted the command of Alpha squad, if not 1st Team itself when the time came.

We also began to grow closer as a unit as well, as demonstrated by our callsigns. "I'm thinking . . . Banjo," I said one evening in the chow hall, looking at Gaines. Standing well over six feet and built like a brick shithouse, he was easily the biggest man in our team.

He scowled at me and remained silent as he ate. Not so our compatriot Angelo Martinez, who laughed. "Good one, Blake."

Kimberly looked over at me, one eyebrow raised in question. I shook my head with a smile, but Eaton piped up from a couple seats down. "Didn't you ever see *Deliverance*, ma'am?" she asked Kim. "It's that song, 'Dueling Banjos'." Kim laughed and Gaines' scowl just deepened, causing Martinez to laugh even more.

"Y'all are right. It is pretty funny," Gaines drawled in his deep, southern Georgia twang. "I still shoot better'n all of ya, though." Dalton Gaines, Gunnery Sergeant (USMC), had outscored nearly everyone in our marksmanship trials, trailing only behind Corporal Eaton and that only by a few points. He glanced her way, and then turned back to Kim.

She may not see it, but this big boy's besotted with her. Probably the only girl ever to beat him in anything.

"I'd prefer 'Gunny', if it's all the same to you, ma'am," Dalton said to the captain.

Kim nodded and Gaines broke out in a big smile. "What about mine?" Kim asked me.

I looked thoughtful. "Well, Alpha Six isn't great, nothing to build on there." The designations were simple: Alpha for the squad, and Six as the commander. Similarly, I was Alpha Five, as her Executive Officer, also known as an XO.

"No, I've got it." I finished the last of my potatoes before answering. "Carrot-top."

That dinner roll barely missed me.

I also learned a great deal about hand-to-hand combat during that time. I'd had some experience with various martial arts when young. After all, what boy didn't want to be a ninja at some point?

None of that mattered now, though. We studied one-on-one techniques as well as multiple-on-one situations, such as when a crowd of zombies might attack a lone or separated soldier. There was training with knives, clubs, police-style batons, and the kukri—a short, curved knife.

We all began to master Kendo, Judo, Tae Kwon Do and Aikido. Many of my teammates had already learned one or more of these arts in their previous positions, but by the time we left the training, we were all as deadly with our hands and feet as we were with rifles or blades.

After a particularly grueling lesson one day near the end of training, I collapsed into the corner as my squad was finally dismissed by our instructor. We sat on benches and the floor, some of us panting more than others. I looked around at my fellow soldiers, and smiled at the pained but prideful expressions. The training had been exceedingly hard, but we were all proud of our accomplishments. Still, I wondered how useful techniques such as these would be against zombies.

My concern must have shown on my face, since Eaton spoke up. "Blake, what's up? You look worried." The rest of the squad turned to look at me.

I shrugged. "It's nothing, really. I'm just wondering how useful some of these techniques will be in the field. I mean, the idea is to keep the walker from biting you, I know that. Better than most, actually. So the throws especially I understand working on. But that only gets you so far. Let me show you what I mean. Barnes?" I turned to find her stretching to one side, and cleared my throat as my thoughts drifted. "Uh, give me a hand?" She stood up and nodded, then glided to the middle of the mat.

"Okay, Barnes here is a walker, and she's going to do everything she can to bite me," I said as I strode forward. She promptly adopted the stance and mannerisms of a zombie, raising her arms and moaning as she moved towards me. "Brains," she drawled as she walked forward. "Brai—" she stopped suddenly, breaking off and turning away. Several of the others laughed as she turned back around, chuckling.

Seeing my puzzled expression, she laughed as well. "Well, obviously I wasn't going to find any brains in *that* direction, was I?" The squad broke up laughing as she stuck her tongue out at me.

I began to laugh myself. "Har, har, har. Very funny." I sobered quickly, though. "Can we focus, please?" She nodded and was instantly the consummate soldier once more. She suddenly came at me, shambling along and moaning, and as I turned to throw her as we had practiced earlier, she made a show of biting me on the arm closest to her. I nodded and bowed to her, then walked back over to the rest of the squad.

"See? Just like that, you're one more soldier down, and there's one more walker to take out, only this one's someone you've fought and lived with." I sighed again. "And that's assuming their arm doesn't just pull right out of the socket or come apart in your hands. They're dead and decomposing, remember."

The squad was silent, realizing the importance of what I had just shown them. From the back of the room came a sharp snort and we all turned quickly to see Maxwell approaching us. None of us had seen him in weeks, and we had been wondering what had happened to him.

"He's right, you know," he said. "All these trainers and instructors are accustomed to training people to deal with normal threats, which doesn't include zombies. Blake, what would you suggest?"

I looked at my squad, who were all waiting for me to answer. "Well, sir, I would suggest that we use the training that we've received as a baseline for further work. I know that my squad has some very well trained martial artists amongst them, and I'm sure the other squads do as well. If we combine their knowledge of our true enemy with the training we've already received, we should be able to work up some more advanced training scenarios. But all this martial arts is—or should be—a secondary consideration, sir."

"Why do you say that?"

"Well, because the whole *point* should be to keep the damned things as far away from us as possible, sir. That's the single most important thing to remember about zombies. At a distance, they're essentially harmless. It's only up close that they become so dangerous. So while the throws and hand-to-hand are a still a good idea, just in case, we really should be focusing on how to escape being grabbed or pinned with these exercises. The knives and clubs and what-not . . . well, ideally we should never get close enough to use them, sir."

Maxwell merely grunted and looked thoughtful.

"One other thing, sir."

"Yes, Blake?"

"We're not just going to be fighting zombies, sir. We're going to be fighting regular people as well. Even our own turned friends and other soldiers. Walkers don't start out as walkers, sir. They're normal people to begin with, and those people will be scared, angry, hurt and more than a little crazy. We need to be prepared to fight not just the walkers, but also those who are infected but not yet turned, not to mention those who might become infected, too."

I looked around at my fellow soldiers and realized that none of them had come to this conclusion yet. It was a startling thing, to realize you would have to deal with the regular people as well as the zombies. Maxwell cleared his throat.

"Well, son, you've given us all something to chew on, haven't you?" I winced at his phrasing, but he continued without noticing. "I'll pass this along, and we'll see what adjustments can be made. Good thinking, Blake. Fall in!"

Without thought, we fell into our standard formation, drilled into us after months of training. Covered in sweat, we were prepared to listen to our commander.

"Part of my responsibility here is to see to it that you are all in tip-top shape at all times, and that includes mentally. Blake here," he said, pointing to me, "has just shown us that hardly any of us are thinking outside of the box on this one, especially us stick-in-the-mud military types. Obviously, we're all too close to this, and we need a break. You've all been working at this non-stop for nearly three months."

"So, we're going to bust you out of your routine and shake you up a bit. As of 2000 hours this evening, you have all been granted a forty-eight-hour pass." Surprise registered on all our faces, but even more so when Maxwell smiled. "You've earned it. Report back to your barracks no later than 2000 hours two days from now, and we'll continue your training. Until then," and he broke into the biggest grin we'd seen from him yet, "consider yourselves ordered to have fun and not think at all about walkers. Dismissed!"

There was a ragged cheer of sorts from the exhausted soldiers—and one civilian—and we fell out to our barracks. As we were leaving, I spotted Doctor Adamsdóttir entering from the side of the room. She and Maxwell were close in conversation, and if I hadn't seen it myself, I never would've believed it.

Ol' George was nervous.

Him? And the doc? No way. Never in a million years . . . I lost my train of thought as Eaton yanked me out of the door, pestering me with questions about the local sightseeing opportunities. Lost in our own conversation, I quickly forgot about our leader and the doctor.

Most of our team spent our first day off in months seeing the sights in Denver or Colorado Springs, or visiting friends and relatives. Alpha squad had little of the latter nearby. I had none, as my parents were long dead, and everyone else I had known had died in Fall Creek. So when Eaton and Barnes suggested that we have a nice dinner out the next night, the rest of us readily agreed.

Reynolds, Gaines, Martinez and I had been seated by a young hostess at one of the better steak restaurants in Denver. I had never been able to afford to eat here, but now that we were on the Army's dime, it seemed the logical choice.

Who knows when we'll get another chance?

We were all in evening wear, having had more than enough of uniforms for the moment and taking the rare opportunity to dress however we wanted. Barnes and Eaton had taken that idea to heart and had informed the other four of us in no uncertain terms that what we—meaning, of course, *they*—really needed was a night out on the town in style.

And damn if they didn't succeed, I thought as the girls entered the restaurant.

On the low side of medium height, Rachel Eaton had long brown hair that was often pulled back into a ponytail, and her brown eyes could pierce like augurs right through those unprepared for the intelligence behind them. She entered rooms like she owned them, and though she didn't monopolize conversations, she made damned sure that you knew she was there. No back seats or sidelines for her.

She had really pulled out all the stops tonight, in a black and white patterned strapless dress that set off her toned arms and prominent collarbones. Her dark hair was pulled half up in a clip, revealing sterling silver and teal earrings that matched her tasteful belt and open-toed heels. A black clutch purse completed the ensemble, and it was a toss-up as to whether she or the captain drew more stares. *Kimberly*, I admonished myself. *Her name is Kim. Not Barnes and not captain. Kim.*

Kim was stunning in a spaghetti-strapped deep green cocktail dress that perfectly matched her eyes. The dress fell to just above her knees, clinging to her slim legs as she moved. Long silver earrings accentuated her graceful neck and tanned shoulders, and her hair fell curling down her back in an auburn cascade. I was too flustered to even notice anything else as she and Eaton moved across the room arm in arm.

She and Eaton—*Rachel*—had outdone all of the guys by leaps and bounds. We were suitably attired, but the girls had every head in the place turning, male and female alike. They had reminded us that they were more than just soldiers, and I doubted any of us would forget that lesson again.

Kim laughed at a comment from Rachel. I looked away as she turned my way, hoping for help from Gaines, who was so obviously trying not to look at Eaton that it was almost pitiful. *He's not going to be any help.*

Somehow we managed to stand at the girls' arrival, and fumble our way through greetings. I tried to think of something debonair or at least mildly interesting to say, but failed because I couldn't seem to take my eyes off Kimberly, who, of course, hadn't noticed and was deep in whispered consultation with Eaton, both sitting across the large table from me.

In desperation, I turned to my left and asked Reynolds—Captain Tom Reynolds, Air Force, 22nd Special Tactics Squadron out of Tacoma, Washington—if he'd ever been here before. He looked back at me with a smirk as he shook his head.

"No, sir. A friend recommended it. You might ask Captain Bar . . . uh, Kim, though. I think she was stationed here at one point." Holding his menu up as though he was having trouble reading it, he nodded in her direction and winked at me as he grinned.

Bastard.

I turned back to Kim, as if I hadn't been practically drooling over her ten seconds before. "Well, Kim? Have you ever been here?"

Her eyes sparkled as she turned my way and flashed me her thousand-watt smile. *Good grief. I'll be useless if I can't get her out of my head.* "Just once, sir. Though it feels like a lifetime ago now."

"Stop calling me sir," I mumbled. I should've given up on it by now, but I couldn't seem to get them to stop. "How was the food?"

"It was amazing, si— David." She had made the effort, and I quickly squashed the little voice inside my head that told me how good it was to hear her say my name. "The T-bone was phenomenal, and the crab cakes, and . . . well, I'm getting even hungrier just thinking about it." She looked around for a waiter, and I sighed.

I just can't. Not now, not with all that's coming. I have to focus, buckle down, and forget how gorgeous she is.

I sighed again as the waiter arrived. "I'll have a Jack-and-Coke." I caught his arm as I noticed the two girls talking quietly across the table. "Make it a double, please," I muttered to him, and caught his slight grin as he nodded.

"Certainly, sir."

As it turned out, our fellow squaddie Reynolds was quite the conversationalist and dinner companion. He kept us entertained throughout the meal with funny anecdotes and critiques on the wine and the food, and always made sure that our glasses were full and our palates delighted by the sensations of the food and drink he suggested. He claimed to have been an engineer in his civilian career, though he did like to entertain.

Kim was right, this food is excellent. I groaned a little later as I leaned back. *I feel like a turkey ready for Thanksgiving dinner. Oof.*

I looked around the table and noted that everyone else also appeared full and in some cases, a bit tipsy. I realized I'd helped go through at least four bottles of wine between the six of us.

"So," I said. "what's next on the schedule?" I asked.

A whispered conversation later, the girls presented us with a united front. I glanced at the other guys and confirmed that they were as nervous about this as I was. What were they planning now?

"We want to go dancing," said Kim.

Rachel piped up, too. "And not somewhere cheap. Someplace nice." She shook her finger at me and I surprised myself by nodding.

"Why not?" I motioned to the waiter and he came over to the table quickly. "Where can we find a nice place for dancing?" I was certain I didn't slur my speech at all, but the waiter looked at me as though trying to translate what I had said.

"Dancing, sir? What kind of dancing did you have in mind?"

Helpless in the face of this most daunting of questions, I gestured to the girls. "Well?"

"Salsa," Kim said, a mischievous glint in her eye.

Evil, evil woman.

The waiter smiled and leaned down to give her what I could only presume were the directions to whatever den of iniquity he had in mind to seal the doom of the men in Alpha squad. Gaines began poking me in the ribs.

"What?" I hissed at him, surreptitiously holding my side where it felt like I'd been stabbed with the blunt end of a screwdriver. I looked up at Gaines to see the most pitiful hang-dog expression you can imagine.

"I can't dance, man. At least not that salsa stuff." Okay, *he* looked scared. I patted him on the shoulder and told him not to worry, I had it on good authority that Colonel Maxwell wouldn't let us go down without a fight, and I'd think of something.

Maybe it had been more than four bottles of wine, after all.

Suddenly, the waiter was gone and we were all standing in preparation for our departure. I grimaced and wondered how I would pull this off. The only time I'd ever danced in my life was at a cousin's wedding, and my date told me I'd left bruises all over her feet. I was not looking forward to this.

I turned to Reynolds to ask him if he could show us a couple of quick steps out of eyeshot of the girls at some point, but he demurred.

"I won't be joining you this evening, sir," he said. He quirked a smile my way. "My tastes lie in . . . other directions."

I followed his quick glance and saw meaningful glances pass between our waiter and Reynolds, out of sight of the others. I looked back at him and realization dawned at that moment. Tom merely smiled.

"Well," I began lamely. "Uh, good luck?"

He laughed and clapped me on the back, turning me to face the others. "My friends, I'm afraid that life calls me elsewhere, and I won't be able to join you. Have fun, and I'll see you tomorrow."

He winked at me, and I mustered everyone outside to the waiting cabs. Again, the girls had insisted on separate transport.

This could not end well.

Somehow, Gaines, Martinez and I managed to arrive before the girls. Much to our surprise, Martinez was able to teach the other two of us a few steps before they arrived. I asked him where he'd learned.

"I grew up in Miami, sir," he answered. "There, if you don't know salsa, you don't know nothing. They taught us in school, too."

I laughed and clapped him on the back. "Good thing for us, *mi hermano.*"

I don't know if it was the drinks, the girls, or the stress we were all under at the time, but I don't remember much after that.

I remember catching my breath yet again as the girls walked in. Dalton was in much the same state, though we both tried—and failed—to appear calm and cool at the table we had selected near the dance floor. Angelo had disappeared into the crowd as it got busier, and we'd let him go.

I remember the girls sitting down and us ordering drinks, starting a tab with our waiter. I clearly remember laughter and conversation while resting between dances. I remember Rachel leaning over to whisper in Dalton's ear, and him flushing as she took his hand and led him out to the dance floor. He glanced at me, and, feeling pretty good, I grinned and gave him a thumbs-up. He smiled, looked down at Rachel smiling back up at him, and whirled her out amongst the other dancers with a confidence I was certain was faked.

Damn him, he was a good faker.

I looked back over at Kim just in time to catch her looking at me, at which point she blushed and looked away. I still don't know where I got the courage, but I offered her a hand. "Care to dance?"

Her eyes shone as she looked back at me, and she led me to the dance floor. I don't remember us getting to the dance floor, but I do remember a slow song starting to play as the salsa band took a break from the usual pace, and her arms wrapped around my neck as we danced, her head resting on my chest.

Suddenly, she chuckled and nodded towards the other dancers, and I saw Rachel and Dalton in a similar pose. The difference in their height didn't seem to bother either of them in the slightest, and I was struck by the change that I'd seen come over my big friend. I looked back at Kim to comment on it, and saw her looking at me thoughtfully once again. This time, she didn't turn away.

That's one of the things I remember most from that night—realizing that the two of them, Rachel and Kim, had planned this whole thing from start to finish. Apparently, the dawning realization was evident on my face, because Kim placed one slim finger across my lips, stifling whatever I had been about to say. Not that I knew what that would have been.

She took in a relaxed breath and nodded almost to herself. "None of us know what's going to happen in the weeks to come, David. You and I both know what our mission means to the rest of the country, possibly to the world. What if we fail? We can't just put off our private lives while we hope that things turn out all right."

I started to object, but she shushed me again. "We didn't plan it, but it looks like some of the women in AEGIS are 'choosing' guys. Rachel and I just found out, and we're not about to get left out of the process. Not all the other girls have come on board with the idea, but we'll find a way to make it work," she said, then paused. "And yes, we know about Reynolds. He's not the only one. It's done."

She bit her lip as she leaned back, looking more fully into my eyes as we moved across the floor, and took another deep breath. "I've . . . I've chosen you, David. Rachel has chosen Dalton." I stopped, awestruck by her words. I felt her tense against me when my silence continued. "I've seen the way you look at me, don't tell me—"

I interrupted her as she had stopped me, with one finger across her lips, and smiled for what felt like the first time in a long time. "I understand." It was her turn to be surprised as I leaned down and gently kissed her, pulling her close to me. Her response was tentative, at first, and then grew more intense as the kiss continued.

No, *that* was what I remembered most from that night.

When we finally came up for air, I nodded across the floor to Dalton and Rachel. "You know he's absolutely head over heels for her, right?"

She laid a hand on my chest, smiling. "I know, but she can't see it. She feels the same way about him, though. Does he know?"

I laughed. "Not in the slightest. He gets nervous just at the mention of her name. It'll be interesting to see who breaks first."

"Yes, yes, it will," she said, smiling.

We danced and laughed and drank and danced some more until they finally kicked us out somewhere on the other side of two in the morning. There was early morning breakfast at some little diner I don't remember the name of, and the stumbling, bumbling walk out to the street to catch two more cabs—though this time the pairings were somewhat different.

We arrived back at the base the next morning in a disheveled state, the girls still looking beautiful and Dalton and I looking happier than pigs in . . . well, pretty darn happy. Reynolds met us at the barracks door, looking nearly as bad off as we were but somehow managing to make it seem dashing rather than reprehensible. Oh, how I hated him for that.

I don't remember seeing Martinez in the barracks, but he was there when we reported to the briefing room. I don't know that any of us were particularly clear-headed, but I noticed a good many more smiles and a generally lighter feel to the room than before our weekend pass.

We managed to pay some attention to that day's briefings, and as we ran through some fairly dry details of historical actions against walkers, I glanced over at Kim to see her looking back at me with a smile.

It was then that I knew we had a fighting chance. A chance to take down this menace before it killed us all. It wasn't going to be easy, and some of us wouldn't make it all the way through, but we had a chance.

No one could ask for more than that.

Chapter Five

FORT CARSON, COLORADO

AS OUR TRAINING CONTINUED, WE learned more about the classifications of walker incursions. It turned out that what happened at Fall Creek was just the tip of the iceberg, and there had been a pattern of behavior by the government to conceal the existence of walkers since the late 1800s. They'd even gone so far as to discredit witnesses who either refused payment in exchange for their silence or spoke out anyway.

One bit of AEGIS history that particularly disturbed me was what had happened to Harry Stafford in the Washington Territory in the 1930s. I shivered when I read his account, feeling close to the man who had gone more than a little mad at what he had seen, and what he had been forced to do.

I hear them, too, Harry. I hear them, too.

I hoped I wouldn't end up as he did. I hoped I was stronger than that. Our stories were too similar for me to completely discount any possibility of my going crazy, but then again, Harry hadn't had a full company of soldiers helping him, either.

There was, of course, no reference to any survivors other than Harry Stafford in the histories and files that we read. It seemed I was unique, and as I told my story again and again to the soldiers, I found it became easier to bear those memories. I would never forget the time I spent during those two days in Fall Creek, but it no longer haunted me as it once had.

One day a couple of weeks after our weekend pass, my team was led into a small room that reminded me of execution viewings.

A large curtained window, closed at the moment, faced two rows of chairs that looked profoundly uncomfortable. A switch on the wall, presumably for the curtain, completed the room's sparse adornments. We took our seats, curious about this new training, but we kept quiet and attentive, ready and able to take on any challenge.

Or so we thought.

We stood to attention as Maxwell entered, waving us back to our seats. He looked us over with a critical eye as always, and then nodded to Anderson, standing near the curtain control.

"I guess they're ready, Frank." Turning back to us, he stepped to one side, motioning to the window. "Ladies and gentlemen, meet Chauncey."

There was a collective gasp as the curtain drew aside to reveal a very old zombie that had rotted away almost to nothing. One of the soldiers in our company bolted out of his chair and was three steps away before even he realized it.

"Siddown, Jones!" Maxwell yelled. "That's bulletproof glass, son. The big scary monster can't get you."

Jones reddened with embarrassment and returned to his seat. *He'll hear about that for weeks.* It was only when we all turned back from Jones' distraction that I realized what the walker—*Chauncey*—was doing, and I wasn't the only one who turned a little green.

Fortunately or unfortunately, depending on your point of view, I'd seen it before. Still, the sight of a zombie feeding wasn't something you could just ignore. I glanced around the room, and saw the iron will these operators embodied as they steeled themselves against the horror.

I just swallowed hard and looked away. I'd seen enough already to last anyone a lifetime. I was trying to emulate these men and women, but even I had my limits. Taking more than a few deep breaths and gathering what resolve I had, I turned back.

Chauncey appeared to have been a male, from the lack of breasts and enlarged upper torso, but as to his age, no one could guess. He was so decrepit and rotten that bits seemed to be dropping off him even as we watched.

"We found dear old Chauncey here thirty-some years ago in eastern California, wandering around a campsite that appeared to have been attacked. By him or some other zombie, we don't know. Unfortunately, we didn't find any bodies or other walkers, except for one poor girl who apparently called it in to the locals but subsequently turned shortly thereafter. We took over the case, and brought Chauncey back here for study. Much of our more recent knowledge about the walkers was learned from him."

"But *feeding* him, colonel?" I asked, surprised as he at my questioning. "Why feed it? It's not as if it would die of starvation, after all. And how did it last this long anyway? Thirty-one years? That's impossible."

"Dr. Adamsdóttir theorizes that the reason it's still . . . alive . . . is that in an enclosed environment like this, the normal decomposition process is slowed to a near crawl. Bacteria and the other bugs don't seem to take to walkers as well as regular humans. The doc thinks it could be something in the blood changed by the prions, but no one knows for sure. No injuries, except for that collar and the wrist restraints. No outside forces like weather, heat, cold, etc. Just the same air conditioning, day in and day out." He shook his head as he looked at the walker.

"As to why they feed them . . . well, the doc has tried to explain it to me several times. Seems to be something about these prions being more active and replicating faster when the walker is feeding or has just finished. They don't give them much, just enough to see whatever it is they're looking for. Frankly, I'd rather they just put him down, but that's not an option. At least not now.

"All of you need to get used to this," he said. "You will all be participating in acclimatization exercises with Chauncey here over the next few weeks, to prepare you for live combat. We need you functional out there, not falling apart in the face of the enemy."

Chauncey had finished his meal, and now stood at the metal table, his hands and neck linked to steel cuffs on chains, their other ends embedded in the reinforced concrete of the lab floor.

A door opened in one wall of Chauncey's cell, and a short, bored and average-looking technician came through with a long pole in one hand. The pole had a hook on one end, and just as I was wondering what he intended to do with it, he hooked a special loop on the bucket of 'food', pulling it toward himself and leaving the room with the feed bucket in hand.

Afterward, Dr. Adamsdóttir gave us a tour, briefing us on some new developments in the labs, designs created specifically by AEGIS technicians. She stopped near a mannequin outfitted with an ACU that was much thicker than normal.

"This is a special type of Kevlar weave we've been looking at incorporating into your uniforms to help with bites from the walkers. It's great for preventing heat and abrasions, but not so good with the way biting combines pressure with tearing. We haven't worked out all the bugs yet."

She held up the jacket for our inspection. "Your new uniforms will be substantially stronger than the classic versions, but they'll also be thicker and heavier. That's something else we're trying to address."

She moved over to a nearby table, covered with what looked for all the world like electronic packs of cigarettes with an elastic band on one side.

"So what we have here, boys and girls, is essentially a mini-computer that tells this gun not to fire at you," she said, pointing at what we now all recognized as an automated M2 'Ma Deuce' .50 caliber machine gun on a ground mount. "Now for a demonstration. Ears please," Mary continued, and we all put on our ear protectors and watched as she pointed down-range.

A training dummy began crossing the range at normal zombie speed, and we watched in amazement as the gun tracked briefly before chattering to life and taking out the target. I was impressed even more by the gun's accuracy, given its automatic targeting—it had fired at head height, and used minimal ammunition.

"Now watch what happens with the device attached to a dummy with a simulated heartbeat." Mary yelled, pointing to the next training dummy, wearing one of the devices around its bicep. The gun tracked the target, but didn't fire.

I looked over at Kim, who was watching the system like a kid in a candy store, and I grinned, giving her a thumbs-up. She returned the gesture and turned back to Mary, pointing at the headsets.

Mary nodded, engaged the gun's safety, and removed her headset, and we followed suit. "Dr. Fanning originally designed them as mobile trauma units, but then he gave them to me when he saw the implications, and I improved on them a bit. So, what do you think?"

Kim was the first one to speak up. "How does it work?"

"It monitors vital signs such as blood pressure and temperature and then transmits that data wirelessly to the system. It also includes a GPS transceiver. We can monitor the vital signs of anyone wearing it. Hence the mobile trauma idea." She pointed at a small computer attached to the side of the gun's mount.

"The defense system compares the transmitted data to a set of specifications that we have programmed into it. If the data falls within the parameters, the gun doesn't fire. If not, it does."

"So if a target is cold, with no blood pressure . . ." I asked.

"Like a zombie . . ." added Rachel.

"Then it gets some more iron in its diet," Mary said, grinning. "A *lot* more."

"How does it track the targets?" asked Angelo. "I mean, inside a building or whatever, if they don't give off heat . . ."

"Ah, good question, Captain. It uses a combination of radar, sound amplification, infrared and other sensors to pick up movement." She paused. "Have you seen *Aliens*?"

He laughed. "Of course, Doc. It's practically required viewing for anyone my age."

"Right, of course. Well, the motion trackers we've built into this system function very much like those in that movie. Granted, not as spiffy-looking, but basically the same thing."

"Sweet."

"What's it called?" I asked.

"We're calling them 'Real-time Enemy Assessor and Physiology Readers.'" There was a snort from Tom Reynolds to one side, and when I looked at him, he just waved off my unspoken question.

"Nothing, sir. Sorry."

I jumped and swore as Mary snuck up behind me and strapped one of the devices on my arm. "Damn woman, you should be one of us."

She shrugged. "Too smart for that, I guess. You all need to know that it works, so you're going to show them. They're not perfect, but we'll get there. George wants them ready for you before your first mission."

She looked over at Reynolds, who by this time was red-faced trying not to laugh. He was practically crying as he held his sides. Mary got a mean look in her eye. "Don't you dare, Reynolds. Don't you dare."

The rest of us looked on in puzzlement as Reynolds tried and failed to contain his laughter one last time. "Sorry, Mary . . . but this is too good." He pointed at my arm. Another warning glance from

Mary just bounced right off. There were groans and guffaws alike as he finally got it out: "Don't fear the REAPR, sir."

Sometimes I hate my squad.

Fast-forward a few days, and we were near the airfield, practicing fast-roping. I'd done so many drops out of Black Hawks and other helicopters at this point that it was almost second-nature. After I piled out of the current bird, I noticed Maxwell observing, and ran over.

"Mr. Blake. What can I do for you?"

"Well, sir, I've been thinking about this for some time now. Our main objective is to stay as far from the walkers as we can when we take them out, but we're still on the ground in most of the scenarios we're practicing."

Kimberly and the others looked interested as they gathered around, the dust from the departing Black Hawk settling down as it moved off.

"Where are you going with this, Blake?"

"Well, sir . . . why don't we use the helos, sir? For more than just transport, I mean."

"You mean like miniguns or snipers mounted in the helos?"

"Yes, sir."

"Walk with me, Blake. The rest of you might as well come, too." He waved off the Humvee driver, and we began the march back to the main part of the base.

"We've thought about using helos and aircraft for a long time, frankly. The problem is that when you're talking about walkers, you've got one of two ways to take them down—a shot to the head, or a leg shot that you can follow-up on later."

"Right, sir. Surely you can do that from a chopper?"

"Son, you've been on the firing line. You know how hard it is to make a headshot in perfect range conditions. Now imagine that you're forty, fifty, a hundred feet in the air, swinging back and forth with the wind." He snorted. "There's maybe thirty guys in the world could make those shots with any reasonable reliability. And they're all spoken for, protecting high-value targets *without* having their butts in a sling a hundred feet in the air.

"Of course, you've got the M240s and rockets and other things, but those are 'spray and pray' at best. You might get one in a hundred headshots, and maybe twenty to thirty in a hundred will take out a leg or two, but either way you've still gotta helluva mess to clean up. And you have to get down there to do it."

"Napalm." Gaines jogged next to us without apparent effort.

The bastard.

"And we can use that, when it's appropriate. Flamethrowers on some tanks and ground troops, etc. The problem with all this is that the most effective tools we have at fighting the enemy also destroy nearly everything around them. Tanks can't really fight effectively in an urban environment—even Humvees have a problem turning in some areas, although we've had good luck with the Bradleys." Maxwell slowed and began walking as we approached his office.

"It's not about the machines and the firepower and everything else. Hell, do you have any idea how much fuel it takes to run a tank like an Abrams?" He turned back to us. "We can run the helos and the tanks and the planes, and take out a lot of zombies—and a lot of civilians and structures at the same time, while we burn through our available fuel like there's no tomorrow—which there won't be if we don't take these bastards out. And we may end up doing that, if the situation gets bad enough.

"But for now, we need surgical strikes. In, out, and done with minimal impact on the surroundings and *especially* minimal impact on civilians. The fewer who know about us, the better." He glanced at us, and then down at his watch. "Now, if I'm not mistaken, it's chow time. And it's chili night. So get going! Dismissed!"

"David, wake up."

I woke up thinking I was in a rocking boat, but as it turns out, it was just Kim shaking me. "Wha'? What is it?"

"It's Tom, David. He's . . . well, you need to see him." Her voice sounded shaken.

What the hell?

I was dressed and out the door headed for the infirmary before I even realized it. Only when we got there did I realize the rest of Alpha squad was with us.

I was only partly surprised to see Mary in the ward this late, attending to our friend. Turning as we rushed in, she held up her hands and ushered us back into the waiting area.

"He's okay for the moment, but he's asleep, and needs it. So none of you are going to wake him up." She motioned to the infirmary's commander, Captain Stephen Drewson, who signed a form and headed over to us.

"He's sedated, for now. Multiple contusions and lacerations on his face and upper body, his jaw is broken in two places, and his nose. Swelling indicates he was hit in the ear several times as well."

I could see Kimberly getting red to match her hair, and laid a hand on her arm. Surprisingly enough, she didn't immediately fling it off, but just took a deep breath.

"Go ahead, Doc," I said.

"Well, he didn't go down easy, I'll say that much for him. Bruises and scrapes on the knuckles as well as some blood that clearly isn't his on his ACU indicates that he put up a hell of a fight. Whoever did this is definitely going to be in pain, from what I can guess. And they haven't shown up here to be treated."

"That's good to know, Doc," said a voice from behind us, and we turned to find Major Matthew Daniels standing there. Fort Carson's Provost Marshal. The man wasn't physically imposing, unless you'd seen him in the training grounds or in the gym. Even Gaines gave the man a wide berth. "Should make it easier to find them."

Rachel spoke up. "I think I know who you can start with, sir." The look on her face made me feel sorry for the fool who engendered such a reaction in Rachel. I wouldn't have wanted to be on the receiving end of whatever she was planning.

Ten minutes later, we watched through one-way glass in the provost's office as Daniels interviewed Petty Officer 3rd Class Edward Ames, a member of Bravo squad. Lieutenant Commander Jake Powell, squadleader for Bravo, had joined us in the viewing room.

"You look like you could use some medical attention," said Daniels.

He wasn't wrong. Ames looked as though he'd been through the wringer and come out the other side hard. Split lip, eyebrow bleeding, and when they brought him in he was limping more than a little.

"Just fell down the stairs, sir."

"Is that right? Which stairs would those be? We have to make sure the facility's safe, after all."

Ames said nothing, and stared straight ahead.

"Do I look stupid to you, kid? Or maybe you think I'm just dumb enough to believe that."

"No, sir."

"No, sir, *what*, soldier?"

"No, sir, I don't believe you're dumb or stupid, sir."

"Well, then, that's a start. Now, you wanna tell me where you really got your injuries? Cause it wasn't from falling down the fucking stairs."

"I . . . It was a fight, sir."

"Oh, I see. A fight. Looks like you need a little more time in the gym, son. Cause you got your ass whupped!"

Ames turned red and shouted. "Bullshit! I kicked that faggot's ass!" Realizing he'd said too much, he slumped back in his chair, looking through the provost as if he didn't exist.

"You really are a moron, aren't you?" Daniels just shook his head. "Why don't you tell me who started it? Save yourself some brig time. Not all of it, mind you, but some."

Ames looked up from under lowered brows. "He did. Prancing fucking fairy!"

The sound was like a thunderclap designed by God himself as Daniels' hand slammed down. "That is enough, Seaman."

"Petty Officer, sir."

"Not if you don't tell me what I want to know, it isn't. Hell, you'll be lucky to end up as a Seaman Apprentice. Wanna go back to swabbing decks, asshole?"

Ames shook his head. "No. No, sir."

"Then tell me what I want to know. Now."

"He hit on me, sir."

"Who did?"

"The fa—Reynolds. After our leave a few weeks back. He was drunk off his ass when he came in the barracks and he hit on me."

I looked over at Kimberly, who was obviously trying to control her temper. Rachel stood beside her, equally pissed.

"Tom would never have done that," Kim whispered to me. "I don't care how drunk he was."

"I know, Kim. Let's just let Daniels handle this."

"What exactly did he say?" asked the provost. "What words did he use to make you think he was hitting on you?"

"Uh, well . . . he said we . . . um, should get drinks some time. And he said it looked like I was losing weight, and I looked good. And some other stuff." Ames looked down at his hands, clenched in his lap.

The door to the interview room slammed open, and Commander Anderson stormed in, looking as pissed as I'd ever seen him. "Thank you, Major," he said to Daniels, who looked stunned. "That will be all for now. I'll take it from here."

"But you can't—This is . . ." Daniels started to protest, but then looked at Anderson's face. "Yes, sir." He stood up and left the room without even the briefest of backward glances.

Anderson walked over and put his fists on the table, leaning forward. "You asshole."

Ames didn't even look up.

"We're fighting a fucking war against the goddamn undead," Anderson continued, his voice never raising. Those of us in the viewing room struggled to hear it through the pickup. "And you go and pull some dumb redneck shit like this. What the fuck is wrong with you?" Anderson leaned closer. "I should feed you to Chauncey right now."

Ames went as pale as I'd ever seen anyone get. He knew that he could be disappeared and no one would ever know. He cowered back in his seat.

"But I'm not going to," the commander said, straightening. "I don't have to. Act like that again, and your own people will take you out. I won't have to lay a finger on you."

I glanced over at Powell, and saw him nodding. I hoped it was an unconscious agreement.

"We need everyone we can get in this fight. Reynolds is ten times the man—ten times the *operator*—that you are. If I had to choose . . . well, it wouldn't be a choice. So let me make myself perfectly clear."

He walked toward the door, turning back to look at the cringing man that had replaced the bigoted jackass who sat there only a few minutes before. "If I ever hear so much as a peep out of anyone that you've tried this shit again, I guarantee you that we *will* have that little meeting with Chauncey. Understood?"

When Ames didn't reply, Anderson continued. "Is that understood, soldier?"

"Yes . . . yes, sir," Ames finally answered.

"Very well." He knocked on the door and Daniels opened it. "Put him in solitary for a week. Let him think about what he's done. He's also offered to forfeit his pay for the next month to some suitable charity. I'm sure you can find one."

Daniels' grin was quick. "Oh, I'm sure I can, sir."

"See to it then," Anderson said, and left.

I turned to the others as Daniels escorted the white-faced Ames from the room. I couldn't help but look at Powell, who was staring into the now empty room, and only turned to face me when he noticed the scrutiny. He came to attention as he turned to Kimberly.

"Captain, on behalf of Bravo squad, I apologize for Ames' actions. I assure you, it won't happen again."

"It better not."

We headed back to the infirmary, anxious to check up on our friend. Still sleeping, Drewson told us, but he assured us that he would inform someone the moment Tom was cleared for visitors.

Several days later, we were sitting in the briefing room, wondering why we'd been summoned. The whole 1st Team—except for the still-recovering Reynolds and his incarcerated assailant Ames—was ready and raring to go. Of course, there were those of us who thought we would be assigned our first mission, but given Commander Anderson's un-stressed attitude, I thought that was unlikely, at best. I knew I'd be at least a little tense if I was sending people to maybe get killed. No, this is something else entirely.

Maxwell walked in, and we all stood at attention, waiting until he reached the front of the room.

"Take your seats." There was a shuffling of feet as we sat at the tables, and he leaned forward on the podium a bit. "I have some good news, folks."

I glanced at Kim, who shrugged. Clearly, she didn't have a clue either.

"We've recorded no walker activity in the last five months, while you've all been in training. I don't know whether this is due to the weather being unseasonably cold, or simply just our dumb luck, but at the moment, we have nothing for you folks to do but stay here and train."

He straightened and began pacing. "Now, I'm all for training until you can do this in your sleep, but we've got our orders." Maxwell glanced at Anderson, who appeared grim and very unhappy at the announcement. "1st Team is hereby moved to 'inactive' status until further notice."

I wasn't the only one to respond with a hearty "Bullshit!" or similar. *This makes no sense, no sense at all. We need to keep training.*

Maxwell waited until we calmed down, then continued. "I know, and I don't like it any more than you do, but these are our orders. The commander and I will stay here to coordinate activities with the research group and the SpecOps teams for any minor incursions that may happen. We'll also be drawing up plans for other teams to start training, when and if we get those orders.

"Let me be clear, folks. I'm not letting this order stand, if I can help it. We all need more training, and more training after that. So don't expect to be gone long."

"What happens now, sir?" asked Rachel. "Where do we go? Not all of us have lives outside of this base."

"I know that. I've been authorized to have our people make arrangements for you, wherever you'd like to live—provided you can be back here in twelve hours if the shit hits the fan. Make an appointment with Nancy, and she'll get everything set up. I'd recommend you stick together as much as possible, but I can't order you to."

He looked over at Anderson. "Anything you want to add, Frank?"

The commander looked thoughtful for a moment. "Maintain operational security at all times. Keep an eye on the news. Keep your phones close. That's it."

"All right, 1st Team, you have your orders. Dismissed!"

Chapter Six

SOMEWHERE IN TEXAS
9 MONTHS LATER

RING

"Hello?"

Cold, electronic tones. "Voice identification confirmed. Code Alpha Five. Authenticate." A short pause. "Authenticate!"

The training took over. "Authentication Delta Tango Bravo. Active."

"Confirmation and activation accepted. Standby."

Click

My hand shook as I hung up. It had finally happened, and there was no going back now. All our careful preparations . . . would they be worth a damn, in what was to come? No time to worry about that now. If we were moving off inactive status, then the shit must have hit the fan somewhere.

I dropped the phone into the pocket of my jeans and snagged my keys from the kitchen's bar, moving at a fast walk down the hallway. Stopping briefly to retrieve a large duffel bag from the hall closet, I opened the door into the garage and took a quick last look around at what had been my home. I hit the garage door opener, and set down the duffel bag next to the covered motorcycle.

Pulling the ripcord quickly let the airtight cover fall away with a soft sigh of inrushing air, leaving me looking at a pristine motorcycle that seemed to exude speed. This one was somewhat modified and could go appreciably faster than the standard model.

Not that we ever tested that, of course. I grinned.

I strapped the duffel tight to the rack mounted on the back and it fit perfectly, as I knew it would. Pulling on the nearby gloves, jacket, and helmet, I added a machete from the wall to a leather holster on the right side of the bike and a small mallet on the left. I hoped I wouldn't need them, but if the balloon really had gone up, there was no way to know. *Better safe than sorry.*

Satisfied that everything was in place, I pulled forward out of the garage and closed the large door. The late afternoon air was breezy and cool, a fine fall day. I looked back once as I pushed the button on the bike—a last minute addition that looked as though it had been bolted on—and saw the inside of the house go dark, a small green light flashing twice in the front window.

I hope I see you again. I accelerated down the street. *I liked living here.*

The bike easily ate up the pavement, gathering speed as I leaned into the turns, headed for the freeway. I gave the instruments a cursory glance, knowing what they would show. Everything was normal—for now.

That'll change soon enough. I sighed. *Everything will, and so few of us are ready to fight.*

Crackling static sounded in my ear, then a voice, through the helmet's earpiece. "Alpha Five, AEGIS Actual. Report."

This time I was ready, but something wasn't right. "Active and on-schedule to Checkpoint One."

"Acknowledged. Be advised, the remainder of Alpha is on schedule. Alpha Six authenticated but has not checked in and is presumed off-mission."

I couldn't let this one go. Even though she'd broken up with me months ago, even though it still hurt every time I thought about her, I couldn't resist the impulse to find out what was going on with her now, at this critical moment. "Request permission to retrieve Alpha Six." A long pause, so long I began to wonder if the connection had been broken. "Repeat, request—"

"Approved. GPS tracking data downloading to you now. Alpha squad will proceed as normal. Retrieval of Alpha Six is a secondary objective. Acknowledge."

I breathed a little easier and glanced at the bike's custom GPS display. "Acknowledged. Tracking data received. Will report when Alpha Six retrieved and en route. Alpha Five out." This was going to be one difficult confrontation, but I couldn't just leave her. Not now. Not after all we'd been through, and all that was still to come.

The blaring horn of the trucker behind me interrupted my reverie, and I twisted the throttle, blasting onto the freeway's entrance ramp. By the time I hit the main lanes, I was already at 95, and weaving in and out of traffic like a madman as I continued accelerating. She was ten minutes away, even at these speeds.

"Dispatch, this is Unit 17, in pursuit of a motorcycle at high speed northbound. Request back-up and run the following plate: Three Victor X-ray Four Three Seven." His siren wailing, the trooper waited for a response. He jerked the wheel suddenly as the motorcycle veered sharply into another lane, then passed the car beside him. As the motorcycle weaved in and out of the mildly congested freeway traffic with only inches to spare in some cases, the trooper began to sweat.

This fool is going to kill someone. And himself!

"Unit 17, Dispatch. Standby."

For a brief moment, he pulled alongside the motorcycle, attempting to edge it towards the shoulder without causing an accident. The rider looked over at him through his jet-black visor. Slowly and deliberately, the rider shook his head at the trooper, then twisted the throttle and roared ahead. *That's impossible. No motorcycle is that fast.*

"Unit 17, Dispatch." The trooper glanced at the radio as a different voice responded to him. He knew that voice. It was the dispatch center's supervisor, but he sounded odd, somehow. "Cease pursuit immediately. Repeat, cease pursuit immediately and resume normal patrol. Do not document this incident in any way. Forget that it ever happened. Is that understood?"

"Understood, Dispatch," said the trooper, in a tone indicating he did not, in fact, understand. He turned off his lights and siren, slowing down to posted speeds and watching the motorcycle continue its maniac course through traffic. "Show me back in service. Unit 17 out."

Several miles away, at the dispatch center, the supervisor turned back to his monitor and the message that had been returned when he had run the plate. "Department of Defense vehicle. Do not pursue. Do not report." The supervisor fumed. *Damn irresponsible running a bike like that.*

His thoughts interrupted by yet another emergency call coming in, the supervisor watched as one of the operators handled it. He pushed the mysterious bike and its rider to the back of his mind. He didn't notice his monitor blanking and the message "Retrieval record deleted" appearing, either.

I smiled to myself as the siren and lights following me fell silent and still, as I knew they would. *I wonder how that conversation went.* I pulled off the freeway and onto side streets as I headed for the tag marked on my GPS unit. She was on the move, but not where she was supposed to be going. I heard the distinctive sound of another bike like mine and coasted to a stop in an alley, shutting off the headlight as she sped by. She turned, and I followed.

Twenty minutes later, the near-moonless night had fallen and it was dark as she turned into an apartment complex in a lower-class neighborhood. Not horrible, but not somewhere I'd want to be alone at night—as I was right now. I pulled into the alley behind a darkened business and shut off the bike, keeping my eye on the apartment complex across the street.

As I moved toward the end of the alley to make my way across, I heard a sound that chilled me to the bone. It was a sound I hadn't heard in years—at least, outside a lab—and one I had hoped never to hear again.

A low, resonating moan came from the figure approaching down the alley. One hand on the machete I'd pulled off the bike—now in its hip holster—I stepped forward to investigate. *Surely they couldn't be here already. We would have been activated long before now.* He didn't appear to notice my movement, instead seeming to concentrate on something between us.

As I closed in, I could see a homeless man in faded Army fatigues and a wool cap, lying on the pavement against the alley wall. He appeared to be either asleep or dead and didn't notice the figure coming at him. Another low moan issued from that creature, along with a strange rumbling noise, and I eased the machete out of its scabbard as I took another look at the creature again, much closer than before.

Just as it passed under the flickering remnants of the alley's one remaining light, I finally got to see its face, very pale and contorted in pain. *Wait. Walkers don't feel—*

Another groan, and this time the figure leaned against the wall and vomited what appeared to be everything he had eaten in the last few days. I relaxed, the machete returning to its holster almost as if by magic and my breathing returning to more normal levels. I shook my head as the poor homeless vet got hit with another burst from the drunkard, and moved to leave the alley.

Out of the corner of my eye, I spotted my quarry entering one of the apartment buildings across the street, and moved to follow her to her destination—wherever that might be. What was she after, here?

I'd never been here before, and she hadn't mentioned it at any time during the time we'd been together.

What other secrets has she hidden from me? It didn't matter now. I had to get her out of here and on the road.

Of the twelve field agents, ten had been successfully activated. "AEGIS Actual" looked up from his terminal and out the window, putting down his headset. His aide stood beside him, listening to his own headset and taking notes furiously on a clipboard.

"That's it, Frank. It's done," said Maxwell.

Anderson murmured one word—"standby"—into his headset and turned to face the colonel, his hands and clipboard folded behind him at exactly the proper at-ease position.

"Yes, sir. We have confirmation on ten, sir. Only Ames hasn't reported." Frank paused for a moment, apparently ill at ease about continuing. "Sir, about Blake . . ."

Maxwell held up a hand to forestall further protest. "Sometimes, Frank, we have to bend the rules to follow them. I'd hoped that you'd see that by now. That man deserves a chance to find her." He turned to look at his long-time friend and colleague, who sighed with resignation.

"George, it's just as much a part of me to question that order as it is for you to give it. You know that. Any less and we wouldn't be where we are today. You know I agree with you."

George nodded and smiled a grim smile. "Still, I had to say something. As you say, it's a part of me." He turned back to the window and his view of the Rockies as he picked up the headset again and put it on, sighing softly. "Still, maybe he can get her back. They're going to need everyone. Have Powell follow up with Ames. If anyone can find out what that asshole's up to, it's him. Are the rest of the protocols in place?"

Frank was all business once again. "Yes, sir. All protocols are in place, ready, and awaiting activation, sir."

George nodded and turned back to his terminal. "AEGIS Actual to all stations. Initiate Protocol AEGIS Five Two, repeat, initiate Protocol AEGIS Five Two. Authorization Golf Hotel Mike seven five."

He looked at Frank, who was issuing the retrieval orders to Powell, then spoke again. "And may God have mercy on our souls."

I moved quietly up the building's stairs, not sure exactly what I was headed into. I had managed to follow her here, but I had no idea *why* she was here, and that made this whole situation dangerous. *I should be past Checkpoint One by now.*

Instead, here I was standing outside an apartment door, trying to hear what the shouting inside was all about.

Love can do funny things to a man.

Suddenly the shouting cut off, the door flew open and I was knocked off my feet by a tall auburn-haired woman with tears in her eyes and a motorcycle helmet in her hand as she exited the apartment.

I sat there trying to get my breath back and mentally checking that nothing was broken as I looked up at her. She stood there, frozen in shock.

"Hello, Kimberly," I said, at length.

A large blond man who looked as if he could crush free weights in his hands just for the fun of it filled the doorway behind her. His young face looked strained and his voice was hoarse, probably from all the yelling. "Who's this, sis?"

It was only then, as I was picking myself up off the ground, that I noticed the clear family resemblance. She wiped the tears away and stared at me in silent defiance. I raised one eyebrow.

When she didn't respond, I sidestepped her and stuck out a hand towards the big man. "David Blake, 1st Alpha, AEGIS. And you are?"

Kimberly was nonplussed as her brother sized me up—much like Maxwell had so long ago—and then clasped my hand in a strong grip. I winced as he introduced himself.

"Name's John, David. John Barnes. So you're from this 'AEGIS' outfit, are you? Then it's all real, what's she's told me?"

I looked at her out of the corner of my eye as she looked down, slumping. "Well, John, I don't know exactly what she's told you, but AEGIS is real, and so am I . . . and she and I have to go."

"I told him everything," she mumbled. "I had to. He's all I have left, David." She looked at me as though imploring me to forgive her transgression. As though I had the right to tell her it was okay that she had lied through her teeth to me, to her unit, and to the Army.

"No, he's not, Kim." My meaning was clear as I looked straight at her, and she looked away. "I told you I was there for you, and you left me. You left whatever it was we had, and I never heard from you. That was *your* choice, not mine."

"Oh? There's one thing she didn't tell me, I guess." John looked at his sister, then back at my unsmiling face, and then shrugged. "I wish it'd lasted, sis. You've always seemed so lonely, after . . ." He broke off and looked down.

He appeared haunted, as though he'd seen something horrible. I knew that look, and I guessed he was thinking of their parent's death, one of the few personal things that Kim had shared with me before she split. *She didn't tell me about him, though. I wonder how much of what she did tell me was the truth?*

John looked back at me. "Well, if you need to go, go. You folks have important things to do, and I won't stand in your way. Not that I could ever talk her out of anything, anyway," he said as he looked at her fondly. "Sis, I'll go to Colorado Springs like you asked. Whenever you get done with this, I'll be there waiting for you."

She looked at him, smiled that huge smile of hers, and hugged him tight. "Thank you, Johnny. I'll leave you some contact info when I know more, if I can. I love you."

His huge arms enfolded her, making her look small. "I love you, too. Be safe. Now go."

"Let's go, David," she said, walking down the corridor. I made to follow, but her brother motioned me over.

"Take care of her," he whispered as I leaned in. "If she dies, you die. If she hurts, you hurt. Understand?" As I straightened, I started to tell him how well she could take care of herself, but he knew that already. He was just being a protective brother, and I could tell how serious he was about that.

In the same somber tones, I answered him. "John, I promise you I will do everything I can to protect her. She will be safe with me." He nodded as though the issue was settled for him, and perhaps it was. I felt certain that he would be in Colorado waiting for her when whatever had happened was all over. As I turned and moved down the stairs to catch up to Kim, I wondered how likely it was that she would ever meet him there.

"What the hell, Kim?" I asked as we neared her bike and she climbed on. "Were you ever planning on telling me about him?"

She fumbled with the straps of her helmet, staring at her hands. "I couldn't. What was I supposed to say? 'Hey, I've got a brother. I have to make sure he's safe. Oh, and, no, I can't leave without telling him everything about our super-secret Army unit?'"

"Maybe not, but I deserved to know." I caught her arm as she put on her helmet, forcing her to look at me.

"I know, David. I'm sorry. We can't talk about this now, though. We're already late."

"I'm parked over there," I said, pointing. "Follow me, and *do not* report in. We're already in enough trouble. I'll handle it."

"Yes, sir," she said with a tentative smile that I didn't return. "Hop on and I'll give you a lift. Better than walking."

I hesitated, but got on, reluctantly putting my hands around her waist, and she sped us over to my bike. She idled as I started it and suited up. I looked at her as I reported in. "AEGIS Actual, Alpha Five. Package retrieved, en route to Checkpoint One, ETA fifteen minutes."

The response was immediate. "Alpha Five, AEGIS. Package retrieval acknowledged, proceed to Checkpoint One ASAP." There was a slight pause, and the commander continued in a quieter tone. "Welcome back, Kim. Good to have you with us."

She bowed her head as she heard him, and she sounded somewhat choked up as she replied. "Good to be back, sir." Her jet-black helmet, visor down, turned towards me, and I nodded. Seconds later, we were twin blurs of speed on the freeway, headed west.

A little while later, we approached Checkpoint One, the local Army National Guard post. As we pulled into the parking lot, we noticed four other similar bikes and parked next to them. As I took off my helmet, I could hear the rotors of a nearby helicopter turning and glanced around.

A very young man in fatigues approached and saluted. "Sir, the chopper is standing by behind the building, sir. I've been ordered to see to your motorcycles and make sure you get on board as fast as humanly possible, sir. Or it's my ass, sir."

I returned the salute and laughed. "At ease, Private. I'm guessing you spoke with Colonel Maxwell, right? And that 'or it's your ass' is a direct quote?"

"Y-yes, sir."

"Thought so. Let me let you in on a little secret, Private. He's a real softy at heart. Besides, I'm not the one you should be saluting. And don't call me sir." I grabbed my gear bag from the back of the bike and threw him my helmet. He managed to catch it, then looked over my shoulder and stopped dead still, staring, mouth gaping like a dying fish. I chuckled because I knew what he was seeing.

"All right, Barnes," I said, chuckling. "Give the poor boy your helmet and let's get going." I heard her laugh too, and her helmet followed mine into the private's arms as he somehow caught the second one as well, without taking his eyes off of Kimberly.

As Kimberly and I rounded the corner of the building, we could see the Black Hawk's rotors begin to spin faster, and the other four members of our unit climbed aboard, giving us a hand as we raced up to the chopper just as the skids left the ground. I pounded Gaines on the back as I climbed in, pointing to his chin where a scraggly growth of beard grew. He blushed and glanced Rachel's way and I laughed. "She likes it, doesn't she?" I yelled over the noise from the rotors and the wind outside, and he nodded.

I felt a pang that they had made it through these nine months and Barnes and I hadn't, but I gave him a thumbs-up and put on my headset, making sure that everyone was secure as I looked towards the crew chief. SILVERA was stitched on his uniform.

"Chief Silvera, how far behind schedule are we?"

He shook his head. "Far enough that my CO just gave me a royal ass-chewing, sir. I hope whatever slowed you down was worth it."

Kim looked at me as I glanced her way, and smiled. I found myself smiling back, bigger than I wanted to. "It was, Chief. It was."

Reynolds looked over at Gaines and Martinez and laughed, pretending to gag. It was as if we were right back to where we were nine months ago. I wasn't sure I'd feel this way again, ever, but it was like we'd never been apart.

Too bad it couldn't last.

We landed just before midnight at some airfield, the name of which I immediately forgot, and were escorted to a fueled and waiting Air Force Learjet. I exchanged glances with my squad as we boarded, wondering just how bad the situation was for them to send a Learjet for us. Granted, a cargo jet, but still, not something you saw every day when flying for the military.

I shrugged and buckled in, just in time for the doors to be closed. We could hear some minor chatter from the cockpit as we strapped in amidst the containers and other materials being transported, not that there appeared to be much of that. Our gear was stowed overhead, and the rumble of the engines increased as we accelerated down the runway and took off.

Leveling off at cruising altitude, the pilot indicated we could stand up and stretch our legs. I decided it was time for that overdue explanation, and looked over at Kim, nodding my head toward the rear. She sighed, nodded, unbuckled herself, and walked back.

As I stood up to follow her, Gaines chuckled, though it turned into a grunt as Eaton dug her elbow into his ribs. I chuckled too as I left them there, him rubbing his side and her glaring at him. Martinez was snoring, and Reynolds, for his part, just looked amused and snagged a magazine from his bag.

Kim didn't look glad to see me as I made my way back through the cargo to the only empty space at the back. She fidgeted and picked at her nails. I leaned against a stack of boxes and waited for her to come around on her own. I'd learned long ago that push-ing her too far to do anything was useless. A nudge here and there, but never the proverbial stick.

If only I'd learned that in time. Ah, well. Que sera, sera.

"I lied to you, David," she said, not looking up.

Well, this is going to go well. I waited for her to continue.

"My parents didn't die in a car crash." She began to pace back and forth. "They told me after it happened that I couldn't tell anyone what I'd really seen, what we had been through. We were so young when it happened."

She sat down on a crate and folded her arms across her chest. "Did you ever wonder why Maxwell and I got along so well?" It occurred to me that she and the colonel had been friendly, but I hadn't noticed anything out of the ordinary, and said so.

"My brother and I lived with him for years. He and his wife Althea took us in after . . . after what happened to our parents. He could have let AEGIS take us away and put us somewhere, but he convinced them that we were better off with him. Johnny stayed with him lon-ger than I did. I joined the Army when I turned eighteen and got out of there. Johnny eventually joined the service too, though he went Marines."

I noticed fierce pride in her voice. "He made Force Recon. I made George promise never to tell my brother what really happened that night, and he didn't. I owe him for that, David. I just told Johnny what I'm going to tell you."

I nodded, taking a seat on a secured crate next to her, letting her tell the story in her own way.

Chapter Seven

Somewhere Over Texas

AS KIM FINISHED TALKING ABOUT her parents' death at the hands of a single walker, I was still trying to process everything. I was able to manage a smile as Kim looked up at me, though. I had moved to sit beside her, one arm around her shoulders and the other holding her hand as she told me how her parents had died. I was saddened not so much by her loss, though that was tragic, but more so by the fact that she and especially her young brother had had to witness such horror.

"The man who seemed so sad to me was, of course, George," she said. "He told me that my mom was dead and that my dad was very sick and might not make it either. He calmed me down and told me that he had arranged for both of us to stay with him for a while, until they could locate some family we could be placed with at least temporarily.

"I told him not to bother. My dad was an only child and his parents had died years before. My mom didn't even remember her parents, having grown up in the foster care system. So there wasn't any family for us to go to.

"I remember he looked even sadder at that, and somehow I realized at that point that I could trust him." She snorted as she continued. "Of course, by that time my dad was already dead and had reanimated, and for defense the helicopter crew had neutralized him before they even put him on the chopper."

The way she said *neutralized* left me cold, and I realized how brutal an experience that must've been for such a young child, and how much it might've warped her world-view if George Maxwell and his wife hadn't been there to help them both through it.

"He took care of us. He took us home and fed us, treated us just like the children he and his wife could never have. He hid the truth from us only because it was so horrible. I saw how he lived and the standards he held himself to, and I knew then that I wanted to be what he was. I knew that the Army was where I wanted to be."

"So when did he finally tell you the truth?"

"I had just finished a tour in Afghanistan, and I came home for a visit. My first in years, actually. He and Althea were very surprised and glad to see me. Johnny even managed to get some leave around the same time, so it was something of a reunion. One night after dinner, George and I were sitting outside on the porch, him with his cigar and me with a glass of wine, and he just started talking.

"He told me the truth about my dad, and even about Jack. The zombie had bitten him too, and I simply hadn't noticed as I rode him off the farm. They saw the bite right away and put him down before the chopper took off with us."

"But animals don't turn . . ."

"We know that now, but at the time they believed that it was a virus, remember. They were afraid it could end up as a carrier of the contagion."

"Did you believe him? Maxwell? It's a big story to swallow if you've never considered it before."

"At first I thought he was just bullshitting me in a weird and hurtful sort of way, but then I realized it was painful for him to tell me all these secrets he'd been hiding." She stood up and walked to the bulkhead, then turned back to me. I didn't believe him, not at first. I mean, I knew *he* believed it, but I still didn't. I couldn't. I mean, zombies? Seriously?

"So he showed me the tapes and the pictures and the videos. Then he asked me to join this new team he was forming, a 'special branch of service,' he called it. He told me I could get revenge for my parents, and I signed on. Johnny got pretty banged up and got an honorable discharge just before I went to Afghanistan, so when they put us on inactive status, I knew where I wanted to go—wherever he was."

She took a deep breath. "And then you and the others were all wanting to stick together, and I thought that would make everything so much easier."

She came back to the crates, sitting next to me and reaching out to hold my hand. She didn't look up at me, though, and when I saw teardrops start to fall, I lifted her chin so I could meet her eyes.

"I'm sorry, David. I didn't want to lie to you, but I didn't know how to tell you the truth. Then it just got so hard to keep all the secrets, and I withdrew, and . . ."

I smiled at her as I wiped the tears away, and I could feel her shiver as I brushed her hair back over her ear.

Can I trust her again? I wondered. After all, she had kept such a huge part of her life secret. *Will I always wonder what else she's hiding from me?*

"I understand why you did what you did, but I can't just forget about it. So let's take it slow, okay?"

Kim nodded and smiled. "Okay."

She smiled as she ran her hand along my cheek. "I missed you, David," she said as she leaned in and kissed me.

I relaxed and held her close, feeling her against me as I had feared I never would again, never wanting to let her go. We were startled out of our kiss by a burst of loud clapping and whistling. We looked up as Eaton, Gaines, Martinez and Reynolds finished rounding the corner into our little nook with huge grins on their faces.

Martinez and Gaines pounded me on the shoulder. Rachel and Kim were hugging and tearing up just a bit, and Tom stood there like a proud parent, watching us all and smiling so hugely he must have been hurting something.

I looked around at my squad, and was happy for the first time in quite a while. "Ready to kick some zombie ass?" I shouted.

The echoing agreement in the plane was deafening.

A tall, thin man met us in front of the main building as we disembarked from the Humvee that had picked us up from the airfield. Dressed nondescriptly in grey, he was the most average-looking man I had ever seen, and when he spoke, I thought I would die from boredom from the nasal drone of his voice.

"Good evening, gentlemen and ladies. My name is Henry Gardner. I'm the new head of the civilian arm of AEGIS, and the Secretary of Defense asked me to introduce myself to you personally. I thought this would be as efficient as any other method." We looked at each other, and then the rest of the squad turned to Kim.

Command is a lonely job. I sighed as she turned to the grey man and held out her hand.

"Captain Barnes, 1st Alpha squad, at your service, sir."

Henry looked down at her hand as if it were some sort of poisonous creature about to bite him, and licked his thin lips. "Yes, well, this way, if you please," he said.

It appeared that introducing himself was just about the limit of old Henry's abilities.

Kim and I exchanged glances, and I heard her whisper, "I've got a bad feeling about this."

"Me, too."

As we entered the building, it seemed as though nothing had changed. I was surprised when Gardner stopped just outside the mess hall, wondering why we weren't headed for the briefing room. Inside, all the chairs and tables had been folded or stacked against the walls, and the room was empty apart from two men I knew well, but hadn't seen in almost a year.

I grinned and there was a lot of chatter as we approached Maxwell and Anderson. They turned and smiled in welcome.

"David! Good to see you, my boy. It's been a long time," boomed Maxwell. He shook my hand as roughly as ever, making me wince, and turned to Kimberly.

For a moment, the tension in the room was palpable, then he held out his arms and she came forward as he embraced her with a huge hug. I smiled as they finally parted, and Maxwell straightened his uniform and cleared his throat.

"Uh, yes, good to see you too, Captain," he said, with a twinkle in his eye as he looked at Kim. "We'll talk later, but for now just tell me this: Is he all right?"

She nodded. "Yes, sir. He's fine, and on his way to the Springs as you suggested."

"Good," he said, the matter closed for now. "Good to see all of you. The rest of your team should be joining you here momentarily. I'm told they're landing just now." He turned to Henry, standing off to one side, looking at the small reunion with vague distaste.

"Henry, perhaps you'd like to greet them as well?"

"Yes, of course, Colonel. I will return shortly." The door closed behind him and Maxwell turned back to us. "That guy gives me the creeps, plain and simple."

I'd swear I heard Anderson snort at that comment, but I couldn't say for sure.

"We've got a bit of a surprise for you folks, but we'll wait until the others get here," said Frank.

"Sir, shouldn't we get right to the briefing?" I asked.

Maxwell's only response was a raised eyebrow.

"Oh, come on, sir. You wouldn't have activated us just for some sort of reunion. We've got a mission."

Maxwell laughed and shook his head. "Steady, Blake. The birds are fueling now, and the quartermaster is prepping your gear. In the meantime, why don't you catch us up on what you've been doing?" The confusion was considerable as we all began talking at once, but eventually everything calmed down, and the only really big news—that Rachel Eaton was soon to become Rachel Gaines—went over extremely well with our superiors. They were both very congratulatory to the pair.

Soon enough, the rest of our team had arrived and filed in, and the process began again, everyone excited to hear what had happened to everyone else in the time we spent apart. The large space was filled with the sounds of laughter and conversation. The only spot of tension was the one we all expected, between Reynolds and Ames. For his part, Tom seemed to believe that Ames simply didn't exist. From his reaction, I believe Ames was just as glad to pretend the same thing. Gradually, the talk died down and our attention was diverted to the front of the room as Maxwell and Anderson moved apart.

"1st Team, it's been a long time." Cheers were cut short as Maxwell lifted a hand. "I wish we had more time to socialize, but instead, we have a surprise for you, then your activation orders." Everyone sobered as we were reminded why we were here in the first place. Maxwell nodded to Anderson, who lifted a radio and spoke briefly into it.

"Send them in."

We turned at the sound of the hall doors opening, and marveled at the sight of soldier after soldier marching through, taking ordered ranks in three separate groups. As the soldiers formed their ranks,

I noticed my team quietly whispering amongst themselves, point-ing and nodding their approval of the new arrivals. The muttering grew louder as we realized that there were now nearly four full teams, including ours, in the dining hall. Colonel Maxwell broke the silence as the last soldiers took their places in the ranks.

"1st Team, fall in!" As though we had never left, we formed our ranks, eyes front and at attention. Maxwell smiled as he saw us form perfect ranks, despite being separated for so long. Not so much as a finger was out of place, and Anderson smirked with pride as well before straightening and also coming to attention. Maxwell paced back and forth before us, something we had all become accustomed to over the course of our tenure at 'zombie boot camp.'

"About face!" Like clockwork mannequins, we pivoted in place, coming to rest viewing the other soldiers. "First Team, meet your fel-low AEGIS personnel." I was stunned as realized what I had missed previously—the patch each of these men and women wore on their shoulders, showing the familiar logo of AEGIS.

"2nd, 3rd, and 4th Teams, take a lesson from 1st Team. They are the example to set yourself by. 1st Team, about face!" We turned again, glad to see nearly forty more recruits added to our roster.

"Operators, as you are aware, we now have a full complement of soldiers. As such, we have been ordered to form the First Com-pany of AEGIS personnel. 1st and 2nd Teams will be deploying today. 2nd Team, get geared up and form up at the airfield. 1st Team will remain here for further orders. The rest of you will fall out to the barracks. Dismissed!"

We remained at attention as the rest of the soldiers filed out, and as the last one shut the door behind him, Maxwell turned to us. "All right, fall out, ya lazy bums." We began talking as we tried to figure out what had happened to cause the sudden surge in man-power. Maxwell came up to me and clapped me on the shoulder. "A word, son?" I nodded and stepped to the side, waiting for the colo-nel to continue.

"I would never ask this of another soldier, but your unique posi-tion in this company provides me with an opportunity that I can't pass up," Maxwell said. "No one has ever had a command quite like this, facing things like this. I need to know, straight up and no bull-shit, if Kimberly can take it."

The answer must have been clear on my face. "Settle down," he said, chuckling. "I was sure of the answer, but I needed to hear it from her *second in command*." I was shaken for a moment. He grinned. "That's right, David. XO is yours. Do us proud."

I marveled yet again at the change that had come over the formerly dour and severe colonel I said goodbye to less than a year ago. He turned and motioned to Commander Anderson, glancing at Kimberly. Anderson looked thoughtful as well, then nodded firmly, grinning.

"1st Team!" Maxwell yelled to get their attention, and I shook my head to clear the ringing. "It's been a while since you were all in training, and it's about time we made it official. Say hello to your XO, David Blake. Major Barnes, front and center."

Kim looked shocked as several people clapped her on the back and a general whooping and hollering rang through the dining hall. She pointed at me, a fierce scowl on her face, then laughed and motioned for everyone to be quiet as she walked up to Maxwell and stood to attention, saluting him.

"Captain Kimberly Barnes, sir."

Maxwell shook his head. "I don't believe you heard me correctly, *Major*."

She swallowed and jerked her chin up at his words. "Sir, yes sir!" Maxwell returned her salute, then smiled and shook her hand.

"Congratulations, Kim. You've earned it."

"Yes, sir. Thank you, sir." We all surrounded Kim, giving her the standard good luck punch on the arm that she deserved. Maxwell gave us a minute, then ordered us to the briefing room.

"Roosevelt, Utah," Maxwell was saying only moments later, showing a map of the city on the briefing room's projector. A small town, with only a handful of streets, a high school, and a couple churches. *Could be anywhere in America*. We all sat at the same tables we had occupied before during another important briefing, and I got a strong sense of déjà vu.

"At 1620 hours local time yesterday, my office was informed of a potential outbreak in the area, based on descriptions of bites and symptoms provided by our contacts at the Centers for Disease

Control and elsewhere. At 2347 hours, another report came in, indicating that the infection had spread, as we expected, to several other wounded.

"According to the latest word we have from Roosevelt, there are approximately ten to fifteen walkers active at the moment that they are aware of, all of which have been sealed inside the local hospital.

"Your mission is straightforward: You will airlift into the area, clean out the walkers in the hospital, and mop up any stragglers. The sheriff's office has already been informed that the National Guard is en route, so you shouldn't have any problems there.

"The locals have been ordered to assist you in any way you need, but primarily they've been asked to return people to their homes and see that they stay there. Once the walkers have been neutralized, standard containment measures will follow."

'Standard containment' was the Army euphemism for burning homes and smaller structures, and thoroughly decontaminating larger ones with chemicals that could kill you with even the most minute exposure.

Glad I'm not those guys.

He turned off the projector and as the lights came back on, he stood with arms folded. "We don't believe this is an isolated incident. I'm not authorized to disclose additional intel at this time, but Commander Anderson will be in command of this op, as requested by our new liaison."

Heads turned to look at Gardner, at one side of the room. He regarded us impassively, as if we were merely bugs . . . or pawns.

Maxwell continued, "The commander will be recording your op, and this will be reviewed by higher. In this case, that means the Secretary and possibly the president himself, gentlemen. So no fuck-ups, clear?"

As one unit, we shouted "Clear!" loud enough that Mr. Gardner spooked and looked nervous, causing more than one of us to grin. Even Commander Anderson flashed a smile that was just as swift in disappearing.

"Report to the quartermaster for gear, then to the hangar. Wheels up in twenty. Dismissed." As we filed out, I glanced over at Mr. Gardner, and found him looking at me. Noticing my glance, he shifted his attention to others.

What exactly is he looking for? Not that it matters. This one's going by the book if I have to kick every ass in the team—assuming

Kim doesn't do it first. I could tell from her expression that Kim was thinking the same thing.

We made it to the C-17 Globemaster in seventeen minutes, geared up and ready for action. I whistled as I stepped out of the Humvee, amazed and feeling more than a little tiny next to the gargantuan airplane. The noise from the turning rotors fit the big beast. It was unbearably loud as we clambered up the back ramp. Several Humvees were chained to the decking, National Guard logos obvious on their sides. I noticed Anderson strapped in near Kimberly, and chose a seat close to them.

"Good to have you with us, sir," I said. "We can sure use another experienced hand here."

He nodded back and grimaced. "Just be glad you don't have to deal with the bean counters, Blake," he said, tapping the camera mounted to his helmet.

I chuckled and shook my head. "That's why you get the big bucks, Commander." He rolled his eyes at me. Moments later we took off, headed at max speed into the pre-dawn darkness. I glanced over at Kim, but she was studying the briefing materials and the map we'd been given with an intensity I had come to recognize. This was going to be her first 'real' action against a serious outbreak, as it would be for the rest of the team, except me. I'd already had my initiation.

Some time later, I awoke suddenly and took a second to get my bearings, and then realized we were still on the plane headed to Roosevelt. I noticed many of the others around me catching cat-naps, except Kim and Commander Anderson, who were having something of an animated conversation.

"So you saw action like this in Central America, sir?" she asked.

Anderson nodded. "SEAL Four was tasked with some anti-narcotic raids deep in the jungle in Panama, a couple hundred klicks east of Panama City. We were trying to get some dirt on Noriega, some sort of proof that he was working both ends against the middle by helping out his dealer friends. Justification for the invasion, you see." He snorted, shaking his head. "That was one of the few times we actually got good intel that wasn't corrupted by some asshole wagging his tongue for a few *balboas.*"

"We put in near Mamitimpo and humped it in. About a klick out, we stopped to recon, and what we found was not what we expected. It looked like a war zone before we even got there. We could see the shacks for processing cocaine, or at least what was left of them. We had no idea what we were in for." He went on to tell us the details of his sojourn in that far-off jungle in such vivid detail that I could see it as though I'd been there myself.

"I was never so quiet in my life as I was during the hike out of there. It took us more than three hours to make it, and we were scared shitless every step of the way," said Anderson. I realized yet again that if this man, this gung-ho, never-say-die, I-can-kill-you-seventeen-ways-with-my-thumb career bad-ass was even a little scared of what he had seen, then it was probably okay that I was, too.

"MacMillan was bitten though, wasn't he?" Kimberly asked.

Anderson nodded and sighed. "He died on the chopper back to JTOC at Fort Sherman. That's where I met the colonel. Hamish's body was placed in the morgue and I was held for debriefing. Less than eight hours later, Hamish had reanimated and been put down by the MPs and the base was under lockdown.

"The colonel debriefed me. He let me know what had happened to Hamish and why. I didn't believe him at first, but when he showed me what was left, I understood. I've been with him ever since."

He looked over at me as he stopped, and there was again that unspoken bond between us.

He's been in the trenches too, and had to kill those he cared about.

I nodded solemnly, a sign of respect from one warrior to another. I turned to look out the window as we crossed the Rockies, the mountains lit by the early-dawn light. I felt calm. We were well-trained, prepared soldiers with the latest military hardware. It never occurred to me that we might return with fewer friends than when we'd left.

It should have.

Chapter Eight

ROOSEVELT, UTAH

I WATCHED AS THE BIG plane roared off down Route 191, five miles east of Roosevelt. As it rose higher, it banked to the northwest, most likely headed for Hill Air Force Base just outside Salt Lake City.

The Humvees were idling in a line headed toward the small town, the barrels of the machine guns glinting dully in the sun.

This early, there wasn't likely to be any traffic coming west toward the town, and the sheriff and his men had already cordoned off those coming from it. All that was left was for us to get in there and take out the walkers. The other two teams had dispersed to their vehicles, and I joined Kim and Commander Anderson in the first vehicle in line.

As I climbed in, our team leader barked orders. "All teams, Alpha Six," she said. "Prepare to move to assigned positions." She nodded at the driver, and we began to move west. "Roll out."

We rumbled down the highway towards the town, checking our weapons and other gear nervously, avoiding at all costs looking each other in the eye. We'd simulated the environment, we'd run the drills, but this was our first live-fire exercise, and it would make or break us as a unit. Each of us needed to deal with that on our own, at least for the moment.

Suddenly we slowed, a sheriff's deputy waving us through the roadblock. I wondered what he must be thinking of these troops rolling into his town, and how worried he must now be about what they had seen and experienced.

A few minutes later there was a slight bump and we came to a stop. The driver looked back at Kim. "We're here, ma'am. Uintah Basin Medical Center."

"Defensive positions. Move out!" Kim was taking to this command thing rather well, it seemed.

We moved to our assigned guard positions as Kim walked over to the sheriff.

The Humvees moved off, disgorging their cargo at the pre-planned locations. The other teams spread out, with the armored transports taking up support positions. I didn't see any walkers, and there were no reports from the other squads. It looked clear . . . for now.

I glanced over at Kim, but couldn't hear anything. She walked back over and motioned for me to join her as the sheriff walked back to his squad car and left.

"He says they've got about ten to fifteen walkers in the hospital, which they've chained shut."

I snorted. That wouldn't hold them for very long, and I would be surprised if all of them were still intact now. Walkers weren't super-strong, but they would push past the normal limits of endurance that living humans had—and that made all the difference. Zombies didn't care if they tore a muscle or sprained something. I started to ask a question, but she shook her head.

"I know, but he can't get any of his people close enough to really check on the chains, not when it's still slightly dark out, anyway. They've heard rumors, and some of them didn't make it out, so they're not about to go back in. At least, that's what he says. I told him to check on his people, make sure they're all where they need to be and that everyone's staying home."

She turned back to the hospital, pulling an overhead photo from a pocket. "We've got primary entrances here, here and here, plus side doors, the loading dock, etc. We'll check the primary exits first, then spread out along the perimeter in teams and look for egress points."

I nodded.

Kim went on, "1st Team: Bravo, north side main entrance. 2nd Team: Charlie east, Delta west. Verify and secure primary exits, then spread out for secondaries and hold."

I whistled, and the other four members of Alpha and I moved forward, Kim at my side. The SCAR machine guns we all carried were held ready as we moved forward in a low crouch. We fanned out as we approached the front of the building, and stopped fifty feet from the front door.

The main entrance, like most hospitals, appeared to be a sliding glass door, though this one had been disabled and its outer handles chained together. I couldn't see any movement through the glass, but the chain looked intact.

Maybe they're all still in there. I grimaced. *Yeah, like our luck is that good.*

"Alpha clear and secure." Kim's voice in my headset was loud and clear, and we waited for similar confirmations from the other squads.

"Bravo, clear and secure."

"Charlie, clear and secure."

We all paused, but there was nothing from Delta. Kim tried again. "Delta, report!"

There was a crackle of static. " . . .piece of shit! Sorry, ma'am. My fucking radio wasn't working. I had to—Wait one." We waited in silence, scanning the still dark interior of the hospital and the surrounding grounds. "Delta here, ma'am. West entrance is *not* secure, repeat, *not* secure. I can see the chain, but it's on the ground and appears to be broken. The door's open; there's blood on the wall."

"Roger, Delta. Mobile Three, move to support Delta and scan that area for movement. Delta, secure that exit." Her voice was cold and hard, and I glanced at this woman who was my commanding officer. Her jaw was set, she looked pissed, and I knew that if anyone could pull this off, she could. *Poor dumb sons of bitches. They've screwed with the wrong soldiers.*

"Delta, moving to secure." We heard a sharp intake of breath. "Walker spotted." A pause, and then a whispered, "Walker down. Door secure."

I let out a breath I didn't realize I'd been holding, and saw Gaines doing something similar to my left. We'd passed our first hurdle. Somehow everything was just a bit more real, now. Even with our training encounters with Chauncey, we hadn't really gotten used to the *reality* of what we were up against.

Kim whispered into her mike, "Good work, Delta. All teams, move to secondary positions and then regroup."

Reynolds, Barnes and I split off and moved to the right, looking for other doors or broken windows that might indicate a zombie had escaped the facility. Not finding anything, we returned to our prior position and were met by Martinez, Gaines and Eaton, who shook their heads as they crouched.

"Alpha, clear." The other squads reported in as they also cleared their sides of the medical center.

"Charlie, clear."

"Delta, clear."

"Bravo, clear." As this last transmission came in, there was the distant crash of breaking glass, and a quick gasp from the radio. "Scratch that, multiple walkers, northeast corner."

Kim swore softly and keyed her mike. "Mobile Two, move to intercept and support. Charlie, assist."

"Roger, Mobile Two moving to engage."

As the strong wind shifted our direction, we finally heard the moaning of the zombies, loud enough to be heard even over that distance. Moaning that was swiftly cut off, followed by a laugh into the mike by Powell, the Bravo squadleader. "Ma'am, all targets down. Mobile Two . . . well, she just ran them over, ma'am."

I couldn't help but grin at the idea, and the others joined me, except for Barnes. "Stay frosty, Bravo Six. Mobile Two, fall back to support position. Bravo, neutralize targets on the ground." Zombies would get back up again unless the brain was destroyed, and despite a half-ton piece of military hardware rolling over them, something was bound to get missed. A few moments later, we heard again from Bravo Six. "Targets neutralized."

"CharlieTeam, reinforce Bravo. Delta, Alpha is headed your way. Mobile units, set up rolling perimeter and activate REAPRs."

I looked down at the REAPR strapped around my forearm to make sure it was on and functioning. The indicators on the device showed green across the board, meaning it was in contact with the base units attached to the big M-2 machine guns on the Humvees.

In simulated combat, we had discovered that it was the single best invention AEGIS had ever had to determine quickly whether a soldier had been turned, completely aside from its usefulness as an overall health and status indicator for the troops in the field.

Zombies had no pulse, hence anything walking around with a REAPR and no pulse could safely be counted on to be a walker. This system, combined with motion-sensing and infrared imaging that indicated moving, cold targets, boasted a 99.8% accuracy rate in the identification of soldiers that had been turned.

We moved forward to the west to join Delta squad as we prepared to enter the hospital. "Delta, be advised Alpha inbound at your three." No sense in having us round the corner only to get shot by our own troops.

"Roger, Alpha. Welcome to the party."

We grouped at the entrance Delta had re-secured. There was a small metal-inlaid security window next to the door, or what had once been a window. The safety glass had shattered and lay on the walkway, presumably broken by walkers trying to escape the facility. The metal door had been bent and twisted by the force of the blows that it had sustained from the inside, and the cheap metal lock had given way.

The chain that someone had locked it with was now wrapped around the door's handle and the steel window frame, allowing only a small space between for anything to enter or exit. Through the window, I could see one crumpled form, and I assumed it was the zombie they had taken out to secure the door.

We crouched there in the now-bright morning sun, with the Humvees moving in their rolling perimeter around the hospital, churning up what little grass there was. The .50 caliber M2 machine gun swiveled atop their turrets, checking for targets in 360 degrees. The rest of the squad and I looked at Kim, ready for her orders.

"Bravo, Charlie, report status," she said.

Powell responded, "Bravo and Charlie are go for entry."

"Initiate sweep and clear. By the numbers."

"Wilco."

I ran forward, staying low as Reynolds moved up beside me to open the door as Martinez opened the lock. Eaton and Gaines covered me while Barnes maintained a rear-guard.

"On three," Reynolds murmured quietly. "One, two, three!" He yanked open the door and I quickly scanned for targets as he and Gaines stepped to my side.

"Clear!" I whispered, hearing similar reports from Bravo and Charlie squads as they moved into their own entrances. I slowly entered the building, carefully rounding the corner of the hallway on my right as the others moved up. A shambling figure caught my eye at the end of the hallway, a flickering light betraying movement just before the signature moan reached us. "Walker spotted," I said quietly, and then fired a three-round burst at the target.

The suppressor on my FN SCAR-H rifle softened the shots to nothing more than a few muffled coughs, and at least one of the bullets connected, showering the wall behind the zombie with blood and brain matter. "Walker down."

We moved slowly through the medical center, carefully checking closed doors and open rooms. A small knock on a closed door would tell us whether it was populated by one of the ghouls or empty, and we put more than a few rounds into walkers that suddenly erupted from nooks and crannies. Fortunately, we had all trained well and knew what we were getting into, and we had no injuries.

This is too easy. We'd only killed four zombies at this point, and Bravo and Charlie had put down another three. *We're missing something, here. Where are all the walkers?*

"Roberts, stand fast!" We all heard Commander Anderson on our radios, and froze where we were, our training having ingrained in us an immediate response to orders from a superior.

"It's all right, commander, I knocked," came Roberts' voice. A second, then two, and suddenly we heard a piercing scream echo down the empty hallways, followed by a crash. The scream was abruptly cut short, and all was quiet once more. We were left looking at each other wondering what had happened.

"Bravo Team, report." Kim kept the fear and agitation she must be feeling out of her voice.

A pause, and Powell responded. "Ma'am, Roberts is down. Repeat, Roberts is down."

"Understood. Mark for retrieval and neutralize."

"Already done, ma'am. Bravo and Charlie squads are continuing sweep."

I looked back at Kim and she motioned for us to continue. We crept through the rest of that section of the hospital, Eaton marking cleared rooms with her phosphorescent paint-stick. These were specially designed to apply paint that would fluoresce in night-vision goggles as well as glow brightly during the day. These were a godsend to the sweep teams, allowing them to avoid having to retrace their steps.

As we moved toward the reception area and our planned rendezvous, we found two more zombies and put them down. At the entrance to reception, we paused at a signal from Kim, then crouched down as she indicated more than ten targets were in sight. I crept up beside her and counted.

Well, this is where they all are. I wondered why we hadn't seen them from outside but realized they happened to be far enough back in the shadows to avoid direct sightlines from the exterior. There had to be at least fifteen zombies standing still and quiet at random spots throughout the reception area—deadly terror given form and shape.

How I hated them.

"Bravo, Charlie squads, report," Kim said.

"Bravo and Charlie clear and moving to reception."

"Be advised, multiple walkers in reception."

"Acknowledged."

We waited motionless until we saw the dark forms of the other teams come to a halt in the shadows across the reception area. Kim signaled again, and we activated the laser sights on our guns, each targeting a walker. Fortunately, the zombies didn't seem to notice the glowing red dots on the sides of their heads.

"Fire," Kim whispered, and a sort of wet crackling noise enveloped us all as the silenced and flash-dampened muzzles of the machine guns sent their deadly cargo into the zombies skulls. Gore splattered the front door of the hospital, and I began to realize how little I envied the AEGIS clean-up crew.

"All teams, reception clear. Split into fire teams and make a final sweep. Commander Anderson, sir, you're with me." Anderson split off from the other group and came over to our side of the reception hall as the others split up to double-check hallways and doors as we headed back out the way we'd come in.

"Mobile units, Alpha Six. The hospital is clear. Report activity."

"No activity, ma'am, though we did have some movement just after you went in. No hostile contact."

"What sort of movement, soldier?"

"Ma'am, it appeared that we might have a walker to the northwest, but the movement wasn't sustained and if it was really there in the first place, we lost it. It might have been nothing, ma'am."

"Very well. Maintain scans of that area, just in case. Mobile Two, Mobile Three maintain patrol. Mobile One prepare for retrieval to north side."

"Acknowledged, Mobile One moving forward for retrieval. ETA one minute."

We left the hospital, ensuring that the facility was clear. There were no surprises, and we exited through the metal side door, leaving it unchained and open.

"Mobile One, patch me through to Sheriff Warren in his car."

"Yes, ma'am. Patch coming up . . . now."

"Hello, Sheriff Warren? Yes, sir, the hospital is clear, sir." Kim paused, listening as we maintained our alert status, scanning the parking lot and open areas of the middle school across the street for any sign of walkers or infected people.

"No, sir," Kim continued. "We didn't find any survivors, sir. Yes, sir, we did a thorough search. Sir, I have to ask—have there been any reports of walkers anywhere else in town, sir? Okay. Okay, I see. No, sir, stay where you are. Thank *you*, sir."

She rolled her eyes as she looked back at Anderson and I. "Like I wouldn't look for survivors. He said there's a small farmhouse to the northwest just past those trees. The Millers live there, and he hasn't been able to get a hold of them. A deputy sent out there to collect them didn't return, and he can't get *him* on the radio, either."

Anderson and I looked at each other, and then back at Kim, who shrugged. "They're dead by now. You both know it and I know it. We've got a job to do, though, so let's get it done." Keying her mike once more, she turned to face northwest. "Mobile units, retrieve the teams and proceed northwest on Mobile One's six." Mobile One rolled over to us moments later and we clambered inside.

There was some jolting as we turned a couple corners sharply, and then we came to a skidding stop on the dirt turn-around of a country farmhouse—or at least that's what it looked like. A cop car with the Roosevelt PD logo was off to one side, its driver-side door standing open and a splatter of dried blood across the window.

"Lieutenant," Kim said, addressing the vehicle's equipment operator. "scan for targets."

"Yes, ma'am. One small heat signature, ma'am, probably a child, approximately ten feet underground in an open area of some sort. It's faint, but it's there."

"Storm cellar. Any others?"

"No, ma'am, no other heat signatures. The computer indicates positive ID on four walkers in the house, one additional on the porch, ma'am."

"*How* positive, Lieutenant?"

"Ninety-four percent probability, ma'am."

Kim hesitated, and I knew what she was thinking in that moment. *If they're not walkers, she'll be consigning those people to their death. Then again, if they're not walkers, why aren't they showing up on the infrared sensors?*

"Very well, Lieutenant. You are authorized weapons hot. Fire."

"Yes, ma'am." The lieutenant reached down and pressed a series of buttons on his controls, and the Humvee shook with the recoil of the big M2 .50 cal machine gun firing above our heads. "Targets eliminated, ma'am."

"Alpha and Bravo teams, into the house. Charlie, set perimeter. Delta, recon for possible stragglers or runners."

The team piled out, each moving to their assigned positions. Alpha and Bravo teams entered the small farmhouse, the gaping bullet holes left by the machine guns drawing our attention only slightly. *At least they'll save on air conditioning.*

Not that there was anyone left to worry about that bill.

As we cleared the lower floors, several team members stopped to put additional rounds into the walkers lying on the floor, one of them in multiple pieces. The sheriff's deputy had clearly had a pretty bad day, his remains scattered across the living room.

"Alpha, with me. You too, Commander." Anderson glanced at me with a quick grin, and I grinned back. Kim was sure taking to her new role, and I was glad that I had confirmed that to Maxwell. This was what she was born to do. "Bravo, secure the second floor. Delta, check that shed out back, too."

Acknowledgments came in from the other squads, and we ran out the back door and around to one side of the house, where Kim motioned for me to open the storm cellar door as she covered the exit from the side. I nodded and on her signal, yanked the handle.

No zombies emerged, and we all breathed a small sigh of relief. As the light filtered down into the cellar, we could see a short ways in. The concrete steps were covered with dust except for some recent footprints, and those were small.

Brave kid. Hid down here not knowing what was going on upstairs except that it was bad. I wonder how long he's been down here.

Kim moved down the steps, slinging her battle rifle out of the way and drawing her pistol with its attached flashlight. "Hello?" she called. "It's all right now, the monsters are gone."

I started down the steps, my SCAR held at the ready. I didn't know why my instincts were telling me to hang onto it, but I knew that there could be others down here. As I moved off the steps into the room, Kim was a few feet in front of me, her flashlight trained on a small child huddling in the corner, still and quiet. Too quiet.

I reached out a hand for Kim, whispering. "Kim, something's not—" She had half-turned towards me when the boy exploded out of the corner, moving faster than any walker I'd ever seen. He had almost reached her when my flying tackle took her out of harm's way, and he tumbled to the ground, spinning and coming back at us with a speed I'd rarely seen in normal humans, much less zombies.

Suddenly there was a burst of gunfire, and the boy went down in a soggy, bloody mess, his corpse landing not five feet from me. I glanced over at Kim, and she was wide-eyed as she looked at me.

"Hold still, David. Do. Not. Move." I froze at the command, not knowing why she said it but trusting in her enough to follow the order without question. From a pocket on her ACU, she drew a small white handkerchief, and slowly dabbed at my left temple, near my eye. As she drew it back, I saw dark, congealed blood and swallowed.

I hadn't been hit, so the blood must've come from the boy. A few centimeters the other direction, and I'd be as dead as he was: infected, I would most likely have been killed by my own squad or, even worse, by Kim herself. She drew another white packet from her uniform, tearing it open with her teeth and applying the moist cloth inside to the same spot on my temple.

Sterilization 101. Just because the blood had been wiped off didn't meant that the risk was all gone. All it took was one tiny little prion in your bloodstream, and you were as good as dead. Once she had finished, we both gave each other a thorough inspection, eliciting a slightly embarrassed cough from Reynolds, standing at the bottom of the cellar stairs with a wisp of smoke trailing from the end of his rifle.

Kim turned beet red as she and I clambered to our feet, and I hid my smile behind one gloved hand. Maybe it had been a little *too* thorough of an inspection, at that. One thing was damned sure, though: I was going to recommend eye protection be included as standard gear for all AEGIS personnel immediately.

We exited the cellar and regrouped at the Humvees. Kim looked at Jake Powell. "Jake, Bravo's on clean-up. Get moving."

Jake didn't look happy, but he knew why she had assigned his team the onerous duty of cleaning up the farmhouse. After the loss of Roberts, Bravo Team and its leader were going to be in more than one commander's doghouse before it was over.

As they began collecting the necessary equipment from the back of their vehicle, I heard the unmistakable crunch of tires over a dirt road, and a spray of dust and pebbles greeted us as Kim and I turned towards the sheriff's car.

Kim half-turned to me, and I held up a hand. "I've got this, go call the colonel." She looked relieved, and walked to the back of the lead Humvee as I met the sheriff, running over to us in his haste to find out what had happened.

"Stop right there, Sheriff." He glared at me and made as if to move around me, and I put one hand on his chest and shoved him backward several feet. The sheriff was not a small man, but neither was I, and he hadn't been trained by U.S. Army Special Forces. He opened his mouth with every intent to berate me, but I went on as if nothing had happened.

"This is a United States Army matter now, sir. For reasons of national security I'm afraid that I can't go into the details, but you will be given information on a need-to-know basis by appropriate personnel.

"For now, I'm ordering you to return to your office and make sure no more calls have come in with similar reports. We need to know right away if there have been some, and you can help us the most by getting back to your post."

There was a *whoosh* behind me, and I felt heat on my back as I watched the sheriff's eyes grow as round as dinner plates, and I could see the flames from the farmhouse reflected. I thought he was going to have a heart attack on the spot when he began spluttering at me. "You can't just go around burnin' people's homes, boy, I don't care who you work for. We've got rights, and no one—not even the Army—can take those away just yet. Now listen here, this is *my* town—"

I almost slapped him at that point. My hand was on its way, but I managed to stop myself as the sheriff's eyes got big once more.

It's not his fault he's just a good ol' boy. He's just protecting his town—as he sees it. He doesn't know what's really going on, and he didn't just lose a friend to a bunch of fucking monsters.

I took a deep breath, and smiled—or at least made the attempt. It must've fallen short, as the sheriff recoiled.

"No, *you* listen here, Sheriff. If you want to tell me how to do my job, then the next time you have crazies eating each other and attacking people, we'll just let *you* take care of it, okay? Until then, just *do your fucking job* and help me." I took another deep breath. "Please?"

I swear I thought I heard him whimper as he walked back to his car, got in, and drove off. There was a guy who was going to have a hefty therapy bill. I turned as Kimberly walked up. "David, did you actually *slap* that man?"

"Absolutely not, ma'am." I struggled to keep from grinning. "I sure wanted to, though." We both looked over at the farmhouse, now a tall pillar of flame that would consume the zombies, the invisible protein that had created them, and all other evidence that they were ever here.

A tragic, tragic accident, and no doubt about it. Still, it's better than John Q. Public figuring out what's really going on.

Commander Anderson joined us and nodded to the deputy's squad car. "I assume that's going to be handled, too? Ah, I see." He appeared pleased as Bravo Team moved the car into the field and placed a small explosive charge inside the trunk.

Another unfortunate accident. They moved away and the charge ignited, incinerating the car and the rest of the evidence. *All these old police cars should be replaced. Absolute deathtraps.*

Anderson turned back to Kim. "Well Major, it wasn't a perfect mission, but all things considered, you did well." We were all somber, knowing that the loss of even one soldier would hit us all soon. Families like the one our team had become didn't take losses lightly.

Kimberly nodded to Commander Anderson. "Yes, sir. I've taken the liberty of contacting base. The colonel has already routed a cleanup crew for the medical center. Their ETA is one hour, sir. As it turns out, a planned renovation project planned is going to get an early start, sir." She smiled at the cover story, and shrugged. "At least they'll still have the hospital."

"Agreed. Let's pack it up, this mission is over. I'll coordinate the cleanup from here, and act as liaison with the sheriff," Anderson said. "Your orders are to proceed with all speed to Hill Air Force Base for extraction back to Fort Carson. You can drop me off at the sheriff's office on the way." He handed her the camera from his helmet. "Make sure that this gets back to Colonel Maxwell. Do *not* give it directly to Mr. Gardner, clear?"

Kimberly and I both came to attention, saluting. "Clear, sir." she said. As he dropped the salute she immediately began recalling everyone to their vehicles. Ten minutes later, we were westbound on 121, headed for Salt Lake City and home. The C-17 ride back was as quiet as any flight on the big birds ever got, leaving the crew shaking their heads and wondering just what the hell had happened, until they saw the body bag strapped carefully in beside us.

They say war is hell. I doubt zombies are what they had in mind, but they're still right.

Chapter Nine

FORT CARSON, COLORADO

WE ALL FILED INTO THE briefing room in a somber state. Losing Roberts—Victor to his friends—was a hard blow to our morale. Even to an experienced, battle-hardened team, a loss is hard to take.

Colonel Maxwell strode in as though he owned the place, like always, and slammed down a stack of reports on the desk at the front of the room. The gunshot-like sound cracked back and forth between the cinderblock walls, and brought us all to attention behind our tables without our even realizing that it had happened until it was done.

Not only had we lost a man, we were all ready to rack out after having been in action or on the way to or from it for the better part of two days. Some of us looked better than others, but none of us were cheery.

"What a sorry bunch of low-life assholes this is. I've scraped better soldiers than you off the bottom of my boot."

For Maxwell, this was practically a compliment. The sad part of it was that he was being literal. His time at Fall Creek had been no easier than mine.

Someone—Powell, I thought—started to say something, but the colonel stopped him short simply by leaning over and placing his hands on the squadleader's table, staring nose to nose with him.

"If I want to hear from you ever again, maggot, I will by-god ask you. The next time you open your mouth it better be to answer a direct question or you will be scrubbing the lab floors with a toothbrush for a month." I doubted even the colonel would consign someone to cleaning the floor of the exam rooms, but you never knew what Maxwell had up his sleeve for someone who had screwed up so profoundly. "You get me, boy?"

Jake nodded and whispered. "Yes, sir," he said, his posture showing more than anything how defeated he felt.

If he stays squad leader, I'll be surprised. I glanced at Kim, and it appeared that she was thinking the same thing. Then she looked over at Reynolds, pity and sadness crossing her face before turning back to Maxwell.

Why would she be especially sad for him?

Returning to his accustomed spot at the front of the room, the colonel took an at-ease stance. "As much as you screwed up today, you've now tasted real combat, some of you for the first time. Now you know what it's like to be in the shit, your life on the line. I'm not glad he's dead—far from it—but Roberts' sacrifice has provided us with a valuable lesson. One I want you all to think about carefully over the next two days while you are restricted to quarters."

He grunted when the expected grumble of discontent didn't appear. "Good. At least you *know* you fucked up." Maxwell sighed and stood easy. "Problem is, so does higher. Or they will soon enough. Those of you with a brain bigger than my thumb will have already noticed a distinct lack of grey suits in this room."

I glanced around, realizing I *hadn't* noticed, trying to confirm what he had already told us. *Boy, we are in the shit today.* Almost all of us turned to look as well. *With attention spans like this, God help us if we got attacked right now. We'd be walker-bait in a heartbeat.*

Just like Roberts.

I don't remember the rest of the debriefing. A sort of grey haze had fallen over me, and I was running purely on automatic at that point. The next thing I knew, there was a quiet knock on my barracks door, and Kimberly entered, looking over her shoulder. She glanced at the room's other bed, empty and bare, and then at me with one raised eyebrow.

I doubt she even realizes how many of Maxwell's mannerisms she copies. I shrugged. "It would've been Roberts', but I traded spots with Reynolds."

She smiled, but I could see her eyes glisten with tears as she sat next to me on the bed. "Victor. His name was Victor," she said, choking the words out as if they were the hardest thing she'd ever had to say.

I slid an arm around her shoulders and held her close to me as she finally broke and collapsed into me, tears streaming freely now. "His name was Victor," I said, just holding her close as her tall frame was racked with sobs. Eventually, the pain had passed somewhat and she was able to look up at me.

"How can you not be crying? Don't you *care*?" she asked, leaning away.

"Of course I care," I said, a little harsher than I intended, and she flinched. I took a deep breath and continued, pulling her back to me. "Of course I care. He was a good friend. A good man. I'll grieve for him, but right now I can't think about it. I have to sort of . . . put it away and forget it for a little while, or I'll lose it."

She sniffed and wiped some of her tears away. "I wonder how Reynolds is doing," she said, her words barely audible.

"I'm sure he's doing about as well as any of us. Why?" I asked, remembering her looking at him in the briefing room.

She sat back up and looked at me, her surprise plain. "You mean you didn't know?"

"Know what?" I said, completely mystified.

"He . . . he and Victor . . . they . . ." She appeared to be on the brink of tears once more as I took her hand, and suddenly, I knew.

"Victor was Tom's 'choice,' wasn't he?" I asked.

She nodded. "He was going to be, but Tom never made the move. He kept saying he would get to it when the time was right, and I never pushed him. I should've made him do it." She shifted closer to me on the bed, laying her head on my shoulder. "I went to his room and knocked, but he's either not answering, or not there."

That doesn't sound like Tom at all. Even now, he'd normally be comforting us too. So either he's not there, or . . .

I stiffened, turning to Kim. "Come on." I said, grabbing her hand and running from the room, pulling her after me. We ran down the short barracks hallway, and I began pounding on Reynolds' door.

"Come on, Tom, answer me. I know you're in there. Just open up so we can talk."

Kim looked at me, worried. Other squad members and personnel were appearing out of barracks rooms and from outside, and Dalton and Rachel popped out of the room next door.

Kim stripped off her ACU jacket to cover Rachel, who blushed as she realized she'd left her room in her distinctly non-Army-issue nightwear. She hid behind Gaines, who looked at me in fear. I didn't see Angelo anywhere, but chances are he was sacked out, dead to the world. So to speak.

No one in the group had ever seen me this focused, this *scared* before, and I think I frightened them as much as myself. I turned to Gaines, and gestured to the door.

"I need this door down now, big guy."

Dalton didn't hesitate, trusting in me to know what was right. One well-aimed kick just above the door's handle, and his massive tree-trunk legs and bare foot slammed the door open, a shower of splinters and a screech of tortured metal announcing our entry. I rushed into the room.

Empty.

"We need to find him. Quick," I said. "Check everywhere."

Barefoot, I exploded out of the barracks door, grabbing the first guard I saw as Kim came out after me.

"Reynolds. Have you seen him?"

"Who, sir?" asked the young guard, perplexed.

"Reynolds! Tom Reynolds!"

"Oh! Captain Reynolds headed toward the lake, sir." I started to run off, but stopped as the guard continued. "Sir, he didn't look . . . Well, sir, he looked a bit off. Had his issue sidearm with him, sir."

Kim and I exchanged glances and took off for the lake. I had a feeling I knew exactly where he was going.

The picnic area was large, but not *that* large. We found Reynolds sitting on top of a park bench, staring towards the lake. I noticed the bottle of Jack Daniels in his left hand, the pistol in his right. Waving Kim back, I approached slowly.

"Hey, buddy," I said, moving closer.

"Stop right there, David," he said, putting the barrel of the gun under his chin, clearly intending to stop me. It worked.

I took a deep breath, and sat down on the grass nearby. "Talk to me, Tom. I'm here to listen."

He looked right through me for a moment, but then brought his eyes to meet mine and I could see them glisten with unshed tears.

"I thought I could do this, David. I thought I could handle it," he said. I said nothing, merely listening and waiting for him to continue. "During the mission, I was okay. I heard him go down, and I was like a robot. Didn't feel anything. Just another resource for us, gone in a heartbeat."

He swallowed, and the tears started to fall. "In the C-17, I was fine. In the briefing room, I was fine. Walking back to the barracks . . . fine. Then I get to my bunk, and I see all his gear, and . . ." He lowered the pistol, pointing it at the ground and scrubbing at his eyes with the back of his other hand, spilling quite a bit of the whiskey in the process.

"I lost it, David. I don't remember when I picked up the gun, but it doesn't matter. How am I supposed to keep this up? What's the point? You've seen the numbers. You know what's going to happen. It's inevitable."

I took another deep breath, and just listened. Rebecca, my long-gone fiancée, had told me I was a great listener. Now was the time to prove it. *That's a conversation I need to have.* I glanced at Kim standing off to the side. *Speaking of secrets never told. Not going to go well, that conversation.*

Unfortunately, Tom saw the look I darted at her, and grimaced. "See? You have someone. I don't. Not anymore. Those damned walkers took him from me. I hate them so much."

"I understand, Tom, believe me."

"You can't understand!" he yelled, swinging the gun in my direction. My heart nearly stopped. "No one can! It's not just the walkers. It's that asshole Ames. Fucking redneck homophobe."

This is it. This is where I come in.

"That motherfucker?" I said. "I'll kill him. If Anderson doesn't do it first. What'd he do now?"

"No, it's not—"

"Screw that," I said, interrupting him. "We've got too much to deal with without having some bigoted shithead causing more problems."

"It's just taunts, David. He's obviously trying to control—"

"Bullshit!" I yelled, as angry as I'd ever been in front of Tom. "I'm tired of this shit. He had his one warning, as far as I'm concerned. I'm going to fuck this asshole up, right now." I stood, moving quickly to Tom's side.

At this point, he was so amazed to see me this angry he wouldn't have noticed a full marching band behind him. He barely flinched as I took the gun from him, racking the slide.

"I'm gonna find him, and when I find him, I'm gonna kill that motherfucker, because this is just too much." I turned to storm off, and got about three paces before I heard a very unexpected sound behind me: laughter.

"Oh, you marvelous bastard," said Tom.

I turned, the pistol held at my side, pointing down.

"Bastard? What did you just call me?" I said, hoping against hope that it had worked.

"You are one crafty son of a bitch, David Blake," he said, all but falling off the park bench as he stood up, taking a swig from the bottle. "You had me going, there. Totally, one hundred percent fooled."

I handed the gun to Kim as she came up next to me, and she turned to head off the crowd who had crept up, including our Alpha squad teammates.

"Why, Mr. Reynolds, whatever do you mean?" I asked, affecting my best—and worst—'southern belle' accent.

Drunk though he was, Tom was still in possession of some of his faculties. "You got the gun away from me."

"I did."

"Because you never get mad."

"Hardly ever."

"So I was surprised."

"You definitely were."

He laughed again, and hugged me so tight I could barely breathe. "Thank you."

"You realize, of course, that I may have shit my pants when you pointed that gun at me."

"Just means you're a pussy."

"Fuck you, man," I said, laughing, and I was relieved when he joined me. "We need you, Tom. All of us, even that asshole Ames, though he doesn't know it. Don't quit on us now, dude."

He looked at me, and I had the sense that once again, that I was being weighed and measured. I must've passed the test, because he nodded and smiled. "Okay. I'll stick around for a while. After all, someone has to save you from yourselves."

"Kiss my ass, ya fuckin' queer."

"Ha! Now you're gettin' it!" One arm around my shoulders, and the other around Kim's, we walked back towards our squadmates, who crowded around us.

Tom slapped Gaines on the back, glancing at the now fully attired Rachel, who rolled her eyes and smiled. *Obviously one of those new bunking situations was working out well.*

Back in the barracks, I sat back down on my bunk, Kim next to me. I wrapped my arms around her and pulled her close. She suddenly looked up at me, worried.

"David, you're shaking! What's wrong?"

I put a hand out in front of me, and I marveled at how shaky it was. "Must be adrenaline, I guess. I've never been so scared."

"How'd you know what to do?"

I snorted. "I didn't have a *clue* what to do, Kim. I wanted to shout at him, to slap him, to tell him anything that would help. He either had to stand or fall on his own, and then I realized that if I could just get to him, just snap him out of that world of grief and pain he'd built for even a second, then maybe I'd have a chance."

"Well, it worked."

"Yeah, I guess it did."

She looked at me sidelong for a moment, and I couldn't read her expression. "Seems like Dalton and Rachel are doing well, doesn't it?"

"Yes, it sure does. Of course, she *is* pretty hot, so . . ."

I laughed as she pinched me and smiled, and then it was her turn to laugh as I tickled her relentlessly. Her giggles had turned into pleas for mercy when there was a loud banging on the wall from next door, and we heard the voice of Powell.

"Keep it down, ya lousy sons-of-bitches!"

Kim and I both turned to the wall and echoed each other without meaning to. "Fuck off, Powell!"

We collapsed laughing, and Powell swore. A few seconds later, we heard his door open and close and his retreating footsteps down the hallway.

"Probably going to sleep in the motor pool," I snickered.

Kim turned to me, and the moonlight coming through my window framed her beauty as she pulled her T-shirt off over her head. "Now that he's gone . . ." She smiled as she pushed me back on the bed, and then squealed as I flipped us over and kissed her.

They say that there's a connection between sex and death. I'm not sure if it's true, but I certainly wasn't going to find out tonight. The base alarm sounded, the loud "whoop, whoop" startling me out of bed so fast I dumped Kim on her ass on the floor.

She didn't even blink as she pulled her shirt back on, along with the rest of her uniform, and she was out the door with me as we mustered in front of the barracks. Commander Anderson came running up to us, and Kim saluted. Anderson returned her salute.

"Well done, Barnes. We've had a breach in the lab section. Outfit your team and get them over to Building 8 ASAP. The other teams are gearing up, but they'll be backup."

"Yes, sir!" Kim said, turning to me even as I was giving the order to gear up. *A good XO knows when to give orders, and when not to.* Kim had taught me that.

"All right, you heard the man. Gear up! Two minutes!" I joined the rush into the barracks, and grabbed my gear and Kim's as Anderson continued the briefing. I was proud of our team as we reassembled with twenty or thirty seconds to spare, ready for action.

Anderson had vanished, evidently gone ahead to take charge of the situation or to meet with the colonel. Kim sized us up.

"Team! Prepare to move out!" We moved into marching order, and I was filled with pride once again as we readied ourselves. "Move out! Double-time!"

We made it to Building 8 in under four minutes, passing through the perimeter that had already been set up by the other teams.

Kim stopped us at the main entrance to the medium-sized building. "Bravo and Delta squads, cover the other two exits."

Janet Turner and Jake Powell took their squads off to either side of the building, and Kim turned to Greer, Charlie squad leader and CO of 2nd Team. "Greer, take the fire escape on the west side. Wait for my signal for entry."

Maxwell trotted up with Anderson in tow as Greer and his team moved out. Anderson raised his radio and the alarm finally cut off.

"Major, we have a serious situation here," said Maxwell.

"Yes, sir. I assumed so, sir."

Kimberly was in her no-nonsense mode, but Maxwell chuckled all the same. "Of course. Apparently one of the technicians responsible for feeding Chauncey got lazy, and got bit."

We all sucked in an involuntary breath at that point, realizing what that could mean for the rest of the lab personnel. *Hopefully containment held. I don't want to have to shoot any more friends.*

"Unfortunately, despite the guard hitting the alarm, the tech managed to get out. Apparently the motor on the secure door was faulty and it didn't close fast enough."

A guard was always on duty near the Army version of a 'panic button,' and all the doors were supposed to close super-fast and automatically. The system was supposedly tested on a regular basis, but sometimes maintenance wasn't done.

Now we've got a brand-new specimen. Won't Gardner be happy.

"He's locked in the main specimen room for the moment. Take him out, along with anyone else who's been compromised."

"Yes, sir."

"Well, Major, don't let me keep you."

Kim didn't even redden. "No, sir. Alpha squad, move out!"

We entered the main doors into the brightly-lit corridors of the scientific heart of AEGIS. Moving fast, we headed towards the rear of the building, where the specimens were all kept. As we passed the main corridor, I noticed the door to Dr. Adamsdóttir's office. It was closed and locked and the lights off. I hoped that she had left for the evening already.

Suddenly we heard screaming from the direction of the specimen room. "Charlie Six, go," Kim whispered into her mike, and waved us forward. We picked up the pace. As we reached the outer door for the room, Reynolds and Gaines covered the hallway, and Eaton and I readied ourselves as Kim reached for the door, Martinez on its other side.

Another scream blasted forth from inside, but none of us were fazed. We might as well have been made of ice for all the effect it had. We had a job to do. Nothing else mattered.

Kim cleared the door, and I wasn't sure whose bullets hit the zombie first, mine or Eaton's. Crouched over the body of another luckless technician, it had turned our way as the door opened, but had time for nothing else as our shots splattered its brains all over the wall behind it.

Why am I completely unsurprised? I recognized the technician I'd seen from my earlier experiences with Chauncey. Or rather, what was left of him. I didn't even recognize the other one.

"Walker down," I muttered as we crouched, creeping into the room in formation, seeming to watch everywhere at once. Reynolds looked calm as he put two rounds in the head of the corpse on the floor.

"Charlie Six, report," Kim whispered into her mic as she scanned the room.

"Charlie is all clear, ma'am. No walkers on the second floor."

"Roger. Rendezvous at east stairwell, first floor."

"On our way."

I looked around the room, but didn't see any other active specimens. There were a few quiescent bodies on tables covered in sheets here and there, but nothing moving. The door to Chauncey's cell was open, and I heard a soft clinking from inside.

Kim glanced at me, and I shrugged. "I think we're clear, ma'am."

"Oh, shit."

This soft comment from Martinez drew my attention, and I saw him looking at Reynolds, who was in turn looking at a sheet-covered body. Or mostly covered, anyway.

Oh, fuck me. They couldn't have . . . I walked up behind Tom and ever so slowly put my hand on his shoulder. He didn't even flinch. Didn't move at all as he looked down at the man who had almost been his lover.

Victor was laid out on the slab as neat as could be, grey and lifeless. I didn't see the bite that had killed him, but the two holes in his forehead from a 'neutralization' order were clear enough.

There were no tears from Reynolds now, just a blank stare. What I saw in that stare scared me. Maybe he'd truly turned a corner and let Victor go that fast, or perhaps he'd just locked away all emotions.

Will we all end up like that? As empty as the walkers? Remorseless, fearless, the only difference being body temperature? God, I hope not.

I pulled Tom away, and sat him down in a nearby chair, where he just stayed still, lost in his own private hell. I looked up at Kim as she came over, gently laying her hand on his other shoulder.

"Gaines, Martinez, go meet up with Greer," Kim said as she touched her mike. "Command, Alpha Six."

"Command here. Go ahead."

"The building is clear, sir. No indications of activity outside the specimen room. Two walkers neutralized."

"Roger, Alpha Six."

We collected Reynolds and moved back outside the main entrance, Gaines, Martinez, Greer and the rest of Charlie squad joining us. Maxwell met us once more.

"Well done, Major," he said as the clean-up crew moved past us in their bright white environmental suits with their flamethrowers.

"Thank you, sir. Permission to speak freely, sir?" He nodded and Kim continued. "Sir, what the *hell* is going on?" Maxwell raised an eyebrow, and Kim flushed. "Sir, walkers don't turn that fast."

"What do you mean, major?"

"Sir, he was practically completely turned by the time we got there. That's, what, *maybe* ten minutes? The fastest I've ever seen—and the fastest recorded in the records you gave us—was well over an hour. So I have to ask: what the hell is going on?"

Though I'd never seen him stunned, I think that was the closest I will ever get. The colonel appeared as though he'd been hit right between the eyes. Poleaxed, my granny would've called it. That expression didn't last long, though, and was quickly replaced by one of anger.

"I am going to have a little *chat* with our dear friend Mr. Gardner," he said, and stalked off. Commander Anderson looked at us and shook his head. *I'm sure as hell glad he's not coming for me. Dude is* pissed.

Commander Anderson dismissed us, and we returned to our barracks, still keyed up from the excitement. No one said a word at Kim following me into my room, and I smiled at her as she turned back to me.

"Now where were we, Mr. Blake?" she asked, running one hand over my chest.

So much for going slow.

Chapter Ten

FORT CARSON, COLORADO

REVEILLE CAME *WAY* TOO EARLY the next morning, and I opened my eyes and sat up to see the dawn breaking.

God, I hate mornings.

I looked down at Kim lying next to me, the sun turning her hair to molten fire, and the half-smile on her lips reminding me just how good a night it had been. I sat and looked at her for a while, amazed at this beauty I'd awoken next to, and remembered the feel of her against me the night before. How we had just seemed to connect on a deeper level than before, and I wondered whether it was just the death of Victor that had caused it, or whether we truly had turned a corner.

A little while later, Kim turned, trying to recapture the warmth I had taken away at sitting up. I smiled as I watched her stretch and yawn as she opened those emerald eyes, and she smiled back.

"How long have you been watching me sleep?" she asked.

"Only an hour or so. It was the snoring that really got to me, though."

"Ass," she responded, giving me a smack on the arm and smiling wider. "If anyone should be complaining it should be me. Where'd you put the cabin, anyway?"

Oh, sawing logs. I get it.

My brain doesn't work too well in the mornings.

"Har, har, har." I ran my hand up her side as the sheet fell away from her body, watching as the cold barracks air and the light touch caused her to flinch. "Hmm, I didn't know you were that ticklish."

I ran my hand under the sheet and squeezed, and she jumped. "Now *that* I knew about," I said, laughing as she smacked my hand and covered herself more fully with the sheet. Just then, there was a brief knock at the door, followed by Tom entering, bearing a tray of steaming food. He raised one eyebrow, smirking, as he set the tray down on the room's only desk.

Two cups for the coffee, I noticed. *Subtle, isn't he?*

I grinned back at him, the grin of every man who'd just spent the night with a beautiful woman and found to his surprise—and possibly hers—that she was still there the next day.

"I was talking to the colonel this morning," Tom said. "He asked me to bring you something to eat. He figured you'd had a hard night, so to speak, and he thought I needed some mindless busy work."

I chuckled, and Kim just shook her head. "Little boys. You're all little boys," she said, sticking her tongue out at Reynolds.

"Don't stick that thing out at me, darling. I know where it's been," he said, grinning ear to ear.

Kim blushed to the roots of her hair and I laughed, which earned me yet another smack. I must be a glutton for punishment.

I glanced up. "Any other messages from the colonel, Tom?"

He straightened and was the professional soldier once more. "Yeah, he wants us all in the briefing room at 0800 for a meeting with *Gardner.*" He sneered the name. "Geez, I hate that guy."

Kim and I groaned.

"Dammit, something about that guy just creeps me right the hell out," I said. "What's his deal, anyway? He's like some sort of paper-pushing robot."

"Well," Tom said, "from what I hear, he's going to be the one doing most of the talking this morning."

Another round of groans, and I waved Tom out so we could get dressed. He chuckled and muttered as he left the room. "So much for *my* good morning!" he laughed as he closed the door.

I waved in the general direction of the drawers that had all our gear in them as I sat back against the wall. "Ladies first."

Kim gave me that look that every man in the free world has seen from one woman or another. I knew I hadn't fooled her a bit, but I wasn't about to admit it.

What can I say? I like looking at beautiful women, and Kim was that and more. She pulled the sheet with her as she left the bed, leaving me scrambling for the blanket to cover myself against the chill air of the room. Snagging a couple pieces of bacon off the tray, she sauntered over to the drawers, letting the sheet fall to the floor as she picked out her clothes for the day.

I could only stare in silence as my brain turned itself off, leaving me to look like a drooling idiot as she dressed. She knew exactly what she was doing, too. A turn of the leg here, a twist of the torso there, and I was mostly a puddle of goo when she was finished.

Mostly.

She giggled and sat down to eat her breakfast as I stood to take my turn at the dresser. I dressed quickly, trying to think of baseball, cold showers, Margaret Thatcher naked on a cold day—*thanks very much for that, Mike Myers*—anything but her as I pulled my T-shirt over my head and salivated over the smell of the fresh coffee on the tray.

"So do you think he'll be okay?" she asked me as I sat down.

"I dunno, really. It took me a long time to get over Rebecca, and this will be just as hard for him . . ." I broke off as I realized what I had said, and looked up to see Kim as stony-faced as I'd ever seen her.

Oops. I'd really put my foot in it this time, and there was no way out but through. *Well, it had to happen sooner or later. Now's as good a time as any.* I sighed and put down the coffee cup.

I composed myself and then looked her straight in the eye. Honesty was *definitely* the best policy here.

"Rebecca was the fifteenth walker I put down, and my fiancée. She and I had met a year or so before it all went to Hell in Fall Creek, and we were happy, for a time."

Rebecca picked up the pale yellow sundress and scowled at it. It wasn't her color, and far too thin, and *short. Trust David to pick out something like this. I really need to work on his fashion sense.* She'd have to wear something else underneath it, or at the very least a jacket, but she also knew she'd have to wear it today, or he'd wonder why.

And she couldn't very well tell him he had the fashion sense God gave Michael Jackson, could she? She sighed and then smiled. *Still, he's the best boyfriend you've ever had, girl. Shut up and wear the damn dress already.*

She had just finished pulling the dress over her head and settling it on her shoulders when she heard and felt Eric bounding up the stairs and around the corner, racing into the room and throwing himself on the bed. Her eight-year-old son looked up at her, his bright blue eyes shining underneath a mop of straw-blond hair.

"Mom, guess what?"

She ruffled his hair. "What, kiddo?" she asked as she pulled a silver watch that her father had given her out of her jewelry box.

"Aw, come on, you're supposed to guess!"

She turned to him, one finger on her lips in a thoughtful pose. "Hmmm, let's see. You've been kidnapped by aliens and they've replaced you with a robot?"

He laughed. "Nope!"

"Um, you're actually a hundred years old but you pretend to be small so you can get out of paying the bills?"

"Nah."

"You saw the scariest monster you've ever seen and now you know what you want to be for Halloween?" She said, grasping at straws as she took out a simple diamond necklace and laid it across her neck. It had been David's Christmas present to her the year before. She hadn't asked him what it cost, but she had snuck a look at the receipt and was astounded that he would spend that much money on her. Suddenly she realized how quiet the room was and turned around. Eric was staring at her, his mouth agape.

"Close your mouth, you'll catch flies," she said automatically, to which he responded as automatically.

"Better than your cooking, anyway." Her lack of culinary skill had been a running joke in their small family for more than six months now. For whatever reason, she found it as funny as they did, and hey, at least it got her out of cooking. "How did you know?" he asked.

"Know what, babe?"

"That I saw a scary monster!"

She was momentarily nonplussed, and ran the conversation back in her head. "Wait, you really did see a scary monster?"

His eyes were huge as he whispered. "He was all gooshy like he'd been dead for weeks or something, and he made this weird moaning noise, and he wouldn't go away. He tried to grab Brandt, but we got away. He was like a movie monster, mom."

Now she was worried. Eric didn't usually make up stories, so he must've seen something. "Where did you see this monster?"

Eric grew shifty, and Rebecca knew he was lying to her. "Um, over by the park."

She walked over to her son and sat down on the edge of the bed. "Now, what have I told you about lying, Eric?"

"I know, it's just . . ." The little boy sighed and sat up, looking at her. "Please don't be mad, Mom. We were riding bikes near the mine, and Brandt thought he saw something moving in the shack."

"Dammit, Eric," Rebecca said, and then calmed herself, taking a deep breath. *Getting mad at him now's not going to help anything.* "You know why I've told you over and over not to play there. Now you almost got grabbed by some homeless man or something!"

"He wasn't a homeless man, Mom! He was a monster! All grey and moaning, it was gross!"

"It doesn't matter *what* he was, you knew you shouldn't be there. Thank you for telling me the truth. You're grounded for two weeks."

"Aw, Mom, I told the truth! You said I wouldn't get in trouble if I told the truth!"

"No, I didn't. I said you'd get in *more* trouble if you *didn't* tell the truth. Now go get in the car. We'll go and see David. He can talk to the sheriff about this *monster* you saw."

Eric jumped off the bed. "Can I start the car?"

She laughed and shook her head. "Not this time, little man. Maybe next time." She gave one more look in the mirror and tossed her long blonde ponytail over her shoulder.

Downstairs, they climbed into her Wrangler, and she made sure Eric was buckled in. It was a short drive to David's shop, but Eric had a habit of taking off the belt, claiming it choked him.

A few minutes later, she pulled onto Main Street and stopped at Magnolia, then turned right and entered the rear parking lot of the small shopping center.

The bell on the door tinkled as she entered the Fall Creek Bookshop. She bypassed the counter, waving at Jenny who worked as David's assistant and kept things organized. Jenny waved back and smiled at Eric, who blushed bright red and ran ahead into the back room.

"He's got a huge crush on you," Rebecca told the younger girl.

"I know, and he's cute, but he's a bit young for me," Jenny said, winking. "David's in the back."

"Thanks, Jenny."

She walked back through the shelves and shelves of old and new books and put her arms around David, sitting at his desk, frowning at his computer monitor.

He looked up at her, and she was struck as always by the deep grey of his eyes, just as Eric careened into his lap for a hug and he smiled at both of them.

How much happier can I get? I can't wait to see what's next.

After Eric finished his story, I looked at him and Rebecca both. "This doesn't sound good, babe. I think I need to tell the sheriff."

"You really think it's that serious?" Rebecca asked, surprised.

"Well, even if he's just a homeless man, he needs to be stopped from attacking people or at least threatening them. And who knows? He could be hurt and just need some help. Either way," I said, turning to Eric. "*You* are not going anywhere near that mine again. Clear?"

He looked down, embarrassed. "Okay." He looked back up at me and met my eyes without flinching. "I promise."

I nodded at him, as one man to another. I'd often found that showing a little respect seemed to go a long way with children, and Eric was no exception. "Okay then."

I looked back at Rebecca, marveling yet again how someone so beautiful could be so taken with me. "I'll talk to the sheriff about this, but I think you and Eric should get home. Do we have enough stuff for dinner at the house?"

Rebecca shook her head. "Not really. I'll stop by the store, and dinner will be ready by the time you get home."

I smiled and pulled her close as I stood. "Thanks. Just make sure to lock the doors, okay? The house is too close to the mine for me to feel comfortable with you two there all alone. I'll try to wrap this up as quickly as I can and get home."

She smiled and laid her hand on my cheek. "You're sweet. We'll be fine, love. See you later." As she kissed me, Eric made the requisite barfing noises of all eight-year-olds, and begged for them to go. Rebecca and I just laughed, and I smiled at her as she left.

It was about two hours later, and I was deep in my work, cataloging the newly arrived books when the sheriff walked in. I looked up as I heard Jenny greet him and he came around the corner of the doorway.

He wasn't a large man, either in height or girth, and he wasn't the sharpest knife in the drawer, but Sheriff Jasper Inson was everything you'd expect from a small-town sheriff. Friendly, tough, kind, all in equal measure, except for the ironclad core of his personality: justice. I'd never met a man so devoted to the ideal as Jasper, and it showed in everything he did.

"Hey there, Sheriff," I said, smiling at the man who worked just two storefronts over. "I'm glad you stopped by. I was actually going to come see you."

Jasper's laugh boomed out of him like he was a natural loudspeaker. "Oh really? Well, how . . . uh . . . fortuitous . . . that I happened to stop by, then." He raised an eyebrow at me, and I nodded, smiling.

Jasper had been trying to expand his vocabulary, and being as this was the only bookshop in town, he'd enlisted my help in providing some fiction that was a bit wordier than your average cop novel. Ever since, he'd been trying out the new words on me when I saw him. Except for the occasional gaffe, he was doing quite well.

"Yep, it certainly was serendipitous," I replied, and chuckled as Jasper snagged the pad from his shirt pocket and made a note. "S-e-r-e-n-d-i-p-i-t-o-u-s," I said, helping him out.

"Ah, got it. Thanks, David." He put the pad away, and was suddenly serious. "What were you coming to see me about?"

"Oh, nothing too important, I think. Just a homeless guy near the mine. Eric and his friend were playing over there and he said this guy tried to grab his friend. Apparently he was moaning, too, so he might've been hurt and just needed some help." I noticed Jasper carefully concealing a quick look of surprise, but I continued as though I hadn't. "Even if he is homeless and hurt, he doesn't need to be bothering a couple of kids."

"And when did this happen?"

Okay, Jasper is serious about this. Something else must've happened. But what? "Eric told Rebecca it was about five or six hours ago, now. Why? What's wrong?"

"Settle down, David, it's probably nothing. I just got a third call about some weird guy hanging out around the east side, about a half mile from the mine. Kenneth Ackerman said he tried to grab his dog, of all things, and the damned thing went crazy, barking as soon as it saw the guy. He's all barricaded in his house now, and I sent Charlie to take a look."

He chuckled. "That guy's almost as bad as Feldon, or getting there. Anyway, I thought you might have heard something about it. Looks like it was a good idea to come talk to you after all."

"Well shit, Jasper! Why didn't you tell me? That's over near my house, man! Rebecca and Eric are there all alone! What if this crazy fucker decides he's going to go after them? I've gotta get over there." I stood up, grabbing my keys and coat.

"Now hold on, David. Charlie will take care of this. There's no need to get all crazy."

"Jasper, that's my girl and my kid over there," I said, moving to go around him as he blocked the doorway. He didn't move, but he put one hand on my arm, and I looked at him, my heart in my eyes. "We're getting married, Jasper."

He looked back at me, searching for something undefined, and nodded, releasing my arm. "Just be careful, David. Who knows what this guy is capable of if he's attacking dogs and kids? Stay in your house, with your family. Okay?"

I nodded as I walked out front. "Will do!" Looking over at Jenny, I stopped for a second. "Jenny, go ahead and get out of here, ok? Lock up, but don't bother with any of the other paperwork. We'll take care of it tomorrow if we need to. Just head home and stay there."

She looked surprised, but shrugged. "Sure thing, boss. See you tomorrow."

"That was the last time I saw her or Eric alive. Or Jasper or Jenny, for that matter." I sat still, lost in memories for who knows how long. Kim took my hand and broke the spell and I smiled at her in thanks.

"I never did find out what happened to Jenny, but I killed Jasper early the next morning. By the time I got to our house, there was no one there. The front door was smashed, but I don't think Rebecca had been home. I think whatever went through the door was after

Eric. I grabbed my rifle and pistol, just in case, and headed out to look for them, but I didn't find them at the grocery store, and things went to hell before I could get back home. You know the rest."

Kim cleared her throat and started to say something, and stopped. She tried again. "What about Eric?" she asked.

I shrugged. "I don't know. They never found him. Or at least, they never found a body. He might've run off, or been—" I broke off and stared at the table, still holding her hand.

She leaned forward and turned me to face her, and I felt like she was looking into my soul with those eyes of hers as she fought back tears. "I'm sorry, David. Sorry that you lost her. That you lost Eric, that you lost all those friends. But you're going to be okay."

I swallowed the lump in my throat and blinked several times, finally getting myself under control. "I . . . I know, babe. It's just hard sometimes, you know?"

She smiled and stroked my face with her hand, then stood and came around the table and pulled me to my feet. "Let's see if we can't make it a bit better, shall we?" She drew me in for a deep kiss, and suddenly all thoughts of Rebecca, Eric, even yesterday's mess fled.

We were only a few minutes late for the briefing, but Maxwell glared at us both as we walked in and took our spots. Commander Anderson, on the other hand, hid a grin, as did Reynolds.

I returned the colonel's glare with a cheery smile, and even that old bastard finally faltered a bit and I saw the hint of a smirk slip through, just before he sighed and stood up.

"Now that we're all here," he said, looking at Kimberly and me. "Let's get started. Mr. Gardner, you have the floor."

The grey man, as I thought of him, stood and moved to the small lectern that had been placed on the desk, clearing his throat and arranging his papers just so before getting started. Just as some of us began to fidget, he cleared his throat *again* and finally started.

"Gentlemen, I must congratulate you on the most successful mission that you had yesterday," he said. "You were able to secure and cleanse the Uintah Basin Medical Center and its environs of zombies with acceptable casualties and minimal structural damage to important buildings."

As he spoke, some of the soldiers and I glanced at each other furtively. *Is this guy for real? Acceptable casualties?*

"The important thing to take away from this mission is the knowledge that you can survive. That, indeed, you can succeed beyond our wildest hopes," Gardner continued. "The REAPRs were also an unqualified success, though it was to be hoped that they could be used to track additional targets. Still, they proved their worth and the remainder of the force will be outfitted with additional units."

He turned to Janet Turner, a young woman with shock-white hair and a severe sort of mien, and gestured at the light switches. "Young lady, if you please." Janet scowled at the man, but reached over and flicked the appropriate switches to turn the lights off and the projector on. I'm guessing Gardner missed the subtle hand gesture she sent his way behind her back, though the rest of the team saw it.

"Thank you, miss."

I could see her visibly grind her teeth in a smile, and stifled a chuckle as Gardner turned to the projected map of the United States. He pointed to a small red dot in northern Utah: Roosevelt. There were several other red dots scattered across the map, even in Alaska. "Unfortunately, even with the success we've had with this mission, we've had recent reports of incursions elsewhere, too, as you can see."

"Except for Roosevelt, all of these incursions were graded Class One, some barely even making that level. Until Roosevelt, your combined military strength hasn't been needed, and conventional troops could be used to deal with the minor number of walkers encountered. As usual, we staged an epidemiological accident as the cause."

I tried not to fall asleep as he droned on and on with statistics, charts, graphs and more esoteric data than I'd ever seen. I could tell from Gardner's attitude that he was in his element now. I could also tell from the looks on the faces of my peers that they were as enthused as I was, and I'd have sworn that Powell was dead asleep, though he was staring straight ahead, eyes open. That was a trick I'd yet to master, as hard as I'd tried.

I snapped back to full alert when Gardner pointed to a new map that I hadn't seen him bring up, overlaying the old one. This showed two blue circles, significantly larger than the red ones. One appeared to be near south-central Wyoming, the other in western Maine.

"This, gentlemen, is our most serious problem. This is why the other teams have been activated and are being armed and outfitted as we speak. They have already received this briefing as of yesterday afternoon." He put down his laser pointer and turned to us, and became more animated than we'd ever seen him. If anything, he appeared . . . *excited.*

Surely not.

"The two areas you see outlined here are confirmed to have experienced a Class Two Outbreak. As expected, AEGIS has been tasked with cleaning up the mess. Teams Three and Four will deal with the outbreak in Farmington, Maine, while Teams One and Two will be tasked with the Rawlins, Wyoming outbreak. Both towns have a population under ten thousand, but local press is expected and, in the case of Rawlins, is already on site.

"Thus far, the cover story has held. We're telling them that the 'illness' causing the attacks is a result of two things: an as-yet-unknown chemical agent introduced to the water supply by illegal dumping, most likely some sort of pesticide, and a food additive that is illegal in this country but wasn't screened out during customs checks, similar to the pet food scare a few years back. Before, you went in as National Guard troops. Now you'll be regular Army— of a sort. How many of you are familiar with USAMRIID?"

There were a few raised hands, but most of us had only heard of the agency at best, much less actually knew details of their operations or what they were charged with doing.

"Very well. For those who aren't aware, the United States Army Medical Research Institute for Infectious Diseases is essentially the Army version of the CDC. They're the top of the heap when it comes to Army responses to biological threats, and more important, *they're known.* Hell, they've even been in a movie or two. We work with USAMRIID for obvious reasons, and their commander is one of the few people outside this room that are aware of the prion disease.

"Oh, one other thing: we need you to be aware of any opportunity you might have to *capture* specimens, rather than destroy them. 'Live'—for lack of a better word—specimens are necessary for further study."

The looks that passed between us at this ridiculous news must've been obvious to Gardner, but he didn't bat an eye at the animosity coming his way.

"You'll be going in as USAMRIID forces, even down to the paint on your Strykers, which we'll be able to use due to the presence of the Army rather than the National Guard. This is standard procedure for big outbreaks, since usually the CDC handles smaller ones. We've got USAMRIID-tagged press releases ready to issue, as well. The important thing here is that *no one* talks to the media except Colonel Maxwell. OpSec is *very* tight on this one."

He paused and looked up at us. "This cover won't hold forever, so you'll need to take care of the situation with as few public encounters as possible. I'm sure you'll be able to handle it adequately. Obviously, we'd prefer not to have this as front-page news, but I really don't see how we can avoid that now. I'll leave it to Colonel Maxwell to fill you in on the details of the mission. Goodbye."

He started to walk away from the table, but I stood, ignoring the glares from Maxwell and Anderson. "You just wait one goddamned minute, Gardner," I said, putting every ounce of loathing and annoyance I felt for the man into my voice. Easy, since *something* about him bothered every particle of my being, not that I knew what it was.

I had thought he was robotic before, but I was sorely mistaken. He stopped, turning to face me without seeming to move his feet, as if he was rotating in a window display. For a brief second, I thought I saw a flash of anger, but it might've been a quirk of the lighting.

And pigs might fly. I'd broken that shell, and he and I both knew it. *This isn't going to be pretty.*

"Yes, Mister . . ."

"Blake, *Mister* Gardner. David Blake." His eyes widened for a moment, just a fraction, but I could tell he recognized the name. *So, point number two for me.*

"You want us to go out there in the middle of a Class Two outbreak and not only take care of it, but take live specimens, too? You do realize that the first recorded Class Two outbreak in the US caused the full and complete destruction of my *whole fucking hometown*, right? As in fifteen. Hundred. People. Gone."

I grew angrier as I moved toward the man in his expertly tailored suit that probably cost more than the combined salaries of this entire room. "But not just gone, Gardner. At least half of them were turned, and at least forty of those were US Army. The very same people you want to send to their deaths trying to get 'specimens' for you."

I didn't notice the colonel and his XO moving toward me at speed until Gardner waved them back, setting his files and notes down. He folded his arms, looking down his nose at me from the depths of his cavernous brow.

"I know exactly how many people died at Fall Creek. After all, I was there, too."

Score one for the grey man.

I tried not to let the shock show on my face. Fortunately, I wasn't exactly slow when it came to thinking on my feet. "Good. I can only assume you were one of the people they brought with them, so you must know, at least partially, what we're dealing with. Before I'll order my team *anywhere*," I said, pausing at a feminine cough behind me. "Before I follow orders to take this team anywhere, I have some questions for you that the colonel may or may not be able to answer."

I glanced over at the colonel, but he and Commander Anderson were simply standing there, arms folded as well, looking intently at the man in the impeccable suit.

Gardner swallowed somewhat nervously as he realized he was faced with a roomful of angry, well-trained, dangerous men and women who could quite easily remove from him the burden that was his life.

I'll say one thing for the grey man. He certainly knew how to pick his battles.

"Very well, Mr. Blake. What would you like to know?"

I glanced at Rachel, who nodded and held up a pen and notebook, as though she had read my mind. "I want to know why *now*."

He appeared slightly confused, which for Gardner meant a raised eyebrow. "Why now?"

"Yeah. Why now? Things have been quiet for more than two years since Fall Creek. No reported sightings, no attacks, no outbreaks. Then suddenly we're activated, and there's at least two incursions already in progress. So I repeat: Why now?"

At first, I would've sworn there was a flash of fear in the man's eyes. But it was there and gone so quickly, I must've imagined it. He started laughing at me. Granted, it was a dry, rasping cough more than a laugh, but I got the point. "You poor, benighted fool." He turned to Maxwell with a questioning look, and the colonel shifted uncomfortably, and then shrugged.

Okay, whoa. I'd seen Maxwell set his own broken bones before without so much as a twitch—field exercises could get rough—but *this* made him uncomfortable?

What the hell is going on?

Chapter Eleven

FORT CARSON, COLORADO

GARDNER SMILED, AND I HOPED for all the world that I would never see it again. It was like being smiled at by a six-foot python that had just decided what to have for its next light snack.

He gestured to the tables. "Please, have a seat. You're going to want to sit down for this." We all sat back down as he moved back to the lectern and took his laser pointer out once more. He accessed a secure file from the network, and suddenly a new map, overlaying the old one, showed up on the screen. A map with, at first glance, over a hundred small green dots, across the entire United States, Canada and even into Mexico.

This can't be good.

"What you are looking at is our most recent historical map. What you see here is a map of every recorded incursion or outbreak in the last hundred and fifty years, since we began tracking the walkers." More than one of the soldiers blanched at this. Commander Anderson turned and began a fierce whispered conversation with Maxwell that ended abruptly as Maxwell cut him off.

Anderson shot out of his chair, and saluted the colonel damn near perfectly. I could forgive him if his hands shook, but I was stunned when he left the room, slamming the door on the way out.

That is going to be an interesting conversation.

"According to our records, in the last hundred and fifty years there have been more than *five hundred* incidents in the United States alone, including all Class One outbreaks." Gardner said, and then pointed to Janet, who had raised a hand in the back. "Yes, miss?"

"What do you mean in the United States alone, Mr. Gardner?"

"You didn't think this was confined to our shores, did you, Ms. Turner?" She flushed as she not only realized that this man knew her last name, but that she had just asked a truly stupid question. "Let me show you something else."

The view zoomed out to a global map, and we all gasped in shock. Green dots covered the surface of the Earth, with the most massive collections in rural Africa, parts of Asia and South America as well as the Middle East. There were even a few in Australia, and near the Arctic Circle in far northern Greenland.

We were stunned into silence at the ramifications of what Gardner had showed us. The entire world had experienced these outbreaks, and yet *no one knew.* Or at the very least, the majority of the public went on in blissful ignorance.

Gardner's smile turned even creepier, somehow. "AEGIS isn't the only agency out there, people. We've been working with other governments for the last, oh, fifty years or so to coordinate our efforts." He made sure he had our attention before he continued.

"*We are losing this war.* And make no mistake, this *is* a war. According to our best estimates, more than five million people worldwide have lost their lives to the walkers, and that's only since we started looking at the history very closely. We put *enemy* numbers at somewhere over fifty thousand, give or take a few. It's hard to estimate given the conditions they can survive in."

Suddenly, quite a few pieces of a puzzle I'd not yet realized I was looking at fell into place for me, and I can only imagine the horror on my face as I turned to look at Gardner who was already staring at me.

"Ah, I see at least one of you senses the true nature of this battle," he said, nodding like some bobblehead on a dashboard. "Tell me, Mr. Blake, what you think you know."

I held up fingers one by one as I ticked off my conclusions.

"One: This problem is *far* more widespread than anyone will *ever* admit publicly.

"Two: Hardly anyone knows what's really going on.

"Three: The government, AEGIS, whoever, has been investing billions of dollars in Hollywood getting Americans and others ready for the idea that zombies are real." I snorted at their confused faces.

"Think about it! All those zombie movies and books and TV shows recently? End-of-days-style stories? Post-apocalyptic is all the rage in film right now. And why is it all pretty much the same?

"Because it's these guys," I said, pointing to Gardner, "getting us ready for the real deal. This way, at least some of us may not freak out as badly when the shit hits the fan. Hell, some of the survivalists or others like them might even make it through, at least for a little while, especially since what we've seen in the movies—like head shots—actually works."

Now for the really scary stuff.

"Four: The shit has hit the fan, or is about to, because—and here's where we get seriously fucked—Five: The so-called 'war on terror' is a cover. We're really fighting a war on walkers." A soft clapping brought everyone's attention to the front of the room again. Gardner folded his arms and leaned forward.

"Oh, well *done*, Mr. Blake! Well done. We've managed to keep that realization from nearly everyone, and you put it together in five minutes flat. I can see how you survived Fall Creek, though I'm not sure that was entirely *your* doing." I flushed as he continued, unaware or immune to the anger on my face.

"In any case, you're right. The war on terror *is* really a war on walkers. It was simply easier to blame the terrorists for all of it and give ourselves a blank check to move men and materiel wherever and however we wanted."

Powell put up his hand, a worried expression on his face. "So Al-Qaeda doesn't exist, then?"

"Oh, to be sure, they do exist, and did cause 9/11, but not for the reasons even they think they did. Osama bin Laden ordered the attacks because he believed that the US and its allies had caused the plague of walkers that's now infecting most of the Middle East. Sure, he *said* it was for religious reasons—or at least that's what we told everyone. You don't really believe that there are *that* many soldiers killed by IEDs, do you?"

The soldiers looked skeptical, and though I understood what was going on better than most, it was hard for me to believe, too.

Gardner's skeletonesque grin got just a bit bigger. "We do have troops in Afghanistan, Iraq, etc. That part is real. Some of them die in truly horrible ways, and the IEDs do claim many lives. They're certainly doing a great job against what they think is the main enemy. Unfortunately, they're wrong."

Powell spoke up. "So you're saying most of it is just made up?"

"Well, Lieutenant, Blake just told you and I've confirmed that we've spent millions if not billions of dollars in Hollywood getting people psychologically ready for the end of the world. Which do you think is more likely? That we couldn't possibly get away with it, or that people don't want to know the truth and will blindly swallow whatever tripe the modern media shovels their way?

"When was the last time you looked really closely at any of the images coming back? Do you even know anyone who has? No one wants to look at gruesome injuries to their own soldiers. Not even the most bloodthirsty journalists and media hounds can stand to look for long, and they refuse to believe what their eyes are showing them."

There was a general shaking of heads, and Gardner sighed.

"I know it's hard to believe. But I've watched AEGIS technicians take a live feed from a roadside attack in Afghanistan and digitally edit out the zombie's remains, replacing them with an insurgent. *And things like that happen all the time.*"

"But surely there have been soldiers and media people who've seen what's really going on," said Reynolds, disbelief still strong in his eyes. "You can't tell me that no one has seen a walker anywhere and reported it."

Gardner's gaze was ice. "I wouldn't tell you that, Captain. Of course they have. Or at least, they've *tried* to report it. Some have listened to reason and retired, others had to be . . . *coerced.*" He left no doubt in my mind exactly what he meant by that. Judging by the faces around me, I could see that the rest of my team got the message, too.

"Where do you think their transmissions go? To satellites. Who controls the satellites? We do. The governments. It's as simple as that. We control the entirety of the information coming through news channels from the Middle East, and everywhere else for that matter."

"What about the Internet, though? I've seen crap like this all the time before Fall Creek," I said.

"You're not seriously suggesting we can't hack whatever we want, are you, Mr. Blake? We're talking about not only the wealthiest country on earth but also arguably the most technologically advanced. We have crypto-analysts and hackers that are good enough . . . Well, let's just say the true extent of their talents would shock even you.

"Or maybe you didn't think that we could have our own people do some posting of our own? In fact, I've got three or four geeks whose sole job is to sit in a room eight hours a day, five days a week, doing nothing but posting misinformation on every forum and website they can find.

"Not everything has to be super-secret spy stuff. Believe me, information control was the first thing we thought of." He paused, and smiled again. "After all, we can't have people running around claiming it's the end of the world, can we?"

I sat down in my chair, stunned and mumbling. Gardner heard it, though.

"What's that? Come, come, share with the rest of us?"

I ignored him, lost in my own little world, until Kim shook my arm roughly. "David, what is it?"

I shook my head and turned to look at Maxwell. "I understand, sir," I said. "I understand why you couldn't tell us." A pained look crossed his craggy face, and he glanced at Gardner, who wouldn't meet his eyes. I looked back at Kim, and something on my face caused her to flinch back, startled.

"They couldn't tell us. I wish I didn't know. I wish none of us knew," I said.

"Knew what, David?" Kim asked, reaching out a hand to lay it on my arm.

"We're going to lose this war. We never had a chance." The silence from Gardner and Maxwell was confirmation enough.

"Is that information that Gardner showed us confirmed, sir?" I asked Maxwell, dreading the answer. "Reports from all continents, I mean."

"Yes, son, it is."

"Well, that's it, then," I said, collapsing into my chair. I could feel the thousand-yard stare creep across my eyes.

"David . . ." Kim asked.

"We're fucked." I glanced at Maxwell. "Sorry, sir."

"Never mind that. What do you mean?"

"Well, if they truly are on every continent, then it's only a matter of time. We'll see sporadic outbreaks across the globe, probably starting in the Third World and Southeast Asia. Places like Laos, China, mid-Africa and the poorer parts of India would all be good bets. Anywhere people are packed in like sardines and have little or no access to quality health care. Not that that would make any difference in this case." I paused and stood up, pacing.

"They'll be Class One outbreaks initially: five walkers at most, with the occasional Class Two to indicate a hotspot or a country with no effective response to the incursions, like AEGIS. This will go on for a while."

Tom broke in. "How do you know this?"

"I don't, not for sure. But we saw the same thing in Fall Creek, just adjusted for our size. A microcosm of what will happen out there," I said, waving my hand vaguely toward the window. "It starts small, with just one or two people affected. Then it grows, primarily because no one will believe what's actually happening. Because, of course, zombies don't exist in the real world.

"What you have to understand here is that *we have lost containment*. If we'd been able to find that first walker, or first couple of them, and put them down, we could've saved the town. But we didn't know what was happening until it was too late. Out there, there is no way in hell we could do that. There's no way to find 'Walker Zero.' And there never will be. There can be no putting the genie back in the bottle on this one.

"The end will happen fast, too. Every walker creates who knows how many others, and their numbers will grow exponentially. We'll see cities overrun, then almost overnight it'll be smaller countries, then several, and finally whole continents. There won't be any safe places to run or hide, because eventually the survivors will make a mistake, or run out of supplies, or just go crazy. And that'll be it.

"In short, we're fucked. We never stood a chance, after it spread this far. And the really screwed up thing is that *this will never end*."

"How so?" asked Maxwell.

"Think about it. Is there any way you could absolutely say for sure and for certain that you could find every single walker out there? Every. Last. One? Every waterlogged bastard hiding out on the ocean floor, every frozen one stuck in waist-deep permafrost somewhere in Washington State or the Arctic? No, there's not. Not now, anyway.

"And that's what you'd have to do to make sure these prions were dead and gone forever. The walkers would have to be wiped from existence completely. And since you could never be sure you'd gotten them all, there would always be the chance that someone, somewhere, somehow could stumble upon one and be turned."

"That's not entirely accurate, Mr. Blake," said Dr. Adamsdóttir. "Walkers decay just like any other organic creature, just much more slowly. *Eventually*, they will literally fall apart, and when that happens . . ."

"When that happens, the prions—which will be dormant at that point, but not dead—will likely make their way into whatever groundwater is nearby their former host's remains. Which means they could end up in *anything*. It might end up in a human who drinks from that water, but it could just as easily end up in any animal as well. Although from what you've told us, most animals seem to somehow sense this disease and stay away.

"We'll never be rid of it, though, not really. Until and unless someone miraculously develops a serum or antidote sometime in the next few years—before we're all dead—this thing is going to be with us forever, and we're going to all need to be willing to put a bullet in and then burn anyone we know. That's the only truly permanent solution—destruction by fire.

"And since setting fire to the entire surface of the planet is probably a bad idea, we've got no options."

The human race was ending, and we had front-row tickets to the big show.

Chapter Twelve

FORT CARSON, COLORADO

GARDNER LEFT, AND WE NOW sat in a loose circle. Colonel Maxwell had joined us, but Commander Anderson was still MIA. That worried me, but I knew that they'd been together for a long damn time and would eventually work it out. I just hoped that they got the chance.

"Sir?" Powell was leaning forward, staring at something only he could see beyond the scratched and dinged tiled floor. "Was what he said true, sir?"

The colonel sighed and stood up, pacing behind his chair. "Yes, Lieutenant, it was. Everything he told you is or has happened."

"Everything?" asked Kimberly, her arms folded and a look that would have sent me running for the hills on her face. Fortunately, it was directed at the colonel.

"Operational security, Major. I was given specific and direct orders by the Secretary himself, on orders from the President, not to divulge the true nature of the walker threat." He scrubbed a hand through the short grey stubble on his head and shrugged. "There was nothing I could do."

"What's the point, sir?" Janet spoke up from the back of the room where she was leaning against the wall. "I mean, if it's as bad as that, why are we bothering to fight at all?"

I turned to Janet, surprised. "We have to, Turner."

She ignored me, staring down the colonel, who finally spoke.

"He's right. We all know how this is going to end. There's too many of them, too spread out, and the only effective weapons we have are in the hands of far too few soldiers and other trained personnel. We can't just run around killing them willy-nilly, either."

"Then why don't we tell people? Tell the truth, I mean."

Maxwell looked at her, dumbfounded. "I happen to know you are not that stupid, soldier. You and I both know what would happen if we did that, and if John Q. Public believed even half of what we told them."

"Panic. Anarchy. Riots, looting, endless chaos, millions if not billions dead." I couldn't keep the terror from my voice as I said it.

Pointing at me, the colonel continued, "Exactly. People are not prepared to deal with a crisis of this magnitude. Hell, we have enough idiots to deal with who actually know what's going on and think we can somehow domesticate or train the things."

He paused as the incredulous looks spread around the room. "Now you know some of the shit that I've been dealing with from Gardner.

"But that's not the issue. People are panicky. We don't need some jackass in Bumfuck, Nebraska going on a shooting spree because he thinks all his neighbors are zombies. And god help us if some zealot or terrorist decided to set off a nuke."

He sat down once more in the circle, and sighed. "We're fighting because we have to. It's the only option we have left. We have to keep them at bay as long as we can, hoping that we have enough time."

"Enough time for what, sir?"

"I don't want anyone here to have any illusions about what we're facing. Still, things may not be as bad as you think."

Maxwell stood and activated the briefing projector once more. "Ladies and gentlemen, I give you Project Phoenix."

He looked around at us, and grinned slightly. "None of you are cleared to know about it, but this hasn't exactly been a day for keeping secrets, has it?" He half-turned toward the hall door and raised his voice. "Okay, Frank, you can come back in now."

Commander Anderson walked into the room, saluted the colonel, and grinned. "Thank you sir. That hall is not made for waiting around in." He took a seat as Maxwell waved his hand in the general direction of his forehead, and relaxed.

The rest of us sat there, confused and uncertain of what had just happened. That was the only time I ever heard Colonel George Maxwell laugh, and just like everything else he did, he laughed *loud*.

"Oh, that's rich. I love the looks on your faces. Frank?"

Anderson was still grinning and chuckling a bit, and nodded. "Definitely, sir. Caught them all by surprise, I think."

"Well, good. It's about time we shook them up a bit. So, Project Phoenix."

"Sir, what was all that about with the commander?" Dalton asked, looking confused.

"All in due time, Gunny. All in due time." He waited until Dalton shrugged, then went on. "Project Phoenix was conceived about twenty years ago once we realized just how bad things had really gotten. They've been actively working on it for the last five or so, after all the bean counters and administrators had their say in the planning."

"Essentially, what's happening is that governments around the world are quickly and above all quietly, building large subterranean bunkers that can house up to about ten thousand people each. Once the situation on the surface gets to the point of no return, those chosen for the bunkers will go underground."

"What happens to those left above?" I asked, already knowing the answer.

"They'll die. Or they'll get bitten and turn. Some may even survive in the mountains or in other cold locations where the walkers slow down some. I imagine quite a few of the survivalist types will make it, but they'll end up as warlords or nomadic tribes or some other such thing, if only because they've got weapons and most know how to use them. But most everyone else will die."

"How could you build these without anyone knowing?"

"Who said we did?" Maxwell chuckled. "They're all in remote areas, to begin with. Second, the best place to hide something is in plain sight. For some of them, it was just another government storage bunker. For others, it was to hold toxic waste, or just about anything we could dream up.

"Sure, there were occasionally those who wandered onto the properties or dug a little too deep, but all in all, it went off without a hitch. Almost all of them are located in places no one cared about, and eventually, the novelty of some massive government project just wore off."

None of us could say anything for a while. We just sat there, processing all the new information with which we'd been inundated, and the idea that the majority of the planet, *eight billion people*, would die horrible, painful deaths. Finally, Reynolds broke the silence.

"So there's a chance, then. Send a bunch of people into the bunkers, presumably to keep working the problem and hopefully finding a cure, and eventually we can come out and repopulate."

Maxwell nodded. "That's the idea, son. How well it works, and whether we have time to get all the bunkers done, is something we can't control. But we can *try*, damn it, and that's why we're fighting. We cannot go quietly into this good night."

"Dylan Thomas, sir?" I asked. "I never would've figured you for a poetry man."

Maxwell chuckled. "I wasn't always a grunt, Mr. Blake." He noticed the others looking confused, sat a little straighter in his chair, and began to speak.

> *Do not go gentle into that good night,*
> *Old age should burn and rage at close of day;*
> *Rage, rage against the dying of the light.*
>
> *Though wise men at their end know dark is right,*
> *Because their words had forked no lightning they*
> *Do not go gentle into that good night.*
>
> *Good men, the last wave by, crying how bright*
> *Their frail deeds might have danced in a green bay,*
> *Rage, rage against the dying of the light.*
>
> *Wild men who caught and sang the sun in flight,*
> *And learn, too late, they grieved it on its way,*
> *Do not go gentle into that good night.*
>
> *Grave men, near death, who see with blinding sight*
> *Blind eyes could blaze like meteors and be gay,*
> *Rage, rage against the dying of the light.*
>
> *And you, my father, there on the sad height,*
> *Curse, bless me now with your fierce tears, I pray.*
> *Do not go gentle into that good night.*
> *Rage, rage against the dying of the light.*

"We fight to give them time to complete the bunkers, where we few may keep the species alive. We fight because we must. Any questions?"

He looked around and saw the set and ready faces around him. The faces of professional soldiers, ready to give their lives in defense of their country, as they'd been trained to do for years upon years.

"Good. One more thing, though. You are not cleared to discuss anything I've just told you with anyone outside this room. Clear?"

"Clear, sir!"

"Very well, dismissed. Report in one hour to the hangar for dust-off to Rawlins. Good luck."

RAWLINS, WYOMING

This is not going well.

I tagged another walker in the head as Reynolds and I covered each other and moved down the hallway, back to back. "Seventeen!" I shouted over my shoulder as we paused for a moment to check ammo and take a breath. "This is insane!"

"Almost feels like a video game at this point, doesn't it?" he replied, spinning and firing from the hip as a walker came through a glass door of the hospital. "Eighteen."

"Yeah. I'm so damn sick of hospitals at this point." I touched the mike at my throat. "Alpha Six, come in."

"Go ahead."

"We're at a count of eighteen, here, and we're almost done with this hallway."

"Roger. Yours is the last for the first floor. Bravo and Charlie have cleared the other two, Delta has the perimeter locked down. Finish your sweep and report back to reception."

"Roger, out here." I stood, and nodded towards the last room in the hall. "That's us, Tom. On three?"

"Got it." He maneuvered to one side of the door while I matched him on the other, keeping an eye on the long dark hallway as well. He knocked softly, and we heard a crash, followed by the moan we'd come to know so well. The rough scratching of dead claws at the other side of the door told us where it was, and I stepped back and covered the hall as Tom faced the door square on, raising his rifle.

The armor-piercing rounds punched through the hollow door as if it were tissue paper and threw splinters of wood and plastic across the hall. We both held our breaths, listening for more sounds from the room, but there was only silence. I reached up and twisted the knob, throwing open the door at the same time I moved back. The walker had once been a young woman, from what I could tell, but the bullets had torn her head from her shoulders and splattered it across the room. We double-checked for stragglers, then jogged back down the hallway, headed for reception.

The rest of Alpha met us on the way, with Bravo and Charlie clattering down the steps moments after we arrived.

"Good work, team," Kim said. "All squads move out to the Strykers. AEGIS Actual, Alpha Six."

Maxwell's voice crackled on the radio as we climbed into the big vehicles. "AEGIS Actual, go."

"Sir, we've finished our sweep of the hospital. Thirty-seven walkers identified, neutralized, and tagged for retrieval."

"Good work," the colonel said, knowing we could hear him. "Proceed to the high school and initiate containment procedures."

"Yes, sir. On our way." Kimberly turned to me. "We'll sweep and clear the high school, then the junior high next door. Thank God he convinced the cops to order everyone back to their homes for safety."

"I still don't envy the man, though," I said. "Not only does he have to work with those new teams, but he's got that holier-than-thou bitch to deal with, too." Kim raised an eyebrow at me, and I chuckled. "What can I say? I hate reporters."

"No, ma'am, I cannot give you any more information than that at this time. As soon as I know something I can tell you, then I will. That's all I can promise." Maxwell gritted his teeth at the reporter from Cheyenne.

I'd rather be out there hunting walkers than dealing with this. At least with zombies you know what you're dealing with. Okay, most of the time. This is why you get the big bucks, George.

"But surely, General, you can—"

"Colonel."

"Colonel then," said the woman, obviously exasperated with all things military and this puffed-up soldier in particular. "Surely you can tell us why the city is sealed off? Why we haven't even been allowed to fly over it?"

Colonel Maxwell rubbed the bridge of his nose with one hand. *This is going to be a real pounder of a headache.* "Ma'am, can I ask *you* a question?"

The cameraman stifled a chuckle as he focused on the colonel's face. Maxwell glanced at him but said nothing.

"Call me Doris," she said, missing the obvious annoyance in the colonel's tone of voice. "Certainly you can ask."

"*Ma'am,*" the colonel said. "Do you want to be sick? To spend the next month or so in quarantine, assuming you survive even the *initial* toxicity of whatever it is that's causing this illness?"

"Of course not, but surely reasonable precautions can be taken to . . ."

"There are no reasonable precautions that I can allow *civilians* to take, ma'am. Civilians don't have the training to handle a situation like this or the respect for danger that comes with it. USAMRIID, on the other hand, does have just this sort of training, and we're working closely with the CDC to get this mess taken care of."

He stepped forward and leaned towards Doris. "Now unless you're volunteering to go into the city without the proper training or protection, then I suggest you get that camera out of my face and let me do my goddamned job."

Doris blanched. "Uh, yes, Colonel. You know where to find me if you have more information. Let's go, Steven."

"Oh, and Ms. Poole, one more thing."

Doris stopped, back straight, and turned to the colonel. "Yes?"

The grin Maxwell gave her was calculated to instill the fear she suddenly felt. "If you or any of your colleagues attempt to enter the city through the perimeter without my personal permission, I will consider that a breach of quarantine and you will join everyone else in town. Understood?"

All the backbone went out of the poor reporter as she nodded and left the trailer.

God, I hate reporters.

She managed to make it back to the news van before she started laughing. Steven just looked at her and sighed. "What's so funny, Doris? He was seriously pissed!"

"Oh, whatever. He was just grandstanding. No, I'm not worried about that. What's funny is he was lying to us."

"What do you mean?"

"Give me the disk, and I'll show you."

He handed her the disk from the camera, and watched as she pulled up the footage from inside the command trailer. "What office did he say he was from?"

"USAMRIID."

"Right. Now look at this." She zoomed in, focusing on one folder lying somewhat askew in a stack of others. "See that symbol?"

"I can't make it out. Looks like a gun and a castle of some kind."

"Right. USAMRIID's logo doesn't look anything like this one. In fact, I've never seen anything like it before. I'm going to do some digging. Something's fishy about all this."

Steven just shook his head. "Doris, that's not a good idea. Can't we just report on what we know?"

She rounded on him, angry and raging. "You moron, reporting on what we know is never going to get us anywhere. You may be satisfied with that, but I'm not. And then that asshole Rick at the station couldn't even give me a seasoned cameraman!

"If you're going to stay in this job for very long, you need to learn a few things. I'm not going to sit behind a desk in the afternoon slot in some podunk little hick town for the rest of my life. This is my shot, and by god I'm going to take it."

Steven sighed and held up his hands in surrender. "Sure, fine. I'm gonna go have a smoke. Just do me a favor and think about it again before you send that to anyone, ok?" He got up, pulling a pack of cigarettes from his pocket and opening the van's door. "I'd hate to see you find out it's nothing."

When she didn't respond, didn't even turn his way, he shrugged and closed the door again, looking at the town beyond the military barricade as he lit up. He moved off into the trees near the road to answer a sudden and urgent call of nature.

He was only marginally startled when a soldier appeared in the trees nearby, camouflaged and blending in so well he'd hadn't seen him, and he'd been waiting and watching.

"So?" the soldier asked him, his eyes scanning the trees closer to the road for potential interruptions.

The cameraman sighed. "She's going to be a problem. Should I handle it?"

The soldier shook his head. "No. Just maintain cover. You'll get exfil instructions."

"Got it. Just wish I didn't have to deal with that bitch anymore."

The soldier grinned. "Don't worry. No one will." Suddenly he was gone, and the man Doris knew as Steven walked out of the trees. She spotted him, beginning another tirade as she marched over from the van.

God, I hate reporters.

I looked down at the bodies, arranged in a line of half-closed body-bags. My squad rested nearby, on guard detail for the moment. Each of the men and women in those bags wore ACUs, and all had two small holes in the middle of their foreheads. Soldiers, trained to destroy the enemy, but they'd become the enemy, instead. *Or would have. None of my team, though.* Somehow, that didn't seem to help as much as I thought it might.

I looked up as Major Shawn Carver from 2nd Team approached. The squad came to attention, saluting. "Never mind that," he said. "Give me a sitrep."

"Yes, sir. We've been ordered to guard detail, sir. Major Barnes and the rest of 1st Team are clearing the remainder of the junior high school now. We expect final sweep clearance within the hour, sir."

"Good, good. Major Barnes is a good soldier. She knows what she's doing," he said, glancing at me.

"Yes, sir."

He chuckled. "Well, we've only had one escape attempt, so I'd say the situation is fairly contained. Pretty boring, actually. I'd hoped we'd get some more action." I'm not sure what look I had on my face when he said that, but obviously it wasn't what he expected.

"Oh, don't get me wrong, kid. I'm just as sad as anyone else about losing these fine soldiers," he said, jerking his chin in the direction of the bodies. "I just can't help but wonder if we could have avoided it with fewer people on the perimeter and more in the thick of it, as it were."

I looked straight ahead. "Sir, I'm sure I can't speak to the colonel's force disposition choices, sir."

Carver rolled his eyes. "Okay, Blake. I get it. You stay sharp over here. After all, we hardly need more bodies on the ground, do we?"

We were startled as the automated .50 cal machine gun on top of the nearby Stryker rotated and began firing into the side of the junior high school, less than two hundred yards away. The rounds blew apart the old brick and mortar construction, and seemed to be tracking toward the corner of the building.

"Multiple targets acquired!" screamed the vehicle's commander from inside. "Automated systems firing!"

As if we hadn't heard the huge gun going off so close that it was painful just to stand near it. Of course, we had all hit the deck at that point and were looking for the targets. I spotted them coming around the corner, and my blood froze as I saw more ACUs and booted feet from the cover of the Stryker's side.

Please don't let one of them be Kim. I can't do that again.

Dalton was the first to fire as the group of zombies came around the corner. "It looks like Charlie squad from 2nd Team!" he said as he chambered another round into his Barrett sniper rifle.

Weighing over thirty pounds, the gun was so heavy that Dalton was the only one in the squad that could hump it and all its ammo. It didn't hurt that he was now the best shot in the team, either.

"Alpha Six, Alpha Five. We are engaged. Make it seven"— the loud *crack* of the sniper rifle was audible even through my ear protection —"correction, six walkers. They appear to be Charlie squad, or at least some of them."

"Roger, do you require backup?"

"No, ma'am, not at this time," I replied as the rifle and machine guns made short work of the rest. "Standby."

I turned to Rachel who, along with Reynolds, was covering our flanks. "Confirm all targets down."

She scooted over to the open hatch of the Stryker, which by now had ceased firing. A moment later, she looked back out at me. "Confirmed, sir. No movement."

"Alpha Six, Alpha Five. Confirm targets down."

"Good work. Tag 'em and bag 'em."

"Yes, ma'am. Alpha squad, tag and bag!" I said.

Reynolds, Martinez and Gaines moved over to the now quiescent bodies of the walkers, and began a swift and thorough check for those that had been incapacitated but not destroyed, their pistols out and double-tap shots ringing out around them.

Eaton was halfway across the grassy space when she suddenly yelled. "Walkers, nine o'clock!" Dropping into a crouch, she began firing in quick, controlled bursts as the guns on the big ICVs swung around and began firing as well. Apparently, the destruction of 2nd Team's Charlie squad had drawn interest.

"Alpha Six, Alpha Five. Multiple walkers spotted."

"Roger. Can you confirm numbers?"

"Rough guess, I'd say thirty to forty, ma'am."

"On our way. We'll come in on your seven o'clock."

"Yes, ma'am," I replied, taking out a walker on the far side of the school's football field as it came around the side of a small outbuilding, heading straight for Reynolds and Gaines and Martinez, who were slowly retreating toward the Strykers while firing.

I glanced to one side, looking for Major Carver. He was crouching against the Stryker, muttering and rocking back and forth.

"Major Carver! Sir, we could really use a hand here!" He flinched violently away. "Sir! Those were your men out there! We need help!" I couldn't believe he would actually crawl under the ICV, but he did.

Well, this is going to get messy.

"Alpha, form on the Stryker!" I switched to single-fire and began sighting carefully as the shambling mass approached.

As many as the Stryker's gun was chewing into bloody pulp, there seemed to be more behind them. Unfortunately the gun wasn't exactly a precision instrument, and couldn't be counted on for consistent head shots.

Maybe thirty or forty was a bit on the low side. The walker ranks seemed to thin out a bit as I felt more than saw my squadmates take their positions on either side of me at the end of the Stryker's open hatch. *This is going to be close.*

Off to the right, across the field, another group of walkers came out of the dark. Only these weren't just walking . . . they were running.

"Holy shit," I yelled. "Runners, four o'clock!"

"Shit!" Rachel turned with me and we began firing as fast as we could, trying to hit the speeding monsters coming our way. "They're just kids, sir!"

I looked more closely, and she was right. The oldest of these had to have been no more than fifteen or sixteen when he was turned.

And this is a high school. Fuck me running.

"I know. Take them down," I yelled, toggling my mike. "Alpha Six, we have *runners*, repeat *runners* in sight. Be advised, they are teenagers, probably students. They're fast, and coming at us."

"Roger, we've seen the same. Standby."

Suddenly I saw a line of white smoke and a massive explosion threw dirt, rock, and pieces of walker and runner alike high into the air as it impacted the group of children running at us.

The Stryker stopped firing, its sensors confused by the sudden increase in movement, and our sporadic fire at the targets gradually slowed as the rest of 1st Team arrived from behind to assist us. Shortly, nothing more remained, and it was time for cleaning up.

Kim approached, waving away a stray cloud of smoke. "So much for Gardner's RPG idea. I think we'll leave them at home next time. All that did was spread bits around. Everyone ok?"

"Yes, ma'am," I said, saluting.

"Very well, begin clean-up."

I shook my head. "Sorry, ma'am, I have something I have to do first." The surprise on her face was plain as I turned and walked to the front of the Stryker and crouched down. Sure enough, there he was. I couldn't quite reach him, though.

That's probably a good thing. I'd like to tear him to pieces with my bare hands.

"Gaines, come over here a minute." He pounded over, and I pointed beneath the ICV. "There's a rat I need you to get for me under there, Gunny. I can't reach him."

He crouched down and looked under the vehicle, then back at me with a grin. "Yes, sir." The rest of the team gathered around as Dalton pulled the squirming Major Carver from beneath the Stryker. He fought like a cornered badger, which affected the massive gunnery sergeant not in the slightest. Hands like iron vises clamped down on the man's shoulders. He was going nowhere.

"Get away, just get away!" he shouted, voice rising to a shriek.

I slapped the major, hard. "Get control of yourself, man! You're a soldier, for fuck's sake!" His head rocked back from the force of the blow, and as his eyes cleared, he glared at me.

"I'll have your ass for that!" I looked back at him coldly, uncaring. Hell, I would've done just about anything for anyone at that moment if it meant this ball-less wonder never commanded troops in the field again.

"No, you won't," said Kim's voice, over my shoulder, and she came to stand next to me, along with the rest of my squad. I glanced at Kim, and she nodded.

"AEGIS Actual, Alpha Five."

There was a pause, and then the colonel was on the line. Carver's eyes widened at my temerity. It wasn't every soldier that could just summon the colonel. "Go ahead."

"Sir, I'm reporting an Article 99."

"I see. On whom?"

"Major Carver, Second Team, sir."

"What happened?"

"Sir, Major Carver crawled under the ICV while we were engaged, and refused a direct request for assistance. We barely fought them off, sir."

"Corroborating witness?"

"Yes, sir. Sergeant Rachel Eaton, 1st Team, sir. I saw it." Before the colonel could respond, the others of my squad also joined in.

"Gunnery Sergeant Dalton Gaines, 1st Team, sir. I saw what happened."

"Captain Thomas Reynolds, 1st Team, sir. I saw it, too."

"Yes, yes. Very good." Maxwell paused, and his voice took on a tone of command I'd only heard him use a few times since I'd been a member of AEGIS. "Major Carver, do you read?"

The major looked sick, having gone pale at the conversation going on around him. He seemed to muster whatever self-esteem he might still have had, and raised his chin as Kim obligingly activated his radio. "Yes, sir. Carver here."

"Very well. Major Carver, you are hereby relieved of your command pending a full investigation. Your XO is Captain Ramos if I remember correctly," Maxwell said, his voice as cold and robotic as I'd ever heard it. "Ramos, come in."

A new voice came on the line, one I didn't recognize. He too was cold and emotionless. "This is Lieutenant Greer, sir. Captain Ramos didn't make it."

"I'm sorry to hear that. You are next up, are you not?"

"Yes, sir."

"Very well. Captain, you are now in command of Second Team, effective immediately."

"Yes, sir," James answered. "It's lieutenant, sir."

"Not anymore."

"Yes, sir. What's left of my men and I will assist with cleanup, sir."

"Very well. Barnes?"

"Here, sir," said Kimberly, unconsciously straightening without actually coming to attention.

"Major Barnes, take Carver into custody until such time as he can be delivered to base MPs at Fort Carson."

"Yes, sir," she replied. "Barnes clear."

I'd seen fury before, but the tight control that Major Carver showed amazed me. I don't know how he kept such anger in check, but it was pointless to wonder.

Kim jerked her head toward the Stryker. "Major Carver, this way please." I motioned to the back of the Stryker, and holding his head high, the major entered the vehicle. The vehicle commander gave me a questioning look.

"Article 99, sir," I said. "Would you have restraints, sir?"

"99?" said the captain. Graves, according to his ACU. "That serious?"

"Sir, you must've been otherwise occupied, sir. He crawled under the Stryker and refused to fire on the enemy, sir."

Graves turned to face the major, a look in his eye that I was sure he reserved for things he wanted to scrape off the bottom of his boot. I'm fairly certain my own expression wasn't much different.

"Well, that *is* serious, isn't it? And stupid, to boot. If we'd needed to maneuver this tub, you would've been grape jelly. Regardless, you realize that an Article 99 is punishable either by death," he paused as Carver cringed, "or such punishment as a court-martial may direct, sir?"

When Carver didn't respond, Captain Graves smiled down at Carver from his raised seat.

"I see. Well, all we have are some tow chains, son, but you're welcome to them." He gestured to a panel inset into the floor.

"Thank you, sir." Five minutes later, Carver was trussed like a Thanksgiving turkey, chained to one of the bulkheads. A truly screwed-up turkey, but a turkey nonetheless.

"We'll keep an eye on him," said Captain Graves, shaking his head at Carver's predicament. "Not like he's going to go very far, anyway." He glanced back up at his monitors. "Looks like your squad could use a hand."

I looked around and noticed that Kim had started the team policing the area as I was dealing with Carver. "Yes, sir. Thank you, sir." I left the Stryker, jogging over to where Reynolds struggled with one of the bodies from Charlie squad, and pulled on the nitrile biohazard gloves we all carried for such tasks, as well as my respirator mask.

No sense taking chances. Reynolds smiled at me thankfully, and then reached down to turn off the poor dead soldier's REAPR unit. "Bastards must've surprised them, sir. I think this is nearly the whole squad."

"I think it's more than that, Captain. Take a look." I said, pointing at one of the other bodies. It was a teenage boy, no more than thirteen or fourteen. Or it had been, once. He grimaced and spat to one side.

"Easy. It's the price we pay. You know that."

"Knowing doesn't make it any easier, sir."

He held up a hand to forestall my comment. "I know, I know. Still . . . sometimes I wish we could just push a button and wipe all of them off the planet." I couldn't help but think of Rebecca and Eric, and sighed as I hefted the other end of the body bag I'd put the first corpse in, and sighed. "You and me both, Tom. You and me both."

CHEYENNE, WYOMING

Damn him. She pulled the news van into the television station's parking lot. *First, that bastard colonel stonewalls me until he leaves, and then his "support staff" isn't allowed to talk to me at all. Support staff, my ass. They were the cleaners, making sure nothing and no one that I could use slipped through the cracks.*

"Hi, Ms. Poole," said the smiling young security guard behind the glass of the lot's security booth. "Find anything interesting out there?"

"No, I didn't," she said harshly. "Open the damn gate already!"

The guard's smile faded, and he pushed a button. "Right away, ma'am." The gate raised and she drove off.

Rick met her as she entered the building, carrying the few disks she'd managed to get out of the damned Army.

"So, Doris . . . Tell me you got something," he said, dry-washing his hands in expectation, looking her up and down in the process.

Ugh, how much creepier can this asshole get? She sighed. *It's my fault, I suppose. I never should've slept with him.*

"Nothing, Rick, okay? Not a damn thing. That jackass colonel gave me nothing but the same old crap, and then he wouldn't let us go into town, and the people he left to clean up the mess are even less helpful. They wouldn't talk to us at all."

"Well, maybe we'll find something we can use in the video." He tried to smile winningly at her, completely unaware that it appeared instead as yet another leer.

Doris narrowed her eyes and glared at him. *How much does this little troll know? Did Steven tell him about that emblem?*

"Oh, I doubt that," she said. "Nothing there, really."

Rick looked around, as though he'd just realized something. "Where's the new guy?"

Doris lost it. "That 'new guy' was worthless, Rick! He couldn't hold the camera steady to save his or my life, he was never ready to roll when I needed him and to top it all off, he asked me to drop him off at his place instead of coming back here. Said he had something 'important' to do. I swear to god if you ever send some useless prick like that out with me again, I'll—"

Rick held out his hands, surrendering. "Okay, okay, Doris. Just come inside and we'll see what you've got on the video."

"You know what, Rick? I don't think I will," she said, hands on her hips. "I've changed my mind. It's been a long goddamned day and I'm going home. We can go over the video tomorrow." She turned and stormed off across the lot to her car, an aging pale blue BMW. Rick just watched her go, shrugging and heading back inside.

Doris sat down in the front seat of the car, the recorded disks resting in a plastic bag on the passenger seat. Pulling out her Blackberry, she texted her sometime "boyfriend" Jason, although that was a huge stretch. He was more *convenient* than anything else.

"Have special project for u. Meet ASAP, my place."

Smiling to herself in triumph, she put the key in the ignition. She never saw the hand that came from the back seat and clamped over her mouth, or the needle that dipped ever so quickly into her neck.

Chapter Thirteen

FORT CARSON, COLORADO

MAXWELL WAVED KIM AND ME into his office, and we remained at attention while he was on the phone.

"No sir, I'm not saying we did everything right. Yes, sir, I realize there were mistakes made. Yes, sir, we'll correct those as soon as we can." The colonel looked up at us and motioned for us to sit, then rolled his eyes, holding the headset away from his ear. We both grinned.

"Yes, sir. No, sir. Absolutely, sir. Mr. Gardner, sir, I'm afraid I have to go—debriefings, you know. Goodbye, sir." I could hear Gardner still talking as Maxwell hung up the phone, but I wasn't about to stop him.

"So, thanks for getting here so quickly," he said, smiling. "I *hate* talking to that guy." He stood up and then came around the desk and perched on one corner of it.

"We lost a lot of good people today. Nearly three-quarters of Second Team."

"Three-quarters, sir? I knew about Charlie squad, but Delta, too?" I asked.

"Oh, they weren't turned or anything. No, unfortunately, they were killed when some redneck tried to cross the barricade and accidentally slammed his jacked up F-350 into their Humvee at about 60 mph." He sighed, shaking his head. "As if we didn't have enough problems with the walkers."

"What was the total on walkers, sir?"

"Three hundred and fifty-two. Another forty or so uninfected are under observation for psychosis, and we had to euthanize twenty-three that had been bitten. All of the bodies are being cremated, of course, with fake ashes returned to their families."

I sighed, not liking it but understanding the necessity. "Any problems with the media?"

Maxwell looked at me sharply for a moment, and then shook his head. "Nothing we couldn't handle, Blake. Damn reporters nosing around. I hate reporters."

"How'd things go in Maine, sir?" asked Kim.

"They went right the hell out the window. Only lost one of ours, but we had to write the whole city off, for the most part."

I swallowed. "Sir? What happened?"

He sighed and moved to his windows, looking out at the sprawling base, his hands clasped behind his back.

"Commander Anderson tells me that our intel from the Maine location was *extremely* unrealistic. There were more than two hundred walkers there when we arrived, and it was only because of their training and superior firepower that they were able to maintain the single casualty. He said that, at the end, they were firing on civilians who were rushing the barricades, scared out of their minds. The country's so open up there that the Strykers burned through two tanks of gas each just on perimeter patrols."

"Scylla and Charybdis, sir," I said, and both he and Kim turned to look at me. "Homer's *Odyssey*, sir? A rock and a hard place. Either get eaten by zombies or shot by the Army. I know which I'd rather choose, sir."

Kim shuddered, nodding. "Too right. No choice there at all."

Maxwell looked thoughtful. "Maybe you're right. In any case, we ended up wiping out most of the town. Called it a gas main explosion. We used a low-yield FAE. I'm afraid there's not much left."

"Holy shit, sir! I thought fuel-air explosives required special presidential authorization."

"Normally they would, but AEGIS has been cleared to use them at our discretion, with the caveat that every use would be investigated later. It was one of my conditions for starting the program."

"Ah, forgiveness is better than permission, right, sir?"

"Exactly. Still, there were more than eight thousand people in Farmington. We rescued fewer than five hundred."

This sobering thought occupied all our attentions for a moment, until I realized something.

"Shit!" I said, still thinking.

"Yes, Mr. Blake?" Maxwell said. "What is it?"

"Something's been bothering me ever since Rawlins, and I just figured out what it was."

"Do tell."

"Charlie squad was overrun. We lost most of them."

"And . . . ?"

"Then they came and attacked us after they were turned."

"That's what you stated in your report."

"So the question is, how the hell did they turn so fast?"

Maxwell thumped back in his seat. "Holy shit."

"Exactly, sir. The only other time we've seen this sort of speed in turning was with that tech that Chauncey got to. He turned before we even made it to the building, sir. Maybe ten to fifteen minutes, at most. Charlie Squad took about the same time, given what we heard."

Kim looked over at Maxwell.

"Sir, did we ever find out anything from Gardner's people on that situation with Chauncey? Maybe there's something they've discovered . . ."

Maxwell was silent, staring down at his desk. I could almost see the thunderclouds forming over his head as his expression turned darker by the moment.

"No, we never did get any information from them, as such, Major," he said. I don't think he realized he was clenching his fists.

"And what about those kids? They were too damned fast. That can't be normal," I said. "Kim and I saw the same thing from that kid in Roosevelt. Just blindingly fast. But only the kids. Any word on that either?"

"No," he said. I had the impression that Mr. Gardner was going to have a very unpleasant conversation, very soon.

Suddenly, there was a knock at the door and Commander Anderson entered, saluting.

"Yes, Commander?" said Maxwell.

"Sir, I've got some bad news," he said, moving forward. "It looks like Tremaine isn't going to make it, sir." His face looked bleak as he turned to us. "Tremaine was in 4th Team up in Maine. We thought he was just ill, but it turns out he was hiding a bite, and is in the last stages of turning."

The ACU-clad walker pounded against the thick bulletproof glass, trying to get to the food it saw on the other side. Several of us stood there, staring at it, wanting more than a little to reach for our side-arms as the creature pounded again and again at the barrier.

I know it would be practically impossible for the thing to break out, but after what happened with Chauncey . . . I shuddered, still hearing the echoing screams of the poor technician who'd slipped up just a bit and ended up as walker bait.

There was a buzz from the security door, and the colonel waved at the small window set into the frame, simultaneously pushing the button that turned the observation glass opaque. There was another buzz, and the door opened to admit Henry Gardner, in a different, yet still dull, grey suit.

"Ah, Mr. Gardner, good to have you with us. I thought you might like to see what your orders have wrought."

Gardner looked at him skeptically. "Yes, well, let's not waste time, Colonel. Where's the specimen?"

"If you'll just step up to the glass, sir, you'll be able to see in just a moment." He looked at Kimberly and me and the other soldiers in the room as Gardner stepped forward, trying to see through the glass, and then pushed the button, turning it transparent once more.

Just as the walker formerly known as Tremaine crashed into the glass again, right in front of the hapless government official.

"Wow," I said, checking Gardner's pulse a moment later. "I've never seen anyone pass out that quickly."

Kim massaged her temples. "Or scream that loud."

"He'll be fine, sir," I told the colonel. I took a capsule of smelling salts from the medkit mounted on the wall nearby, and broke them open under the poor man's nose, waking him. "You're fine, Mr. Gard-ner. You just had a bit of a fright."

Gardner stood, needlessly straightening his necktie and comb-ing back his hair. "I . . ." he paused, then took a deep breath and continued. "I wasn't expecting that. You might have warned me, Colonel."

Maxwell gave him a look of studied innocence. "Oops."

I studiously ignored Kimberly, knowing if I even glanced her way we'd both be laughing for quite some time over that.

The walker was still clattering against the glass in its attempt to get to us, and once he'd composed himself, Gardner moved forward to study it.

"Yes, yes, I think this will do just fine. Assuming the proper precautions are taken, I believe we can study this specimen *quite* successfully. This is a great day, gentlemen. We've rarely had such an opportunity. Especially with such a *fresh* specimen! This is truly a cause for excitement." He turned back to us, his eagerness to get started plain.

I slowly turned to look at Maxwell. "Sir?" I said, my voice strained. Kim looked as though she was about to chew through her lip to keep from saying something.

"I'll handle this," he said, his voice cold and remote, as it had been when ordering Major Carver's relief. He strode over to Gardner, stopping an inch or so away from the grey man, who, being backed up against the glass, had nowhere to go. The walker became frantic trying to reach him, and Gardner turned almost as grey as his suit.

"*Mister* Gardner, that creature in there was once a decorated soldier of these United States. He and nine other men and women gave their lives today, defending their people and their country, and you *will* respect their sacrifice," he said, his iron gaze wilting the government man where he stood.

"Because the next time I hear you even begin to disrespect one of our fighting men or women in any way, shape or form, I will personally feed you to Tremaine here, a piece at a time. Clear?"

Scylla and Charybdis, indeed.

Gardner nodded mutely, and Maxwell moved back. "Very well," he said. Pushing another button on the table, he spoke into a small speaker. "Mary, you can come in now."

Dr. Adamsdóttir entered the room and I listened as Mary talked with the colonel and Gardner.

"Well, we've gotten more out of Mr. Tremaine than from other walkers, as we had his baseline genetic code already from earlier blood tests and other samples. Now we have what remains in the veins of the cadaver, as well as behavioral observations, etc." She paused, thoughtful.

"I'm not sure what we'll get out of that last, though. We have complete studies of adult-turned subjects from prior specimens, and none of them are different from any of the others. I mean, it's not like we can train them to do even menial tasks. Really, once the biological samples have been obtained, I'd recommend destroying the specimen to prevent potential accidents or other issues, such as what happened with Chauncey."

Everyone in the room—even Gardner—winced at that memory.

"Agreed," said Maxwell. "Let me know when you've retrieved all you can from Tremaine, then I'll take care of it from there."

"Colonel, surely you can see the value in retaining a specimen such as this!" said a startled Gardner. "Beyond the purely physical aspects such as DNA, think of the potential for other uses. Despite Dr. Adamsdóttir's clearly biased *opinion*, several specialists believe that they *can* be trained to do menial work, and then there's the bio-weapons potential—"

Gardner broke off as he caught the look in Maxwell's eye.

"This specimen is to be destroyed *immediately* once Dr. Adamsdóttir is finished collecting samples. Is that clear, Mr. Gardner?" said the colonel.

"Colonel Maxwell, may I remind you that despite its overly authorized level of autonomy, AEGIS is still under the command of the Department of Defense and the Secretary, and that as his personal representative and liaison here, I retain—"

"Shut up, Gardner," I said, the loathing in my voice never more evident than it was right then.

Gardner spluttered to a halt, as shocked as I'd ever seen him, which was saying something. He looked as stunned as if I'd slapped him in front of God and everybody. "How *dare* you speak to me like that? I'll have you arrested! Court-martialled!"

I leaned toward him, and though I was not the most physically intimidating of men, something in my attitude made him pause.

"Gardner, you should know as well as anyone that Colonel Maxwell is in full command of this base, at least when it comes to security. The buck stops with him. And if he were to decide that Tremaine here is a threat to that security, then he has every right—he has the *duty*—to see to the walker's destruction. He has the *duty* to see to the elimination of *any* threat to this base.

"Besides, you can't court-martial me. You could *fire* me, sure. Even have me arrested. But then you'd lose one of your most valuable sources of intel, wouldn't you? I'm not sure if you'd get rid of me anyway, but I *know* that the rest of my team wouldn't like that. Not at all. And while you might think we dislike you now, just wait till you lose them *another* team member."

I saw the light of understanding flicker in Gardner's eyes, and the look of cold calculation that replaced it as he glanced at the others in the room and back to me. He saw that no one here was on his side.

Maxwell just stared at him, looking bored. Creepy Gardner might be, but he wasn't stupid. No, not by a long shot. If he wasn't my enemy before, though, he damned sure was now. It was amazing how little I cared about that.

Standing up straighter and straightening his tie once more, the grey man nodded slightly, almost to himself.

"Very well, Colonel. I understand completely. Thank you for allowing me to view the specimen." With that, he left the room, and Kimberly and I glanced at each other.

I turned to the colonel. "Sir, I—"

"Save it, Blake. I don't trust him, either. Mary, you understand the necessity of the specimen's destruction, don't you?"

She nodded. "Of course, Colonel. I'll see to it myself."

"Thanks very much, Mary. I did have one or two other questions for you, if you don't mind?" he asked, motioning to the outer office. I caught a little smile pass between them as they left.

I had to ask, but first I turned and set the glass to opaque once more. "There's only so many zombies I can take in one day," I said when Kim looked at me curiously. "By the way, did you get the impression that there's something going on between those two?"

"Who, the colonel and the doc?" she asked.

"No, Gardner and the walker. Of course the colonel and the doc."

"Well, I should hope so. They've only been dating for six months." She laughed at my dropped jaw and bemused expression. "What, you didn't know?"

"I thought he was married . . ." I said.

"He *was* married. Althea died almost two years ago, shortly after I began working with AEGIS. She had cancer."

"I'm so sorry," I said, knowing she and her adoptive mother had been close.

"It's okay," she said. "Even she didn't know, until the end. She went quickly, without a lot of pain. It was easier on all of us than so many others I've seen."

I shook my head, amazed at the things I missed. "Maxwell and the doc. I never realized."

"I wouldn't have expected you to."

"Why's that?"

"Well, because you're a man," she said, and then started laughing as I chased her out of the room.

Gardner fumed as he stalked back to his office, muttering to himself. "How dare that upstart colonel talk to me like that? Who the hell does he think he is? And Blake? I'll have that little bastard's head on a goddamned platter!" He stormed into the small waiting room of his office, then shouted at his assistant as he slammed his inner office door. "Get me the Secretary!"

"Yes, sir," said the poor private who'd been assigned to the liaison. He dialed the office of the Secretary of Defense, also keying a certain code on a small device sitting next to the phone.

Gardner would flip out if he knew he was being recorded. Good thing he's a jackass and deserves it. Of course, it doesn't hurt that those are my orders, either.

The Secretary's assistant answered. "Secretary Tate's office. This is Madeline."

"Madeline, it's Sam. Go secure, please."

There was a hum on the line, then nothing. "We're secure, Sam."

"Great. I'm calling for Mr. Gardner. Is the Secretary in?"

The cheery voice on the other end of the line lost some of its enthusiasm. "I'll check. When are you going to start working for someone nicer, Sam?"

"I know, Maddy, I know. Believe me."

"Just a minute, kiddo." Sam winced. Madeline Norville was only a bit older and liked to call him 'kiddo' and 'sport,' but from what he remembered of the one government function he'd attended where they met, she had a hell of a figure and was nice to boot. *Too bad she's all the way out there in Washington.* "Patch him through, Sammy," Madeline said as she came back on the line.

"Okay." He punched another button, and Gardner picked up. "I have the Secretary for you, sir."

"Well, quit your lollygagging and put him through, then!"

"Yes, sir." Sam transferred the call, and sat back, watching the mini-recorder's activity light flash as the conversation continued, wishing he was somewhere else.

"It looks like we've caught a break, gentlemen. There've been no new outbreaks for the last three weeks, so we're cycling everyone through for some R&R. Now we can't let everyone go at once, so we're starting with 1st and 3rd," Maxwell broke off as the dining hall erupted with cheers from the named teams.

"Followed by 2nd and 4th teams." Good-natured grumbling was received as expected, but generally, everyone seemed to be in a good mood, despite our recent losses. With 2nd just now back up to full strength, Maxwell would probably have them training for the whole next week.

"Those teams who are on leave will be expected to depart within twenty-four hours and not return until one week from that time." Maxwell put the clipboard he'd been looking at down on a table. "Let me be clear here, folks. I will not have my troops going crazy because they've not had enough time off. Every commander worth a damn has seen the point of R&R, and I'm not about to buck that tradition."

He began pacing back and forth behind the table where the team leaders and Commander Anderson sat. "Things are ramping up, overall. Attacks are happening more frequently despite the present lull, and it may be a while before we get another chance, so take advantage of this opportunity. The MPs have orders not to permit anyone on leave to return to base before one week's time, unless countermanded by Commander Anderson or myself.

"So take your vacation. You've earned it." He smiled. "And try not to kill anyone while you're gone, all right? Team leaders and XOs stay behind. Everyone else fall out to your barracks. Dismissed!"

I joined the small group of soldiers at the table, and we all took seats, looking at the colonel and commander.

"First things first: you've all done very well recently. 4th Team especially showed courage in Farmington, and I know that was a difficult mission. The fact that you only lost one soldier does you credit, as hard as that might be to hear."

4th Team's leader, a rough-looking sort named Malcolm Dagger, nodded silently.

"Before I release those of you on leave though, I have been ordered to pass along some new information regarding future plans for this organization. I had to argue to get your names on the list, and you all know how much I hate arguing." There was a chorus of good-natured chuckling around the table.

"AEGIS and various civilian companies operating under strict OpSec rules have begun construction of ten massive underground bunkers throughout the US. Planning took two years, and actual construction started nearly three years ago. Frank?" The colonel motioned to the commander, who turned on the projector, showing us a map of the US.

"Each bunker will house roughly ten thousand people, as well as all the support materials needed to survive for up to twenty years. Power, hydroponics, vehicles, seeds, everything."

"Only ten thousand, sir?" said Captain Greer, newly confirmed team leader for 2nd Team.

"From what I've been told, they could've fit more people in, but they wouldn't have been able to last as long. More years equals fewer people. Apparently, based on a number of factors—including construction time and locations—ten thousand was the best number they could work out. Bunkers like this are being constructed around the world, but even with them all stocked and fully functional we'll only be able to guarantee the safety of less than half a percent of the total global population."

The stunned faces from the other teams mirrored our own from weeks before when we're discovered the truth of everything. The loss of more than six *billion* people was not an easy thing to grasp, even for those of us who knew the reasons behind it.

"So that's it?" said Greer. "They're gonna build these bunkers and just forget about everyone up top?"

"They're not going to forget about them, Captain, but I want you to get one thing straight right now: Not everyone will survive. Our world is going to end, and damned quick once these things start spreading. Even AEGIS can't catch every one of the bastards, and it only takes one to start a new outbreak in a new town hundreds of miles from the original source. We've already seen that happen."

"We're not going to forget about them, but there's damned little we can do for them. What I've been told is that once the situation is live, meaning that the public is aware and at least generally believing in what's going on, then the various armed forces will begin specialized training for volunteers in various cities across the US.

"Additionally, what resources can be spared from the Corps of Engineers will be used to begin erecting pointless fortifications around some of our more important locations."

"Pointless, sir?"

"Of course they're pointless! You can't put up a ten-foot-high concrete wall around a city to keep out the zombies and then not screen everyone inside as well as those who come in or out. And I can tell you that *that* little procedural item is not going to go over well with everyone. Oh, some people will be okay with it, maybe even suggest it themselves. But overall? No way in hell. And just imagine what it'll be like when we start euthanizing those who've already been bitten. 'Oh, but Granpa just got a tiny bite, he'll be okay, surely!' Bah!"

"The majority of people will die, especially in large population centers," I said, not speaking to anyone in particular. "They simply cannot grasp the idea that once they are bitten, they're already dead. If they can, their neighbors won't. If somehow they all did, the last place they'd want to be is trapped with a bunch of other people who might or might not be sick. So they're going to try to get out. But they won't be able to because of the barricades. So they'll be stuck, pissed off and more than a little scared.

"It'll be a slaughterhouse. And once everyone inside is dead, it'll be a deathtrap for anyone trying to go back in. He's right, it's pointless to try and defend them, especially the big cities. It only takes one bite. You all know that, some better than others." I looked at Dagger, who sighed. Tremaine had been a friend of his.

Maxwell evidently agreed. "That's it exactly. We'll help people hold out as long as they can on the surface, but eventually every major position will be overrun. Oh, there'll be a few survivalists and whatnot who might organize their friends and make a go of it, but they'll be under constant siege, and eventually they'll go, too. If not to walkers, then to 'warlords' or militias. The only true salvation will be those who are underground, where no one gets in without being screened and everyone is working for a more permanent solution.

"Part of your duties once the shit hits the fan and we all go under will be to train some of the people from each of these bunkers to be an internal police force," Maxwell continued. "Each of the teams will be assigned to one of the bunkers. 1st Team, you'll be in the Mount Rainier location, near Seattle. It's the closest to being completed.

"There are others being built near Taos, Philadelphia, Rapid City, Mount Whitney in California, Austin, Texas, Mississippi and elsewhere. To staff them, we're ramping up our recruiting. We should have another six teams within six to eight months, assuming the same rates of infection we've been seeing.

"I'll give you more details when I get them, but for now you'll all remain here, assigned to outbreaks on rotation as they occur. That's it. Any questions?"

Dagger raised his hand, looking thoughtful.

"Yes?"

"Just one question, sir," he said, and smiled. "How do I get out of this chickenshit outfit, sir?"

A burst of laughter answered his question, and Maxwell smiled.

"I think you've seen that movie one too many times, son, but you ain't the only one. There's more than a few similarities between those alien bastards and our walkers. Anyone else?" No more hands showed, and the colonel nodded. "Very well. Dismissed!"

As Kim and I turned to leave, Maxwell motioned us over. Curious, we followed him to one side as the rest of the soldiers headed back to their respective barracks.

If it was any other man, I'd have said the colonel was flustered and nervous. He didn't seem to know where to put his hands, and he was sweating up a storm. I was concerned at first, but Kim touched my hand and shook her head, and I decided to let it play out.

"Sir?" she said, her voice betraying that hint of mischievousness I'd come to recognize.

"Major . . . uh, Kim . . . I . . . That is . . ."

I was beside myself with shock at seeing this man so uncomfortable, and only realized my mouth was hanging open in surprise when Kim jabbed her elbow into my ribs.

"What is it, George?" she said. "What's wrong?"

"Oh, nothing, nothing's wrong. It's just that I . . ." he fumbled, then visibly got hold of himself and straightened. "I asked Mary to, er, marry me. She said yes."

I'd never seen a smile from Kim that big before. *Well, once, but that was different. Damn him for getting a bigger smile than me.*

Kim threw her arms around the old soldier's neck and hugged him tight. Surprisingly, he hugged her back just as fiercely. "I'm so happy for you!" she said, and I could see a tear or two starting to well up in their eyes. "When is the big day?"

"Well, that's the thing. I was hoping that you and Mr. Blake might help me out with that."

I was dumbfounded and couldn't speak, but it turned out I didn't need to.

"Of course we will," Kim said. "What do you need from us?"

"Well, Mary doesn't have any family, and someone's got to stay here in command, which leaves out Frank, so I was hoping that you would be my best man, David. Kim, Mary told me to ask you if you would be her maid of honor." Before I could begin to formulate a response, Kim was already nodding in agreement. Maxwell went on, "We're getting married in Hawai'i in three days."

"Hawai'i sir?" I asked. "I can't really afford that . . ."

Kim slapped me on the shoulder. "Silly, we'll just take one of the cargo jets. Surely there's a pressing need for AEGIS personnel over there for *something*. And if not, after all that you've done and lost for this country, George, the least they can do is buy you a damned plane ticket."

Maxwell and I looked at each other surprised, and laughed. "Trust her to see the easy way out, sir." I said. "If you just sit back and enjoy the ride, I'm sure she and Mary will have everything planned before we even land, and all we'll need to know is where to stand."

Kim stuck her tongue out at me, and laughed. "Yep, we'll take care of everything."

I raised one eyebrow as I looked at the colonel. "So, just when you happen to need us, 1st Team gets a week of leave, eh, sir?"

He grinned. "Rank hath its privileges."

MAUI, HAWAII

Three days later, I was looking at the red-orange sunset over the water, Kimberly lying in my arms on the oversize lounge chair. I must've been quieter than usual, because she turned and looked up at me.

"Penny for your thoughts?"

I gazed down at this gorgeous woman, and wondered how I could possibly have been this lucky.

Well, you were spectacularly unlucky, so it fits, said that little voice I hadn't heard in so long.

Bite me.

"I was just thinking about everything that has brought me to this point. Two years ago, I was happily working in Fall Creek, sure and certain that I knew where my life was headed and that everything would, eventually, be okay. Now, I know that the world is going to end no matter what I do, and that days like this are numbered," I said, waving my hand in the general direction of the ocean. "Days like this, when I can hold a beautiful woman in my arms, watching a beautiful sunset, after being in a good friend's beautiful wedding ceremony . . ."

She laughed and I smiled. "I need to stop saying beautiful, don't I?" Kim shook her head and smiled at me, her green eyes drawing me in and comforting me.

"No, you don't. You just need to realize that however many days we have left, they're going to be great because we've got each other." She kissed me and then snuggled closer, the night air cooling us after the heat of the day. "And I don't just mean you and me, either. All the others in AEGIS, the other people going in the bunkers, we'll fix this. We've got a chance to start over, even if it is a one-in-a-billion shot."

I held her tighter, and tried to stop thinking of anything as I closed my eyes and felt the warmth of her nearness, the last few moments of sunlight on my face, and listened to the sound of the waves on the beach.

Suddenly, Kim broke free from my grasp and stood up, unwrapping the sarong she was wearing and tying it carefully around one arm of the chair, leaving it to blow in the breeze. I marveled again at her body, as I always did, the sunset light playing over the soft-yet-defined muscles of her stomach and hips, the curve of her legs, and the way her hair flew softly around her face as she reached for my hand.

"Come on, I want another swim before bed," she said, smiling.

"It's not bedtime yet . . ." I said, and laughed as she grinned even wider. "Gotcha," I said. I pulled the light linen shirt over my head and we walked together into the surf, letting the cool salt water splash over us, and diving through the rolling swells.

"David," Kim said, and as I turned her way, she came into my arms once more, wrapping her arms around my neck as she turned that oh-so-powerful gaze on me once more. I leaned down for a kiss, but she stopped with a finger on my lips, just as she had years before. We floated there for a moment, bodies pressed together as the waves moved us back and forth, but she didn't say anything. I looked back at her, losing myself in her eyes and smile.

"I love you, David," she said it quietly, almost as if to herself, a worried look briefly crossing her face.

I smiled, and reached up to gently move an unruly curl of auburn hair out of the way. "I love you too, Kim." I bent to kiss her once more, and this time, she didn't stop me.

Chapter Fourteen

FORT CARSON, COLORADO

THE SHOUTING CUT OFF AND the door flew open as Maxwell marched past me and out of Gardner's office. Private Sam Lansford endeavored to make himself as invisible as possible as the graying colonel stormed out, the neon oranges, reds, and yellows of his oh-so-bright Hawaiian shirt searing the eye and his sandals flopping.

It ruined not a bit of his dramatic exit.

I caught Lansford's eye as the outer door slammed shut, and winked. He covered a smile as Gardner walked out and motioned to me to follow him. I sighed and shrugged, following the grey suit into the office and taking a seat as he shut the door once more.

As he sat behind the large desk, Gardner looked at me, his grey eyes seeming cold and calculating. Hardly a surprise, but I'd never dealt with him this close before, at least not alone. He was unnerving in a way I'd never experienced.

As his basilisk stare continued, I realized he was playing a waiting game, hoping the uncomfortable silence would make me break first. As it was, I took the opportunity to look around the room.

It didn't take very long, and was exactly what I expected. The office was empty of all decoration or any personal touches of any kind, except for a small 'ego wall' including a diploma from Columbia University—Political Science, naturally—and a framed photo of Richard Nixon.

Well that certainly explains a lot about our dear Mr. Gardner. He's just one huge cliché, isn't he? He was still staring at me when I looked back his way. *Good luck. I'm nothing if not patient, Mr. Gardner.*

After several minutes, Gardner sighed and sat back in his chair, steepling his fingers. I couldn't decide if he thought it made him appear menacing or thoughtful. In reality, it just made him look like a cheesy sixties spy-movie villain.

"Mr. Blake. You're unique in this group, as I'm sure you realize. What you may not realize is the usefulness that uniqueness could bring to the organization as a whole. Your talent for killing zombies is great, but the experience you've garnered while doing so has surely made you aware of the seriousness of the situation."

Oh, boy. What kind of crap is this? What the hell is Gardner about to pull?

"I'd like you to consider coming over to our side of the organization, Mr. Blake. We could certainly use your knowledge and expertise with the walkers. Naturally, we'd increase your compensation for such a change. After all, you deserve more than just a simple grunt. Of course, certain other *considerations* would need to be made on your part."

Ah, so that's the game. Let's see how far he's willing to take this.

"Well, Mr. Gardner . . ."

"Call me Henry, please."

"Let me get this straight, *Gardner*. You want me to come work for you and leave my teammates—my girlfriend—behind in danger every minute? And I'm just spit-balling here, but I'd bet this expertise you want me to use has nothing to do with *killing* walkers."

"Not as such, no."

"Ah, ok. Just checking," I said, shaking my head. "Well, the answer is no. In fact, not just no, but hell no."

That creepy reptilian smile was back. "I was most certain that you might say that, so I'd like to offer you an alternative opportunity, instead."

He leaned forward, resting his arms on the desk. "Professionally, you're a valuable asset. Personally, I'd rather you not come to work for us on this side, anyway. You're far too *volatile* for my tastes. Still, you retain a certain special position in your unit, and have apparently endeared yourself to the colonel.

"So here's what you'll do, instead of joining us: I want you to expand upon your relationship with the colonel and with Commander Anderson. You're going to be pals, friends, compatriots with them."

The smile vanished, and I felt more like a specimen to be evaluated, studied and dissected more than ever before. "And then you're going to tell me everything they do, Mr. Blake. Everything."

I laughed, and if it was a bit hysterically, well, no one else was sitting in that seat and staring into those dead eyes. "You're crazy, Gardner. Even if I didn't believe you already had your sources inside 'our side,' as you call it, I'd never inform on them to you. If anything, I'll tell the colonel exactly what you've asked me to do here, and we'll see how fast he can have you replaced, shall we?"

Oddly, Gardner laughed too, or what passed for a laugh for him. He sat back in his chair and toyed with a pen on his desk before returning it to its exact spot. "Oh, I don't think you will, Mr. Blake. You see, I've got something you want. Perhaps even need. At the very least, I know you won't turn down my offer after you've seen it."

"Good grief, Gardner," I said. "You couldn't be a more stereotypical bad guy if you had a monocle and a white Persian cat. Now comes the blackmail, I'm guessing. What, you've got a 'soon-to-be-dead' ex-girlfriend of mine as a hostage somewhere? Destruction of my hometown or harm to my family? How about something more conventional, like threatening me with exposure of something embarrassing. Crap like that always works in the movies. There's just one problem with that methodology for you."

"Oh? What would that be, Mr. Blake?"

"I don't have any more ex-girlfriends. My hometown is gone, and my family is long dead. I have no skeletons in my closet. Or rather, I do, quite literally. But everyone already knows about them," I said, and paused before laughing again. "Or maybe you think threatening Kim would work? If so, I'd pay money to see that. She'll kick your ass—or just kill you—faster than any two men I know. So bring it on, grey man."

Gardner smiled once more. "Well, that was a fine speech, Mr. Blake. Really very useless, though."

"I hardly think so."

"Well, of course not. This wouldn't be any fun, otherwise." He leaned forward and turned his computer monitor around to face me, then punched a sequence of commands on his keyboard. The screen lit with a view of what appeared to be a small cell. "You see, poor Mr. Tremaine wasn't the only active specimen we've retrieved in the last few years. I think you'll find I'm rather more than a spy-movie villain, Mr. Blake."

The short, scrawny figure standing in the corner with the messy hair and the torn T-shirt was all too familiar.

Oh, shit.

Commander Frank Anderson sighed and looked down at the orders on the desk for what felt like the hundred and fiftieth time. They hadn't changed since his first glance, but he kept hoping they might. Just as he started to pick up the phone, the colonel slammed open the office door and stomped into the room.

"Have you heard about this crap?" he yelled, throwing his hands in the air in frustration.

"Calm down, George, and have a seat." He raised his voice. "Penny, get the colonel and me some coffee, please." A short, matronly brunette peeked around the door to the inner office and nodded. "And Penny? Make them strong. Thanks."

The commander's assistant raised a hand in acknowledgement before she disappeared down the hallway. Anderson stood, coming around the desk to take a seat on the small couch off to one side, while Maxwell was still pacing and fuming.

"George, you're going to have another heart attack. For god's sake man, you just got married. You should be taking it easy. Why are you even here? You had another day. You should be home, with your wife."

Maxwell finally calmed down enough to take a seat, but still fidgeted and was obviously still very angry.

"Fucking Gardner. It's all his fault. He went to the Secretary, Frank! Who promptly talked to his good ol' pal the president!"

Frank knew not to push too hard, or Maxwell would most likely do something they would *both* regret later. "And?"

"And? *And*? You mean you *haven't* heard?"

"No, George, obviously I haven't heard. It's not as if I'm in Gardner's back pocket. He knows I detest him."

"That *snake* went over both our heads as far up the chain as it goes, Frank. We've got a new priority for all missions now."

"Oh, that."

"'Oh, that'? That's all you have to say? We're now *required* to bring back 'live' walkers from every outbreak and all you can say is 'Oh, that'? And to top it off, they've got some new 'shock' sort of weapon they want us to use. Apparently it paralyzes the walker long enough to restrain it."

"They're not just expecting us to use harsh language and zip-cuffs, George."

Maxwell smiled grimly. "No, they've got some new steel cuffs for us to use, along with a helmet-looking thing to keep them from biting."

Anderson shook his head. "I wonder if they realize how many people we'll lose trying to capture these things?"

"Oh, they know. I told them. Their own people told them."

"And they're still doing it?"

"They call it *acceptable losses*." Maxwell snorted. "I told them to go fuck themselves. I'm not putting my men through that."

"Yet you're still here."

"He said that based on the situation, my leaving could be construed as treason." He looked up at his long-time friend. "He threatened Mary, Frank. Told me that neither of us would be safe if I left. He as much as came out and said they'd kill one or both of us."

Before Frank could respond, Penny arrived, placing a tray between the two men on the small coffee table, then leaving and closing the door behind her. They waited until they also heard the outer office door shut once more before both men reached for the coffee. Frank took a sip of his first and winced.

"She follows orders, I'll give her that. This sludge could just about beat me over the head with my own spoon," he said, stirring a ridiculous amount of sugar into his cup. "George, I know you're pissed about this. You have every right. The fact that he threatened Mary . . ." Anderson shook his head.

"What the hell is going on, Frank? That's my *wife!*"

Anderson shook his head slightly, catching Maxwell's eye. A subtle shift of the head and a slight nod toward the ceiling, and George stiffened, then relaxed somewhat and winked as he sat back with his cup of coffee.

"We'll deal with this through channels, George. Just like we always have. There's a reason for procedures. We'll follow them and everything will work out fine, I'm certain." Frank looked at the colonel over his cup. "Now, what else is changing? Certainly that's not all . . ."

George sighed. "No, not by a long shot. We're getting our other six teams."

"This early, sir?"

"Yep. We're going to wind up a short battalion a lot faster than I thought. Apparently, higher has decided that losing as many as we're going to is enough reason to give us more meat."

"That's what they'll be, too, sir. Fresh meat."

"I know, Commander, I know."

CHEYENNE, WYOMING

Jason Horner walked across the parking lot of the upscale apartment complex. He realized he was whistling as he trotted up the stairs, and stopped as he knocked on the door to 406. *Wouldn't want to appear too eager after all.* When there was no response, he looked back down at the parking lot and verified that her car was nearby. She was home, but not answering. *Maybe it's a surprise.*

Grinning, he took the key she'd finally given him and opened the door, closing it quickly behind him. The apartment was a mess, but that wasn't particularly unusual. Doris hadn't exactly been Martha Stewart, and after the second time he'd brought it up and she'd threatened to break off their arrangement, he'd stopped trying. She was too good in bed to pass up for some trash and a few dirty clothes. Okay, a *lot* of trash and dirty clothes. Didn't the woman ever do laundry?

"Honey, I'm home!" he said, throwing his jacket on the couch and moving toward the small kitchen. Empty. As was the bedroom and bathroom. There weren't too many places to hide in a small one-bedroom like this. She wasn't here.

It's not like it's the first time she's stood you up. He sighed and sat down to wait, taking out his phone and looking at her text message. *ASAP, my ass. I'm not waiting all night. Not again.*

LARAMIE, WYOMING

"No, no, that's fine, Shelly. Get him prepped for surgery and I'll be up after consulting with Dr. Horne. Five minutes, I promise." His nurse nodded and went back into the patient's room as Martin glanced up the hallway at some commotion. Someone strapped to a gurney, obviously resisting treatment. *Looks like they need a hand.* He checked his watch and moved towards the altercation.

Three nurses were attempting to hold down the hysterical woman's arms and legs as a fourth wheeled her into Exam Room Three.

"What've we got?" he asked, clamping a hand down on the woman's left leg, earning a grateful look from one of the nurses, who then finished attaching the restraints as they moved the woman onto the exam room bed.

"She's going crazy, doctor. She came in saying her husband bit her, and then just started twitching and yelling."

Martin jerked back as if her leg had stung him. "Bitten?" He'd seen the advisory and knew what it could mean. "Where's she from?"

The head nurse looked at him. "Saratoga, Doctor. They sent her here, since Rawlins was out of commission." The other nurses had restrained the struggling woman by this point. One held a needle, about to start an IV when Martin grabbed her arm.

"Don't. I want everyone out of this room now. Code Orange."

The nurses looked at each for a moment, then burst from the room, dropping whatever they held as they ran for the nearest decontamination showers. Martin followed, locking the exam room door. He approached the nurses' station, and without a word, ripped the health advisory off the bulletin board and dialed the number printed.

Hopefully we caught it in time.

STEAMBOAT SPRINGS, COLORADO

Rachel massaged her fiancé's shoulders. She was working out the tension she could feel even now, nearly a week after Rawlins had become a memory.

Dalton didn't seem to know she was there, engrossed in the view from the hotel window at the snow-covered peaks of the Rockies.

Winter was one of her favorite times in the mountains, and Steamboat Springs was perfect for a weeklong getaway that was just close enough to the base if they were recalled.

Plus, the skiing here is awesome. She finished her massage and sat next to him, putting her head on his shoulder. Absent-mindedly, he took one of her hands in his.

Suddenly, he turned to her. "Sure wish we could stay here forever."

"I know, D. Me too."

"Then let's do it. Let's not go back. They can take care of this thing without us. We'll go hide somewhere. Find a hole and pull it in after us, ya know?"

Rachel smiled and ran a hand across the big man's cheek, noticing that his brow furrowed with concern for her. She was still amazed that two people as different as they had found each other.

If only we could, love. If only.

"You know we can't do that, Dalton. You know neither Martinez nor Reynolds can hit the broad side of a barn with a .50 cal, and with Blake and Barnes too wrapped up in each other to pay any attention, the rest of the team is a goner." She smiled again, and kissed his hand. "We'll get through this."

He smiled back and leaned down to kiss her. Just as things were beginning to get more interesting, both of their AEGIS-issue cellphones began ringing and vibrating, rattling the cheap wooden table under the hotel room's large window.

"Eaton here." Rachel said, just as Dalton began a similar conversation from steps away. "Yes, sir, right away, sir."

They looked at each other as they hung up the phones, and Rachel scowled, a fierce look in her eye as she took his hands in hers.

"You are going to marry me, Dalton Horatio Gaines, and no fucking walker is going to stop that. Clear?"

Dalton just smiled.

FORT CARSON, COLORADO

The dining hall was packed, full of every AEGIS soldier currently on the base, and more were trickling in as they arrived following the recall. Anderson was checking them off one by one as they entered, and Maxwell was in the middle of a short hurried conference with the other team leaders to one side of the impromptu podium.

As I entered and Anderson checked my name off the list, I noticed Gardner standing to one side behind the podium. He smiled at me. I scowled and moved to take a seat with the rest of my team.

A few moments later, the doors boomed closed, Anderson gave Maxwell a thumbs-up, and the four team leaders took their seats next to their XO's at the provided tables. Maxwell motioned to one of the soldiers standing near a portable projector, and another turned off the lights as some sort of futuristic-looking rifle appeared on the screen.

"Gentlemen and ladies, this is the X-29 rifle, the newest weapon in the AEGIS arsenal. Based on the proven technology of the Taser and the stun gun, this rifle fires a round similar to the Taser, in that it has two electrodes. In the original models developed by Taser and the DOD, the small battery/capacitor setup in each round delivered a charge that is similar to the one in a Taser or stun gun, around 50,000 volts at less than 1 amp. The X-29 was developed specifically for AEGIS, and the rounds are somewhat more powerful," he said, pausing to emphasize his point.

"Each round from the X-29 delivers a charge of 200,000 volts at 5 amps. One shot from one of these rifles will kill any living human instantly. Fried to a crisp. Zombies, on the other hand, will be a twitching, spasming wreck for at least twenty to thirty minutes, if the charge doesn't burn out what nervous system might remain. Hopefully that'll be long enough for you to use these."

Another image appeared on screen. It appeared for all the world to be an iron mask, similar in form, if not function, to Alexandre Dumas' classic fictional construct.

He can't be serious. We're actually going to capture them? I noticed Gardner at the side of the room carefully studying our reactions. *No, it's not Maxwell. It's that asshole Gardner that's done this.*

"These masks are made of high-strength aluminum, and are very light. Each squad will be equipped with four of these, along with similar wrist-cuffs and chains." A muttering grew in the hall, and Maxwell turned back to the crowd. "You've probably all guessed by now, but we now have orders to capture—not kill—as many walkers as we can in our next few operations."

The muttering became a riot. Soldiers from every team were on their feet, shouting and angry, while their team leaders were trying and failing to keep them under control. Maxwell and Anderson had each taken to shouting as well, their orders flying unheeded. The soldiers were having none of it, of course, and the situation was only going to get worse. They'd all been in action, and all of us had seen what happened when someone got bit, courtesy of Tremaine. Not to mention Chauncey.

The first few rounds went almost unnoticed in the noise and confusion, but by the sixth or seventh crack of my pistol, I had gotten everyone's attention. More than a few pistols were pointed my way, and I lowered the gun slowly so as not to get anyone excited or get myself shot in the process.

"Blake! Just what in the hell do you think you're doing?" shouted Maxwell from the podium, where he had taken cover.

"Getting their attention, sir," I replied, holstering my pistol, allowing the remainder of my fellow soldiers to holster theirs. "I thought it was the fastest way." I glanced up. "Gonna need some new ceiling tiles, though."

Maxwell looked at me as if I'd lost my mind, and then shook his head. "Some days you make me wish I'd never gotten out of bed. Or at the very least never brought you in to AEGIS."

I smiled. "I know, sir." My smile faltered as I caught Gardner nodding at me from his shadowy perch at the side of the room. *Bastard. One day, Gardner. One day.*

"All right, back to your seats everyone." We took our seats once more, and although it wasn't at the level it had been, the muttering remained. "Knock that shit off, right now!" Maxwell yelled, pounding his fist on the podium. "You all know our primary mission. To find a cure or vaccine for the virus. Well, our science teams can't do that without specimens to test their work on."

He took a deep breath. "We are all soldiers, we have our orders, and we will do our jobs. Is that clear?" It seemed as though no one wanted to be the first to acknowledge the suicidal nature of the orders. I was as surprised as any to hear the voice from beside me call out loud and strong.

"Clear, sir!" Kim said.

"Well, I see I still have *one* soldier, anyway. Anyone else?" This time the walls *shook* with the response. We might be grunts, and suicidal grunts at that, but by god, we were going to do our jobs.

Even if it killed us.

Chapter Fifteen

LARAMIE, WYOMING

"SO THIS IS LARAMIE, HUH?" shouted Greer, looking out over the sprawling city of nearly thirty thousand. The Strykers were being unloaded from the C-17s behind us, the roar of the many huge engines overpowering normal conversation.

Hell, I can't even hear the Strykers engines over that big-ass plane. That alone means I should be wearing earplugs.

I looked over at Greer and pointed into the distance. "See the stadium?"

"Yeah, what is that?"

"University of Wyoming. You're looking at the third largest city in the state."

"No way. That little town is the third largest?"

"It's a nice place, Greer. I've been here several times, back when . . ." I saw Kimberly walking towards us. "A long time ago, anyway. Too bad. I liked this town."

Kim raised an eyebrow at me and jerked a thumb over her shoulder. "Mount up, boys."

"Yes, ma'am," I said, and Greer and I headed for our respective Strykers. I noticed the ICVs from 3rd Team forming up alongside our own. I thought about 2nd Team, with most of their men still in training after their pasting in Wyoming, and hoped they'd rejoin us soon. Still, if four Strykers and thirty or so highly-trained soldiers couldn't handle this small outbreak, we'd better kiss our collective asses goodbye right now.

I climbed into the vehicle and did a double-take. "Good to see you again, sir," I said, saluting Captain Graves in his command chair.

"You too, Mr. Blake. I hope we have better luck this time."

"Me, too, sir. Me, too." I glanced back at the rear hatch as Kim and Commander Anderson climbed in. "Sir, ma'am, I have a suggestion. I don't think we should go in with the Strykers, at least not at first."

"Oh?" Anderson asked. "Why not?"

"For one, four of these things rolling down the small streets here will probably scare the bejeezus out of everyone, sir. Could even start a panic. And that's the last thing we need, especially with those media folks already at the hospital. And so soon after Rawlins, sir? Not a good idea."

"Good point. Anything else?"

"How many walkers are we dealing with, sir? The colonel's briefing indicated that there was just the one patient, sir. We shouldn't need more than a couple squads to deal with that. Certainly not two full teams, sir. At least not until the infection spreads, if it even does. It's good to have 3rd Team here, just in case, but I don't think we need them just yet."

Anderson glanced over at Kim. She shrugged and he chuckled, turning back to me. "The infection *always* spreads, Blake, and this town has just under thirty-thousand people. We've got the others here just in case, as you said. You seem to have thought this out, though. How would you handle it?"

"Sir, I would take a minimal force, in civilian cars but staying in uniform. Make it appear a serious situation but not serious enough to bring in armored trucks or machine guns. We can even test out some of those new X-29s, sir."

I gritted my teeth but continued. *Damn you, Gardner.*

"Those should help a lot in us capturing the walkers, and it would be good to see how they work in the field, sir."

Kim and Anderson both looked surprised. "I didn't think you approved of our new directive, Mr. Blake," said Anderson, looking at me cryptically.

"Let's just say that I've had a chance to go over some of the background on the weapons and gear, sir, and I believe this is our best course of action for now."

Kim narrowed her eyes at me, but didn't say anything. I had the feeling she was going to be asking me some questions later that I couldn't answer.

I wish I could. God, how I wish I could.

Frank looked at the monitors, then across the tarmac to the line of Strykers. "Very well. Go conscript us a few rental cars—but only enough for your Alpha and Bravo squads. We'll load up and head in. Hopefully we won't scare anybody off."

"Yes, sir."

Ten minutes later we were on our way to Ivinson Memorial Hospital, a train of four white Ford Fusions snaking through the town. Kim drove the lead car, with Eaton calling directions from the rear. The men simply held on, knuckles white on their respective oh-shit handles as Kim took corners like Mario Andretti on crack.

I thought for sure we'd take out at least one or two pedestrians as we crossed the police barricades, Anderson holding up his completely genuine, if meaningless, USAMRIID badge. Somehow, we managed to avoid even the press, and careened to a stop outside the main hospital entrance. I fought the urge to kneel down and kiss the ground in relief as I got out of the car, and noticed Anderson and Gaines seemed a bit green around the gills as well.

"Next time, I'm driving," I muttered, and saw a flash of a grin from Kim. I had no doubt she'd done it on purpose. *She's probably mad at me for supporting Gardner's pet projects.*

Two men approached. One I took to be the chief of police from his uniform, the other a doctor, possibly the hospital administrator.

"Commander Anderson?" the chief asked, looking at Frank, who nodded and shook the man's outstretched hand. "Chief Palmer, Laramie Police. This is Doctor Drake, hospital administrator."

"What's the situation, gentlemen?"

The older doctor answered first. "From what Martin said, there was just the one patient. Apparently, she was bitten by her husband, and she came here since the hospital in Rawlins was closed. But I guess you fellas probably already know about that."

Commander Anderson nodded. "Yes, we're aware of that. You say her husband bit her?"

"That's what one of the nurses said when Dr. Underwood asked her. We don't know what happened to the husband. Chances are he's still at their house. Underwood says that no one did anything to her but apply restraints before he realized what was going on and called the number on the health advisory from Rawlins." The man swallowed, very nervous. "He ordered the Code Orange immediately and put everyone who'd touched the woman through decontamination showers. Twice."

"Excellent work on his part. He may have saved the lives of those nurses. I'm assuming the Code Orange initiates a complete lockdown of the facility? All doors lock automatically, that sort of thing?" As Dr. Drake nodded, Frank smiled. "Good! Have you still got the line inside?"

"Sir, we've got that set up over here," said Palmer, pointing to a newish van that looked like an oversized ambulance. "We're treating it as a hostage situation, sir."

As the chief opened the back of the large van, I whistled. It was a complete state of the art communications and operations rig, and I was impressed. "Jasper was always talking about getting one of these," I muttered to myself.

"Who's Jasper?" asked Kim.

"That sheriff I was telling you about. The friend of mine in Fall Creek."

"What the hell would Fall Creek need with one of these? You barely had fifteen hundred people."

"He knew that. He just wanted one anyway. Besides, they can be used for anything, not just hostage negotiations. As witnessed by the chief's actions."

"We've put the government's stimulus money to good use in these here parts," said Palmer. "Homeland Security grants have helped out too, but this one we were very excited to get. As you said, it's not just for hostage negotiations."

A sudden shouting drew my attention to the small yet growing crowd of people surrounding the police barricades. Someone had shoved someone else, it seemed, and a *very* expensive-looking news camera now lay shattered on the pavement.

Too bad they're not all busted. I counted six or seven other cameras at a glance.

Anderson had picked up the phone and was speaking quietly into the handset, his demeanor growing more focused as he listened. "I understand, Dr. Underwood. No, sir, you did the right thing. Just make sure to let us know if you find anyone . . . yes, sir.

That's right, sir. Biohazard Level Four. I know, Dr. Underwood, just do the best you can. Stay away from anyone that appears to be acting strangely or hurt. They're probably infected. Call if you need anything else."

He hung up and turned to face the doctor and police chief. "Gentlemen, if you'd excuse us, please." The men looked surprised, and Drake at least appeared as though he were going to argue, but Palmer must've caught the look in the commander's eye, and shoved the doctor out the door of the trailer. Once they were out of earshot, Anderson turned back to us. "He says it's just the one patient so far, and she's not managed to break out of her restraints yet, but she has apparently fully turned."

"It's only a matter of time, Commander," said Kim. "Those restraints weren't meant to hold walkers. If she's not out already, she will be by the time we get inside."

"I agree. So here's what we'll do. Alpha squad will enter and proceed directly to the Emergency Room. Bravo will maintain perimeter on the outside, and we'll only call in the others as a last resort. I'll remain here and coordinate with the chief and Drs. Drake and Underwood in case either needs something." He jerked his head toward the press mob. "I'll handle them somehow, too. Clear?"

"Clear, sir!"

"Oh, and take at least two of the X-29s with you, Barnes. We might as well *try* and appease Gardner if we can." He looked at me, but I couldn't read his expression.

Not good. Not good at all. How the hell was I going to get out of this? And more importantly, how was I going to get rid of Gardner?

"Yes, sir," I said.

We trotted off to the cars, signaling for the soldiers inside to gear up. The muttering and shouting from the crowd grew as soldiers in urban camouflage piled out of the innocuous cars, strapping on body armor and checking their magazines. The rifles were obvious, and there was no point in hiding them, and more than one person I saw in the crowd left at that point.

"You and I take the X-29s, ma'am?" I asked Kim, moving into professional mode as we readied for what would hopefully be a short and easy battle.

"Hmm, good idea." She popped open the trunk on the lead car and unlatched the case for the experimental weapons, throwing one to me and slamming a magazine home into the one in her other hand. "The guns feel solid enough, but I don't know about these," she said, waving her hand at the other contents of the case, the cuffs and the mask.

"We'll probably only need the one mask, but let's take two just to be safe. And at least four pairs of the cuffs. Maybe we can figure out a way to transport the thing that doesn't involve one of us getting turned," I said, trying to sound only somewhat upset at having to use the restraints.

Kim snorted. "Yeah, they didn't think of *that* particular detail, did they? I know, let's have the chief or one of his officers loan us their car. We can throw the walker in the back and get her to the airport with minimal fuss."

"Good idea, ma'am." I finished loading and arming the X-29 and turned to find the rest of the team lined up and ready, in formation. "Bravo squad, set up a perimeter. Nothing gets in or out of this place but us. Alpha squad, we've got point on this one. Let's go, people!"

With the speed and efficiency that only military training can provide, the two squads broke to their assigned positions, with the rest of Alpha squad and I waiting at the Emergency Room door for the Bravo's signal.

"Alpha Six, Bravo Six. In place, perimeter secure."

"Roger, breaching now."

We moved up to the emergency room doors, and a frightened young nurse unlocked and pushed them open. We hadn't been expecting her, and she almost got shot for her trouble. Fortunately, no one fired.

"Martinez, secure that door," Kim said as we entered the brightly lit building. It smelled like every other hospital I've ever been in, like death with a hint of Lysol.

"Roger." Angelo closed the door, and I noticed him relock it and pocket the key. The nurse was wide-eyed, and I knew she was thinking about running. She didn't have the chance though, as Kim put a hand on her shoulder, looking the girl in the eye.

"Where's Exam Room Three? And where's Doctor Underwood?"

The girl began crying as she pointed down the hallway, and a stocky man of average height with a full beard appeared out of a doorway. I noticed the name stitched on his lab coat and tapped Kim on the shoulder, pointing his way.

The doctor walked up to Kim and smiled, his teeth even and white above the jet-black beard. "Oh good, you're here! We've been so worried."

Great, a good-looking doctor. Just what I need. Kim flushed, and she and Rachel both gave him appreciative looks as though neither Dalton nor I were standing right there. *Probably thought we wouldn't notice.*

Gaines looked over at me out of view of the doctor, rolling his eyes and making heaving motions. I stifled a snicker and we were both the picture of innocence when the girls' heads whipped around.

Kim cleared her throat, turning back to Dr. Underwood. "Doctor, where is the infected patient? Where is the rest of your staff?"

"The staff and the patients we could move have all gathered in the cafeteria, on the other side of the hospital. There's about sixty or so in there. Only Shelly and I stayed to let you in after the lockdown. I thought it might be useful to have someone to run messages back to the rest of the staff, just in case."

Underwood began moving down the hallway. "The patient's in Exam Room Three, just down the hall on your left. I wouldn't go in there unless you absolutely have to, though. She's dangerous, and from what I can tell is very infectious."

"What do you mean, 'from what you can tell,' doctor?" I asked. My whole squad froze, looking at the doctor.

"One of the new candy stripers made it past the nurse's station somehow when we were all busy, and got into the room. She wasn't exactly the sharpest knife in the drawer, if you know what I mean. Probably never knew what the Code Orange even meant. The woman apparently spit and moaned at her, and some spittle entered her eye," he said.

When he noticed we weren't following, he turned back. "There's nothing to fear. She's been sedated and moved to another room, where we put her in the same restraints, just in case. After all, she wasn't even bitten."

I looked at Kim, who shook her head. "Not now, with only the one squad. We'll deal with that one after."

A quick nod and I had the squad on the move once more. "Eyes and ears, people. Shelly, you stay with the doc." The nurse scooted ahead to grab hold of one of Underwood's arms, obviously clinging to the last piece of her sanity she could find readily accessible.

He just stood there, wondering what was going on, so I hauled him along with us.

"Listen, Doc, all it takes is one bit of bodily fluid to be infected. Ever hear of prions?"

"You're saying this is BSE? Mad cow disease?"

"Not exactly, but it's still prions. And don't look at me like that. What do you think I do all fucking day? A prion disease. That's what this is. Just one prion, and then you become what your initial patient became. That's why we wear these, just in case." I said, pointing to the wraparound safety glasses I wore.

"It's been something of a crazy morning. I'm afraid I wasn't thinking all that clearly," he grated. "Still, you would normally have to ingest tainted brain tissue for this—"

"Like I said Doc, this isn't your garden-variety prion." I sighed and lightened up. "That's okay, Doc. Let's just try to get out of this alive, ok?"

He paled, realizing for maybe the first time how dangerous the situation was. He pulled the nurse closer to him as we moved down the hallway.

We moved fast, rifles tracking in sweep patterns as we followed our training, regardless of the lack of reported walkers. I hefted the X-29. The damn thing was about twice the weight of my SCAR.

I already hate this piece of crap. I just hope it works. Of course, it if doesn't, then I'll have one more thing on Gardner—if I live through it.

We rounded the corner near Exam Room Three, and we could hear the creature moaning from inside. Reynolds and Gaines set to cover the hallways, with Kim behind me and Martinez and Eaton flanking us on the other side.

Underwood perked up as we approached the exam room. "Now, as you'll see, the patient is experiencing severe dementia and violent tendencies, as mentioned in the advisory," Underwood said as he glanced through the door's small inset window. Shelly crouched down against the wall, her arms around her knees, not making a sound though her cheeks were wet with tears. "Well, that's odd," Underwood said. "She was strapped down a moment ago—"

I couldn't react fast enough as he opened the door, and swore as a grasping clawed hand came through the doorway, throwing the door wide and yanking the doctor inside. Shelly screamed, and there was a flash, then the smell of burning ozone and more than a little cooked meat. The doctor came flying back through the doorway at the same moment, impacting the wall opposite and falling to the ground in a crumpled heap.

I looked up at Kim, who was reloading her weapon, and she smiled. "Well, at least we know it works. Tag and bag. Eaton, see to the doc."

I shook myself out of my surprise and moved into the room, gasping and choking at the smell of charred walker. The electrodes from Kim's shot still protruded from the walker's chest, and it shook and quivered as though it was having a seizure.

I nearly gagged on the stench and it took every bit of self-discipline I had to reach into my pack and withdraw the mask and cuffs. Fortunately, my gloves were non-conductive, so I didn't feel any of the residual shocks as I placed the mask over the monster's head and jaws, securing it tight, then did the same with its wrists.

"AEGIS Five, Alpha Six."

"Go ahead, Alpha Six."

"Primary package has been wrapped, sir. At least one secondary has been identified and we are moving to secure."

"Very well. Keep me updated."

"Yes, sir."

"Gunny, get in here and help me with this," I said. Dalton came in a moment later, and we managed to tear down one of the privacy curtains for the exam room, rolling the walker into it like some sort of still-twitching undead burrito. The curtain might be made of low-grade plastic, but the multiple layers wrapped around it should hold long enough for our purposes. Together, we dragged the body out into the hallway.

I nodded towards Underwood and looked at Kim. "How is he?"

She shook her head and grimaced. "Eaton says he's got burns all over his arm where the thing was holding onto him and a severe concussion from the impact with the wall, but as far as she can tell—" She broke off then reached down and hauled the still screaming Shelly to her feet, slapping her so hard she nearly spun into the wall.

"Knock that crap off! I was five years younger than you when I saw my first walker, and I didn't go screaming my damned head off."

That's my girl, a softie through and through.

"Where's the other room? The one with the candy-striper?" The girl pointed two doors down and across the hall, sobbing and trying to wipe her eyes.

"Uh, ma'am, perhaps we should . . ." I began, but Kim dropped the poor girl, who immediately fell back into a motionless lump on the floor. At least she'd stopped screaming.

"Leave him, Eaton. We'll come back for him later." Rachel stood up from the still form of Underwood, and was death walking once more as we all moved to the door where the other assumed walker was being held.

Curiously, there was no noise from inside, and I began to wonder if she'd been infected after all. Maybe it was just some other illness. It didn't really matter, though. Zombie prion or not, we needed to find out. I knocked and stood back from the door, giving Kim a clear field of fire while still keeping my eyes on the door itself.

Again, no moans, and I looked over at Kim, then pointed at the door handle and hinges. An outward-swinging door that closed automatically—provided nothing pushed against the no-resistance handle from the inside—and no lock. Great.

She nodded once to me, and moved into a firing stance, ready for anything that might come through the door, human or undead.

I signaled a countdown and at one I threw the door open and dived out of the way. Turns out there was no need. The room was empty, and as I covered Kim, she picked up something on the exam table, passing it to me as she moved out into the corridor.

A piece of a standard hospital restraint. It appeared to have been ripped in two, the leather, metal and plastic wrenched and twisted beyond the breaking point.

"Oh, shit." I whispered.

"Alpha Six to all teams, alert one. We have a rogue walker."

"Roger, Alpha Six." Commander Anderson's voice on the line was calm, almost as if he had expected something like this. Maybe he had. He'd been fighting walkers longer than any of us except the colonel himself. "AEGIS Five to Mobile One, prepare to roll out and proceed at speed to our location for immediate reinforcement on my order."

"Mobile One here." Captain Graves voice was taut and controlled, just like Anderson's. Two consummate professionals, just going to work. I was glad to have them on my side. "Order acknowledged, sir. We are ready on your go."

I could only imagine the looks on the faces of the people of Laramie as the sixteen-ton APCs began rolling through town towards us. So much for low-profile. Hopefully we wouldn't need the backup, but it was prudent to have the other teams ready if we did.

"Alpha Six, AEGIS Five."

"Go ahead."

"Proceed with search, but carefully, Major. We don't need any more bodies out there."

"Yes, sir. Out here."

"Ma'am, Dr. Underwood." Rachel said, and I turned to see the doctor was moving towards us, a hand against the wall to support him, Martinez on his other side. To their credit, Reynolds and Gaines never took their eyes off their assigned hallways, keeping watch just in case.

The doctor sagged and looked up at us. "Shelly?" he asked, and I simply pointed to the weeping girl. He crossed the hall, putting one hand on her shoulder as he knelt down, the pain from his brief flight and powerful impact obvious. She flinched away from him violently, then realized who it was, and clung to him. He pulled her to her feet, and they moved back to join us, Martinez taking up his rear-guard position.

"What happened to the candy striper?" the doctor asked.

"We don't know, but this gives us some idea," I said, holding out the broken restraint for him. He was shocked as he took it.

"This is impossible," he said. "These things take hundreds of pounds of force to break. I've never seen any patient, even the truly crazy ones, come close to doing this."

"These aren't your garden-variety patients, Doc, as we might have mentioned," drawled Gaines over his shoulder. Reynolds grunted in agreement.

"I can see that."

"You didn't see or hear anything, Doctor?" asked Kim. "Nothing to indicate an escape?"

"Uh, no. I was in my office," he said, glancing down at Shelly. "I was, uh, waiting for the call from the chief or from your people."

I covered a smile and turned away. *Stress makes people do crazy things, I guess. She's young enough to be his daughter!*

Kim shook her head in disgust. "We're just going to have to do this the hard way, then. Bravo Six, Alpha Six."

"Bravo Six."

"Any movement outside?"

"No, ma'am. It's all quiet out here. Well, except for the press."

"Good. Stay sharp."

"Yes, ma'am."

"AEGIS Five, Alpha Six. Sir, I think we should move the press lines back. If we get a breakout here and have to put some down . . ."

She left the sentence hanging, but we all knew what she meant. Secrecy would be out the door. It was one thing to edit and suppress reports coming from Afghanistan. It was a completely different story to do it here on our own soil. *At least, that's what I'll tell myself.*

"Good idea. I'll get on it right now."

"Out here." Kim turned back to us. "All right, squad, we're moving to hunting protocol as of now. Gaines, you're on point. Eaton, cover the doc and the girl. Martinez and Reynolds, on our six. We're headed for the cafeteria. That's the last source of food for this thing. Everyone stay frosty. Let's move."

We had cleared about half the floor towards the cafeteria when we heard the scream, cut off abruptly. Ahead of us, no doubt headed for the same place as we were.

"Well, I guess we know where it is, ma'am," I said, sighing.

"Eaton, find a place to stow the doc and his nurse. Give him a weapon." Kim turned to the doctor as Eaton moved to the last storeroom we'd cleared, double-checking it for walkers. "Listen Doc, I can't keep you with us. You're going to slow us way down and we need maximum mobility for this hunt. Still, I can't just leave you, so here's what we'll do." She took the offered sidearm from Eaton, checked the magazine and handed it to the doctor.

"You ever fired one of these?" she asked.

The doctor straightened. "I was in the National Guard in college. I've had the appropriate training."

"Good. You're going to need it. I want you both to get in that room and lock it behind you. If anything tries to get in without identifying as one of us, you shoot it. These rounds will go right through that door. Aim high," she said, indicating average head height on the door. The doctor nodded and helped Shelly toward the room.

"Oh, and Doctor?" He turned back to Kim. "Save the last two rounds. Just in case. Clear?"

The doctor blanched, but nodded after a moment. "Thank you."

"Don't mention it. Stay safe."

She waited till he'd locked the door, and then signaled for us to move out. We immediately began moving more quickly, toward the source of the scream we'd heard, ignoring the rooms around us.

Now was the time for hunting, not clearing.

We were reasonably sure there were only two active walkers now—the candy striper and whomever had screamed—and we didn't need to search every room.

We came around yet another corner, stopped, and crouched down below the windows of the hospital pharmacy. The sounds coming from inside were gruesome, and I realized that we might only have the one walker, after all. This one sounded *hungry*.

Kim tapped me on the shoulder, and signaled that she wanted eyes inside the room. I pulled a small fiber-optic periscope from a pocket, easing the tiny lens over the ledge of the pharmacy counter, just enough to see inside the room.

I wish I hadn't.

I'd seen some horrible sights in Fall Creek, but I'd managed to put them behind me. Now, they'd all come back. It felt wrong for a zombie to be wearing that particular uniform while bent over, chewing and tearing at the guts that it had ripped from the poor pharmacy technician's stomach. Blood was everywhere, and I nearly heaved my lunch all over the floor.

What the hell was he doing in there, anyway? He should've evacuated with the . . . *oh ho, now I get it*. I sighed as I saw the bag next to him full of prescription bottles. Who'd worry about a little missing Oxycontin or Vicodin when it's all over? Not him, anyway.

I must've been more than a little green as Kim put a hand on my shoulder to steady me, and I shook my head. I pressed the charging trigger on my X-29 and backed away from the window, then stood. Fortunately, the walker's back was to me, and it didn't hear or see anything before the twin electrodes from one of my rounds impacted between the shoulder blades, causing it to convulse for several seconds.

The blood obscured the white on her uniform. *Not much of a candy-striper now. Not much of anything now.*

I nodded to Kim and the rest of the squad moved into the room, Gaines pulling a set of cuffs and the other mask assigned to the squad from his pack. This one too was trussed, although we didn't have a handy privacy curtain to wrap her. Kim had Reynolds and Martinez fetch a bedspread and sheets from the nearest private room, and we carefully rolled her into it, making sure to avoid the blood from both victims, though this proved difficult due to the sheer volume of it.

Once that was done, Rachel stepped forward and put two rounds into the pharmacy tech's head. That was one potential zombie that wasn't coming back.

"Ma'am, would you mind running us through splatter checks?"

"Good idea. Everyone, splatter check."

We inspected each other for random drops of potentially infected blood. Gaines and I disposed of our gloves, replacing them with fresh ones from our packs. There was no way they'd be usable again, not with all that infectious blood. That's when I realized a fatal flaw in the plan to capture these things: the blood.

It doesn't matter what Gardner wants. We can't capture these things alive.

I turned back to Kim. "Ma'am, we can't take these with us."

"Oh?" she said, surprised. "What do you mean?"

"We'll have to leave these for a clean-up crew. We don't have the equipment to transport these things. Just look at all the blood that's on this one."

All of us turned to look back at the twitching zombie form, and the bloody stain that was rapidly spreading through the covering. There was blood everywhere.

"Shit. Shit shit shit. AEGIS Five, Alpha Six."

"AEGIS Five here."

"Sir, this isn't going to work. We can't transport these walkers. We can put them down and immobilize them, for a while anyway, but we can't take them anywhere."

"Why not?"

"The blood, sir. It's all over everything. We'd have to have some sort of biohazard container to take them out in."

"Shit. I hadn't thought of that, and I'm betting neither did Gardner or his people." Anderson paused. "Well, we're not going to put the cleanup crew through that without procedures tested and in-hand. Neutralize both walkers."

"Sir?"

"On my authority, Major. That's an order."

"Yes, sir." Kim straightened as if the world had come back into its proper place. "All squads, capture protocol rescinded. Neutralize all walkers on sight."

More than a few muttered comments came over the radio, and I agreed with them as I muttered under my breath. "Finally."

I turned to Kim. "Do you think we should check out the cafeteria, just in case?"

"Hmmm, maybe . . ." Kim was interrupted as a single gunshot sounded from down the main hallway, in the direction we'd left the doctor. "Shit. Martinez, neutralize that one. Let's move."

Martinez nodded, putting two quick slugs into the zombie's head through the wrapping. We all ducked as ricochets caromed off the thick mask and zinged down the hallway to bury themselves in plaster.

"Fuck!" I said, looking wide-eyed at Angelo, who blushed and shrugged. I unwrapped the sheets carefully around the head, and he took a more well-placed shot this time. *Stupid shit like that is going to get one or more of us dead.*

I shook my head as we jogged back to the storeroom where we'd left the doctor and the nurse. *One shot? Just one? No way.* The door was closed, but I didn't trust that.

"Eaton, cover me." She and Kim took up a covering position as I knocked on the door, standing to one side. "Doc, it's Blake. Open the door, please." No sound could be heard, and I looked at Kim, who signaled for me to knock again.

"Doctor Underwood, please open the door. Shelly, if you're okay, please open the door." I glanced down and saw blood leaking from under the door, moving toward my boot and the others. I jumped back as the door opened, Shelly's bright white sneakers tracking through the blood, her face devoid of emotion.

"He said he was sick. Said he'd never get better and didn't want to be one of them. I asked him not to do it, but he didn't listen. I'm going to my station, now." She walked down the hallway toward the nurse's station, but stopped when Kim gestured at Eaton, who put an arm around her and started whispering in her ear.

I looked back into the room, and wasn't surprised at all to see Doctor Underwood lying back against the blood-splattered wall, the white-painted concrete bricks dripping with bits of brain and skull. Eaton's pistol was still clutched in his hand, and I could see the flash-burn marks under his chin where he'd shoved the barrel of the gun before pulling the trigger.

I also saw the bite mark on his arm, partially obscured by the burns he'd suffered earlier. He'd seen the bites on the woman brought in and probably heard what had happened to the candy striper, and knew what would happen. I didn't blame him at all. I'd have done the same thing. Or my squad would, for me, when the time came.

"Bravo Six, Alpha Six."

"Go ahead, Alpha."

"Proceed to the northwest corner entrance and secure the cafeteria. Estimate between forty and fifty staff have taken refuge there."

"On our way, ma'am."

"AEGIS Five, Alpha Six."

"Go ahead, Alpha Six."

"Second package neutralized. Three casualties, civilian, including the walkers. One survivor, civilian."

"Roger. What's the status of the other staff and patients?"

"Unknown at this time. Bravo team is securing the cafeteria."

"Acknowledged. Get the survivor out of there and begin standard sweep and clear once Bravo team has secured the others."

"Yes, sir. Out here." Kim turned to the nurse, who had left bloody footprints down the hallway from her sneakers. "Shelly? We need to get you out of here, but I'm going to need you to do something for me, first, ok?"

The girl looked blankly at Kim.

"Ma'am, I don't think she's here with us right now." Eaton said, passing a flashlight in front of the nurse's eyes. "No dilation. She's gone, ma'am."

"Shit." Kim sighed. "Take off her shoes and do a splatter check. Gaines, pack her out of here. Reynolds, get the door. Martinez, on point. We'll follow up with Bravo once she's secure."

"Yes, ma'am," chorused the other members of the squad, moving off to their assigned jobs. Gaines, for his part, merely picked the girl up and laid her over one of his shoulders like a sack of potatoes after Rachel cleared her for splatter. I doubt the girl even noticed, judging from the complete lack of expression on her face. Off in her own little world, and maybe never coming back.

Seeing your boyfriend attacked and bitten by a zombie, then watching him blow his own head off to keep from turning into one had a tendency to do that.

Chapter Sixteen

CHEYENNE, WYOMING

HE'D NEVER BEEN ONE TO follow the news very much, but it had been a week since he'd heard from Doris, and Jason was nervous. First, there was the cryptic text message about something important to show him, and she stands him up. Then she doesn't call, text, or email for a week. As far as he could tell, her car hadn't moved from her parking lot in all that time, either.

He'd called the police, but they couldn't or wouldn't do anything. She'd gone off without telling anyone before, she had no next of kin, and there was nothing suspicious.

Not to them, anyway. But I know Doris, and something isn't right. This whole thing is suspicious.

He raised the expensive digital camera he'd snagged from her kitchen table and took a few photos of the soldiers standing around, as well as the one talking to the police chief. There was nothing that indicated that they were anything other than what they were supposed to be, but he was far too paranoid for that.

You didn't get to be on the government's cyber crimes watch list by believing everything they told you.

Still, there was a connection here. Doris had been talking to this same group—USAMRIID—last week when the toxins spilled up in Rawlins. *What a lame-ass cover-up that was. This is no toxic spill, but these same USAMRIID guys are here. For one lousy sick person? Right.*

Suddenly the emergency room door opened, and the group of soldiers that had gone in an hour before emerged, and it appeared that the big one was carrying someone over his shoulder.

He zoomed in with the camera, along with the rest of the crowd, and saw that it was a nurse in pink scrubs. *Where the hell are her shoes? And why is this guy carrying her?* Suddenly he noticed one of the rifles he'd spotted earlier, carried by the tall redhead. He found himself forgetting about Doris for a moment, as her looks put Doris to shame, and he wondered why she'd chosen the Army when she could just as easily have been on the cover of any fashion magazine.

Focus! What the hell type of rifle is that?

He wrenched his attention back to the rifle, and zoomed in with the camera. Now that he was getting a good view of it as the big soldier loaded the nearly passed-out nurse into the back of the police chief's car, he realized it didn't just *look* futuristic. This was an actual, functioning weapon, and he took several photos of it.

Suddenly, he noticed that the redhead was looking his way, and gesturing at one of the other men in the group. The tall, greying soldier with movie-star looks shook his head and began jogging toward the barricades.

Jason was no fool. He knew what came next. Pretending to tie his shoe, he slipped the memory card out of the camera and into his sock. As he stood up, he pulled another from his pocket and slipped it into the camera, turning around just in time to see the soldier arrive at the barricade.

Damn, he's tall. Jason looked for a name on the man's uniform but failed to find anything other than the USAMRIID logo. He noticed several scars on the man's forearms, and he could tell this was not someone to screw with.

Ever.

The soldier cupped his hands around his mouth and yelled. "If I could have everyone's attention over here for a moment, please." The crowd quieted down somewhat, and several reporters pushed their way to the front. Jason was only too happy to let them, easing his way back to the rear of the crowd as the soldier continued.

"For reasons of national security, I'm going to need to confiscate all recording media as of right now." The crowd roared with disapproval, but the soldier merely stood there and held up his hands.

"You've all seen this drill before. You'll get your tapes, discs, flash drives and whatnot back before you leave here today, but we need to make sure that we've got all the information we can about this potential illness."

Again, the crowd roared, questions peppering the soldier, who simply ignored them.

"As I said, this is a matter of national security, and you *will* comply with this order. USAMRIID will see that your materials are returned to you." Another two soldiers trotted up, one carrying a canvas bag and the other a notebook of some kind.

"Please turn over all of your materials to these two. You will be issued a receipt. If you prefer not to wait for the return of your materials here, they will be mailed back to you."

Jason snorted as he reached the back of the crowd. *Sure they would. Empty, no doubt, with some glitch blamed for them being wiped. This ain't my first rodeo, soldier-boy.*

He had a slight smile on his face as he turned to move away from the crowd and ran smack into the immovable wall of the large soldier he'd seen before.

"And just where do you think you're going, kid?" drawled the big man, one huge hand coming down on Jason's shoulder. "I saw that camera, there. We're gonna need the memory card from that, buddy."

"Uh, sure, mister. I get it, national security and all. Here ya go," he said, pulling the memory card from the camera and handing it to the soldier.

"Sorry, kid, it ain't that easy." Jason jumped a bit as a short, dark-haired woman appeared at his side. "You look like a smart one, and smart ones always have a backup plan."

She then proceeded to give him the most thorough search he'd ever experienced. When she pulled the extra memory cards from his jeans, he had the wit to seem chagrined as she arched one eyebrow at him.

"What?" he said. "They're spares." The female soldier shook her head and handed them to the other, who smiled.

"All right, kid, you can go. Just make sure to talk with the guy over there to get your receipt. Assuming you want these back, of course."

"Nah, they're my ex's. I could give a shit if she gets them back. She's not even paying me for this."

The soldier shrugged and moved off through the crowd towards the others, and Jason breathed a sigh of relief, feeling the real memory card against his ankle. *Just what in the hell is on there that they didn't want me to see?*

Gaines chuckled as he walked back to the rental cars, bouncing the memory cards in his palm. Rachel smiled up at him, but managed to look concerned at the same time. "Do you think these were the only ones he had?"

"Not even for a second, babe. But we could hardly strip-search him there in the parking lot, could we? I got his picture while you were busy searching him," he said, holding up his phone. "I don't think he even noticed, what with your hands all over the place."

He grinned down at her as she rounded on him in anger. She snorted as she realized he was pushing her buttons, and punched him in the arm. "Ass. So, what? We just let him walk away?"

"Hardly. I'll make sure that the major or the commander gets his photo. I'm sure there's some way to track this kid down and find out who he is. Once we do that, we can put a team on him to monitor his movements, internet usage, the works. Whatever it was that he found, he's not going to be able to use it."

Rachel sighed. "I wish we didn't have to do crap like this. I'd rather just be out killing zombies. All this political crap is too much for my fragile little military mind."

This time it was Gaines that snorted. "Fragile and little are not words I'd use to describe you, darlin'," he said. "Now *short*, on the other hand . . ."

She hit him harder.

"Alpha Six here, go ahead, Bravo Six."

"Ma'am, we've found the cafeteria, but no one's here."

Kim paled as the radio squawked, and looked at me. "Maybe they went somewhere else? The kitchen, the freezer, who knows?" I said, trying to ease the tension just a bit.

"Bravo Six, confirm evidence of walkers in the cafeteria."

"No, ma'am. There's no blood, at least that we can see. No dead or dying. It's just empty, ma'am."

"Spread out and check all exits from that location. Those people must've gone somewhere, Lieutenant."

"Yes, ma'am, we're already looking."

"Shit, shit, shit. Underwood said there were maybe sixty people in that cafeteria," she said, looking at Anderson. "Where the hell did they all go?"

The radio crackled once more. "Alpha Six, Bravo Six."

"What've you found?"

"Ma'am, we found a roof access ladder at the back of the kitchen. Looks like it's been used recently. Arkady is on his way up now to check it out."

"Acknowledged." She looked at me. "The roof?"

I shrugged. "That's probably what I would've done. Walkers can't climb ladders, so that's one of the safest places they could be."

"Surely we would've seen something by now—at least someone peeking over the edge."

"Not necessarily. They could be hiding, waiting for an all clear from Doctor Underwood." An all clear that would never come, now.

"Bravo Six here, we've found them, ma'am. They're all on the roof. They seem a bit dazed. One of the nurses was scared but in charge. It was her idea to get everyone up here."

"Get them down here, but bring them around the outside of the building. And I want to meet this nurse."

"Yes, ma'am, on our way."

Kim turned to Anderson. "Sir, I'd like to send these vehicles back and get 3rd Team so we can finish clearing the hospital."

"Make it happen, Major."

Kim assigned Rachel, Dalton, and me to drive the rental cars back to the airport, and we managed to pick up Echo and Foxtrot squads. Although there was some squishing involved, we made it back to the hospital in what I believed to be record time. I noticed Kim talking to a tall brunette in scrubs as we pulled up, but I didn't have time to think about who that might be. Kim was obviously busy, so I took charge. After all, that was my job as her XO.

"All right, Bravo and Echo squads are on point for this final sweep. Foxtrot, maintain the perimeter. Take these four with you," I said, pointing at Angelo, Dalton, Rachel and Tom. "I don't want anyone else dying today, so be careful, people. Move!" The fine professional soldiers that they were, 1st and 3rd Teams moved out in almost preternatural silence to their assigned tasks.

"Looks like something's got the gawkers spooked," Anderson said, coming to stand next to me as I waited for the major to finish her chat with the nurse. I looked over at the barricades. He was right, something had the press and the rest of them more agitated than before, and it wasn't just that we'd taken all their disks, drives, and media.

"My father always taught me never to wonder when you can just ask, sir," I replied.

Anderson snorted. "Right. Let's take a little of that advice, shall we?" I started to move towards the barricade, but he stopped me. "I've got this one. Why don't you see what that's all about?" he asked, jerking a thumb in the at the now-finished gabfest behind us.

Yippee. Just don't let me walk in on something I'd be better off not hearing. "Yes, sir," I said as he moved off to the barricades, and turned to find Kim and the new girl approaching.

"David, I want you to meet the nurse that took all those people to the roof. This is Morena Forrest." It took everything I had to keep from leaping backward in fear when I turned around. She wasn't alarming to look at. Far from it. She was tall, maybe five-seven or five-eight, with startling blue eyes and long raven-black hair. That wasn't what frightened me. What I was scared of was that except for the hair color, I knew this woman.

It was Rebecca.

It's not her. My mind screamed at me. *It can't be her.*

That damned voice was back with his helpful little addition to the twisted mess that was my thoughts at that moment. *It can't be Rebecca, because you* killed *Rebecca, remember?* The few seconds that had passed seemed like years as I tried to figure out what to do, what to say. Eventually my overheating brain gave up and just went into default mode.

"Hi, I'm David," I said, reaching out to shake her hand. "Nice to meet you."

"Hi, David, good to meet you, too." Then she did the oddest thing I'd ever seen anyone do after being stuck in a hospital with zombies for hours.

She smiled.

I realized I was still holding Morena's hand, and I let go like I'd grabbed a live power line. At least, that's what it felt like. Of course, that was also the same moment that I noticed a dangerous glint in Kim's eye, so perhaps it was merely self-preservation, at that.

"Uh, so, good job with the staff and patients," I stammered, trying to look nonchalant and failing.

Morena appeared worried. "Did you get all the other ones out, though?"

Kim and I glanced at each other and looked back at Morena. "What others?" I asked. "We thought all the staff and patients were in the—" I broke off and looked back at Kim. "Oh fuck, that's not what he said at all."

"What who said?" Kim asked as I ran a few steps toward the building.

"Bravo and Echo teams, be advised there are more targets in the hospital. Say again, more targets in the building," I yelled, turning back to Kim. "Underwood. He said 'the rest of the staff and all the patients *we could move.*' Morena, how many weren't you able to move?"

Morena and Kim reached the same conclusion as I did, and as Morena paled, Kim whirled and shouted orders through her mike.

"I'm not sure exactly," Morena said, taking obvious control of her fear.

Impressive for someone who hadn't known what she was going to be getting into when she clocked in this morning.

"There were four in the critical care unit, and at least two others in emergency. I know that Shelly was prepping one of them for surgery, and there was another that was in surgical recovery. We did what we could, but—"

"You did the right thing, Morena. I just hope they're still all right," I said, one hand on her shoulder in consolation. I turned to catch up with Kim, but she was already coming back.

"Looks like Echo found one guy near emergency. He's dead." She shook her head at a quick look from me. "No, not turned. Santos thinks he died of respiratory arrest. Something to do with his surgery, she guesses. He was already cold when she got there."

"Morena says there were four in the critical care unit, too, and another one somewhere in emergency."

Kim wasted no time. "Echo Six, Alpha Six."

"Echo Six here."

"Be advised there may be another target in the emergency area as well as surgical recovery."

"Roger."

"Bravo Six, Alpha Six."

"Got another one for me too, boss?"

"Four more targets, critical care unit. All teams confirm walker status before kills. No friendly fire here, people."

"Bravo moving to critical care unit. Out here."

Kim turned back to us. "Ms. Forrest, the patient being prepped for surgery didn't make it. I'm sorry."

To her credit, Morena's voice only stammered slightly. "Was he . . . did he . . ."

Kim shook her head. "No, he wasn't, uh, infected. Our corpsman thinks he died of respiratory arrest, long before they ever got to him."

Morena sighed. "That's really unfortunate. He was a very nice man. Still, better to die that way than turn into a zombie." Kim and I exchanged startled looks, causing Morena to raise an eyebrow. "Oh, what? You don't think I watch movies? Sure, they're mostly made up, but that's what those things looked like to me."

Kim and I avoided looking at each other, trying to stifle grins as Morena looked back and forth between us. "Wait, you're not saying what I think you're saying, are you?" she asked. "These really *are*— Oh, shit." She clapped a hand over her mouth and blushed.

Rebecca used to do the same thing. I swore under my breath and turned away, checking Foxtrot's perimeter. *Thank God she's just a civilian.*

"Alpha Six, Echo Six."

"Go ahead, Echo Six."

"We have retrieved two more survivors and are evac'ing them now. ETA your position two minutes. Request medic."

"Roger Echo Six, confirm evac and medic request." I glanced at Kim and saw her jaw set. If Echo was asking for a medic, then something had happened to them that was bad enough that our resident field medic—Corpsman Lucia Santos, USMC—couldn't handle it. Hopefully, it was just a regular injury. "Ms. Forrest, could you help us out here? We've got wounded on their way."

Morena nodded, almost coming to attention as she straightened. "Call me Morena, please. And yes. Where do you need us?"

Kim drew her closer to the emergency room doors, talking quietly. Morena nodded and whistled. "Saunders, McElroy, get over here with those e-packs!" She yelled louder than Kim, her voice carrying into the parking lot. Two of the nurses milling around the emergency vehicles looked over, grabbed emergency kits out of a nearby ambulance, and sprinted over to the head nurse, who began organizing a field trauma station.

Kim chuckled as she came back over. "That one's a force to be reckoned with. I'm keeping my eye on her." I ignored the sideways glance she gave me, knowing it wasn't just Morena she was going to be keeping her eye on.

I pointed at the doors as 3rd Team came bursting out, two patients on stretchers and one of the soldiers leaning on the arm of the last man out, Captain James—also known as Echo Six, squadleader for half of 3rd Team.

Well, that explains the need for the medics. I watched James ease Santos to a resting position on one of the impromptu tables set up by Morena's people.

"Looks like Santos is hurt," I said as Kim and I got closer, staying well clear of the working medical personnel.

"How is she, Morena?" Kim asked, pulling her pistol from its holster.

Morena didn't look around. "She's not bitten, major."

Santos spoke up. "*Madre de Dios*, that hurts. I'm fine, ma'am. That jackass attacked me with a bone saw," she said, jerking her head at one of the patients they'd brought out on a stretcher. "He was in surgical recovery. I guess he thought I was a walker, sir. He'd barricaded himself in the room. He just forgot that the door opened outward."

Kim put her pistol back in the holster and snorted. "Lemme guess, you decked him." I noticed the oh-so-evident bruise on the man's jaw, and turned to hide a smile from the corpsman.

"Yes, ma'am, I did," she said, shrugging. "We didn't have time to deal with him going crazy, so I figured that was the fastest way. I'd keep him pretty well sedated, if I were you, at least until medical clears him," she said to Morena.

"Don't worry. He's out for a while. I gave him a nice cocktail." The two medics shared a smile, and even Kim grinned a bit, some of the tension easing from the group.

Too bad it didn't last.

"Alpha Six, Bravo Five." I wondered why Arkady was calling in instead of Commander Powell, but as I heard the muted cough of the silenced battle rifles in the background—as well as Powell's fluent cursing—I realized why. "Alert three, ma'am. We're engaged with what appears to be at least four, possibly six or seven walkers."

"Maintain your position, Bravo Five. Alpha squad, move to reinforce Bravo."

"Acknowledged," Reynolds said, and I saw four figures break off from the perimeter at the other end of the hospital and move inside in staggered formation, covering each other. *That's my team.* Foxtrot squad reconfigured to provide maximum coverage as they left.

A few minutes went by, and there was a crackle of static and Bravo Six came on the radio. "—cking thing, dammit! Alpha Six, Bravo Six."

"Alpha Six here, go ahead."

"Five walkers confirmed down, ma'am, with one other infected, also confirmed down. One survivor. We're finishing our sweep now."

"Acknowledged. Send the survivor out with Alpha, through the emergency room doors."

"Roger, Bravo Six clear."

Kim turned to Morena, who held up a hand. "I heard. We'll take care of it. Looks like you might have some unpleasantness headed your way though," she said, looking over our shoulders. We turned to see Anderson striding toward us, and if ever a man could be said to look murderous, that was our commander.

I just hoped *I* wasn't the reason he was pissed.

"Problem, sir?" I asked as he got closer.

"One of those little bastards with a camera got away. One of the other idiots swears up and down that he saw the little shit put something in his shoe. Fuck! There goes OpSec."

"Sir, it may not be that bad." Kim and Anderson both looked at me, startled. "Surely someone got video of the crowd, right?"

"I believe Gaines and Eaton were collecting the tapes and disks and whatnot from those assholes. Where are they?"

"Sir, they're escorting another survivor out of the building while Bravo and Charlie finish their sweep," Kim answered.

"Good. Have them report—" He broke off, looking over my shoulder. "Never mind."

He strode off, leaving us to catch up as he walked toward the field trauma unit, where the rest of Alpha squad had appeared and left their survivor. I waved Tom and the others over.

"Gunny, I need those memory cards," Anderson said without preamble.

"Yes, sir," Gaines said, and trotted off towards the rental car, and Eaton turned to Anderson.

"Sir, we don't have the facilities here to analyze them fully."

"Are you telling me no one here has a laptop? That we can't borrow a computer from the hospital for a bit?"

Rachel flushed. "Of course not, sir. It's just—"

Anderson held up a hand. "I don't need to analyze them completely, Sergeant. I just need to look for someone who's disappeared, apparently."

Eaton grinned. "Lemme guess, sir. Tallish, skinny, sandy hair? Looks about twenty-five?"

Anderson was stunned. "How the hell did you know that?"

"Oh, you know, sir. Women's intuition and all that." She held out a hand as Gaines ran back up with a bulging sack of electronic media. "That, and pictures, sir. D, I need your phone."

Gaines shrugged and pulled the phone from his pocket, handing it to her. Eaton opened the phone, punched a button and held it out to the commander. "Him, sir?"

Anderson grinned. "Excellent work, Sergeant, Gunny."

"We thought he was a bit fishy, sir, we just didn't have a chance to report yet."

"I'll see you get this back, Gaines." Anderson moved off, opening his own phone and making a call.

"I guess I can put these back, then?" Dalton asked, his tone suggesting he'd rather leave them there until they rotted.

"Absolutely," I said, smiling as Gaines grimaced and trotted back to the car. The five of us turned to look back at the hospital. "How was it in there, Angelo?"

"We had it kinda rough, man. They were coming out of nowhere. Not a place I'd want to have to secure again." Martinez was thoughtful, then frowned. "It's a damn shame about the kid, though."

"The kid?" asked Kim.

"Yeah, the survivor we found. Can't be more than seven or eight. He's pretty messed up. We found him hiding in a closet. Think he was visiting someone, but we don't know who. He won't talk to anyone."

"Lemme try, boss," I said, turning to Kim. "I'm good with kids. Maybe I can help him some, ease some of the trauma a bit."

She shrugged. "Knock yourself out."

I walked over to the tables the nurses had set up, and glanced around. I didn't see any kids at first, but then one of the nurses turned and I saw a small arm lying on the table, still. As I got closer, I saw the boy look up at me. Morena had an arm around him, and suddenly I stumbled, sinking to my knees, my eyes locked on the pair.

This . . . this can't be. It's impossible!

Kim rushed over calling for a medic. I dimly heard her calling to me, as though from miles away, but I couldn't think about that right now. All I could think of was that this boy and the woman taking care of him were the spitting image of Rebecca and her son Eric.

Not possible. You shot one, and the other is—I cringed, and tore my gaze away from the boy, somehow reaching for and finding Kim, who drew me to her.

I didn't hear myself mumbling over and over. "It's not them. It's not them."

She heard a voice from behind her as she stared at the car. "Ma'am, will he be all right?" *That would be Reynolds.*

She scrubbed a hand across her eyes to get rid of the tears she'd refused to let fall, and turned to him. "I hope so, Captain. I don't know what happened. You saw as much as I did. He just sort of sat down and started mumbling to himself."

"What was he saying, ma'am?"

"'It's not them.'"

"What the hell does *that* mean?" asked Gaines, who was watching Eaton as she knelt by the open door of the rental car, talking quietly to David.

"I think I know Gunny, but I can't tell you." She shook her head as he looked up. "I really can't." The sergeant subsided but still looked worried. She thought all of them were probably looking the same way.

"Everything all right here, Major?" asked Commander Anderson as he walked up.

"I hope so, sir," she said as she turned to face him. "Bravo and Echo squads have finished their sweep, and are on their way out now. I've got Foxtrot retaining the perimeter, just in case. I've already called in the cleanup teams, they should be here within the hour. Turns out the colonel had them trucking up I-25 at the same time we took off."

"Great, then we won't have to wait forever for them to get here. What's with Blake?"

"He . . . he had something of a scare, sir." A worried look flashed across her face and was gone. "I think he'll be fine, but we need to get him back to base." She looked at him suddenly. "Sir, what about that guy with the camera?"

Anderson grinned in a way that said bad things were going to happen to the little shit soon.

"The techs have identified him based on your pic, Gaines. His name's Jason Horner. He was already a person of interest for us after a little fiasco we had with the press up in Rawlins. They're deconstructing his life right now. They'll know everything there is to know about him by the time we get home." He glanced over to the nurses packing and cleaning the area where they'd set up their mobile trauma unit. "So what's going on with this nurse, then?"

Kim shrugged. "She's good, sir. Very, very good. At least as a field medic. She has no military background, but she's learned things that I've never seen a hospital nurse do, sir." She stood tall and looked him square in the eye. "I want her for AEGIS, sir. But not on my team. I need to make sure David is okay, too. He had some sort of reaction when he saw them."

"Reaction?"

"Went catatonic, sir. He's being looked after." Kim sighed. "Forrest's tough, and she can handle herself. We should keep her around at the base and put her through training, but not on field duty yet, or at least not with 1st Team. And nowhere near David."

Anderson stared back, expressionless. "Family? Friends?"

"No family, sir, and she said she's just moved here, so no friends to speak of that would miss her that much."

"Can she handle it, do you think?"

"Yes, sir, I believe she can. She led over forty people to the roof, and went back twice to look for more." She chuckled. "She said she would've kept going back down, but one of the men threatened to knock her out if she did. So she stayed and made sure everyone was ok. She's seen them, sir, and not only lived to tell but came out without any obvious major psychosis. And we need medics, sir."

Anderson grunted agreement. "That we do, and badly. All right, Barnes, bring her over."

"Yes, sir."

Morena looked up as she approached, and Kim waved her over. "My commander wants to talk to you. Do you have a moment?" she asked the nurse, who appeared startled.

"Uh, sure. Did he say what he wanted?"

"In my experience, Morena, it's better to do first and ask questions later. If you get the chance."

"Gotcha. Lead on."

Gaines and Reynolds stood behind the commander in flanking positions as the two women approached, and Kim could see that Morena was nervous. She put a hand on her shoulder and flashed a quick smile, and the nurse straightened, heartened by the thoughtful gesture.

"You wanted to see me, Commander?" Morena asked.

"Yes, Ms. Forrest. I've had reports from my soldiers here, but I'd like you to tell me in your own words what you think happened here today."

"I just need one word, sir: zombies."

Anderson raised an eyebrow and glanced at Kim, who shook her head and tried her best to stifle a grin.

"Zombies? That's ridiculous."

"Well, *of course*, zombies." She began to count points on her hand. "One, they're dead, then they come back to some sort of life, if you can call it that. Two, if they bite you, you turn into one of them. Three, they don't seem to be hurt by anything other than head shots. Four, the moaning. The goddamn moaning. What else could they be?"

Gaines and Reynolds were doing their best to hide smiles and outright laughter, and Anderson's smile turned up slightly in a grin himself. "Well, I guess that settles that, then."

"Settles what, sir?"

"Ms. Forrest, we'd like you to come work for us."

Morena's mouth dropped open, and Anderson smiled. "Work? For you?" Morena asked.

"Indeed. We'd put you through combat training and assign you to a squad for field operations. We can always use more medics, and from what I've heard, you're one of the best the major here has seen in quite some time."

Morena glanced at Kim, who was also smiling. "But I don't know the first thing about being a soldier!"

"Somehow I doubt that. Major Barnes says she personally observed you performing procedures that we know only military-trained field medics are usually skilled in performing. So what was it? National Guard? Army Reserve?"

Morena flushed and looked down. "I . . . I knew someone once who taught me some things. He was . . . well, he was a soldier." The way she said it left little doubt as to just what kind of soldier her friend had been, but Anderson just shook his head.

"I don't care if he was a merc or a true-blue American soldier, Ms. Forrest. We *need* your help. You'd be moved to our base, paid well, and given certain other perks. But you wouldn't be allowed to tell anyone what you do." Anderson leaned in and brought his eyes level with hers from about four inches away, dead serious. "Ever."

Morena gulped. "Well, in that case . . ." She closed her eyes and took a deep breath. She kept them closed for a few moments, considering the offer. When she opened them again, she was decision and dedication incarnate, and even Anderson was impressed. "Yes, sir, I would be honored to join. I just have one condition."

Kim stood a little straighter, surprised. Anderson quirked an eyebrow at the forceful nurse. "And what would that be?"

"I want to bring Michael with us, sir."

"Who's Michael?"

In answer, Morena yelled over her shoulder. "Michael, come here, please." The little boy that Kim had seen on the medical table came running towards them with a grin, then stopped and hid behind the nurse as he caught sight of the others nearby.

Morena looked down at him. "This is Michael, Commander. His mother was one of the ones in the critical care unit, and his father was the one your men found near surgery." She continued in a whisper. "Car accident, sir. He has no one, sir, no family at all."

Anderson squatted down to put himself at eye level with the child, and smiled. "It's ok, son. I won't hurt you." The little boy peeked out from behind the nurse's scrubs. "That's all right, kiddo. You and I will have plenty of time to get to know each other." He stood back up and laid his hand on Morena's shoulder.

"We'll see if we can't get someone to look after him when you can't. There's plenty of on-base personnel, so it shouldn't be that much of a problem. Your skills—and more importantly, your psychological strength—are certainly worth the effort." Anderson glanced at Kimberly, and smiled. "And AEGIS has some experience with orphaned children, Ms. Forrest."

Kim smiled back at Anderson. "Sir, I'd be willing to bet that Mary would help out with that."

Anderson nodded. "You're probably right, Barnes. I'll check with her when we get back. As for you," he said, looking at Morena. "I can't bring you in off the field as an officer, but we'll fix that soon enough. We'll take care of all the paperwork when we get back, but I'm guessing you'll be an E-4, Hospital Corpsman Third Class, until we get everything straightened out. Assuming you like the Marines, that is. How's that sound?"

"Just fine, sir," she said, and snapped into a reasonably respectable salute, which Anderson returned, grinning.

"Very well. Major, see that she and the boy get what they need stowed aboard the Globemasters. We'll be wheels up twenty minutes after the cleaning crew gets here."

"Yes, sir." Anderson walked away, and Kim hugged Morena. "Congratulations!"

Morena smiled back and held on tight to Michael, who started to squirm as Eaton walked up.

"What'd I miss?" asked the sergeant.

"Morena's going to be one of us, Rachel."

"Great! Lord knows we could use someone who actually knows something about medicine," she said, laughing. "I've been doing some of the heavy lifting with medical needs, but I don't know my ass from a hole in the ground when it comes to true field work. Santos is going to be *so* glad to have you with us."

Morena nodded towards the car where Blake now lay against the backseat. "What about him?"

Eaton chuckled, a mischievous grin plastered on her face. "He never saw the Mickey I slipped him, major."

"Well done, Sergeant." Kim could hear his snores from where she was standing, and forced herself to smile. "I'm sure he'll be fine. He probably just needed some rest."

At least I hope that was all he needed. She looked at Morena and the child. *Please, let that be all he needs.*

Chapter Seventeen

Fort Carson, Colorado

"I THINK I KNOW WHAT it is, Kim," said Dr. Adamsdóttir. Kim turned away from her sleeping lover. David had been sedated for about thirty hours now. He'd been in the infirmary since they'd returned from Laramie, and she still had no idea why he'd snapped.

I can't have him on the team like this, though. I need everyone at 100%, if not 110%.

Kim looked at the doctor and found, to her surprise, not even a hint of the irrational jealousy she'd felt towards her before.

Maybe it's that she's married now. And happily, from what I hear.

"Oh?" she said. "What've you got?"

"We did the normal psychological profile when he came on board with AEGIS, and he was given a pretty thorough going-over after Fall Creek, too," Mary said.

Kim nodded. "We all got that. At least the first part. I assumed he was cleared, or he wouldn't have made the team. Are you saying there was a problem?"

"Not initially. At least, I don't see any red flags." Mary paused and looked at Kim. "I really shouldn't be telling you this, Kim. It's all confidential stuff."

Kim sighed. "I see. Just do what you think is best, then."

"I will. That's why I'm going to tell you what I found. Come look at this."

Kim walked over and looked at the computer as Mary pointed to a graph. "These are his psych profile scores," she said. "See that spike there? That indicates some sort of repressed or blocked memory, something he doesn't want to talk about. The shrinks he talked to didn't get much out of him about Fall Creek other than what we all know. I thought there might be more to the story, so I did some digging through his records, and what I found—"

"Let me guess," Kim said. "It's about Rebecca."

Mary was startled. "You know about her?"

"He told me about her a few days ago. He said he killed her after she'd turned."

"Then you know most of the story, but you still need to see this. I found a picture of her in the city records. Apparently she worked for the mayor's office."

Mary turned back to the computer, and brought up a photo on the monitor. A young woman with blonde hair and a bright smile appeared, and Kim's breath caught in her chest. She sat down hard on a lab stool, frozen by what she saw.

"That's insane," she whispered after a few minutes, and Mary's eyes softened in sympathy. "It can't be her," she whispered.

"I thought so, too. So I had a friend at an outside lab compare this with Morena's AEGIS processing photo. He sent me the results of the comparison."

She punched a command into her computer, and the two photos appeared side-by-side. The results were obvious, and Kim shook her head in disbelief.

"They're a ninety-three percent match, according to facial structure, height, estimated weight, and a whole host of other factors," said Mary. "Other than their hair color, the women are nearly identical. We're looking at proof that everyone has a twin *somewhere* in the world."

"Oh my God. No wonder . . ."

"It gets worse," Mary said, and entered another command. "It's the same for the kid. You know that National Child Registry thing that the FBI was trying to get going a few years back? Well, as it turns out, they still do things like it in various places, and Fall Creek was one of those.

"Eric had his picture, blood type and fingerprints entered into their system, which was then uploaded to the FBI. I looked through their data, found his picture, and I had that compared to the kid we found in Laramie, Michael."

This time there were shots of Eric and Michael being compared. Once again, they were almost identical. "This one was only an eighty-nine percent match, but you can take it from there."

"No wonder. No *fucking* wonder," Kim said. "His fiancée and son—both dead—might as well have come back to life. That would be enough to send anyone over the edge."

"Normally, I would agree with you. But given his psych eval and his interviews, I believe David has a much stronger psyche than the average person does. I don't think that was all it took. I believe he is, or at least *was*, level-headed enough to deal with even that."

"If that's the case, then why . . ."

Mary shook her head. "I don't know. Something must've happened to add to his existing trauma, something we don't know about. Judging from the overall strength of his psyche, I'd have to say it happened fairly recently and was pretty major. Otherwise he would've had time to fully assimilate whatever it was."

Kim sighed. "We need him, Mary. *I* need him."

Mary laid a hand on Kim's arm. "I know you do. I think he'll come back from this, but until he's ok—or we know he will be—I think we should keep him sedated and resting here."

Kim wiped a nascent tear from her eye and smiled at Mary. "That's a good idea," she said, looking over at him. She sighed and closed her eyes. "I have to brief the colonel."

Mary shook her head. "I don't think—"

"No, I have to, Mary. Maybe not everything, but he needs to know what's going on, at least generally. He may even know what it was that sent David over the edge like this."

Mary nodded slowly. "All right. I'll let you know of any changes in his condition, and I would suggest that you keep visiting him. It seems to help a great deal in these kinds of cases." She paused as Kim stood to leave. "And Kim . . . you know I'm always here to talk if you need me, right?"

Kim smiled again and hugged her friend. "I know. Thanks, Mary."

Mary looked over at David as Kim walked out. "What's going on in there? Come back to us, my friend." But David just remained silent and still.

"So that's it, sir. Neither of us knows what the proverbial final straw was, but it must've been big." Kim sat in Maxwell's office, a large cup of coffee in her hand as she looked across the desk at the man who was, for all intents and purposes, her father.

"Holy shit," said Anderson, perched on the edge of the colonel's desk. "No wonder he reacted like that. Hell, George, even you or I would've had a similar reaction."

Maxwell grunted and continued looking out his office window. Barnes and Anderson glanced at each other when no other comment seemed to be forthcoming. Just as Anderson was about to break the awkward silence, the colonel spoke.

"How long?"

"Sir?" asked Kim, setting down her coffee.

The colonel turned away from his view of the Rockies out the window and fixed the major with a questioning look. "How long has he been acting out-of-character, major?"

Kim thought. "It was before Laramie, sir. Not long, though . . . maybe a few days. Whatever it was it happened beforehand, sir."

Maxwell grunted, remembering Blake's antics during the uproar. "Frank, are you thinking what I'm thinking?"

Kim looked to the commander, who grimaced. "I hope not, sir." he said. "We're not ready, yet."

"Ready or not, we may not have much choice. Start making the calls, Frank. Get them prepared."

Anderson stood to attention next to the colonel's desk and saluted. "Yes, sir."

As he left, Kim looked back at Maxwell in confusion. "Calls, sir?"

Maxwell sighed as he scrubbed a hand across the stubble on his scalp.

"Too many years, Major. Too many memories." His expression hardened, and Kim forced herself not to sit back in her chair and straighten out of sheer reflex.

"Too many friends and comrades left on the field. It has to end." Kim sat still, not wanting to draw out the anger she saw on her adopted father's face.

"Dismissed, Major."

Kim stood, saluted and turned to leave. As the door opened, Maxwell spoke, and she turned to see him looking at her in a way she would call kindly if it were any other man.

"We'll figure it out, Kim. I'll get him back to you. I promise."

She nodded and strode out the door. *I believe him. God help the poor fool who gets in his way.*

CHEYENNE, WYOMING

Jason swore and threw the wireless keyboard down on his desk, spinning out of his chair to pace the well-worn carpet. Given his basement apartment's dimensions, he was barely able to get in three strides before having to turn again, but it served to calm his nerves . . . usually.

Nothing! I can't believe there's nothing about these assholes anywhere! It's like they don't exist. That shouldn't really surprise me.

He sighed and flopped down in the chair once more. More than thirty-six hours he'd spent sitting there, searching for some sign of this mystery military unit that had showed up out of nowhere in Wyoming. *Twice.*

Thirty-six hours, and he had nothing to show for it, except some vague pictures of guys in camouflage taking bodies out of a hospital, and no more idea who they were than before.

He'd used every bit of his illicit skill in computers to try and track down even the smallest shred of information, and ended up with nothing.

He sighed again and opened a desk drawer, taking a cell phone out of its pristine packaging and turning it on. Keying in a number from memory, he waited a few seconds until he heard a click from the other end, and then silence.

"It's Jason. I need to see you. I'll be there in an hour." He waited for some response, but when the silence continued, he closed the phone and grabbed his car keys on the way out of the apartment.

He locked the front door and flipped the phone into the garbage truck that was collecting out front as he walked past. He heard the satisfying crunch of the phone's destruction as he climbed into his beat-up Jeep Wrangler. *Trace that, ya bastards*, he thought as he pulled out into the street.

The agents in the car across the street glanced at each other, and the driver started the car. "Watchdog to Base. Target is on the move."

"Roger, Watchdog. Apprehend the target and return to base. Quietly."

FORT CARSON, COLORADO

"I'd suggest you leave right now, *cabrón*," said Angelo, stepping into the other man's personal space, noses an inch apart.

"Fuck you, Martinez. Stay out of this. I got no beef with you." Ames glared at Angelo as though trying to bore a hole in his head.

"You got a beef with *mi hermano*, you got a beef with me, *pendejo*."

"Then tell him to stop swaggering around here like some damned puffed-up, glory-hole wannabe."

"Angelo, let this go, he's not worth it."

"Fuck that. This asshole thinks he can pull this shit and get away with it."

"He didn't do anything. He's all talk, man. Just let it go."

"Maybe I should give him a reminder?"

"You think you can, you little wetback? Bring it!" There was the sound of a scuffle.

And that's my cue.

He walked around the corner and pretended not to notice as Ames and Martinez let go of each other's ACU and backed away. Reynolds, as cool as ever, just leaned back against the barracks wall.

"What the shit is this?" Anderson said, folding his arms and giving the men the evil eye he'd perfected in the SEALs. "Ten-hut!"

All three snapped to attention, saluting. "Now which one of you wants to tell me just what in the bloody blue fuck is going on here?" When this elicited no response from any of them, Anderson shook his head. "Just what I expected." He stepped in front of Martinez, so close he could smell what the man had for lunch. *Pizza would be my guess.*

"Captain? Nothing?"

"Just a friendly discussion, sir."

"Bullshit. You don't think I know what bullshit smells like, soldier? I know *exactly* what it smells like, and I know when I'm being fed a line of it for dinner." He glared at Ames. "And you! Petty Officer Second Class Ames himself. A Navy man. What do you have to say for yourself?"

"As the captain said, sir. Just a friendly discussion."

"Mr. Reynolds, I imagine you'll give me the same bullshit line, won't you?"

"Yes, sir."

"I thought so." Anderson turned and paced away a step, then came back. "You know, I do believe the latrines in these barracks haven't been cleaned properly in some time. You will now take care of that oversight. Requisition toothbrushes from the PX. You'll need to make sure and get them spotless." None of the men moved. "Did I stutter?" yelled Anderson. "Perhaps you're hard of hearing! Clean those fucking latrines! Now!"

As the men started to move off, Anderson grabbed Ames by one arm. "Not you." Ames stopped where he was, watching Martinez and Reynolds run off.

"I have just about had it with you, Ames."

"Sir?"

"You know exactly what I'm talking about. Enough with the bullshit. I've had my daily quota. I don't know why you have such a problem with Reynolds, and I really don't give a shit." Anderson leaned forward, staring Ames straight in the eye. "If I could, I'd follow through on our discussion from the last time. You remember, right? Chauncey's been looking a bit hungry."

Ames paled.

"Except that we can't spare your gun from the line now. So here's what you'll do. You will cease this crap immediately. If I hear even one more word, one more *idea* of a thought of a plan of a word, you will be off this base faster than I can spit. And it won't be to some nice cushy post like Greenland. I will send you somewhere *truly* horrible. Or maybe you can stay on base, and I'll have you reassigned to the Test Subject Pen over in Gardner's section."

Anderson stepped back. "That's if the others in your team don't tear you apart first, of course. Because they will know exactly what you've done here, and I can't imagine they'll be pleased. Now off you go. That latrine isn't gonna clean itself." Walking off, Anderson soon disappeared, and Ames was left to make the walk to the PX for his toothbrush.

"They're on the list now," Ames muttered. "That shithead and Reynolds will both get what's coming to em." Had anyone seen it, the smile on his face would've been reason alone to run for the hills.

"The list is growing, Colonel. We have confirmed cases in twenty-seven states now. Most of them are small outbreaks—Class One at best. Our field agents can take care of those without your teams getting involved. But we're also seeing more and more Class Two situations, and this has the Pentagon and the president worried. Greatly worried."

Gardner relaxed in the chair across from Maxwell's desk. A certain sense of superiority emanated from the man in waves, and from the way he looked around the room. The colonel guessed Gardner was sizing it up for its next occupant—himself.

Over my dead body. Of course, that may not be very far from the truth, given what's coming. With a mental snort, he turned his attention back to the man across the desk.

"What's your point, Mr. Gardner?"

"My point, Colonel?"

"Yes, your point. I'm not sure what more we can do. I've got four teams of men and women fighting to save every life they can, knowing that at any moment, they could be called on to kill one of their own from something as insignificant as a bit of saliva." Gardner sat more upright at the steel in the colonel's tone.

"I've got another six teams working up right now, and who knows how many of them will be dead in a month. That's a hundred and twenty men and women ready to fight and die for a losing cause, *Mister* Gardner. These same men and women fly all over the country, fighting monsters straight out of every horror movie you've ever seen. Things that shouldn't exist, but somehow do. And they don't just do it once, they do it over and over and over again. To protect you. To protect me. To try and save as many of the rest of us as we can." The colonel sat back in his chair, looking at Gardner. "Now, tell me just what more you think I can do."

"Ah, yes . . . well . . ." Gardner stammered under the full force of Maxwell's glare. "I'm certain you're doing all you can, but surely there are some ways to increase efficiency while at the same time providing greater research capabilities and—"

He broke off when he saw the look on the colonel's face. "I understand that the little fiasco with our last research orders caused some problems—"

Maxwell's voice was icy calm, collected and toneless as he spoke. "Some problems, Mr. Gardner?"

"I have it on good authority that it was, in fact, Mr. Blake's idea to curtail the specimen-capture order, and that he convinced Commander Anderson to rescind the order for the capture protocol."

Gardner pressed his obvious advantage. "Indeed, it seems now that Mr. Blake's mental condition is highly erratic, and therefore I've been ordered to remove him and see that he gets the best . . . care . . . possible . . ." Gardner trailed off as he realized the colonel had gone completely silent. "Colonel?"

Only more years of military discipline than he'd care to count kept Maxwell in his seat at the realization that had come with Gardner's news. *That's what he's been after all along. Gardner wants Blake for some reason. Who knows why, but I'll be damned if I'll sign him over to this . . . this . . . demon.*

"We're done here, Mr. Gardner," he said, standing.

Gardner was far too practiced a bureaucrat to show any sign that he was flustered. He stood smoothly, buttoning his jacket. "I see. Well then, please have Mr. Blake available for transport to Washington as soon as possible."

"Mr. Blake is in no condition to travel at the moment, Mr. Gardner. I will see to it that you are informed the moment that changes." Both men knew exactly what was happening. Still, perception was everything.

"Very well, Colonel. Good evening."

"Good evening, Mr. Gardner."

The colonel's assistant poked her head in the office. "Need me for anything more tonight, sir?"

"Yes, Nancy. One more thing, on your way out. Tell Frank that I'd like him to join me for my run in the morning."

"Yes, sir. Good night, sir."

Maxwell sat back at his desk, gazing out the window at the Colorado sunset. *Got you now, you bastard.*

"Hello, I'm Tabitha Greene, and this is a HealthWatch Special Report. We now have over fifty cases of a new flu outbreak confirmed in several states," said the news anchor. "I'm joined today by Dr. Alicia Givens from the Emergency Operations Center at the CDC. Thank you for being with us today, Dr. Givens."

"Thank you for having me."

"So Doctor, what can you tell us about this latest bug? And most importantly, should we be worried?"

"Well, I can tell you this. It's not the epidemic that some are calling it. Fifty cases *nationwide* is a concern, obviously, but at the same time, it's still a vanishingly small percentage of the population. We don't need to be running for the gas masks and bunkers just yet," she said with a smile, earning one in return from the news anchor.

"What people should take away from this is the same thing they should do whenever anyone is sick with a serious illness. In this case, however, there is a certain amount of special care that needs to be taken to ensure that the illness can be contained as quickly as possible.

"What we're urging everyone to do if they believe they know someone who may have contracted this illness is to call the 800 number that's on your screen now. We have been working closely with local health officials to make sure that correct procedures are followed."

"So why should they call an 800 number instead of taking the infected straight to the hospital?"

"We've been able to determine that this particular strain is extremely infectious, for one thing. Also, it can cause abnormal and yes, sometimes violent behavior in those afflicted.

"We've got special teams set up in various areas of the country, ready to take on these cases, but we want to keep the rest of the person's family or friends from coming down with it, too."

Dr. Givens looked straight at the camera. "I cannot stress this point enough: you must isolate the infected person immediately, and *then* call the 800 number.

"Someone from your area will collect them for transport to a local health facility that is equipped to handle such cases. *Do not ignore these signs. This is a very serious illness and can quickly spread.*"

The anchor swallowed hard, picking up on some of the seriousness from Dr. Givens. "Thank you for your time, Doctor."

"Absolutely not a problem."

The anchor turned back to the camera. "We'll be keeping that 800 number up for the next ten minutes, and you can also find it on our website. In other news . . ."

Alicia Givens let them lead her off the set and remove all the accoutrements of the interview. Heading for the craft table, she poured herself a cup of coffee and then pulled a small flask from her jacket pocket. Just as she splashed a dollop of the strong liquor into the dark brown liquid, she noticed the anchor standing next to her.

"Is it that bad, Dr. Givens?"

Alicia sighed and returned the flask to her pocket. "Let me put it this way, Tabitha: do you have someplace you can get away from everything and everyone?"

Tabitha nodded, puzzled. "Yes, my husband and I have a place up in the mountains we like."

"Get him and go there. Today. Take everything you'll need for a *long* stay."

Tabitha chuckled at first, but grew silent and pale when Alicia didn't join her. "R-really? That bad?" The rictus grin Alicia gave her didn't frighten her near as much as her next words.

"And, Tabby? Learn to shoot."

ESCALERO, TEXAS

The west Texas sun beat down hard on the dry plains, and a haze fell over everything. Waves of heat radiated off the tarmac of the small airstrip, and it hadn't taken more than ten minutes after they stepped off the plane before all of them were soaked in sweat.

Barnes shaded her eyes and looked down the long slope towards the town as Reynolds lay next to her, binoculars raised. *God, it's hot. I can't see a damn thing, and Martinez looks more at home than I've ever seen him.*

The skinny Army Ranger was lounging against one of the Humvees, not even breaking a sweat as his sunglasses reflected the near-desert conditions around them.

"Hot like this in L.A., Captain?" she asked him, and he grinned.

"Not really. It's hotter than this in Oaxaca, but there's sometimes a breeze from the mountains."

"I really hate you, you know." When he just grinned back at her, she chuckled. "Gunny, you got anything?" she whispered into her throat mike.

"No, ma'am. No shot at this time."

"Rachel?"

"No, ma'am. Nothing here."

Reynolds just shook his head as she glanced his way. *Well, shit. So much for easy.*

"All squads move to position." 1st Team ran down the hill, taking advantage of what cover they could. Not much of that out here, though. *Sawgrass and tumbleweeds won't stop much.*

It was a small town of about 400 people, at least four of which were confirmed to have been infected. Two stoplights, a crapload of outlying farms, and one "main street" a hundred and eighty-five miles from the nearest major city, and still close enough that the big Strykers would've caused too much attention.

So she had 1st Team to take care of the infestation. Since all of the infected were supposedly in the doctor's office, according to the sheriff, this would've been an easy mission.

Of course, nothing in this outfit is ever easy. Not that I expect that, either. I just wish David was here. Or that we knew exactly what the situation was with these rednecks.

When word got out—as it does in a town that small—that some of the folks had gotten sick, a group of 'patriots' had decided that this was just the beginning of the end, and had made good and damn sure that no 'rotten, socialist, corrupt regime' was going to send them off to meet their maker.

These good ol' boys had appropriated the local supermarket and liquor store and the nearby Escalero Guns 'N Ammo. After calling the 800 number, letting the CDC know what was going on and assuring all the infected were secure, the local sheriff had tried to intervene.

They shot him down in the middle of the street, claiming he was trying to 'poison their minds with government filth.' The fact that he had known all of them their whole lives didn't seem to make much difference. Luckily, his deputy hadn't been quite as willing to put his life on the line, and had provided them with an update when they called the station on their arrival.

"Alpha Six, Bravo Six. In position." The confirmation brought Barnes back to reality as she lay on the last ridge just north of the town. She could see pretty much the whole thing from here, not that there was much to see. She counted fifteen, maybe sixteen shops, and a few houses here and there. Bravo was approaching town from the southwest. "Two tangos in sight."

Barnes swore. Bravo team was in the best position for a direct assault on the two stores, but she hadn't expected to encounter the survivalists outside the buildings.

Maybe it's a patrol or something.

"Roger. Hold for my signal. Out."

She motioned to Reynolds, who handed her the binoculars, and she took a look at the supermarket and gun store. The supermarket lay at the top of a T intersection, the only intersection in town.

The main street ran east-west, then dead-ended at the market, and split to the north and south. The small doctor's office was next door to the supermarket, right in between it and the gun store. Bravo was sitting about half a klick southwest of the market, according to their plan.

"Gunny?" The scope on the gunnery sergeant's rifle was at least as good as her binoculars, if not better. Now that they were closer, maybe he'd have better luck.

"Two on the roof, ma'am, armed to the teeth by the looks of 'em. I count one inside the market at the front. I can't get a visual inside the ammo store. No other movement on the street, ma'am."

"What about the doctor's office?"

"No movement that I can see, ma'am."

Barnes thought for a moment. Everyone must have fled when the rednecks took over the market. *Good for us, though. Means little or no collateral damage. Not that this town's that big anyway. They probably roll up the sidewalks after work.* She sighed and pulled out her cellphone. Checking the number on her wrist, she dialed the supermarket.

"Who is this?"

"Who is *this*?" asked Barnes. She could hear the nervousness in the man's voice, along with no small amount of Texas twang.

"Junior."

Of course it is. "Well, Junior, this is Major Barnes with the United States Army."

"Uh, did you say the Army, ma'am?" She wasn't sure, but Barnes thought she heard his voice break, ever so slightly. *This guy couldn't be much out of his teens. No wonder they call him Junior.*

"I did, indeed. So why don't you put me on to the guy calling the shots there, ok?"

"Yes'm. One minute, ma'am."

At least he's polite.

"This is Orin Wilson. You're from the Army?"

"Yes, sir. I am. I need to talk to you about what's going on here."

"Well, this ain't any of y'all's affair! We know what y'all are trying to do here, poisoning us off so you can take our land and drill for oil or mine gold or some other such crap. Trying to keep us from our rightful piece of the profit, too."

Barnes stared at the phone, glancing at Reynolds, also puzzled. *What the hell?*

"Uh, Mr. Wilson, we were given to understand that you had a disagreement with us about trying to kill off the whole town."

"One second, Ms. Barnes." She heard the sound of the receiver being covered with a hand, then a muffled, "Go on now, git! I'll call ya if I need ya," followed by a slamming door.

"My apologies, Ms. Barnes. Some things are better discussed without the ears of one's compatriots."

Kim was only mildly surprised at this point. "Yes, sir, they are. So if I read you correctly, you're not particularly interested in what's happening to these townsfolk?"

"Not even slightly, ma'am."

"Well, let's make one thing perfectly clear. I'm not here for you."

It was Wilson's turn to pause for thought. "I see."

"So, I'll make you a deal, Mr. Wilson. If you bring all your boys back inside, and let my people take care of our business, we just might miss you slippin' out the back door, if you take my meaning." She paused for a moment, and continued in a somewhat more forceful tone and manner. "Otherwise, Mr. Wilson, we are going to come in and kill every last one of you."

Silence greeted her demand for a moment. "I see. I must say, Ms. Barnes, this is not the negotiating style I was expecting to be dealing with today."

"I imagine not. There is one caveat, though, Mr. Wilson."

"Let me guess: you want the man who shot Sheriff Calton."

"Indeed."

"Well, I think that can be arranged, Ms. Barnes. When should I be expecting the festivities to start?"

"As soon as you withdraw your men and I've confirmed that."

"We'll leave the overly enthusiastic young man who shot Sheriff Calton inside for you when we leave. Do with him as you will. Goodbye, Ms. Barnes."

"Goodbye, Mr. Wilson."

Reynolds just shrugged when she looked over at him. "We have more important shit to worry about, ma'am."

"Yes, we do, Tommy. Yes, we do." She raised her binos again, and whispered into her mike. "Gunny, can you confirm they're leaving the roof?"

"Yes, ma'am. I can't see any of the targets, ma'am."

"Very well. Bravo Six, Alpha Six."

"Bravo Six, go."

"All right, Jake, here's the deal." She explained the situation, including her deal with Orin Wilson and the changes to the plan, and heard him snort. "Problems, soldier?"

"No, ma'am. We'll move in and take up positions, then retrieve the package once they've left."

"Right. As far as I know, all of the infected are still in the doctor's office. We'll move on that target and keep you apprised."

"Yes, ma'am. Bravo out."

A moment later, there was a transmission from Gaines. "Movement," he said. "Friendlies."

"Alpha, go!"

Alpha squad swept down from the ridgeline and onto the street. Gaines clambered up a fire escape and took position on the roof of one of the buildings, Eaton ever-present at his side—in this case, serving as his spotter.

A sudden scream from one side riveted Kim's attention and stopped the forward progress of the whole team. "Martinez, Reynolds, go."

"Roger," said Angelo. The pair peeled away to investigate the noise as the squads surrounded the doctor's office. Barnes could see Bravo moving into position on her right as she crouched across the street from the doctor's, covering the front door.

"Alpha Six, Alpha Four."

"Go ahead, Angelo."

"Turns out it was a lady hiding in one of the shops, ma'am. She saw us and thought we were with the others." The scorn in his voice was evident. "I guess the uniforms didn't make an impression."

"Let her go and take position out here."

"Yes, ma'am."

"Alpha Six, Bravo Six."

"Go ahead."

"Package is secure, tangos have amscrayed."

"Roger, standby," she said. "Alpha squad, engage."

The AEGIS personnel were maintaining a perimeter around the doctor's office now that everything was said and done, and Barnes smiled as Commander Powell walked up with his protesting prisoner.

"I didn't do nothin', officer. Not a thing. They hornswaggled me into this here crap!"

I'd recognize the break in that voice anywhere. He can't be any more than twenty. She shook her head and chuckled as Powell released him in front of her.

"Let me guess: Junior, is it?" she said, smiling.

He gulped and nodded. "Uh, yes'm. Please, *please* don't kill me, ma'am."

"Settle down, kid. I'm not going to kill you. I'm going to go out on a limb here and figure you aren't the one that shot Sheriff Calton, either."

Junior's eyes widened and he fell to his knees, still handcuffed, and started blubbering. "No! I never shot no one before! I *liked* the sheriff! He was always nice to me."

Kim shook her head, and looked west toward the market as the squeal of tires came from down the block. What was surely the only sheriff's car in the county came roaring around the corner and stopped short when the machine guns of nearly all the Army soldiers were suddenly leveled at it.

Very, very slowly, the largest black man Barnes had ever seen opened the door and got out, his hands on his head. His badge marked him as a deputy, but none of the AEGIS personnel were moved in the slightest.

"Stand fast! Lower your weapons!" shouted Barnes, in her best parade-ground imitation of Colonel Maxwell. *Not bad, if I do say so myself.*

The soldiers lowered their weapons.

She motioned the deputy over, and he shook himself as if to reconcile the reality of the Army in his small town, and . . . well, *moseyed* on over. *That's the first time I've ever seen anyone do that in person. It looks . . . uncomfortable.*

"Deputy Brentwood, I presume?" she asked, holding out a hand. As he shook it, she could tell he was being careful not to squeeze too tight. It wasn't often that she had to look up at a man, but this big boy was every bit of six-four, if not six-six.

"Yes'm, that'd be me. But y'all can call me Justin," he said, smiling. "I see you've cleaned up our mess hereabouts."

"Something like that. We'll be taking those folks with us," she said, nodding in the direction of the doctor's office. "Nothing more to be done for them now. This guy, however . . ." Turning to Junior, she pulled him onto his feet. "He's all yours. One of the boys from the supermarket earlier."

Deputy Brentwood scowled. "I see." He appeared to be fighting the urge to deck the kid right there, but before he could, Barnes took his arm and led him a short distance away.

"Before you go all 'Texas justice' on him, Deputy Brentwood—"

"Call me Justin, please."

"Okay, Justin, I believe that this kid had absolutely nothing to do with the shooting of the sheriff, and little to do with the market at all. He says he was forced to join, and I, for one, believe him.

I mean, look at him." They both glanced back at the kid and Brentwood snorted as they turned their backs to him.

"What can you tell me?"

"Orin Wilson."

Barnes grinned as the deputy's eyebrows shot up.

"I guess you know him. I would bet you money that he's the man that shot Calton. And it doesn't have anything to do with the government or any of that. He wanted a ransom, pure and simple."

Justin looked thoughtful. "You're probably right. Still, we need to do something with him. Where is he?"

Kim sighed. "I had to let him go," she said, staring him down as he grew angry. "*I had to*, Justin. Or else we'd be dealing with who knows how many dead bodies instead of just six."

It was the deputy's turn to sigh as she explained what had happened. She glossed over the part about walkers, mentioning only that they'd found the infected all deceased, and would be returning them to the CDC for analysis. He calmed down, and took his hat off and ran a hand over his thinning hair.

"All right," he said, putting his hat back on. "I'll lock this kid up, put him through the wringer a bit, and see if I can't flush out Wilson that way. If not, I'll let him go, but only when I know for sure I'll never see him in my jail again."

"Good. Now, have you had any reports of anything else like this in the area?" she asked, pointing to the bagged dead. "Anything even *sort of* similar?"

The deputy shook his head. "No, ma'am. As far as I know, everyone who was sick was brought here. There were a couple more between the time we called and the time y'all got here, but I guess you know that. Say, why is the Army involved in all of this?"

"Have you ever heard of USAMRIID, Deputy?"

"No, ma'am, I have not."

"Well, then, to keep it simple, we're helping out our friends at the CDC with some extra manpower. This is a pretty nasty one, and they're not equipped to handle some of the violence we've seen from the infected." She glanced around as a muffled *whoosh* came from the doctor's office, and laid a hand on the deputy's arm as he started to call for the fire department.

"Justin, like I said, this is a very nasty bug."

He looked at her, searching for the lie, and when he didn't find it, settled down.

"You'll need to let the office there burn itself out. Since it's free-standing and there's plenty of space around it, you should be fine. Bring in your fire team to keep it from spreading, but make sure they let it burn all the way. There's no sense taking a chance at infection."

He sighed again. "Okay. I guess y'all know what's going on better than I do."

Barnes nodded and shook his hand. "You're a good man, *Sheriff* Brentwood."

Justin shook his head as they walked back to the others. "No, ma'am. But I'm gonna try."

"Sometimes, Justin, that's all we can do."

Chapter Eighteen

FORT CARSON, COLORADO

"IS THIS LINE SECURE, MR. Gardner?"

"I assure you, sir, this line is as secure as they come."

"Good, very good. Then I can assume from your call that you have acquired more of the items we discussed?"

"Yes, sir, Mr. Hwong. Quite a few, actually."

"I see. First or second type, Mr. Gardner?"

"The first type, sir. Unfortunately, it has proven . . . difficult to obtain the second type recently."

"You are aware that we seek those most of all, are you not?"

"Of course, sir. Of course. I am most appreciative of your patience in the matter, sir. I expect that we shall be able to collect more . . . items . . . for you soon, with the situation being what it is."

"As you should be. It seems we could conduct our own operations nearby, what with current events. Therefore, we have decided to offer you somewhat less for future purchases, Mr. Gardner. I'm sure you can understand. It's simple supply and demand, after all."

Gardner maintained the even tone in his voice and put on a show for his buyer. *Like I give a damn about the money.*

"That is unfortunate news, sir, but it will not deter me from providing you with top-quality items."

"Very well, Mr. Gardner. We shall expect the next shipment soon."

"Already on its way, sir."

"Good. You will receive payment per our agreement. Good day, Mr. Gardner."

"And you, sir."

"Sir! I have something for you, sir," said Sam Lansford as he entered Colonel Maxwell's office. He noted the presence of Commander Anderson and snapped to a salute, realizing his mistake. Maxwell glanced at Anderson, who was trying to hide a smile with his back turned to the young private, and returned the salute.

"Yes, Private, I'm sure you do. Walk with us, will you?"

For the first time, Lansford noticed that Maxwell and Anderson were dressed in sweats and hoodies, obviously preparing for a morning run. He sighed, preparing to run with them as all three walked outside. Nancy nodded at them and continued her phone call—supply requisitions, from the sound of it.

As they reached the path outside the office, the two officers broke into a slow jog, forcing Lansford to keep up with them.

"Well, Sam, what have you got for me?" asked Maxwell. When the private glanced at Anderson, he continued. "Don't worry, Sam. He's cleared."

"Yes, sir," said the private, already beginning to feel the strain of unfamiliar exercise creeping in. *That's what a desk job buys you, I guess.* "It appears that Gardner is now involved with North Korea, sir." He held out the small tape player for Maxwell, who took it and pressed Play.

As the conversation continued, Maxwell's face got darker, and Anderson's—well, the private had thought the commander's face was chiseled in stone before, but now it actually scared him a bit.

"Very well, Private. You're dismissed."

Lansford gave a running salute and stopped, breathing hard, staring in wonder at the two older men who hadn't even broken a sweat. *I need more exercise.* He headed back to his office.

"Well, Frank, what do you think?" said Maxwell.

"I think the fecal matter is about to impact the rotary air impeller, sir."

"I think you're right, and for once it's not going to be us standing in front it getting covered. Have you talked to the others?"

"Most of them. I'm still waiting on two or three, but I expect them to confirm in the next day or so."

"Good. Hopefully we'll be ready to go by the end of the week." He sighed, shaking his head as they made the turn by the mess hall. "Did you ever think it would come to this, Frank?"

"I didn't want to sir, but, yes, I thought it might."

"You knew Gardner was dirty?"

"Not him specifically, sir, but if it wasn't him it would've been someone else. It's human nature, sir."

Maxwell glanced at his executive officer. "Sometimes, Frank, you really depress the shit out of me, you know that?"

"Yes, sir. It's my job, sir."

"Welcome to HealthWatch. I'm Tabitha Greene. Tonight, our top story is from southeast Asia, where a massive outbreak of the new flu virus is being reported in southern Cambodia."

She turned just slightly to face another camera, and a helpful map of Cambodia appeared on-screen.

"Seventy miles south of Phnom Penh, a small community named Phumĭ Rôménh has been decimated by what some are calling the next biblical plague. Of the approximately six hundred residents, nearly all have been confirmed to have this new strain of flu.

"The Royal Cambodian Army has been mobilized to cordon off and quarantine the area, and no one is being allowed in or out. Food, water and medical supplies are being air-dropped." Another turn, and a general map of Southeast Asia appeared over Tabitha's shoulder.

"Reports continue to come in from other countries as the flu outbreak spreads. The current global death toll is well into the hundreds, with nearly half of those in the US. The CDC has asked that we remind all citizens who think that they or someone they know may have contracted this illness to report it immediately to the 800 number on your screen. Remember, this is a *highly* contagious illness, so isolation is imperative.

"I'm Tabitha Greene, and this is HealthWatch."

NORTHWEST WASHINGTON STATE

"Do you think this looks anything like what Captain Trace saw way back when?" asked Gaines as he and the rest of Alpha squad trudged through the snow.

"I doubt it, Gunny," said Reynolds. "I keep feeling like the next time I turn around I'll see the Space Needle."

"It's too cold up here, man. People weren't meant to live in conditions like this," said Martinez. "What the fuck is wrong with *gringos*?"

"If you ladies will stop jawing for half a damn minute, I need to report in," said Eaton, and ignored the resulting snickers. "Alpha Six, Alpha Three."

"Alpha Six, go ahead."

"No contacts, ma'am, and, respectfully, we're freezing our balls off out here."

"At least we know who has 'em now," Reynolds stage-whispered to Martinez, who chuckled. This, of course, earned them both glares from the corporal and Gaines.

"Acknowledged. You are clear to RTB."

"Roger, Alpha Six, we are RTB."

"Yes! Last one to the Hummer buys the beer." Reynolds shot off like a cannon. Even Eaton laughed as she raced ahead of Martinez and Gaines, who was packing the fifty-pound sniper rifle. They pounded through the snow toward the parked Humvee, and, as expected, Gaines was last. Throwing their gear in the back, they piled in and roared off, slipping and sliding down a steep embankment. Minutes later, they arrived back at the temporary command post set up just outside the small mountain town of Jackson River, population 1,312—and falling.

"Sergeant Eaton reporting as ordered, ma'am," said Rachel as she arrived in the command tent. Kimberly looked over at her and nodded.

"Good. I need Alpha squad here, at the doctor's," said the tall team commander, pointing at a tactical map spread on the table. She looked over at 2nd Team's commander, Lawrence Greer. "Captain, it seems the highest concentration of walkers is around the mall, here. What do you think about having Charlie secure that location?"

Captain Greer looked over the map and ran a hand over his shaved scalp. "Well, it's a smallish structure, so it can't hold too many of them. Do we have a free hand here?" he asked, looking up.

Barnes nodded. "That's what the colonel said. 'Use any and all means.' What are you thinking?"

"To be honest, I don't know that it's worth our time to secure the inside of it, or that it would be safe with just the one squad. I say we secure a perimeter, then lase it and blow the whole damned thing."

Barnes thought for barely a minute. "Agreed, but let's see if we can find out if there are any survivors in there first. Can we tap into the security systems? Where's Ivanovich?"

Jake Powell, commander of Bravo squad, stepped outside to shout and whistle sharply. Moments later, a slim young man trotted into the command tent and saluted Kimberly. "Yes, ma'am."

Barnes returned the salute. "Arkady, I need to know—can you break into the CCTV signal of the mall?"

With a huge grin, the young man nodded. "Easy as pie, ma'am."

"Good. You're temporarily detached to Captain Greer."

"Yes, ma'am," he said, saluting again. "I'll go get my gear, ma'am."

"What about the perimeter, Major?" Greer asked, turning back to Kimberly.

"Let's keep Bravo on it for now. Contact once you've secured the mall, Captain."

It was Greer's turn to salute. "Yes, ma'am!" he said, then about-faced and left. Kim looked at her remaining squad leaders.

"Jake, I know I don't have to tell you this, but I'm going to anyway. I want you to watch Forrest, and watch *out* for her. Whatever she's seen now, she's not fully trained, so it's touch and go at this point. Keep an eye out."

"Yes, ma'am."

"You all know your assignments. Dismissed."

As her people dispersed, Kim walked out of the tent and looked out over the river valley where the town was located. It had been easy to quarantine the town, even with only two teams. Hell, there was only one road in. The hard part was the back side of the town: it was all forest. Delta squad was not going to have a good patrol out there.

Kim began to wonder about Captain Trace, as well, as she envisioned the hunting camps that had no doubt been in this area over a hundred years prior. *This is where it began. AEGIS was created here.*

Looking down at the town, she felt fortunate in a small way. *At least we're not fighting them with muskets.*

"Major?" came a call from the tent.

Kim took a deep breath and turned around. "Yes, Specialist?" The comm specialist Maxwell had sent with her handed her a small note. "Flash traffic from command, ma'am."

Kim took the note and glanced at it, sighing as she read it. "Thank you, Sergeant."

"Yes, ma'am."

Kim read the note again, then destroyed it and toggled her microphone. "Bravo Six, Alpha Six."

"Bravo Six, go ahead."

"Flash traffic from command. There are confirmed cases in all fifty states now. Florida is reporting ten cases, Jake."

Another pause. "Yes, ma'am."

"I'm sure your family is fine. Most of the cases are outside of Tallahassee."

"I hope so, ma'am. Ma'am, we've reached the mall."

"Very well. Continue your mission."

"Yes, ma'am. And . . . thank you, ma'am."

"You're welcome."

FORT CARSON, COLORADO

"Success, Major?" asked Colonel Maxwell.

"Yes, sir. We didn't lose anyone, not even to frostbite—although there were times we thought that might not be the case, sir."

Maxwell chuckled. "They can be a bitch, those winter patrols. I'm glad you got out of it okay, though."

"Yes, sir."

"How'd the new girl do? Forrest?"

"Yes, sir. She did very well, sir. We didn't have any injuries on this go-round, so we didn't get to see her treat anyone, but she was right there in the thick of it with the rest of Bravo Squad. She had a count of four with two assists, if I remember correctly, sir."

Maxwell's eyebrows rose. "Fired on six of 'em, did she? Well, it appears you chose well, Major."

"Yes, sir. It appears so, sir."

Maxwell sighed and motioned for Kim to sit as he took his own chair. "Unfortunately for us all, things aren't going so well everywhere else. We're getting more and more calls and we're spread too thin. We got word from higher today," he said, sliding a memo across his desk.

As she took and read it, she began nodding. "Fifth through Tenth teams are now officially activated as of 0800 hours today. They didn't have the training opportunities the rest of you did, so we'll have to watch them a little closer. Especially since we lost Chauncey."

Kim shuddered at her own memories of the 'acclimatization training' she'd undergone with the captive walker. "Have they been through everything else?"

Maxwell shook his head. "Pretty much just the basics. Briefing on the history, facts about the walkers, the same background material the first four teams got. Beyond that, they're on their own. There's just no time to train them adequately before getting them out there. We're too short-handed now."

"All we can do is try, sir," Kim said, putting down the activation order just as the phone rang and, at the same time, there was a knock at the door.

Maxwell picked up the phone first. "Just a sec, Nancy," he said into the receiver. "Enter!" he called to the door. Anderson entered and sat down at Maxwell's indication.

"Go ahead, Nancy," Maxwell said into the phone. "Put him through, please." Maxwell sat up straight in his chair, and Anderson and Barnes shared a glance.

"Higher?" she whispered. Anderson nodded and smiled. "What? What is it?" Anderson shook his head, putting a finger across his lips and pointing at the phone in Maxwell's hand.

"Yes, sir. I see. And these notifications will start next week? Yes, sir. You too, sir." Maxwell started to hang up, but the voice on the other end continued. "Sir? Yes, sir, he's here. Yes, sir."

Maxwell punched the speakerphone button and placed the handset in its cradle, looking curiously at Anderson across the desk. As though at the bottom of a well, the voice from what Kim could only assume was the Pentagon echoed in the smallish office.

"Commander Anderson, this is General Morrison. Are you ready?"

"Yes, sir."

"Very well. You may give it to him now." Anderson stood, saluted, and standing ramrod-straight, slid a small box across the desk to Maxwell. Barnes stood as well, standing at attention after a nod from Anderson. As he, too, stood, Maxwell opened the box. Kim could see the glint from two silver stars, and couldn't help but smile.

"Colonel George Maxwell," continued Morrison, "for conduct consistently and continuously exemplifying everything that the United States Army stands for over the course of more than twenty years, and for your commitment to the safety and prosperity of this nation and her people, I hereby announce your promotion to the grade of brigadier general."

Commander Anderson moved around the desk, taking the box from the general and pinning the stars to the lapels on Maxwell's uniform after removing the birds already there.

"Congratulations, George. I would have rather done it in person, but you understand," continued Morrison.

"Yes, sir. Thank you, sir," Maxwell managed to choke out a second later, his face pink.

"Now take me off speaker."

"Yes, sir." Maxwell picked up the phone. "Yes, sir. No sir. Will do, sir. Thank you, sir. You too, sir." He hung up the phone and turned to Anderson, demanding, "How long have you known, Frank?"

Anderson was grinning ear to ear as he took his seat. "Oh, about a week, ever since I got your stars in the post. Nancy knew, since the paperwork came to her, of course. But Morrison wanted it to be a surprise, so he ordered me not to mention it, sir."

Maxwell chuckled. "I bet. He's like that." He took his seat and allowed himself to bask for just a moment in the unexpected good news, sharing a pleased-as-punch grin with his old friends.

Soon enough, Maxwell took a deep breath and shook it off.

"As nice as this is, folks, it doesn't change anything. We're still short-handed and things are just going to get worse from here." He handed Anderson a small packet of papers. "Frank, I want you to share this with the rest of the team leaders, but since Kim's here already . . ."

He stood and walked to the window. "It's starting next week. Notification letters are going out—hand-delivered, no less—to those scientists and specialists who have been pre-selected to go into the AEGIS bunkers. It details the situation, what's really going on, that is, and what we're doing to survive."

"Why so early, sir?" asked Kim.

"We're giving them the chance to say no, Major," Anderson replied as he glanced over the paperwork.

"Is that a good idea, sir?"

"What else can we do, Kim?" said Maxwell. "Lock them up if they don't agree to go along with us? I'm ashamed to say that the idea was considered, but some of us still remember the stories of our fathers about the Japanese internment camps during WWII. We're not going to make the same mistake again."

"What if they go public with what they know, then?'

"Then we discredit them. As loudly and as publicly as possible. Make up wild stories so even their own husbands and wives won't believe them."

Kim nodded. "I suppose that could work. Still, if enough of them banded together . . ."

Maxwell turned and looked at her, his face as grim as she'd ever seen it. "We can't allow a mass panic before we officially release the news, Kim. The president has authorized Gardner and his people, and by extension us, to use whatever means are necessary to ensure public order until that time. And we all know what that means."

Kim was dumbstruck. "But . . . but that's *monstrous*! Killing our own people? Who the hell does he think he is to authorize something like that? What gives him the right?"

Maxwell raised an eyebrow at her. "*We* gave him the right, Kim, when we elected him. It's a national security matter, clear and present danger, that sort of thing."

Getting a hold on herself, Kim took some deep breaths. "Yes, sir. I see your point, sir. Permission to speak freely, sir?"

Maxwell glanced at Anderson, standing behind Barnes, who shrugged.

"Go ahead, Major."

"This fucking sucks, sir. And I have to say, I will refuse any order that requires me to fire on unarmed, non-infected civilians, except in self-defense." Kim was caught by surprise again as Maxwell smiled, winked at her, then pointed to the ceiling and cupped his ear.

His office is bugged. Holy shit.

"Major, in future, I'd watch your tone, even when 'speaking freely.'" Maxwell admonished, still smiling. "You will follow all orders as they are given or I will have you arrested. Do you understand me, soldier?"

"Yes, sir."

"Good. Then you are dismissed, Major." Catching her eye, he tapped his watch slowly with three fingers. She looked confused for a second and then nodded.

"Yes, sir," she said, exiting the office. Maxwell looked over at Anderson, who nodded and smiled, then followed Barnes out the door. As the door shut behind them, Maxwell turned back to the window.

There's no going back now. Let's hope she's still the super-smart little girl from Arizona that I met all those years ago.

Chapter Nineteen

Fort Carson, Colorado

ON HER WAY OUT OF the barracks moments later, Kim was surprised to see Anderson just outside the exit door. "Ready to go, Major?" he asked.

She nodded. "Yes, sir."

"Good. Get in," he said, indicating the waiting Humvee. As she took the shotgun seat, Anderson walked around to the driver. "Helipad 4, Private."

"Yes, sir."

Anderson watched the Humvee as it headed off, spraying snow and muck. *I hope George knows what he's doing.*

As they neared Helipad 4, Kim saw a Black Hawk warming up, the rotors turning slow. It wasn't until she climbed aboard that she saw Maxwell inside at the controls. He indicated for her to take the co-pilot seat.

"Sir, I'm not checked out on this aircraft."

"Don't worry about it, Major. I've had well over a thousand hours in these birds. We'll be fine."

Kim buckled on the extra helmet and settled the seat's straps around her, snugging them good and tight. She took a deep breath. "Yes, sir. Ready when you are."

Maxwell got clearance from the tower and they took off, headed west. As they flew out over foothills, the day turned to evening. The sunset was gorgeous. It looked like Maxwell was also enjoying it, and she realized just how few sunsets she might be seeing.

Better make the most of it.

Maxwell lowered the helicopter until they touched down in a small meadow, and motioned for her to get out. They stepped away from the chopper and Barnes noticed a folder in his hand.

"Long way to come for a briefing, sir," she said, looking at him with a raised eyebrow.

"This ain't your typical mission brief, Major. And we can't exactly talk in my office, or in most of the base, for that matter. Take a seat," he said, motioning to a nearby rock formation, sitting down as well.

"Major . . . Kim . . . the full extent of what I'm about to tell you is known only to two people other than you and me: Commander Anderson and the president. There are others who know some of it, but the whole enchilada is just between us. Is that understood?"

Kim nodded. "Understood, sir."

"Good," he said, and handed her the file. He watched her as she opened it and paged through the information inside. Her expression darkened with every page, until he could see that she was shaking with rage.

"Damn Gardner. Damn him straight to hell."

"Calm down, Major."

Kim looked back up at him, and Maxwell recoiled, if only a bit. *I've never seen her this pissed off. And it's only going to get worse.* He held her gaze until she sat back and took another deep breath and calmed down, at least somewhat.

"There's something you haven't seen yet, Kimberly."

"Is it worse than that smug, self-centered, arrogant and idiotic bastard actually selling zombies to the North Koreans? Or deliberately experimenting on our own people?"

"Yes."

She snorted, and he continued. "Maybe not for the world, but for you, yes. There is worse."

She sobered, then glanced down. "Do I want to keep going?"

"As your father," he said, "I don't want you to. But I know you, and I know you couldn't live with yourself if you didn't know it all. I just want you to know before you go down this particular rabbit hole that I'm here for you, and so is Mary. And Johnny. Not to mention David."

Kim nodded. "That means a lot."

"Good."

As she continued to read the file, Maxwell could see she was getting upset again, and then suddenly she stopped as she reached what he knew would either send her over the edge or galvanize her into action. He hoped it was the latter, but you could never tell.

It was a full-size 8x10 glossy image of a brightly-lit cell, with a small prisoner standing in one corner. There was no bed, no toilet, nothing other than four blank walls and some chains leading to the diminutive figure's wrists and ankles from rings bolted into the wall.

Kim looked up at Maxwell, and the tears in her eyes shone with the reflected sunset's light. "How could he? Is he even human?"

"We just got this a couple days ago. That's why you're hearing about this now."

"You know this . . . this is what broke David, right? All the other stuff he could handle, but this . . ." She reached out a hand as though to stroke the hair of the small boy pictured on the page.

"Oh, Eric. Oh, God." Dropping the folder on the ground, Kim staggered off, wrapping her arms around herself to ward off not the cold mountain air, but the chill from inside. Maxwell started to follow, and then stood where he was when Kim stopped a few yards away and fell to her knees.

She has to win this fight on her own. I can't help her with this.

He was never sure how long they stood there like that, his adopted daughter in pain and suffering while he could do nothing but watch.

Eventually, Kim stood up and wiped her eyes, then came back over and helped Maxwell collect the remnants of the file.

"That's what caused that lab tech Chauncey got hold of to turn so quickly."

Maxwell nodded. "That's what we believe. He and his people have modified a sample from Eric to attempt to make a version of the disease that makes walkers faster. We believe the idea was to use them as biological weapons. Chauncey was one of their first experiments."

"What does Eric have to do with that, though?"

"We believe that because of the hormones in children's bodies, especially as they approach puberty, the prion acts differently on their systems. Rather than causing them to deteriorate and slowly putrefy, it appears to stimulate muscle growth and adrenaline reflexes, making them much faster."

"No wonder he wanted us to capture them 'alive.' He needed more subjects."

"Exactly, and he needs more *fast* ones if he's going to make them adequate biological weapons. Imagine the terror the average walker would cause if it was dropped on a unit . . . then picture a whole squad or platoon of them . . . then imagine how much worse it'd be if they could *all* move that fast."

Kim shuddered at the thought. "When did you know, sir?" She paused, and reached out to him. "Oh God, was Mary—did she—she couldn't—"

Maxwell shook his head. "No, she didn't know and she wasn't a part of it. She still doesn't know. Gardner sectioned off part of the lab with those he could trust to work on his little side projects, and she never got in. The fact that he did that was enough to raise some red flags for her, though, and she let me and Frank know, too. She helped us as much as she could, but I wanted to spare her this."

"She deserves to know the truth."

"She does. And I'll tell her. Eventually. But right now, I need her focused on helping to get the research ready for transport, and keeping Gardner in the dark about everything, even if she doesn't know she's doing it."

"But you and Frank. When did you two figure it out?"

"Frank and I suspected something from the beginning, actually. How could anyone meet Gardner and *not* think he was up to something? The day he arrived on the base and took over from Mary—this was while 1st Team was inactive—we started getting a nasty vibe from him. But we never had anything concrete. Not until he went off the deep end and tried to get me court-martialed or transferred after I fought him on the whole Tremaine thing."

"He didn't!"

"He did. He went all the way up the chain, as far as he could. Which is pretty far, considering. The Secretary is practically in his back pocket at this point."

Kim snorted. "I don't know who to feel sorry for, there."

"I know what you mean. Problem is, Gardner and his cronies managed to snag some of the top spots in Bunker Five—the president's bunker in Pennsylvania—using his connections."

"But not the president, sir?"

Maxwell grinned. "Nope, although Gardner thinks SecDef has his ear. He's our man, though, and saw right through Gardner's bullshit as fast as Frank and I did."

"So what's the plan, then?"

"We've got a few high-placed friends in various outfits. Frank has been getting in touch with them for a couple of weeks, and getting them ready to move against Gardner's people. We've identified quite a few—most of them, we think—thanks to Lansford, but Frank's also been cozying up to Gardner just in case."

"That storm-out a while back?"

"All part of the plan. Gardner brought him in on some minor things after that, thinking he could turn him, since Frank was so obviously pissed."

"When do we move?"

"We're biding our time, waiting until everything's in place. We're going to need concrete evidence of more than just some experiments on walkers to take Gardner down for good. We have a lot of evidence, but it's all circumstantial. We don't have anything on him *directly*. We've got eyes on him almost all the time, though. So it shouldn't be too long. He's arrogant and over-confident, and we're using that against him."

"Good. How can I help?"

"I'll need you there when it all goes down, Kim. I promise you'll be a part of it. But, for now, what I really need you to do is get David back to us. Now that we know what sent him over, I'm thinking we can bring him back. Talk to Forrest and see if she'd be willing to give you a hand. Maybe something familiar can help." Maxwell sighed and put a hand on her shoulder.

"Where I'm *really* going to need your help, though, is when and if we *do* get him back: one way or another, he's going to find out about Gardner, if he doesn't know already."

"Shit. I hadn't thought of that. He's going to . . . well, sir, I wouldn't want to be Gardner."

"I know he's going to have other ideas about what needs to happen, and that's the problem. Gardner's the only one who knows where all the bodies are buried . . . in this case, literally. We need him alive. I'm asking you to see to it that he stays that way."

Seeing the expression on her face, his own softened. "I know that won't be easy, and I know I'm asking you to make a supremely difficult choice. But it has to be done. We have to do this the right way, Kim."

Kim hesitated. "Sir, I . . ." She paused. "Yes, sir."

"Good. Now let's get back. I'm freezing my ass off out here."

"Yes, sir."

"So that's the long and the short of it, Morena," said Kim, sitting on the edge of Morena Forrest's bunk in the barracks. Michael played on the floor as the two women talked.

"So you think that seeing us brought back memories and sent him into a catatonic state?" asked Morena.

"Mary and I are fairly sure of it."

"And you want us to talk to him, to try and break him out of it?"

"Yes. We need him back, Morena. He's still the most experienced one of us, and he's in a unique position to help us fight this war."

"I'm not sure this is a good idea. What if he gets attached to us, or somehow wakes up and thinks that I'm . . . Rebecca? Or that Michael is Eric?"

"I have to admit that the thought crossed my mind, and Dr. Adamsdóttir thinks it's a possibility, but a very remote one. And we have to try."

Morena looked at Michael, so happy in that moment, and realized what she would give to stay in that happiness forever, with no thoughts of zombies or the end of the world or any of it. *But that can't happen. Not for any of us. Not anymore.*

Kim put a hand on Morena's shoulder, recapturing her attention. Kim had tears in her eyes, and couldn't seem to bring herself to speak. She looked down, picking at her nails. "It's more than the mission, though," she finally said, her voice breaking. "I need him back, Morena. I miss him."

Morena took one of Kim's hands and held it tightly. "I know, Kim. I know. But this . . ." She sighed, and released Kim's hand. "I . . . I'll think about it. That's all I can promise you now."

Kim wiped the tears from her eyes and smiled. "That's all I can ask. Just don't take too long thinking. We don't have a lot of time."

"Is the new subject ready?" Gardner asked one of the faceless—at least to him—technicians who populated his labs. He looked through the glass at the walker. The suit and tie were all but shreds at this point, but it still stood tall and gruesome.

"Yes, sir. We've prepared the training room as per your orders." The technician swallowed. "Sir, about this configuration—"

Gardner turned to the technician, bringing the full force of his glaring persona to bear on the hapless little man. "Yes?"

To his credit, this tech was braver than the others.

"Well, sir, it's just that if the soldiers aren't *very* careful, then this sort of configuration could lead to an accide—" He broke off as Gardner moved forward, overshadowing the small man by a good six to eight inches.

He could only imagine what the technician saw in his gaze. He'd spent years working on perfecting that reptilian glare, and it had a different impact on everyone.

For this man, it was the same as for so many: a tremor in his hands, an inability to meet that same glare. "Shhh, there, there," Gardner said. "No need to worry. Let's take a walk and we can discuss it. Just give me a second here."

The taller man leaned over his desk, checking the guard's duty roster lying next to his computer. *Perfect. I don't know how this little shit is piecing this stuff together, but we can't have that, now can we, Hank, old buddy? No, we can't.*

"So you can see . . ." Gardner said, pausing. "I'm sorry, your name again?"

"Williams, sir."

"So you can see, Williams, that everything will be just fine. I'll take care of any lingering issues and we'll get this addressed as soon as we can."

As they walked down the hallway, his arm around the young technician's shoulders in a friendly, if unnerving, gesture, Gardner noticed the door at the end and the guard leaving his post a bit early.

Just as I'd hoped. Incompetence, just when I need it.

"Anyway, Williams . . . can I call you Brett? Anyway, Brett, I'm sure you'll see this was all just a misunderstanding. One second, please." He palmed open the security lock for the door, blocking Brett's view into the room as it opened. "At least, that's what I'll tell everyone."

He stepped to the side and shoved the technician through the door, palming the lock again just as the screams began, only to be cut off by the heavy soundproofing as the door closed once more.

Last damn time he'll argue with me. He nodded to the replacement guard just walking up to take his post.

"Evening, sir. Colonel Maxwell wanted me to give you this, sir." The guard extended a folded message.

"Very well," Gardner said, taking the paper and placing it in his coat pocket. As Gardner turned to walk away, the guard spoke again. "Sir, he seemed rather . . . insistent. Said it was urgent, sir."

Gardner sighed. "I see. Thank you." He opened the message as he began walking back to his office. *Paperwork? Now? What the hell is he thinking?*

He stopped at a nearby desk and picked up the phone, dialing the colonel's extension from memory. "Listen, George, I'm afraid I can't . . . No, I don't . . . There's an urgent . . . Look, you can't talk to me . . . I see. Well, that's that then. I'm on my way."

Gardner glanced up at the camera facing the door he'd just come from, the one marked "DANGER: Test Subject Pen." *It's not like anyone knows*, he thought. *I can always erase the footage later.* He strode off toward the colonel's office.

As he sat back down at his desk an hour later, Gardner tensed as he looked at his desk. *Something isn't right . . . something's been moved . . .*

In a panic, he accessed the security logs from the surveillance system. *Nothing. The file's still there, and hasn't been tampered with.* He relaxed—for Gardner—and proceeded to erase several files at random intervals from the camera outside the test pen, including the one from earlier that evening. Then he pressed the intercom on his phone.

"Sam, come in here, would you?"

The skinny youth came into the office and, at Gardner's urging, sat down at one of the chairs in front of the desk. Gardner studied him in silence for a moment.

"Sam, can you tell me the status of the repair order on the security camera outside the Test Pen?"

"Sir?" said Lansford, confused. "What repair order, sir?"

"The one I asked you to issue three months ago, Mr. Lansford. I've just been through the files on the surveillance system, and there are many files missing or corrupted. That's an important camera, Sam. We need to make sure it gets fixed immediately. Make this a priority."

"Yes, sir."

"That's all. You can go."

"Yes, sir." Sam stood and left Gardner's office, fuming the whole way and hiding it like the expert he had to be. "He's up to something. Time to call the colonel."

As it turned out, the colonel already knew.

"Did you get it?" Maxwell's voice echoed in a darkened corridor on the other side of the base.

"Yes, sir. It's all there, sir. The whole file, on that flash drive."

"Good man. I wasn't sure we could pull this off that quickly."

"Me, either, sir. How'd you do it?"

Maxwell grinned as he looked at the guard who had by pure coincidence left his post a bit early that evening. "The bane of servicemen everywhere, Lieutenant. Paperwork."

The guard laughed. "Imagine that asshole brought down by something like paperwork. *That* is fitting, sir."

"I agree, Lieutenant. Dismissed."

Chapter Twenty

"HELLO, THIS IS HEALTHWATCH, AND I'm Tabitha Greene." With dark circles under her eyes and her hair in disarray, Tabby had obviously seen better days. *Be careful what you wish for. You just might get it. I wanted more exposure, but this . . .*

"The 'new flu' has now claimed several hundred lives here in the United States, with hundreds more infected. The mortality rate is unusually high, and the Centers for Disease Control remind everyone to take extreme care when dealing with anyone who is or may have become infected. We will now be displaying the number you see on the bottom of your screen twenty-four hours a day for reports of outbreaks of this illness."

Tabitha paused for a moment, consulting her notes as footage from various cities around the country was shown, with many people wearing masks. "Worldwide cases have also increased, with Southeast Asia being hardest hit. The Cambodian government reports that its quarantine of the small city of Phumĭ Rôménh has been successful thus far, though casualties from the incident are high, with even more expected in the next few days.

"The governments of Thailand, Vietnam and Laos have all expressed concern over the outbreaks in their respective regions, and all are currently in a declared state of emergency. Tensions are also high with neighboring China and Myanmar, which have officially closed their borders in an attempt to maintain their isolation from the spread of this illness.

"One piece of good news is that the CDC and USAMRIID—the Army version of the CDC—have reached an agreement to work together to provide assistance to those whose family members may have been exposed. There are multiple patient-care facilities being set up around the country to help with the massive influx of this highly-contagious disease. The list of these facilities is now available on the CDC's website as well as on our own site.

"Again, we must stress that anyone infected or believed to be infected by the 'new flu' should seek immediate treatment at one of these patient-care facilities. If they are unable to be moved or are otherwise incapacitated, please call the 800 number to arrange for help. Remember: immediate isolation is the best way to keep you and your loved ones safe from an infected person.

"This was a HealthWatch Special Report. I'm Tabitha Greene."

"What progress have you made, Stevens?"

"We have several crates of samples ready for transport, Mr. Gardner. And we should have several more soon, given the rate of infection we're seeing."

Gardner smiled, and Stevens fought the urge to react on camera. Gardner made him nauseous, and he wasn't thrilled about having a face-to-face via webcam with the man.

"Good," Gardner said. "I wouldn't have thought that Lincoln, Nebraska, of all places, would be such a hotspot."

"It's not. It's just that this is the only place within a couple hundred miles that some of these folks can go. Plus, this is where the National Guard is bringing all the others from the region."

"The ones that can't or won't drive in?"

"Exactly."

"I see. Well, this still bodes well for our research efforts. Any security violations?"

Not that I'm going to tell you about, anyway. "Nope. Everything's locked down tight as a drum here. Per your orders, we've exhumed some local bodies and cremated them to provide ashes for family members who are particularly obstinate. Most of the others seem to accept that their relatives or friends are too infectious to see."

"Sheep will do that, Mr. Stevens. Give them a plausible reason— even one that's only *slightly* plausible—and they'll fill in the details themselves. It's really quite convenient." Gardner tapped a finger on the desk as he thought. "Have all the samples you've collected thus far, including the blood, flown out immediately, Stevens. I have an urgent need for them."

"I'll have them on the plane today."

"Good, good." Gardner signed off, and Stevens walked outside as if to clear his head. He looked around for observers and ducked into a nearby alley, pulling the sat-phone from his pocket and dialing a number from memory. It rang once.

"Secure."

"Sir, another transport at 1500hrs local."

"Quantity?"

"Four, sir. Sir?"

"Yes?"

"What's our timetable?"

"Soon, Specialist. Soon. Hang tight, son. We're almost ready."

"Very well, sir. Out here." Stevens put the phone away and went back into the tent, hoping that Maxwell knew what he was doing.

It's a dangerous game, playing with someone like Gardner. Then again, the general has been playing even longer. Let's just hope we come out on top.

"Who are these guys?" asked Porter, one of the soldiers of the freshly-minted 8th Team. He nodded toward the observation room, off to one side, where a small group of technicians stood talking. A thick black curtain screened part of the main room from the soldiers sitting in rows.

"Just some lab geeks, probably here to analyze our reactions or something. I've heard this can get pretty wild," said another. His uniform read MASTERS.

"Whatever. It's just some 'monster' behind bulletproof glass."

"Really? Then riddle me this, genius. Do you see any other glass in here?"

The soldier's eyes widened slightly as he realized the import of his compatriot's words. "Surely they wouldn't—"

He was interrupted as a dull clinking sound emerged from behind the thick curtain. A low moan followed, and the noise in the room from talking soldiers vanished as if a switch had been thrown. None of the soldiers saw the technicians in the observation room watching them as one pushed a button, and the curtain slid aside. None of the soldiers had seen active duty against walkers, but they were all experienced veterans of some of the finest units the world has ever known.

None of it mattered now.

The walker came lurching forward, only restrained by the chains around its neck, wrists and waist. As one man, the soldiers flinched back, several covering their noses and mouths as the stench of rotting flesh overpowered them.

"Holy shit!" yelled Porter. "Fuck me, fuck me! What the fuck?" Some of the soldiers had abandoned their chairs and backed away from the walker, only coming to grips with what they were seeing as they realized that it was chained to the wall.

One brave soul among them moved forward, staying just out of reach of the creature, his curiosity getting the better of him. He could still see the remnants of the suit the man had been wearing.

Some sort of businessman. What the hell he was doing when—

"Look out!" Masters came rocketing in from the side, knocking the other soldier off his feet just as the walker took another swipe . . . one which would have connected if he'd been there. It was only then that some of them noticed what Masters had already seen: the concrete on the wall that secured its anchor chain, which held all of the rest of the chains, had crumbled.

With yet another moan, the walker pulled the ring out of the wall and fell upon the nearest soldier, who raised his arm to ward off his attacker. It grabbed the arm and bit into the meaty banquet it had been provided.

The soldier screamed and fell back, wrenching his arm from the walker's grip. The rest were trying the door, only to find it locked.

Several banged on the windows of the observation room, where the technicians were frozen in fear, one of them in a bundle on the floor, rocking back and forth and crying.

Two of the more enterprising veterans attempted to use the chairs as improvised weapons, but they were bolted to the floor.

"For fuck's sake, people!" yelled Masters, and dived behind the walker, rolling and coming up in a crouch. Grimacing as he caught hold of the creature's legs, he pulled hard, and there was sickening crunch as its head hit the concrete floor. It wasn't out of the fight, though, and it struggled to attack as Masters stood up, still holding its feet.

Masters swung it around hard, not letting go as its head impacted the observation room window, splattering gore across the glass and the wall beside it.

The technicians inside flinched back and one finally snapped out of it and hit the base alarm. Masters made sure the walker stopped twitching before glaring at the technicians through the glass.

As he turned back to the room, he saw two men—one of them the luckless Porter—administering first-aid to the wounded soldier. Suddenly, the wounded man moaned and sat up, with the other two helping him.

"Stop! Get out of there, before—" Masters shouted, but he was too late. The wounded man had turned, and began biting and clawing at Porter, whose reflexes weren't *nearly* fast enough to avoid the attack.

"Son of a bitch!" Masters yelled. "Haven't any of you ever seen a damn zombie movie?" He shoved the uninjured paramedic wannabe away and dragged the walker away from Porter, toward the front of the room, where he kicked it in the head until it stopped twitching.

There was a crash from the door, and Masters saw Echo team— the first to respond to the scene—come through the door. Major James assessed the situation, and without pausing put two rounds into Porter. The man didn't even have time to register what was happening before he was gone.

Probably better that way, thought Masters.

James nodded to Santos, who took care of the one Masters had kicked into oblivion. "Anyone else bit?" asked James. When there was no response, he grunted. "Fine. Do a splatter check. I have some business to take care of."

The remainder of 8th Team began checking themselves and each other for infectious blood as James stepped up to the observation room window and looked at the technicians inside.

Masters took one look at the major's face, and decided that being somewhere else—*anywhere* else—was a good idea. Suiting action to thought, he got the rest of his team out of there.

They made a ridiculous parade down the hallways: some clad only in their underwear, having removed their contaminated clothing, and some of them weren't even in that much.

Back in the gore-drenched room, James finished memorizing the technician's faces, and turned back to his team. "All right, show's over. Get the clean-up crew in here."

"Already on the way, sir," said Santos. "I called them as soon as we arrived."

"Good." He eyed the remains of the original zombie, noting the force with which it hit the window. *That Masters is one formidable, stone-cold son-of-a-bitch. The general is gonna want to meet him.*

"Final numbers?" asked Maxwell.

"Two dead, not including the original walker," replied Anderson, sitting across the desk from the general.

"Damn him. Damn that man straight to Hell."

"Yes, sir. I'd say he's seen to that himself, sir."

"Do we know how this happened, yet?"

"Best guess at this time is shoddy construction work, sir. The anchor ring apparently just came out of the wall. I'm looking into it. As for the rest, it appears Masters took the initiative and kicked some serious ass."

"Okay, so we've got shoddy construction in an acclimatization room built to Gardner's order, almost a whole team shitting their pants, and two recruits of a brand-new team dead."

"Essentially, sir. That's it in a nutshell. Except . . ."

"Except what?"

"That recruit turned in *seconds*, sir. Not even minutes. I think it was a setup. I think Gardner was running an experiment and meant for them to be attacked."

Maxwell looked up, and the ever-stoic Anderson swallowed hard. *I do not want to be Gardner right now. I've never seen that look before. God willing, I never will again.*

"It's time, Frank. Send the activation. Make it 1000 hours tomorrow." Maxwell's voice was cold and hard, as hard as Anderson had ever heard it. "All of them, Frank. No mistakes. And don't miss your flight."

"Yes, sir. No, sir." Anderson stood, saluted, and left, leaving the door open.

"Nancy, get me Barnes," Maxwell yelled. "And the president."

"The tests exceeded even our wildest expectations, sir. The subject turned in less than one minute, with only being exposed to one bite."

The technician sat with a clipboard on his lap, his face devoid of expression. "Unfortunately, the delivery specimen was destroyed during the experiment, but I am confident that we can replicate it if needed."

"Good work, Hodges," said Gardner, leaning back in his chair. "Good work, indeed. I'd like to see if we can—"

He was interrupted by the thick wooden door of his well-furnished office slamming open, cracking back against the wall and leaving deep holes in the plaster as Maxwell stormed in and glared at the technician.

Gardner sighed, and waved one hand at the poor lab tech. "You may go, Hodges."

Hodges stood and bolted from the room, cowering in fear.

Hardly unexpected. Not with a Neanderthal like Maxwell looming over him.

"Have a seat, *General*," he said, putting as much loathing into that single word as he could. "I'll make sure and have my secretary invoice you for the repairs to the door and the wall."

Maxwell sat down, directing a cold, predatory grin at Gardner.

"Henry, that's not something you're ever going to have to worry about again."

It wasn't so much *what* Maxwell said, as the cold, toneless way in which he said it, that gave Gardner the chill that went up his back. *Something's up . . . but what?*

"You fucked up, Henry. But good, this time. Really put your ass in a sling with this one, boy."

Gardner was seething, but it wouldn't do to let Maxwell know that. "Why, whatever do you mean, General?"

"I'm talking about your little unauthorized experiment with my team yesterday, Henry."

"I'm still not following you."

"That acclimatization exercise that you set up? The one where I lost two of my men? The one that ended with three walkers dead and a helluva mess for the cleanup crews? That one."

"Ah, yes. I did hear about an accident in one of the testing areas yesterday. I haven't had time to look at the full report yet, but from what I understand, one of our technicians got a little careless. He's been disciplined by his supervisor and is no longer employed here."

"Carelessness? That's really what you're going with?" Maxwell shook his head. "I shouldn't be surprised."

"I will, of course, order my people to investigate the matter more fully, and we will work with your team more closely in the future to see that this sort of thing doesn't happen again."

"Of course you will, of course. I'm not sure that will be necessary anymore, though." That cold, calculating smile was back. "'Cause I wanted to let you in on a secret of my own."

Maxwell stood up, leaning over the desk, his face inches from Gardner's. Henry flinched back, and hated himself for it, but he stood—or rather, sat—his ground, meeting the general's glare.

"Oh? And what's that, exactly?"

"I. Know. Everything," Maxwell said, punctuating each word with a thump of his finger on the desk.

Gardner went cold and dead calm. *Careful now, Hank, old buddy. He can't possibly know* everything. *Keep him talking to find out, so you can plug the leaks later.*

"I'm sure I don't know what you're referring to, General."

"Maybe," said Maxwell, taking a seat again in the chair, but not before pulling a sheaf of paperwork from a pocket. "Or maybe not." Maxwell threw the packet of paper at Gardner, striking him square in the face as the papers fluttered to the top of the desk.

Invoices for shipments, contents marked "Biohazard—Do not open." Photos of walker samples being loaded onto trucks and even a train, in one case, marked 'Destination: Classified.'

A series of recent photos from one of the "patient care centers" Gardner had set up, showing a technician deliberately gassing a patient who was still conscious, then restraining him against the inevitable turning.

Transcripts of his calls to North Korea.

Maxwell stood and snapped his fingers. Masters entered the room, a portable DVD player in one hand. He stood at attention.

"I even know about those two you abducted because they got too close. The reporter and the kid." Maxwell looked over at Masters. "What were their names?"

"Doris Poole and Jason Horner, sir."

"That's them. Granted, that reporter was a pain in the ass, but she didn't deserve what you did to her. *No one* deserves to be experimented on like that, Henry. Not even you." He paused, and tapped the desktop again. "But that's not all. I told you, I know *everything*. Go ahead, Masters. Show him," Maxwell said.

The soldier opened the DVD player, spinning it around on the desk to face Gardner as it started playing. On the screen, a hallway appeared, a door at one end with a lone guard outside.

"Thank you, Masters. Wait here."

"Sir!" Masters saluted and stood to one side. Gardner didn't notice, his gaze fixed on the screen, where he was walking down a hallway with the now-dead Brett Williams, clearly and unmistakably throwing him into the Test Subject Pen with his own hands.

He could just make out the claws reaching out before the door slammed shut and the video ended.

Gardner took an instant to compose himself, and then looked up at Maxwell.

"What is this? Some sort of hoax? Clearly, that video was edited."

"Oh, come off it, Gardner. You know exactly what that is. Two of your own guards saw you in that hallway with Williams. One of them saw you just before he went off-shift." Maxwell grinned again. "Except that guard wasn't *yours* at all, Henry. He was mine."

"He's lying. They both are."

He really does know everything, except . . .

It was Maxwell's turn to blink as Gardner stood suddenly, buttoning his suit jacket and smiling an even grimmer smile.

"I think you'll find that none of this matters, General. Even if you did somehow have the balls to arrest me, you couldn't make it stick. You see, my orders come from the Secretary of Defense himself, who takes *his* orders from the president, who is fully aware of what goes on here." Gardner motioned to the door. "Now, if you'll excuse me, I have a meeting."

"Not anymore, you don't. That's what I've really come to tell you, Henry." Maxwell grinned. "You're fired."

Gardner smiled back. "You can't fire me, you ridiculous old goat."

"Sam?" Maxwell raised his voice and looked at his watch. "I think it's about time. Put through SecDef's office, will you? They should be calling any—"

Gardner's desk phone rang, and when the grey man didn't pick it up, Maxwell leaned over and punched the Speaker button. "Henry Gardner's office," he said.

"Good to hear your voice, sir," answered Anderson.

"Yours, too, Frank." Maxwell turned to Gardner. "In case you were wondering, that's Commander Frank Anderson, my XO. He's got something to tell you, Henry. Go ahead, Frank."

"Yes, sir. Henry Gardner, under Homeland Security Presidential Directive 118, you, the Secretary of Defense, and any others found to be in collusion with yourselves are hereby placed under arrest on the charges of high treason, murder, conspiracy to commit murder, and assorted other crimes.

"You are hereby remanded to the custody of the Military Police at Fort Carson until such time as you are further remanded to civilian authorities, where you will await a fair and impartial jury trial to judge you for your crimes against the people of this nation and this world."

Gardner had only listened with half an ear to the voice on the phone, having guessed what was happening. He had no intention of sticking around to find out how it ended, and made a break toward the door.

"Barnes," said Maxwell.

Suddenly, Gardner's escape was blocked by the imposing figure of Major Kimberly Barnes, and the even more imposing figures at her back of Tom Reynolds and Dalton Gaines, both armed, their rifles aimed at Gardner. He could almost feel the red dots of their laser scopes on his forehead.

"Get out of my way," he said, just managing to keep his voice from breaking at the end.

"Fuck you," said Kimberly, and her fist flew. Gardner took the punch on his jaw, and its power flipped him around and made him rebound off the desk and the wall before he came to rest on the concrete floor. Fortunately for him, he was out cold before he got that far.

"That'll be all, Barnes," said Maxwell. "Frank, we're done here."

"Here, too, sir," replied Anderson. George could hear yelling in the background, presumably from the former Secretary of Defense. "He was *not* happy."

"I expect not. One second, Frank." Maxwell stepped aside as two very large MPs hauled the unconscious Gardner to his feet and cuffed him.

"He goes in the Hole, boys. No visitors, for any reason, my order."

He turned back to the phone as Barnes and the rest of 1st Team's Alpha squad entered the room.

"How'd the rest go, Frank?" asked Maxwell.

"Spot-on, sir. I don't think any of them had even an inkling that we knew anything, sir."

"Good. How many of Gardner's people did we get?"

"All told, nearly two hundred, sir."

"Holy shit," said Barnes. "Sorry, sir."

"No problem, Major. I said the same thing when the commander gave me his final report."

"We believe that's all of them, sir. There could be more, but with most of them gone . . ."

"Right. Get everything rounded up there, and then get your ass back here."

"Yes, sir. Right away, sir."

"He's right in here, Morena."

Mary Adamsdóttir led the raven-haired former nurse into the lab, directing her toward a bed surrounded by blinking, beeping machines.

On the bed, David Blake lay in quiet repose.

Morena Forrest was a study of mixed emotions as she approached the bed of this man she had met so briefly. Michael, her adopted son, stood next to her, holding her hand and looking around.

"I only met him once, you know," she said, her voice sounding hollow.

"It was in Laramie, wasn't it?" asked Mary, one hand on Morena's shoulder.

"Yeah. He had just helped us realize that we had a bunch more walkers in the hospital. He was . . . nice. But when he saw Michael, he just lost it. Started babbling. What am I supposed to do?" she asked, turning to Mary. "How can I . . . how can we help him?"

"Just talk to him. Even though he can't respond, he'll hear you. Many, many studies have shown that coma patients react well to people talking to them, holding their hand, any outside stimulus."

"He's in a coma?"

"Not exactly. He's technically catatonic. That means he's theoretically aware of everything going on around him, but just can't or won't respond for reasons known only to him. That's what we're hoping you can help us with."

Morena stood a moment longer, looking at this man that she hadn't really known.

"So I really look like her? And he looks like Eric?"

"It's uncanny. Here, I can show you." Mary grabbed her laptop off her desk and brought up the comparisons. "You can see why this might have happened."

It's like looking in a mirror. Only I have blonde hair.

"Creepy," she said. "No wonder it messed him up."

"We have no way of knowing whether you sound anything like her, but I would caution against pretending to actually *be* her. That could only worsen the situation, and send him even further from us if he did wake up."

"Okay," Morena said, taking a chair and bringing it over to David's bedside. She pulled Michael onto her lap. "Michael, do you know why we're here?"

The little boy nodded. "To make the sick man feel better."

"Right. So we're going to talk to him, and see if we can help. Okay?"

"Okay."

Morena reached out and took David's hand in hers. "Mr. Blake? David? My name is Morena Forrest. This is Michael."

"Hello," piped up Michael.

"We want to help you get better, David. I know that wherever you are, it's a safe place, where nothing can hurt you. I know that you went there at least a little because of us, because we look like Rebecca and Eric."

She looked for some vague indication that David knew she was there, that she was making any impact on him, but found nothing.

"I don't know if you can even hear me, but I owe it to you, and to Kim, to try. You saved our lives, David."

Michael reached over and laid his hand on David's. "Please, mister, please wake up."

Mary turned away, wiping a tear from her eye, and noticed Kimberly standing at the door to the medical bay, one hand over her mouth and tears running down her face. Mary walked over to her and let the taller woman lean on her shoulder as she sobbed.

"It's okay, Kim," she said. "You don't always have to be so strong."

A few moments went by, and Kimberly slowly got herself back under control enough to be able to watch Morena and David again. Mary handed her a tissue from a box nearby.

"Thanks," Kim said. She looked intently at the pair still talking to David. "I'm glad they're here. How long?"

"Only a few moments before you arrived. I haven't seen any response yet, and nothing on the monitors."

"Maybe I've got the answer. We arrested Gardner." She looked back at Mary. "He's holding—*was* holding—Eric in a cell, Mary."

Mary's shock was palpable. "Holy—"

"Exactly. It gets worse, though. Much worse." Kim laid out the details of everything they'd found on Gardner. "As soon as I found out about Eric, I knew that's what sent him over the edge."

"No shit!" said Mary. She blushed bright red and covered her mouth. "Sorry."

"Oh, please," Kim said. "Mary, George has known for a while. He didn't tell you—"

"He didn't tell me because he needed my help but wanted to protect me." She rolled her eyes. "One of these days, that man will protect me to death."

"He doesn't mean—"

"Oh, I know. I'm just bitching to keep from thinking about how close I was to that much . . . well, evil is really the only word for it."

Kim looked over at the only occupied bed in the ward. "I'm just wondering if I should tell David."

"Yes!" Mary said, grabbing Kim by both arms. "Of course you should! That might be just the thing!"

Mary dragged Kim over to David's bed, where Morena was winding down, running out of things to talk about. Kim nodded to her, and ruffled Michael's hair. He smiled and stuck his tongue out at her, causing her to grin.

Suddenly, there was a louder beep from one of the monitors, and Mary bent to check it out. Straightening again, she looked at Kim.

"Tell him, Kim."

"Tell him what?" Morena asked, standing up to let Kim sit down. Mary drew her a step away and explained the situation as Kim looked at the man she loved, lying unresponsive once more. Michael stood near her shoulder, as though standing watch.

He's seen enough soldiers do it. Maybe that's just what he's doing.

She took a deep breath, then held David's hand in both of hers, trying not to cry again.

"David, it's me. I hope you can hear me." She glanced at the monitors, but there was no response. "We got him, David. Gardner. We arrested him, and the Secretary of Defense, and everyone involved. The president authorized it."

Still no change that she could see. *Time for the big guns.*

"We know where Eric is, David. We found him. Once we got him in a cell of his own, Gardner spilled his guts to keep us from executing him on the spot."

A beep from the machine, then two more. Adamsdóttir checked the machine, then motioned for Kim to continue.

"We can get him back, David. We can put him out of his misery. No more pain, for either of you."

More beeps, and David groaned.

"Please, David. Come back to me. I can't do this without you. Please." She was crying all-out now, squeezing his hand so hard she thought she'd break it.

More beeps, and Mary smiled down at her. "Keep going."

Morena came back over, putting a hand on Kim's shoulder as Michael added his voice as well. "Please wake up, mister," he said.

"David, we need you with us," said Morena.

Even Adamsdóttir joined in. "Come on, David, you can do it. Fight it. We're all here for you."

Kim was voiceless now, her forehead pressed to David's, her tears running over both their faces. She kissed him over and over again, murmuring words so low no one could hear them.

"K-Kim?" His voice was a barely audible rasp. Mary grabbed a cup of water and handed it to Kim.

"I'm here, David. I'm here," Kim said, holding a straw to his dry, chapped lips. "Drink some of this." He managed a few difficult swallows of the water.

"Kim," he said again, forcing his eyes open and blinking against the light. He raised his free hand to touch her hair. "You're here." He managed a lopsided grin.

"Of course I am. Where else would I be?"

David Blake looked around the room at those who had cheered him on. He flinched when his eyes rested on Morena, but Kim was ready for that and squeezed his hand. He smiled up at her. "Don't worry. I'm still here. And I'm not going anywhere again."

"Hey, little man," he said, looking over at Michael. "I heard you, you know."

Michael's eyes widened. "Really?"

"Yep." David coughed, his voice still straining. "I heard you, and Morena, and Mary . . . thank you."

"You're welcome, sir!" said Michael.

Drawing himself to a passable imitation of attention, the kid saluted. David saluted back, and winked at Kim, who looked over at Mary.

Mary smiled and nodded, taking little Michael and Morena with her and giving the two some privacy.

Kim looked down at David. "You're not going anywhere?"

David shook his head. "Never. I love you, Kimberly Barnes."

She smiled again, tears shining in her eyes. "Good. Cause I'll kill you if you put me through that again."

David laughed weakly. "Noted, Major," he said, running a hand down her face. With the last of his strength, he drew her in for a kiss. "Never again."

Chapter Twenty-one

FORT CARSON, COLORADO

THE NEXT TWO WEEKS WERE difficult, as I came back to the land of the living. I didn't have to learn how to walk again or anything that dramatic, but I *had* been asleep for nearly a month, and that takes it out of you. Still, I was running each morning, a little further every day, and working out in the gym, gaining back my strength and catching up on what had happened in the meantime. I spent a lot of time with Kim, and we were both glad when Maxwell ordered her, with a wink, to take some time off.

Towards the end of my recovery, we went along on several missions with Alpha and Bravo teams, strictly as an observer in my case, as command in Kim's. She was learning fast, and I could tell that Maxwell had chosen the right person for the job. She would make an excellent general some day, provided we still needed those in a few years.

Maxwell ordered us to his office one afternoon, along with Commander Anderson. As they explained it, Gardner had kept everything about his ultimate plans as close to the vest as he could. None of his lackeys knew the whole truth, not even the Secretary of Defense.

He had told them just enough to get what he needed from them, and no more. After weeks of thorough interrogation, the general had ordered most of them released, excepting only those who were guilty of heinous crimes.

Even without knowing Gardner's ultimate goal, some things were just too awful to let slide.

Attacks were getting worse the world over. I was glued to Health-Watch every time it aired, as it became the *de facto* news source for the public on the outbreaks worldwide. Practically everyone on base watched, although most of us were wondering how much longer the cover story would hold up to such continued scrutiny.

"Hello, and welcome to HealthWatch. I'm Tabitha Greene. Grim news tonight: The global death toll from the 'new flu' is now estimated in the tens of thousands, with hundreds more being infected every day. Nearly a thousand are confirmed dead here in the US, with many more infected. The CDC and USAMRIID are working to combat this outbreak as well as they can, and have set up additional patient treatment centers in many areas across the country.

"In Southeast Asia, the news is much, much worse: the quarantine attempts in Thailand, Laos, Vietnam and Cambodia have all failed completely. Under siege from refugees fleeing infection, both Myanmar and China have mobilized their armed forces to protect and defend their borders, which were closed weeks ago. No one is being let in or out, infected or not. Government services in those countries are virtually non-existent at this point.

"According to our latest reports, all uninfected American citizens have been evacuated by heavily-armed military forces. Reports of mass executions and the slaughter of refugees attempting to cross the borders of both Myanmar and China are rampant, with thousands more dead."

Tabitha turned to face another camera, and a map of the region appeared next to her. "We have reports from the White House and the State Department that China has issued a warning to the United Nations: If the situation worsens, China will use tactical nuclear weapons to defend themselves and their country.

"If this happens, it will be the first nuclear detonation outside of experimental testing since the Hiroshima and Nagasaki bombs were dropped more than seventy years ago." Another turn and she looked back at the camera.

"We have scattered and unconfirmed reports from South Africa, Angola, the Sudan, Nigeria, Cameroon and as far north as the Sahara of outbreaks on that continent as well. Added to that, still more unconfirmed reports have come in from Brazil and Venezuela, and even from some Eastern European countries, though the outbreaks are smaller there. This is truly a global crisis, and medical and bio-science teams the world over are pooling their resources to fight this plague.

"Last week, there was a demonstration outside of the CDC headquarters in Atlanta, and several protestors were arrested for vandalism. Additional protests have been held near the USAMRIID main base at Fort Detrick, Maryland, although these have been somewhat smaller due to the restricted access at that location.

"Most of the protestors are calling for more work on this outbreak, saying that no progress has yet been made. A small number of protestors have been calling for the government to *stop* all work on a cure for the virus, saying that 'to attempt to cure that which God has wrought is a sin.'

"This small yet vocal group appears to be led by this man, Reverend Sebastian Wright, from Boston." A calm, well-groomed man sporting a clerical collar and clutching a crucifix appeared on screen, speaking to a group of men and women outside a church.

"'Brothers and sisters! This is not a plague of the end times! This is not Armageddon! This is *justice*! God has sent us this divine retribution to test us, to show us that our evilness and wicked ways will no longer be tolerated! This cleansing of the sinners among us must be allowed to continue, or we will have sinned ourselves in the very light of our salvation!'

"This was the scene yesterday outside the First Church of the Divine Judgment in Boston, newly created by Reverend Wright in the last month," said Tabitha, as the feed returned to the live studio. "He has called for the governments of the world to cease all research into a cure, believing that only those who are worthy will be spared.

"Work continues unabated behind the doors of the CDC and USAMRIID. We remind all our viewers to take precautions for your own safety. If you are near a Red Cross Patient Care Facility, you may bring the infected person or persons to those locations if you can do so safely.

"Red Cross Patient Care Facilities also offer free screenings. If you cannot bring the person to a PCF, you must isolate the infected if at all possible and call the 800 number on your screen. You will be given further instructions and assistance at that time.

"Stay tuned for the latest news on the 'new flu,' and good luck to us all. This has been a HealthWatch Special Report. I'm Tabitha Greene."

"Stop that!" Rachel giggled and swatted at Dalton's hand as he tried to tickle her. Dalton smiled and picked his fiancée up, swinging her around and trapping her arms at her sides, then throwing her onto their bed. "Make me."

"Oh, I will, you can count on that." She sprang off the bed at him, but he easily caught her, folding her over his shoulder like nothing more than a sack of potatoes.

A sack of potatoes with a great ass that just happens to be in swatting range.

Suiting thought to deed, he gave her a good smack as she struggled, eliciting a startled yelp and more pounding on his back. She twisted and squirmed, but couldn't break free.

"All right, fine. You win." She relaxed her body, and he nodded in triumph as he set her back down on the bed, where she kneeled and glowered at him, still just shy of his height.

He smiled down at her. She smiled sweetly back and he had just enough time to worry before she socked him in the gut, hard.

Breathing hard, he reached for her, but she stuck her tongue out and scooted backwards on the bed, then gave him *the look*. He smiled and moved towards her, one knee on the end of the bed.

This was, of course, when the alert sounded.

"Goddamn you, Maxwell," he grumbled, buckling back on his uniform. Rachel was already holding the door for him, and they ran for the briefing room, pulling on their jackets as they went. She shot a look at Gaines as they rounded the corner. "We'll finish our discussion later." It was not a question.

Dalton grunted, and reached out a hand to swat her on the ass again, but she dodged and made it into the briefing room just ahead of him. He smiled as they took their seats. *Even with all this shit, there are still a few good things happening.*

Maxwell walked in, Commander Anderson at his side. Though they were deep in discussion, Dalton could see that the commander was keeping an eye on the soldiers filing into the room. He noticed that the room was filling up fast. There must be a big mission on, as he recognized members from 2nd and 5th Teams as well as the rest of his own 1st Team. He glanced at Rachel, who shrugged and nodded towards the front of the room just as Anderson yelled.

"Ten-hut!"

The soldiers stood at attention.

"At ease, men. Take your seats, if you can. Lights!" The lights were turned off, and a projector map of what looked to Dalton like a seaport somewhere was shown on the large screen at the front of the room.

"Gentlemen and ladies, this is the Port of San Diego."

Maxwell turned and used his laser pointer to indicate a section of the map. "*This* area is the Tenth Avenue Marine Terminal. As you can see, it's less than half a mile from downtown San Diego.

"San Diego is home to 1.3 million people. This port ships nearly 3 million metric tons of cargo each year, from all over the world. Two days ago, a cargo ship arrived at the port and began unloading."

The map disappeared as Maxwell nodded at Anderson, who was controlling the presentation from the briefing table. A photo of a container ship appeared, the name VTC *Dragon* on its prow.

"The VTC *Dragon*'s last port of call was Ho Chi Minh City, in Vietnam." Maxwell nodded as the news sank home. "Exactly. We only received the reports from the Coast Guard on the ship's inspection one hour ago.

"Prominently featured in these reports was the severe illness of several of her crew members. The inspectors didn't know what to look for, but we did. Doctor?"

Mary Adamsdóttir walked forward, nodding to Anderson who changed slides again. This time, the soldiers were rewarded with views of the wounded Vietnamese sailors, several of whom had obvious bite marks.

"We can determine from the report that at least three of the sailors are infected, with the possibility of at least four or five more that came in contact with the virus. All wounded crew were transferred to a local hospital for treatment."

There was a general murmur in the room that broke off when the doctor continued.

"The whereabouts of all of these potentially infected are not currently known. We know where the three original sailors are—locked in a hospital ward at the moment. The others are at large."

Maxwell took over. "As soon as we received the report, I ordered an immediate lockdown of the port, through the CO of the naval base that's practically next door. That has been our one saving grace in this. The squids were able to close it up tight. So far, the only people we know have been in contact with the infected are all accounted for, except those four or five that the good doctor mentioned."

Another click, and another slide, this one of row after row of warehouses.

"This is the problem. There's over a million square feet of warehouses, sheds, and other storage areas at the terminal alone. The Navy boys managed to lock it down so no one's getting in or out, but that still leaves a lot of ground to cover. Commander?"

Anderson stood up as another slide appeared, showing the overall strategic action map. "We'll be using four teams for this op: 1st, 2nd, 5th and 8th. I'd like it if we had more, but the other teams are at other incursion sites. We'll go in small—twos or squads, working fast. That doesn't mean we take chances, but we're going to be light on boots with this one, and we need to make every minute count.

"7th Team will be assisting the on-site Naval personnel with securing the perimeter, as well as helping with the screening. We've got a med team en route already to help with that, but they'll need backup, and 7th has gone with them.

"They'll also pick up the walkers at the hospital and make sure no one there has been infected. Hopefully, by the time we touch down, most of the civilians in the port will have been screened and we can get them out of there. Lights!

"All yours, sir," he said to the general, resuming his seat at the briefing table.

Dalton glanced around the room. *Thirty-five operators, searching a million square feet of warehouses. This is insane.*

Maxwell set his jaw and grimaced as though he'd thought the exact same thing. "All right folks, you know your jobs. You've trained for this. You're ready. All the same, this is deep shit. I want your heads right, your game faces on. No fuck-ups, or the *last* thing you'll need to worry about is a walker getting to you. Clear?"

"Clear, sir!"

"Good. Now grab your gear and report to the airfield on the double. Dismissed."

SAN DIEGO, CALIFORNIA
WAREHOUSE DISTRICT

It felt good to be back in action, on the ground against my old foe once more. I knew that was crazy, but I'd been asleep for more than a month. Anyone was liable to be antsy after that.

"Will you calm down?" asked Kimberly. "You're making me nervous."

We were huddled against the wall of the warehouse, our backs resting against the cool metal. Fluorescent light glared down from the fixtures overhead, but it never seemed to penetrate everywhere, leaving small pools of shadow here and there.

I chuckled and took a few deep breaths, slowing my heart rate. I felt like I'd had a whole pot of coffee, without the pleasure of actually drinking it. I turned to take up guard position as Kim shook her head and called in.

"Alpha Six, east section clear."

"Roger, Alpha Six." Commander Anderson was controlling the op, and his voice sounded tinny and strained.

Probably needs to get some sleep.

"Proceed to checkpoint three."

"Acknowledged," said Kim. We moved to the northeastern edge of the warehouse, clearing the door there and proceeding to the next warehouse over, where we began another sweep. Other duos were clearing other buildings, so we didn't worry that we'd left something behind us. Anderson knew the search grid, so we left it in his hands.

"Eaton, Gaines, status?" asked Kim as we moved down the rows of stacked merchandise. Dalton and Rachel were both supposed to be in this building as well, clearing it from the other side, working both ends against the middle.

"On site, sir. Beginning sweep now."

"Roger. Reynolds?"

"Angelo and I are about halfway done with our sweep, sir. Ames and Turner are on the east side."

"Roger. Six out."

I stopped and crouched at the end of the current row of whatever it was in these boxes, and looked at Kim. "Are you thinking what I'm thinking?"

"What, that Ames and Reynolds in the same building is a recipe for disaster?"

"Yeah, that."

"They're professionals. They can handle it."

I scowled. "Tom is. Ames isn't." I sighed. "I guess there's nothing for it, though. Let's get this finished." I hefted the SCAR and cleared the left side as we continued on.

Tom will just have to take care of himself on this one.

"Contact left."

A soft whisper from Eaton. Dalton looked and didn't see it right away, but remained still, and eventually spotted it. There was no way that guy was still alive, despite the fact that he was walking around. "Two tangos."

Shit, there's another one on the ground. Must've been a snack for the other. He went to one knee and sighted in on the mobile one. A sound like a muted cough, and it was just more dead flesh. Highly contagious dead flesh, but no longer a walker, and that's all that matters.

He moved up a few feet until he had a clear shot and took out the other one as well. "Alpha Six, two tangos down."

"Roger, continue your sweep."

"Acknowledged."

He was turning back to Rachel when he saw it. She was looking in his direction, smiling at him, instead of keeping watch. Otherwise, she would have seen it, too. He didn't even have time to shout a warning, just brought his gun up and fired at the walker that was coming up behind her.

The flash of fear and surprise that crossed her face was etched in his mind as his bullet struck the walker in the cheek, taking out the right side of its head and sending it flying backward.

Eaton ducked out of pure reflex as the shot went past and she felt it brush her collar without being slowed in the slightest. She rolled away from the walker, coming up facing it, gun ready. She knew she should be shaking, but she didn't care why she wasn't. All that mattered was that she was alive, and so was Dalton.

She turned back to him just as he reached her, lifting her in a crushing bear hug. "Can't . . . breathe . . ." she managed to choke out, and he put her back down.

"Are you ok? Did he get you? Let me do a splatter check . . ." He began looking her over, searching for even the smallest drop of blood.

Under other circumstances, I'd welcome this much attention. Now, though, it's not helping.

"I'm fine, D. Really. Let's move out."

"Okay, but only if you're sure."

"I'm sure. Carry on, soldier. That's an order!"

He snorted, and moved to the next row as she reached for her throat mike and spoke. "Alpha Six, one more down. Clea—"

It wasn't so much the bite that hurt, it was the knowledge that something as simple as that was all it took to end . . . well, everything. Her life, her plans for marriage, all of it.

"Fuck!" she shouted, slamming her weapon into the zombie's gut, feeling its teeth tear a scrap of fabric from her ACU sleeve. "You son of a bitch!" She didn't remember switching her SCAR to full-auto, but the stream of bullets she unloaded on the walker was evidence enough.

She didn't know Dalton could move so fast, but he was by her side—or at least so it seemed—in less time than it took her to blink.

"What happened? Where did . . ." She saw his eyes catch on the ripped uniform, and he stared. "No," he whispered. "No."

Picking her up, he moved to the center of an aisle, where the light was brightest. Ripping the rest of her sleeve from her uniform jacket as though it were tissue paper, he carefully inspected the wound. It was clear even to Rachel that the bite had gone through the fabric and the skin. The teeth marks were clear, but it was the blood that mattered.

Bright red. Flowing. Her blood.

Infected blood.

She looked up at Dalton, who had broken out his first aid kit and was swabbing the wound with enough antibacterial, anti-fungal, and anti-viral meds to kill a small village full of diseases. At least he had remembered to put on gloves. She ran her free hand over his cheek, smiling sadly, and reached for her mike.

"Alpha Six, Eaton. Code white. Repeat, code white."

Dalton stopped what he was doing for a second, but then shook his head and continued. She could see his tears falling on her arm as he fought to resist the truth of what had happened.

"Ack—" came the halting reply from Barnes. "Acknowledged. We're on our way. Stay there."

"Roger."

Tom looked over at Angelo Martinez, his partner in the next warehouse over. "Did I hear that correctly?"

Angelo swore in Spanish and nodded, once. "*Si.*"

Now it was Reynolds turn to swear. A minute, then two, and he got himself under control.

"What now, *hermano*?" asked Martinez. "Do we go to them?"

Reynolds debated the idea for a moment, but his military training took over. "No. Nothing we can do for her now, anyway. Barnes will handle it. Let's finish the sweep."

"Roger."

They moved off into the warehouse, checking row after row of boxes. There were some offices on the other end, but Ames and Turner were taking care of those.

Why couldn't it have been that homophobic asshole, instead? Why did it have to be Rachel? What the fuck is wrong with this world?

He continued down the row to the end, where he signaled Martinez to hold.

"Contact right," whispered Martinez. "Friendly."

Tom glanced in that direction and noticed Janet Turner exiting one of the offices. *Ames has gotta be close. Might as well give them some cover, just in case.*

He motioned for Martinez to scout the next row, and indicated he would cover Turner and Ames. Angelo nodded and moved off as Tom took up position to cover the others.

Fuck this, thought Ames. *This little bitch thinks she's hot shit cause she's seen more action than I have. I'd like to show her some action . . .*

He was following Turner, checking every other office in a staggered clear operation, a standard method for small offices like these, especially when time was of the essence. He knocked and opened the door when he heard nothing from inside the room. Unfortunately, the blinds on the office were down, so he couldn't just look inside.

Who the hell puts blinds on an office window that's inside a warehouse? Dumbasses. He glanced around the room, noting the closet in the corner but not bothering to open it. No blood, no walker. *Next!*

He left the room, crouching as he took a slug of cool water from his CamelBak reservoir. Noticing movement across the way, he saw Reynolds take up a position at the end of a row, looking to his right at Turner as she exited an office. He raised his SCAR, looking at Reynolds through the scope. It was then that the realization hit him.

This is it. I could take out that bastard faggot now, claim I thought he was a walker and I shot to defend Turner. No one could argue that.

He heard the voice of his father again, ranting and raving about all the evils of the world, chief among them all the "homo-sex-yuls" taking over. He didn't even notice his finger tightening on the trigger, his aim correcting to take Reynolds in the head.

Suddenly, Reynolds glanced his way and did a double-take as he saw the rifle in Ames's hands pointed at him. Reynolds responded by training his own rifle on Ames, aiming through his own scope.

Son of a bitch! That asshole has the same idea!

Time seemed to slow for daddy's boy Eddie Ames as he saw the muzzle flash from Reynolds gun, and he squeezed off a couple shots himself as he dived forward, rolling and coming up in a crouch, still aimed at Reynolds, who was now ducked behind some boxes.

One of Reynolds' fingers crept up above his cover and pointed twice to where Ames had been. A cold chill ran down Ames' spine.

With uncontrollable nightmare slowness, he turned to look behind him, expecting to feel the sharp bite of a walker at any moment.

Instead, he saw one lying on the ground with its head missing, the brains and other remnants sliding down the window with the blinds he'd been so pissed off about earlier.

Holy— He couldn't finish the thought. Turning back, he saw Reynolds glance out from cover, then move more fully into the light, his rifle trained square on Ames, who swallowed hard.

Pointing his weapon straight up, Ames looked at Reynolds and nodded once, in thanks. He could see the other man hesitate, then lower his weapon and nod as well. Both men moved to join their partners, a catastrophe only narrowly avoided.

"Any chance she's wrong?" I whispered to Kim, glancing at Rachel.

"None." Kim leaned into me for a moment, and I thought for a second that she was going to break. I should've known better. "She . . . she's done, David."

I sighed, feeling the weight of another friend lost land hard on my shoulders. And she wasn't even really gone yet. That made it so much harder. Just that one smallish bandage on her arm and the missing sleeve to indicate anything was out of the ordinary.

Nothing will ever be ordinary again.

"Who's it going to be?" I asked her in a whisper.

"I'll do it," she said. To her credit, it was without any hesitation.

I nodded. "If you can't—"

"I said, I'll do it." She softened the harshness with a brittle smile, then turned and knelt next to Rachel, who was sitting on a crate with Dalton hovering over her. "Rachel? How're you doing?"

"Well, except for the fact that I'll be dead soon, I'm peachy-keen, ma'am. You?"

Kim just smiled and shook her head. "That's why I love ya. Always looking on the bright side."

"You know me, Major."

Kim fiddled with her hands, not knowing what to do with them, and unholstered her side-arm. "Rachel—"

"No," said Dalton quietly. "I'll do it."

All of us turned to look at him, but he was staring at the ground.

"D—" For once, Rachel didn't seem to know what to say. She stood still, looking at her fiancé as he took a step closer.

"I won't let anyone else do this," he said, reaching out to take her hand, but still not meeting her gaze. "I won't let you go alone."

A tear ran down Rachel's face as she lifted Dalton's chin slightly with one slim hand, so that she could see his eyes.

I looked away as the tears in the big man's eyes became evident, and then Rachel was giving me a fierce hug.

"I'm going to miss you, Mr. Blake. You take care of my girl here or I'll come back and haunt you. Got it?" My laugh came out as a choked-up sob as I hugged her back, just as hard.

"Oh," she continued. "and tell Tom that I'm gonna miss his cooking. He was the best of the best. And Angelo . . . well, just tell him *hasta luego*." She turned to Kim.

"And you, you listen to him once in a while, ok? You can't always be the boss," she said. "Although sometimes that's fun."

The two women embraced, and there were more than a few tears from both.

"You're going to make it, I can tell. Take care of him, too, and you'll both make it."

Kim nodded, and held my hand as Rachel took Dalton's arm and they walked off among the darkened rows.

"I don't know if I can do this."

The big man was openly weeping now, clutching her to his chest. "I can't do it. I just can't."

Without breaking their embrace, she looked up at him, drawing his eyes down to meet hers. "Dalton Horatio Gaines, look at me."

Despite himself, he smiled a little at her use of his full name, and made an attempt to wipe away some of his tears. "Yeah?"

"I love you. I need your help. Will you help me?"

I feel like I'm drowning in those eyes of hers. How can I not help the love of my life? Feeling like he was breaking apart, he nodded.

"If you need my help, I'll help."

"Good." She turned from him, her arms crossed over her chest and her head bowed.

"I love you, Dalton. And I always will." She heard the soft scrape of his sidearm leaving its holster, and his whispered reply.

"I love you, too."

Reynolds jogged up and saluted Kimberly, Angelo at his side. "Reporting as ordered, ma'am."

"As ordered?"

"Commander Anderson, ma'am. He ordered Martinez and I here when our sweep was finished."

I looked over at Kim. Who knew that scary old bastard had such a soft heart after all?

"Where's Rach—" Tom started to ask, but was interrupted by the soft cough of a gunshot around the corner. It was such a quiet sound, yet it seemed to reverberate through all of us. Tom turned to me, and I shook my head as I put a hand on his shoulder.

"She's gone, Tom. There was nothing we could do."

I didn't think anyone could look that sad, but I was wrong. Ever the professional, Tom confined his grief to a look of loss that made me want to cry, as well as a single tear and a painful squeeze on my hand. We all looked around a few minutes later as Dalton came back down the aisle, his steps slow and measured.

He carried a small, still form shrouded in a foul-weather poncho in his arms, and the look on his face . . . well, granite had more expression than he did in that moment.

As if we didn't have enough to deal with right then, another soldier trotted up out of the darkness in between the rows, and saluted Kimberly. We were all amazed when we saw it was Edward Ames.

I don't know who moved first, me or Martinez, but I know that it was Tom who held us both back, one hand on each of our shoulders. Both of us looked at him, as incredulous as we could possibly be, but he just shook his head, his eyes never leaving Ames, who hadn't even glanced our way.

"Petty Officer Second Class Edward Ames reporting, ma'am."

Kim returned his salute. "What can I do for you?"

Ames continued to stand ramrod-straight, as though he was filming an instructional video for perfect posture. I still wanted to beat him senseless after what he'd done to Tom, but I was also curious as to why he was here now.

"Permission to speak to Captain Reynolds, ma'am."

Kim raised an eyebrow in Tom's direction, and he nodded again, ever so slightly. Ames gave no sign he saw the exchange. "Permission granted."

Ames took several precise steps over to Reynolds and saluted him. The rest of us exchanged startled and unbelieving glances.

What the hell is going on?

Tom was the only one of us who didn't react, other than to come to attention and return the salute.

"Yes?" he said, more than a little curiosity in his voice.

"Sir," Ames began, looking Reynolds straight in the eye. "I owe you an apology. I was seriously out of line in many ways, and I know that I can never make up for the harm that I've done to you or this team. All I can do is apologize, and promise that I will, from this moment on, be better. I can't change overnight, but I can do my best. I hope you'll help me with that. It would be my honor to continue to serve with you, if you'll have me." Ames held out a hand to Reynolds and kept it there, waiting.

Tom never glanced at it, but we all began to wonder as the moments slipped by and he didn't shake it. It was an old-fashioned stare-down, with neither man looking away. Finally, Tom took a deep breath and shook Ames's hand. There was a palpable sense of relief in the air, and Ames smiled, obviously relieved.

"I owe you my life. I won't forget that. Hope you can forgive me."

"Already done, Ed."

Ames turned back to Kim and saluted. "I'd best return to my squad, ma'am."

Kim returned the salute. "Off you go."

Ames jogged off, and we all congregated around Gaines, still holding Rachel's body in his arms. He hadn't made a sound, never even seeming to notice what had happened with Ames. He was completely unresponsive to us, and as I glanced at Kim, she shook her head.

Solve one problem, gain another. When will it end?

I was going to find out all too soon, I knew. We all were.

Chapter Twenty-two

FORT CARSON, COLORADO

I APPROACHED GAINES SLOWLY AS he sat on top of the picnic bench near our barracks, looking out over the Front Range in the rising sun. We had a great view from up here. I just wished we had something nicer to look at than the city of Colorado Springs. I didn't think it was a bad town, but it wasn't exactly as gorgeous as the mountains behind us.

"Mind if I join you, big guy?" I asked. When he didn't respond, I took his silence for acquiescence and sat down as well. We sat there for quite some time. He didn't move a muscle, just stared at the sun as it rose, bathing everything in a golden glow.

"It was a nice service. Simple, no frippery. Just what she would've wanted, I think."

Neither of us said anything for a while, but eventually, I glanced over at him and cleared my throat. "You know, D, if you ever need to talk . . ."

I'd thought I'd gotten through to him when he slowly turned my way, but the look on his face was the same as it had been since we returned from San Diego—nothingness. He was functioning on autopilot, not really seeing anything or anyone around him.

"I don't need to talk, David. I had to kill my fiancée. I had to shoot her so she wouldn't become one of *them*. What could you possibly say that would help with that?" He turned away, dismissing me as though I didn't exist.

I'll admit, his casual dismissal of my own pain pissed me off.

Until I realized a simple fact: He didn't know about Rebecca or Eric. "I may be the only person here who can truly understand what you're going through."

I didn't expect what happened next. How could I?

One minute, we're sitting on the picnic table, watching the sun come up.

The next, he had me in a choke hold—with one hand, no less—against the wall of the barracks, my feet drumming on the wall six inches off the ground.

"You. Don't. Know. Anything," he said, his face a mask of rage and pain.

I don't know how, but I managed to choke out a few words. "I killed Rebecca."

He didn't let me go, but his iron grip on my throat relaxed a minute fraction, enough for me to get in a gasp of air.

"Who?"

"Rebecca. My fiancée."

I caught myself just in time as he let me go, turning back to the sunrise, as though nothing had happened, climbing once more up onto the table. I shook my head and coughed a little to make sure everything was still attached and working, then joined him again, sheer stubbornness keeping me at it.

"We had been living together for over a year, and were gonna get married in about six months," I said, my voice rasping out of my bruised throat. *To say nothing of my ego.* "She was bitten, and I had to shoot her. She had already turned, but I couldn't leave her like that."

I thought Dalton may have sighed a bit, but couldn't be sure.

"It was the hardest thing I've ever done, or will ever do, pulling that trigger. I'd seen her less than a day before, bright and beautiful, but to see her like that . . . to *leave* her like that . . . that was more than I could bear. So I did what had to be done."

I put my hand on the big man's shoulder, and he didn't flinch or draw away. "You did the same thing for Rachel, D. What she asked. She knew the score. She knew what would happen. You saved her from that."

"How do you live with it?" he asked, so quiet I barely heard it.

"I take it a day at a time, same as anyone else. Some days are harder than others." I sighed. "It's a bit worse for me, though."

Anger clouded his features and I held up a hand.

"Just listen," I said, taking a deep breath, and then another. "You were there when Gardner was arrested, right?"

He nodded. "Yeah, that bastard got the surprise of his life when Kim decked him," he said.

"Well, did Kim tell you *why* he was being arrested?"

"Not really, just that they had evidence he'd done some pretty awful stuff."

"That's putting it mildly. One of the awful things he did was to take a little boy and keep him locked up in a cell."

I looked at the rising sun, unable to hide the tears in my eyes as I remembered.

"That little boy was gonna be my stepson. His name was Eric Campbell. Gardner kept him to experiment on. He had been turned as well, back in Fall Creek."

"Holy shit."

"Yeah."

"No wonder you—" He trailed off, unable to finish the sentence. I didn't blame him.

"Went wacko? Three fries short of a Happy Meal? Yeah. That combined with seeing Michael and Morena . . ."

"Morena? The new chick? What about her?"

"Kim didn't tell you? I'm not surprised, really," I said, pausing as I remembered the day I'd lost it. "Morena and Michael are dead ringers for Rebecca and Eric." I snorted. "Poor turn of phrase, but you know what I mean. Put a blonde wig on Morena and she'd be Rebecca."

Gaines had no response this time. "So you see, when I say that I know what you're going through, I mean it." I put a hand on his shoulder once more. "Any time you need to talk, I'm here. And so are the others." I stood up, dusting off my ACU, then turned back to him once more as he stared toward the rising sun. "Just remember this one thing, D. You're not alone."

I didn't say anything more as I left, but I did notice a tear fall, and I was glad. At least he was grieving properly, and not going batshit insane for a month or so like me.

Now if we can all just keep it together, we might just make it out of this mess.

WASHINGTON, D.C.

"What'd you do, Keith? Straight-up copy this from *Deep Impact*?" The president's chief of staff was incensed, yelling at the younger man with a wadded up copy of the speech in his hand. "What happened to the version I reviewed yesterday?"

"Look, Jack," said the speechwriter. "There's only so many ways you can write an end-of-the-world speech, ok? *Anything* I write is going to sound like it came from *Deep Impact*, or *Armageddon*, or something! And the one yesterday was crap. You and I both know it."

Jack took a deep breath, then let it out.

"Well, this one *is* a damned good speech, and better than yesterday's. And it *is* the end of the world. Let's just hope he doesn't start ad-libbing. Again."

"Ladies and gentlemen, the President of the United States."

The podium was cleared, and for a brief moment the seal of the White House was visible behind it before it was washed out in a blaze of flashbulbs. The president stepped up and bowed his head, as if praying.

Maybe that's appropriate, given the content of this speech. Only a few people in the room knew the full nature of what he was going to say, while others "in the know" hadn't made it this far. He'd already had several staffers quit to go be with their families.

Not that I blame them for that. That's where I'd rather be, too. He looked up from the podium, square into the camera and into the eyes of most of the world.

"My fellow Americans, and citizens of the world: By now, it will have come to your attention that this broadcast is coming to you live, over every channel. Every satellite, every radio station, every TV and news outlet online is carrying this message in the hope of reaching as many of you as possible.

"Our great nation has been beset by a horror the likes of which none of us have ever seen, and could only imagine in the worst of our nightmares. Our families and loved ones have fallen ill, and none of them have returned to us.

"We have told you that this is due to a new type of influenza. In truth, we have withheld certain information to protect as many of you as we could, and to give us time to work on a solution, including searching for a cure. While we have not, as yet, found that cure, we do have an alternative that is even now being activated.

"You have all seen the news reports from HealthWatch and other sources, noting the rising number of dead in our cities and from around the world, all attributed to the 'new flu.' You have been told to stay in your homes, to isolate the infected, and to avoid contact with anyone who may be infected at all costs.

"This is, quite simply, not enough. For what we are dealing with, there are no half-measures. The truth is stark, certain, and like nothing you have imagined. Or, more accurately, it's *exactly* what you have imagined, but never thought possible.

"I know that what I'm about to tell you will sound like science fiction. When I was first informed, I thought the same. But there is evidence—as I will show you—and there can be no doubt as to its veracity. This is not a spoof, not a comedy skit, not an error. The threat is real, and very, very deadly."

The president paused, leaning on the podium in a classic politician's "I'm one of you guys" pose.

The speechwriter closed his eyes. *I hate it when he improvises.*

"Look, you folks know me by now. You know I don't beat around the bush or pull any punches, much to the chagrin of my staff and administration. I don't see any reason to change that now. So I'm going to give it to you straight. They want me to call these things some sort of made-up scientific name, or use a politically-correct term, but that's not what you need right now.

"What I think you all need is the truth, something you can understand without having a doctorate, something that actually tells you what we're facing here. You *deserve* to know the truth, so that you can protect yourselves and your families as you see fit.

"So I'm trusting you with this information, knowing that you will live up to my faith in you. With that in mind, ladies and gentlemen, what we are dealing with is—and I say this with utmost sincerity—zombies."

The president was interrupted by a wave of somewhat relieved laughter that swept the room, picked up by the video cameras and transmitted around the world. People in their living rooms and around their dinner tables relaxed, sure that despite his words, this was all an elaborate hoax.

It was only when the journalists and TV crews in the White House Press Room realized that neither the president's staffers nor the president himself were laughing, that they began to sober. The president held up a hand for quiet as the questions began to fly.

"Please hold all your questions until the end, although I know how difficult that must be. We have a lot to get through." He faced the cameras once more, square-jawed and calm.

"I realize that some of you may believe that this is the biggest hoax since the famous *War of the Worlds* radio broadcast by Orson Welles in 1938. Sadly, it is the truth.

"As you know, this illness is not confined to our corner of the globe. Other nations around the world are being notified at this moment by their leaders, who have been working closely with us since the beginning of this crisis. This disease is a global pandemic. Medical facilities, cities, towns and even whole countries are being overrun by the infected.

"Many of you are familiar with Mad Cow Disease. The agent which causes this disease—a prion—is a natural protein that has become twisted from its normal form." In the case of this 'new flu,' however, the situation is much more dire. The prion will kill its host within sixteen to twenty-four hours after initial infection. Once dead, the host will then re-animate and seek out new hosts.

"There is no cure." The president paused for effect, letting the realization sink in for his listeners. "Once infected, the host will die and reanimate. This process may take more or less time, depending on where on their body the victim was bitten. And yes, the primary mode of transmission is through bites, although any contact with bodily fluids will also result in infection.

"I don't have to tell any of you what a zombie is. You've seen the movies and TV shows and read the comic books. What we are dealing with here is nothing short of a horror movie come to life. The dead are walking, and they're hungry."

Medics were moving through the crowd now, attending to several who had fainted. *That's just the start. Wait till they see the video.*

"In case there are any who still disbelieve, I have ordered that video proof be made available online. I will not show it now due to the graphic nature of the content. Please play it when my speech concludes, but do *not* allow your children to watch it. However, as bad as this may seem, all is not lost, and even now a long-planned series of actions are taking place to safeguard our way of life."

A screen came down beside the president, who pointed to the basic graphic. "What you see here is a drawing of a bunker, built into the side of a mountain. This bunker will hold thousands of people, including all the food, water, and other facilities necessary to shelter them for up to twenty years. We call this Project Phoenix.

"There are ten such bunkers spread across our nation. I can't tell you exactly where, for security reasons. These bunkers are at this moment being stocked with supplies, as well as priceless historical and artistic treasures of our culture.

"Obviously, we cannot all take refuge there. Using information collected over the last five years from various sources, a list has been compiled of the best of us, in all fields of human endeavor and from all walks of life, together with their families. A list of 100,000 people who will save our way of life. Those selected are receiving notification as we speak. Please understand that there is no possible way to steal a notification or to impersonate someone who has been chosen. Do not try.

"Let me be clear. *We will survive.* The human race has resisted every attempt in our long history to destroy us. We will survive this as well. These bunkers have been outfitted with the latest in scientific equipment, and those who are chosen will work night and day to find a cure, a way for us to return to the surface of our world, and to save those left behind.

"Until then, we will fight. We will not go gently into that good night. A special unit of our Army has been formed to help in the evacuation of those who have been selected, and to train those who must remain behind."

The president leaned forward once more, his stare intense and direct. "As of now, martial law is declared in the United States of America. All borders are closed, all airports and seaports are locked down. No unauthorized travel is permitted by air, land or sea.

"Stay in your homes. Await your selection notification. Isolate the infected. Violence against military personnel or each other will be dealt with swiftly and harshly. Looting of any kind will be considered a capital crime."

Standing tall again, the president looked at the cameras one last time. "We will survive. We will go on. Life will prevail. In this, our darkest hour, I pray that God is with us all. Thank you."

A knock sounded on our barracks room door, and Kim looked over at me as I swam up from the brief nap I'd been taking over my paperwork. What could I say? Comparing equipment lists wasn't exactly the most exciting thing in the world. I looked back at her and shrugged, then got up and cracked open the door.

I could not possibly have been more surprised than I was at that moment.

"Who is it, David?" Kimberly asked, and I fought hard to keep a smile from my face as I turned to answer her.

"Oh, no one important, I guess."

"Says you, fella," said the very large man on the other side of the door. "She might feel differently."

"That can't be . . ." Kim looked stunned. "Not . . ."

I stepped out of the way as Jonathan Michael Barnes, Jr. moved into the room, ducking his head to avoid the doorframe.

Yeah, he was *that* big.

Looking back, I'm fairly certain that it was words of some sort that came out of Kim's mouth as she rocketed across the room to fly into her brother's arms, but I've never been able to figure out what they were. Not like it mattered.

"Hey, ease up, sis. Those are my ribs, ya know."

She laughed and smacked him on the arm as she let him go and stepped back. It was only then that she noticed what I had seen an instant before. Johnny was wearing an ACU with an AEGIS patch on it. Kim ran her hand over it, then looked up, tears in her eyes as she realized that he would be putting his life on the line along with the rest of us. "No, Johnny . . ."

He took both her hands in his, sat her down at the table, and squatted beside her. As tall as he was, he was still at eye level. I took the other seat and waited.

"George called me," Johnny said. "I don't know how he found me, but it isn't important anyway. He said he had a spot open on a team, and that he could use my help. That *you* could use my help, Kimmy."

Kim looked overwhelmed, and I'm not sure she was really listening at that point. "Which team did he put you on?" I asked. He glanced my way and gave me his own version of the Barnes' trademark thousand-watt smile I'd seen from Kim so many times.

"1st, of course. I'm in Alpha squad."

"Of course, you realize what this means, babe," I said, smiling as well.

"What?"

"He's going to be with us. In Bunker One."

Kim sort of lost it then, happy and hugging her brother close. This was the most emotional I'd ever seen her, and I can only imagine what that must've felt like. But I held out one hand as we all stood. "Good to have you along, bro," I said. He looked at me sideways for a moment and turned to Kim.

"Bro?"

She laughed, and patted him on the chest. "There's a lot to tell you, Johnny." I smiled as she pulled him toward the door. "But first, let me tell you about Rachel . . ."

SEATTLE, WASHINGTON

Tom Reynolds looked out over the city as his plane and 8th Team came in low and heavy into McChord Air Force Base. Loaded down with two Strykers, several cargo trucks, provisions and various personnel, the Globemaster was really pulling its weight this time.

I hate this part. He winced as the big plane touched down hard and then bounced once before rolling down the tarmac. *Although that was as good as anyone could've done it, as overloaded as we are.*

"Ever been here before, sir?" asked Larkin. He was one of the new recruits to 8th Team, having taken the place of the unfortunate Porter.

"You could say that. If you look out the right side over there, you can probably see the house I grew up in. It's a funny old world, Larkin. I joined the Air Force to get away from this place, now I'm being assigned back here for the next twenty years."

"You're damn lucky, if I may say so, sir."

"Oh?"

"Hell, yes!" Larkin said, shaking his head. "We got Texas, sir. Out in the middle of nowhere, not a speck of green as far as the eye can see, or so I've heard." Then he shook his head. "Not that it'll matter, what with being underground for twenty years."

"Not exactly what you signed up for, is it?"

"No, sir. Not by a long shot."

"There's another way to look at it, Larkin."

"Sir?"

"You could be staying topside for twenty years."

The young soldier nodded. "Point taken, sir."

Tom looked at the commercial planes sitting at their terminal gates. *How many will be left sitting there to rot when it goes down? Hundreds? Thousands?* He noticed a column of smoke to the south, black and thick. Then another, some distance away. *What the hell?*

"Captain Reynolds, sir?" said the Globemaster's crew chief. "Got some flash traffic for you, sir," he said, handing over the note.

"Fuck a duck in the ass," Tom muttered as he read.

"Sir?" asked Masters, who had appeared next to the captain as if by magic. *Spooky, this guy.*

"Get your men geared up, Lieutenant. And have your drivers prep their Strykers." Tom glanced at the columns of smoke. "This is gonna be ugly."

FORT CARSON, COLORADO

"No, sir. I understand, sir. Yes, sir." Maxwell's voice was quiet as he hung up the phone. "That was the president," he said.

Anderson waited as Maxwell sat back in his chair. The general would talk when he was ready. Anderson had been around long enough to know when to wait, and when to speak up. This was definitely one of the former. "There's been some rioting in Seattle."

"How bad?"

"Couple hundred dead, several square miles or so cordoned off by the police. Fires, looting, the works."

"That's not good at all. Have they found the bunker?"

"As far as we can tell, no. Probably some of the locals noticed the construction and may have put two and two together, but nothing's come of it yet. The cops are handling it fairly well, though Governor Phillips has called in her National Guard troops and put them in strategic areas."

"Probably a good idea."

"Very. Still, the main problem is that the rioting is worst right where 8th needs to go. Just our dumb fucking luck that they're in the way."

"Reynolds is with them, isn't he?"

"Yeah, I wanted him to keep an eye on them, especially since he knows the area so well. I already sent him orders to take command of the team and get those supplies to the mountain by whatever means necessary."

"I see. You realize what this means." Anderson's voice was cold.

"Yes, Frank, I know. We have no choice. That convoy has to make it to the mountain, come hell or high water. I have to think about the people that are going to be in that bunker. And so does Tom."

"He'll do what he needs to, sir. He's a good man."

"I know. I just hope they make it."

SEATTLE, WASHINGTON

"Fire!" yelled Reynolds.

8th Team began firing into the air, just short of the makeshift barricade that had been erected across the road.

"Cease fire!" Reynolds shouted. The rifles from the other team members quieted, and he looked back at the man standing atop the pile of debris.

"That's just a demonstration, sir. Our weapons are live, and we will use them. Remove the barricade, or we will go through it."

"It's you and your kind that have caused this plague, evil-doer! Reverend Wright said so, and we believe him." A chorus of agreement sounded from those behind the barricade.

Evil-doer? Who talks like that? Reverend Wright is a moron! He started to say that to this jackass standing atop a couple empty gasoline drums, but thought better of it. *Not going to get out of here that way. I need to talk this guy down.*

"I understand the fear you're all feeling," Reynolds said as he walked a few steps closer. "I felt it too, the first time I found out what's going on. But we're not zombies, as you can plainly see. Last time I checked, zombies didn't hold conversations."

"That doesn't matter. You're as bad as they are. Hell, you're *worse!* It's you and the rest like you that have brought this evil down on us, with your wars and your 'experiments.' God is punishing you, and we will *not* keep you from his divine sight! No, sir! You will burn, and you will burn *now!*"

Reynolds jumped back as a Molotov cocktail landed at his feet, a fast-spreading pool of fire approaching the front of the lead Stryker. A single shot sounded from above, and a man fell from the top of one of the nearby buildings, his next improvised grenade clutched in one hand, splashing around him as the bottle broke.

"Cease fire! Cease—" More shots sounded as other rioters lobbed more Molotovs at his men, and he realized that the situation had changed irrevocably. He had to get his people through to the bunker, and talking hadn't cut it. More direct means were required now.

He ran for the first Medium Tactical Vehicle, a cargo truck with a container on the back and an armored cab up front. Small arms fire plinked off the cab as he jumped inside and turned to the soldier manning the machine gun in its berth atop the cab. "Return fire!"

He grabbed the radio off the dash. "Alpha Two to all vehicles. Return fire. Mobile One, take us in."

"There's really no way around this, sir?" asked Larkin from the driver's seat. "They're just people, sir. They're *our citizens.*"

"I know that, Larkin. They've left us no choice. We don't have time to go around them and we don't know if the other roads are even clear."

"Yes, sir." Larkin threw the vehicle into drive as the Stryker in front crushed the flimsy barricade under its oversized tires. Reynolds could see the .50 caliber machine gun on its roof tracking back and forth, spitting rounds as it found its targets. "I just wish there was a different way, sir."

"Me, too, son. Me, too. Just make sure your REAPR is on in case we have to bail."

Suddenly a blast rocked the street, and a building to their right began to crumble and burn. As the smoke began to clear somewhat,

Reynolds could see the Stryker ahead moving forward, its right side dented, scarred and blackened.

Holy shit. IEDs.

"All units, all units. Watch for IEDs."

"Say again. IEDs?" A voice crackled over the radio. "Seriously?"

"That's affirmative, IEDs."

Another blast, this time from the left side of the street, and the Stryker ground to a halt. This explosion had been much, much closer. They were still taking some small arms fire from the roofs and others running down the street toward them.

"Mobile One, report."

"They got our axle on that one, sir. Not sure how, but from what I can see, the whole wheel is shredded."

"Roger that. Prepare for evac."

"Roger."

"Mobile Two, move up. MTVs, heads-up. They'll be coming for you. There may be more on the—"

Reynolds didn't so much hear the explosion as feel it. It lifted the truck off the ground, slamming it forward into the rear of the broken Stryker. *What the hell was that?*

Glancing over at Larkin, Reynolds noticed the star pattern on the windshield where the man's head had impacted, and saw the crazy angle at which his head now rested. Unreasoned anger boiled in him. *Dumb shit. Why weren't you wearing your seat belt?*

He unbuckled his own belt and checked the gunner behind him, who was moaning but alive. "Up and at 'em, soldier. Let's find out just what the hell is going on back—" Reynolds was interrupted again as another massive explosion ripped through the convoy.

"Son of a bitch!" He pulled the cab gunner to one side and stood up, taking his position, trying to see what was going on behind him and not get shot at the same time. As his sightline cleared the top of the big container behind him, he was dumbstruck.

Mobile Two was on its side, on fire, two of 8th Team's Marines trying to rescue a third from the Stryker while a fourth provided covering fire. The two other MTVs were burning wrecks, their contents spewed across the street, their drivers . . . one of them was pulled from the burning wreckage by several men, then thrown to the ground. They beat and kicked him until a smattering of shots from the Marines near the Stryker took them out.

His ears still ringing from the explosions, Tom turned as he heard shots from his right, where Masters and the rest of the men in Mobile One were moving back along the convoy in a tight squad formation, taking down their attackers as they came at them. Masters glanced up at Reynolds.

"Sir, we should get out of here." Reynolds was amazed at the calm way the young man spoke, firing a single shot that took out an oncoming rioter even as he did so. "Now, sir."

That was enough to break his daze, and Reynolds snatched his rifle from the floorboard, checking on the gunner he had moved. It was only then that he saw the wound on the man's neck. Bright red, spurting blood coating the floorboards and making it slick.

The soldier's eyes were glazed, and Tom knew he was gone. *No time for that now.* He turned and dove out the driver's side to take up a position with Masters' squad.

"Let's go, Lieutenant."

"Yes, sir."

The squad moved toward the rear of the convoy, maintaining their tight formation. Tom took down two would-be snipers from upper stories as they made their way, and lost count of how many the other squad shot.

As they reached what was left of Mobile Two, Masters looked at the two Marines still struggling with their trapped comrade. Tom could see that the trapped man was dead, the life gone from his eyes. He put a hand on one of the men's shoulders. "He's gone, leave him."

The Marine snarled, throwing off the hand and turning back to his task. The other never even acknowledged him.

Reynolds was about to pull the man away, but Masters got there before he could, with a right hook to the Marine's jaw that sent him flying back a pace and landing on his ass. Masters put a boot on his chest before the Marine could move, and pointed his pistol at the man's face. Reynolds hadn't even seen him draw the gun.

"Get up, soldier. Retrieve your weapon and take your position." He leaned down. "Understood?"

The Marine looked at the gun, at the lieutenant, and then back at the dead trapped soldier. His eyes cleared, and he seemed to wake up. "Yes . . . yes, sir."

Masters nodded and moved to talk to one of his men. Reynolds just shook his head and took his place in the formation. *That is one hard son of a bitch.*

"Orders, sir?" asked the younger soldier.

"Form up, and we'll take up a position in that building," he said, pointing to what appeared to be a clothing store of some kind.

"Yes, sir. You heard him, boys. Move out!"

The squad moved as one into the damaged shop, then further back into the store room and office area. "Masters, secure a perimeter and get me your radio operator."

"Yes, sir. Can't, sir. He died in Mobile One."

"Fuck. All right then, just the perimeter."

"Yes, sir."

Reynolds found the office phone—cordless, fortunately, and still powered—and dialed as he maneuvered out to the front of the shop, keeping to what cover he could find as he surveyed the street outside. From this vantage point, he actually had a good view of the wreckage of the convoy and the intersection.

"Maxwell, go."

"Sir, this line is unsecured."

"Roger that. What's your status?"

"Sir, the convoy has been destroyed. I've lost half of 8th. We've secured a perimeter for the moment, but without any vehicles or additional support, I'm not sure how long we can hold out. Estimate forty to fifty hostiles in our immediate area. Requesting air cover, sir."

"Understood. Help is on the way, ASAP."

"Yes, sir. Thank you, sir. We'll hold out—" Reynolds broke off as he saw, coming around the corner of the street ahead, a mob of what had to be a hundred or more.

Give them torches and pitchforks, and it'd be right out of a movie.

They were headed straight for the convoy, and it was only a matter of time before they reached his position. "Holy shit," Tom whispered, forgetting he still held the phone.

"What was that, son?" asked Maxwell.

"Sir, I'd just like to say it was an honor serving with you." Checking the magazine in his rifle, he moved back into the office as the crowd approached.

"Captain?"

"That estimate of hostiles, sir? It was a bit low. Tell my team goodbye for me, sir."

He could hear Maxwell take a deep breath. "Will do, soldier. The honor was all mine. Good luck. Maxwell out."

"Masters!" Reynolds flinched only slightly as the man appeared as if by magic at his side. "Bring everybody back. We'll need them."

"Sir?" The lieutenant glanced at the approaching mob. "Yes, sir."

Reynolds began firing as the mob noticed him crouched in the shadows. One shot, one kill. Their voices raised in fury, they rushed him. He could hear shots from behind as the crunch of a door being torn off its hinges echoed from the rear of the store.

Funny, I always thought it'd be a walker that punched my ticket.

FORT CARSON, COLORADO

"No word from them, sir."

"What about the Black Hawks?"

"The pilots said they found what was left of the convoy, but it wasn't much, sir. The Strykers were fairly intact, such as they were, but the trucks were destroyed. There was no sign of any AEGIS personnel or the supplies, sir. They reported at least a hundred hostiles in the area, though it appeared they were dispersing."

"So the whole team?"

"We believe so, sir. Until it cools down, we can't get any men on the ground."

"See that you do, Commander. No one gets left behind."

"Roger that, sir." Anderson stood to leave. "Will there be anything else, sir?"

Maxwell sighed. "Yeah. Get 1st Team in here. I want to tell them myself."

Anderson nodded. "Yes, sir." Saluting, the commander turned and walked out of the general's office as Maxwell turned to the window, staring out at the beautiful Colorado sunset.

The irony of so much beauty and so much horror co-existing in the same world did not escape him. *I'm beginning to wonder if any of us will live through this. But if not us, who?*

The colors and shapes of the sunset continued to shift, ignorant of the heartache and pain of those watching, as it always had.

Chapter Twenty-three

FORT CARSON, COLORADO

NO FURNITURE, NO SINK, NO drain. Four solid concrete walls framed the rectangular room, one of them inset with a heavy steel door. A row of thick one-way observation windows covered one wall, and flimsy fluorescent light fixtures dangled high overhead. It was an empty cell.

Well, mostly empty.

If I hadn't been completely distracted by the contents of the cell I would have been interested in the construction of the floor. It looked like carbon fiber, and it wasn't so much a floor as it was a grid. A pattern of small circular holes formed the entire walking surface and went three rows up onto the wall. Even though I knew what the holes were for, it still looked odd to me.

But I *was* completely distracted by the contents of the cell: its sole inhabitant, which stood staring at the door, with thick chains around its wrists bolted to a ring set in the wall.

My radio crackled. "We're ready."

"Okay," I said, my voice breaking. "Give me a second."

I reached a hand out to the small figure, but he didn't see me. He didn't see much of anything. My hand spread across the glass as if I could pull him back with sheer willpower.

It's my duty to save him. But first things first. Can I live with myself if I go through with it?

"Do it," I said, dropping my hand from the window.

The steel door in the side of the chamber slid open, revealing a man in a hood—and what appeared to be a very nice suit—who was thrust inside the room. The smaller figure snarled and charged, only to be brought up short by the shackles on his wrists. The door clanged shut, and the man freed himself of the hood.

I depolarized the observation windows so that Gardner could see me. He took no notice of me at first. He was busy cringing back from the still-snarling form of Eric, who should have become my son, as the chains made sharp snapping and jingling sounds in the air. Gardner huddled into a corner by the door.

Finally catching his breath and looking around, once he saw that the chains were secure, Gardner spotted me through the window and flinched as I gazed at him with no emotion. He started speaking, and I punched another button on the wall-mounted control panel beside the window to turn on the communication system.

"—can come to some sort of accommodation, surely. There's no need for any dramatics. You've made your point, Mr. Blake."

When I didn't respond, I could see his Adam's apple bob up and down on that scrawny neck and the sweat that appeared on his forehead as he tried to ignore the screaming, clawing zombie that raged not three feet from where he crouched.

"Really, this is unnecessary."

I cocked my head at him, as though inspecting a heretofore unknown species of insect.

"Do you recognize the room?" I asked. "You should. You had it specially built, didn't you?"

Gardner looked around at the room, seeing the grid of round holes in the floor as if for the first time, and he swallowed again.

"You wouldn't . . ."

My hand hovered over the console again, and I saw the look in Gardner's eyes as he realized that there was no escape for him this time. He stood up straight and tall then, obviously intending to meet his fate with some dignity. *Good for him.* Still, there were two unanswered questions, and I had to know.

"Why me? Why go to so much trouble over me?" I asked.

"Because you're infected, Mr. Blake," he said impatiently, as if I were an idiot for not already knowing.

For a split second, I reeled. *Impossible! Me, infected?* As fast as the shock came, though, I realized what he was doing: playing me, yet again.

"That's impossible, and you know it."

"Is it? Think back, all the way back to Fall Creek. You were injured, weren't you? A splinter of wood, I believe. In your report, you mention a little girl . . ."

I thought back to that little girl in the yard that night. *Could she have infected me? No, it just wasn't possible.*

"You're just trying to save your own skin now, Gardner. You'd say anything."

"Hardly. It's obvious that I won't change your mind about this. What reason would I have to lie at this stage?" He folded his arms and leaned back against the wall, the picture of confidence.

"This is nonsense. If what you're saying was true, I'd have become a walker a long time ago."

Gardner moved forward toward the window, suddenly animated, but still careful to keep out of reach of Eric.

"Exactly, Mr. Blake! Now you understand. What makes you immune to this? How do you walk around with these prions inside you—and we've verified that in your blood samples, by the way—without turning into a walker?"

He shook his head. "If only I'd been able to get you on the examination table, we might have discovered the truth. I know more than any other scientist on the planet about this disease, Mr. Blake. I could have found the answer. That'll never happen now, though."

He turned away and moved back to his corner, but I knew he was watching for my reaction out of the corner of his eye.

I wasn't about to give him the satisfaction. It was such an obvious ploy. He just wanted to find a reason for me not to push the button at my fingertips. And I could not imagine any reason in the world powerful enough to stop me, though I gave him points for creativity.

Since I wasn't going to get a real answer, I changed the subject. "What about everything else, then? Why all that?"

"Why what?" he answered.

"All of it! The secret experiments, selling the samples to North Korea, all of it. You had to know what would happen. You had to know what you would help create, and what you would destroy."

He laughed. Then he shook his head. "You're hardly worthy of the trouble of explaining it," he said dismissively. I casually tapped my fingers near the buttons on the console until he noticed and took a deep breath.

"Fine," he said. "You see all the puzzle pieces together, *finally*, and you still can't see the picture it makes? You want to know *why* I did it?"

"I do."

"Why, Mr. Blake, for the only reason in the world that means anything at all." His smile was chilling, this time. As if I gazed on pure evil. "Power."

"How does killing off the human race give you . . ." I stopped, forgetting for a moment the button that would end his life and my misery. In an instant, it all became clear. "Oh, I see."

"Ah, yes. There it is, the light of understanding, be it ever so dim." He clapped his hands softly and slowly, a 'golf clap' if ever there was one.

"Only a hundred thousand of us left. And you've got a spot in the bunkers," I said. "And not just *any* old bunker—the *presidential* bunker. With SecDef and the rest of them. With only ten thousand people to deal with, consolidating your power would be easy.

"You'd probably claim credit for Project Phoenix as a whole, or something similar. And once you were done with that bunker, there would only be nine others to bring under your control. A hundred thousand people, all owing their survival to Henry Gardner."

I snorted. "Henry Gardner, ruler of the New United States."

He turned and spat, sneering. "As if I would cheapen this great nation with all that rabble. I would have selected my followers carefully, and only they would have seen the light of the surface again.

"This country—this *world*—has allowed itself to be dumbed-down by generation after generation of idiots and whores. The world I was creating was to be an intellectual paradise, free of the fallacies of all the morons that had gone before, with pure untainted stock—"

"Shut up, Henry." He spluttered to a halt as I took the opportunity to laugh, sickened as I was. "You really are a spy-movie villain, you know."

"How so?"

"I've caught you monologuing."

I pressed one button, and the special explosive bolts in Eric's chains blew, letting him loose in the room. Gardner shrieked as the child came flying at him, far faster than any other walker I'd seen out there in the world.

No wonder he wanted to experiment on Eric. Someone like him could see so much potential in that sort of speed.

To Gardner's credit, he fought the kid off for a few seconds, kicking and trying to run away. But there was nowhere to go and he knew it. It took only one misstep, his immaculate and expensive loafers tripping him up, and Eric was on him in a heartbeat.

That was when my buddy Henry *really* started screaming.

I was wrong. The question isn't whether I can live with myself if I do this. Almost of its own volition, my hand lifted to the large red button on the wall marked "Flash Activation."

The question is, how could I live with myself if I don't?

I punched the button, staring into Gardner's now-sightless eyes as Eric feasted on him, not looking away as the 3,000° F flames roared by the window, consuming everything and everyone inside.

After a full five minutes, the flames shut off and the room was visible once more by the light of the observation room. Everything temporary—the chains, the lighting fixtures, and especially Eric and Gardner—were gone, as if they never existed. Only blackened and cracked concrete remained.

I knew that I would be haunted for years by my actions here today, regardless of their outcome, and by Gardner's. It felt like I had heard the cries of all of his victims. I'd dispensed a horrific justice for them, to be sure, but it was the least that he'd deserved. And what about all his *future* victims? Those whose only defender had chosen to stop his crimes before they'd even begun?

Yes, I will be haunted. But if that's the price I have to pay for me to know that his evil is gone, then so be it. I can bear that pain, for Eric. And for all the others, past and future.

The door to my right opened and I could feel Kim standing there, though I didn't turn.

"It's done," I said, almost whispering.

"Are you back?"

I had to take a deep breath before I could answer, but it was time to put my demons to rest, once and for all. "Yes."

I turned to her and smiled, finally at peace with Rebecca and Eric's death, and knowing that I would fight and, if necessary, die to protect those who remained.

Kim nodded. It was a hard thing I'd asked her to do, but she had only hesitated for a moment. She'd seen the right of it, and knew the cost as well as I did.

We'll pay it together, I hope. With her by my side, I feel like I can withstand anything. That will just have to be enough.

Suddenly our radios squawked. "Blake, Barnes, report to the general's office on the double." Commander Anderson's voice. Kim half-turned toward the door, cocking one eyebrow at me. I took a deep breath and let it out, then walked out with her.

I had left the past behind me, and it felt good. Time to focus on the future, now. Although, I would definitely be stopping by Dr. Adamsdöttir's office to have my blood tested the first chance I got. Couldn't hurt to check up on ol' Henry, after all.

"Sir, I have something I think you need to see."

The young soldier stood at ease in front of General Maxwell's desk, while Commander Anderson leaned against the wall nearby.

"Oh? And what would that be, Sergeant?" Maxwell asked.

"Sir, I . . . I was ordered to keep an eye on the labs, since Mr. Gardner's detention, sir. I was walking through the security area and saw something on the monitor . . ."

The kid turned a bit pale, but continued. "I just think you should see this, sir," he said, laying a flash drive on the general's desk. Maxwell glanced at Anderson, who nodded slightly.

"Very well, Sergeant. You're dismissed."

"Thank you, sir," the soldier said, saluting and exiting the office as Maxwell fitted the drive into his computer and brought up the only file on the device. A few minutes later, Maxwell turned off the video of the security feed from the lab cameras and sat back in his chair. He glanced over at Anderson, still leaning against the wall. The stone-faced commander was silent, as he had been throughout what they had just witnessed.

"Nothing to say, Frank?"

"No, sir. I'd say it was the least he deserved. Not something I would've done—or you—but Blake? Of all of us, he had more reason to do it than anyone."

"Well, what about Kimberly?"

"They're a pair now, sir. Joined at the hip, as it were. She pulled him back from a near coma, sir. I'll bet she hesitated when he asked, but not long. After all, it was *him* pushing the buttons, not her."

Maxwell grimaced. "Be that as it may—and I agree with you—the fact is that they disobeyed direct orders. I'm in a mess of shit now. I'll have to justify this to the president, you realize. He's going to want to know what happened to the bastard."

Frank stared at the general, not moving from his perch near the window. "Permission to speak freely, sir?"

"Always, Frank. You know that."

"Sir, I'd say if the president doesn't see the right of this, then fuck him, sir. We've got too many other things to worry about than the death of some asshole who should've been shot a long time ago."

Maxwell laughed. "Well, you *did* say 'freely,' didn't you?"

Anderson's lips twitched in what Maxwell thought might be the ghost of a smile.

"Fact is, you're right. Too much other crap. Better bring 'em in, then." He picked up the phone on his desk and punched a button. "Nancy, send them in, please."

Anderson moved around behind Maxwell as the entirety of 1st Team filed in, taking spots wherever they could. It wasn't a big office, and space was at a premium, even with all nine of them standing at attention. As the senior operator present, Powell stood forward and saluted. "First Team, reporting as ordered, sir."

"At ease, men." Maxwell tapped a pencil on his desk as his crème de la crème fell into parade rest. He could see Powell was a bit nervous, and decided to be nice . . . for once. "Don't worry, they'll be here in a minute."

Jake couldn't help but glance at the general, then returned to eyes-forward. "Uh, yes sir." As if on cue, they all heard the rhythmic thump of boots running into the hallway outside, clearly moving at top speed. A short mumbled conversation later, and Barnes and Blake arrived.

"Good of you to join us, Major. Mr. Blake."

MOBILE, ALABAMA

A coalition of Baptist ministers and deacons organized their followers to protect the outlying areas of the city and its suburbs. Congregating in one of the larger churches, this fellowship stocked the church with food and other supplies sufficient to last them for months, if not years.

Construction began shortly after on a wall surrounding the property and a fortified structure in the rear of the church to house all the people and the supplies. One of the ministers gathered a couple of the farmers and walked them around a section of the land, explaining where he wanted the large garden to go.

The poor and destitute weren't turned away, and helped to construct the fortifications and protect the followers from those who fear what they see coming. The clergy extended invitations to anyone willing to work, and promised safety and security.

One man arrived a few days after construction began with his sick wife and child, and the senior minister at the time turned him away, saying that they would pray for the survival of the small family, but couldn't accept the sick.

Tears streamed down the minister's face as the man turned away with nowhere to go and all hope lost, but he stood his ground and just shook his head when the man looked back one last time.

The only others he turned away were a group of young men who drove up in a rusty pickup, piling out with their rifles and pistols, drunk and boisterous.

The senior minister, a large southern man, wasn't flustered.

"What can I do fo' you boys?" he asked.

"We's here lookin fo' the Church of the Divine Judgment. Y'all them?" One particularly feisty-looking young man stepped forward.

The minister looked at the boys, considering. He spat on the ground, a stream of dirty brown juice.

"We ain't them. Don't have no truck with that nonsense. You boys look like you're from good folk. Hell, I even know some of ya." He nodded toward one of the young men, standing at the back, who flushed and looked away. "Yeah, I know your ma and pa, Darrell. What would they say about this?"

When none of the men responded, the minister spat again. "Well, if ya ain't gonna help, you can be on your merry. Lord save you boys."

The leader of the men judged the will of the minister, one old man against his young pack, and gestured to the truck. "Load up, boys, let's go find 'em."

The minister waited until they were out of sight and then glanced skyward with a murmured, "Thanks, Lord."

Soon, the ten-foot cinder-block wall was finished, and the construction crew focused on the barracks. They worked hard. It seemed that they knew that they worked for the survival of everyone.

FORT CARSON, COLORADO

"So that's the situation. We've managed to get some search and rescue crews into the area, but other than the wreckage of the convoy, they didn't find anything of use. Just shredded pieces of uniform and some spent shell casings. No equipment, no bodies, nothing."

I felt like I'd been punched in the gut as I listened to the general tell us about 8th Team's fight in Washington.

Tom is gone. Probably dead. How many more will die?

"Sir, there's a chance—" I said.

"They were surrounded by a couple hundred screaming, angry, crazy religious people last I heard, son," Maxwell replied, putting his foot down hard on any hope we might be harboring for our fallen comrades.

"Tom Reynolds and Adrian Masters were two of the toughest sons of bitches I've ever met, but even they couldn't pull their asses out of that fire. No, they're gone. And that's the end of it. Clear?"

"Yes, sir," I said, getting the message. "So, if we can't truck the supplies in—"

"Choppers. We've conscripted every Chinook and Skycrane we could find, in and out of the service. Those bad boys can move more than ten tons each, and we're getting nearly a hundred of them."

"What about their bunker, sir?" asked Kimberly.

"Bunker Eight is a hundred klicks or so outside Austin, Texas. Frank and I have already discussed this, and he's headed there to recruit any likely folks he can and get them trained up. He'll be staying with them there. It's the only thing we can do."

Maxwell stood up and began pacing behind his desk. "There's something else you need to know. Evacuations of lottery selectees have already started. They will continue until everyone is inside and lockdown is initiated. We're not sure when that'll be, but things are progressing even faster than we expected."

"Any idea at all when we'll be going, sir?" I asked, hoping I didn't already know the answer.

"Soon, Mr. Blake, soon. We've completely lost southeastern Asia, it appears. Africa is bad, as is South America. No reports out of China, but that's not a surprise. Australia is holding on, lots of people retreating to the Outback." He snorted. "That's a helluva comeuppance for them, having to depend on the aborigines for once."

Maxwell stopped pacing and turned back to us. "Our best analysts have put our most optimistic timetable at a month, maybe two at the absolute most. Personally, I think that's horseshit. I expect us to get the evac orders within a couple weeks. But asking questions isn't why we get the big bucks, is it?"

A few chuckled, and Maxwell nodded. "Good, at least some of you can still find some humor in something. That's all for now. General briefing in one hour. I expect you all to be there. Dismissed."

We stood and saluted, filing out. I looked at Kim as we crossed the field toward the barracks.

"You think he's right?"

"I don't know. I hope not," she said. "But there's something to be said for being safe and secure inside a bunker. Better than not knowing if you're going to live through the next day."

"True enough. Still, we've got each other."

She half-turned and flashed me that radiant smile. "You bet your sweet ass we do." She grabbed my hand as we continued walking, squeezing it tight. "I miss Tom. And Rachel. And Victor."

"Me, too, love." I could see tears in her eyes, and put my arm around her shoulder. "Me, too."

APPLE VALLEY, MINNESOTA

Just outside Minneapolis, a stranger spies a roadside revival tent city. His walking staff in hand and his pistol weighing heavy in its concealed holster, he enters the haphazard layout, joining a few other stragglers still approaching the event, and finds a stage of some sort set up just outside the biggest tent.

A man is on the stage in front of a crowd of hundreds, preaching about the end of the world and how only the truly good shall be saved from the divine retribution overtaking the land. The stranger waits at the edge of the crowd, watching the rapt faces of the preacher's listeners and wondering how they could be so blind to the truth.

The preacher's going full-steam now, and his speech and gestures grow more and more wild, culminating in a roar as he commands the crowd to attend to the "salvation arena."

Intrigued despite his better judgment, the stranger follows the crowd to the other side of the tent city and is astonished to see a temporary cattle corral set up with several walkers crashing against the barriers. His hand darts to his pistol, but he stops when he notices the barrier's concrete bases. He glances at the makeshift stage set to one side, overlooking the corral, where the maddened preacher now holds a young girl by the arm.

More preaching, more deranged ravings, and the stranger grows nervous as the rantings take a darker turn, the clergyman demanding a trial of salvation. It's now clear what the madman intends, and the stranger uses his walking staff to clear a path to the stage. Several members of the crowd nurse large bruises by the time he arrives.

Dropping the staff and taking the few steps of the stage in a single bound, he grabs the girl's other arm, swinging her back onto the stage just as the preacher flings her forward into the corral.

In an instant, utter quiet descends over the crowd, except for the moaning of the undead below, eager for their feast. The stranger stares at the preacher, his contempt and disgust clear.

Gently, he says to the girl, "You're safe now, miss," and she collapses against his chest, sobbing. He never takes his eyes off the revival preacher, who seethes at the interruption.

"How dare you?" he roars. "You have forsaken your salvation with this desecration of a sacred rite!"

"Sacred, my ass," says the stranger, and unzips his jacket to reveal a clerical collar and a cross around his neck. "There's nothing sacred about human sacrifice."

A gasp rises from the crowd at this new revelation, and the preacher snarls. "If she was truly pure, she would not be harmed! You are a traitor to your faith!"

The stranger shakes his head, steps to one side away from the girl, and draws his pistol. In the blink of an eye, the .357 Magnum roars three times, dispatching all three walkers in the corral with a shot to the head for each. He then turns back to the preacher.

"No more."

Completely insane now, the preacher screams and charges, but the stranger sidesteps and lets him fall into the corral. He addresses the crowd.

"You're not evil, if that's what you're thinking," he says as they stare at him, struck nervless by his actions. "You've just been deceived by someone who's very, very good at it. This plague is evil, not a divine judgment. If you're bit, you will die, no matter how many times a day you pray. Now go home. Pray. Pray for us all. Be with your families. Or better yet, evacuate with the National Guard and the Army."

He stands there a moment longer, putting away his pistol and checking the girl for bite marks and other injuries. Finding none, he whispers calming words to her, and she thanks him as she runs off.

Headed for home, I hope.

The crowd disperses, and as he zips his coat once more over the now-holstered pistol, he hears a faint cry for help from the corral. He glances back, and sees there were four walkers in the corral, not three. The fourth crawls along the ground toward the dazed preacher. Its legs are those of a crippled person, shriveled and useless.

Another victim?

He turns his back on the corral, picks up his walking stick, and sstrides out of the tent city. He is at the edge of the last row when the screams begin.

He doesn't turn back.

"I say again, brothers and sisters, that this is our time to unite against the evils of this world, brought upon us by the military and industrial demons of our past. They have sown evil for hundreds of years, despite our warnings, and now the reaping has come!"

Reverend Sebastian Wright had never looked more stately, more *godly* than he did at that moment, preaching to his followers from every radio and television station and satellite channel he could get his hands on.

"Let the future know us as the ones who redeemed this foul, cruel, *evil* world! Let them not remember the failed sinners who have succumbed to the righteous justice that is this plague upon the world! Let the naysayers and so-called 'scientists' talk about prions and illness. We know the truth of our Lord God when we hear it!"

His message reached large groups of followers throughout the United States and the world. In Maryland, they chanted slogans and hurled insults outside the offices of USAMRIID. In Washington, DC, hundreds had been arrested outside the White House and on the steps of Congress. Military installations across the country were on their highest alerts, and more than a few followers of the Church of the Divine Judgment had been killed in self-defense by those who did not believe as they did.

In Atlanta, soldiers from the Georgia National Guard were supplemented by those from Fort McPherson to the southwest. They patrolled the grounds of the Centers for Disease Control and Prevention after some Church members attacked personnel there, claiming that it was God's will that the plague go uncured.

"We shall overcome this plague, just as the last one, my children. For we are chosen, the Chosen of God himself. Uninfected by this judgment, we are instead filled with the light of the Heavenly Father and the Son. We are his instruments on Earth to bring about this change, helping to keep those who would do evil from stopping his grand design."

In Seattle and Tacoma, the mob had grown by hundreds in past weeks, then by the day. More and more adherents of the Church flocked to the only thing they still had: faith.

"We will survive, chosen. Not because we're better, but because we *believe.* We are not evil, and therefore we will not be purged. We will rise up and cast down the sinners, the unbelievers, and the faithless. They will burn in the fiery pits of their own making and, yes, we will watch and laugh. For it is joyous to witness the end to sin, and that can only happen with the Lord's righteous fury.

"Let not evil survive among you, my children. Seek out he who would hide his evil from our sight, who would cover the marks of the devil and the filthy lusting for the flesh of his kin. Seek out those who hide themselves among you, pretending their evil does not exist. Find them and show them no mercy, for they are of the devil and must be destroyed."

Wright had really worked himself into a lather, and was nearly foaming at the mouth.

"All the power and the glory be to God, to Jesus and to His Holy followers! Long live the Church of the Divine Judgment!"

Chapter Twenty-four

"THIS IS A HEALTHWATCH SPECIAL Report. I'm—" Tabitha broke down for a moment, her face in her hands, her shoulders shaking. She wiped the tears from her eyes, and continued in a breaking voice. "I'm Tabitha Greene.

"This is our final report. We will be going off the air in a few moments, as will all satellite and television stations. We will leave our channels broadcasting emergency service messages around the clock as long as the equipment continues to function.

"Here's what we know: Zombie outbreaks have occurred in every major city, in every country and on every continent around the globe, with scattered civilian resistance. Here in the US, the Army and National Guard are on full alert, helping to evacuate overrun cities and coordinating defense plans for others.

"There are some areas in some of the larger cities that have been cordoned off. What reports we have from inside seem to indicate that these areas are under the control of local militias, many of whom are well-armed and self-trained, and who are holding their own against the zombies outside the barricades. Those who seek to join these militia-controlled areas are cautioned that living persons have been reported to have been cast out of them to the zombies for reasons unknown.

"The list of cities that have not and cannot now be evacuated is too long to provide. Here are brief reports on the largest cities. Chicago, New York, and Houston have succumbed.

"In Manhattan, both tunnels to New Jersey and all of the bridges have been deliberately collapsed by the Army Corps of Engineers.

Please be advised that there is no longer any passage to or from the island."

"San Diego, Denver, and Atlanta have reported massive outbreaks in the last twenty-four hours. Seattle and its suburb of Tacoma are a raging inferno, as is Los Angeles.

"Oklahoma City, Kansas City, and Minneapolis are reporting successful evacuations in progress. Dallas and Fort Worth are gone, as are Memphis, New Orleans, and Detroit. Here in Washington, DC, we have had several large outbreaks.

"There have been reports of civilian attacks on the entrances to the government bunkers, but these attacks have been met with overwhelming force. Thousands are dead, many left lying where they fell as the Army continues to defend humanity's last hope for survival. For your own safety, please do *not* attempt to force your way into a bunker."

She took a deep breath. "It has been reported that the president and top government officials have begun evacuations to their bunker. Latest reports tell us that nearly ninety percent of those selected for Project Phoenix have arrived at the bunkers or been accounted for. If you have received a notification letter or phone call, government sources tell us that you must arrive at the bunkers in short order or the doors will be closed.

"For those of you still watching and not evacuating: Remember to isolate anyone who is infected. Bar your doors. Collect what water and food you can. Pool your resources, but only with those willing to prove that they are uninfected. Store drinking water in your bathtubs—" Tabitha broke off and put one hand to her ear, listening through her earpiece. Her face turned ashen. Her voice was halting as she continued.

"Ladies and gentlemen . . ." she said, and paused once more, taking several deep breaths but failing to get herself under control. "Ladies and gentlemen, I've just been informed that China has made good on their threat. Seven minutes ago, multiple nuclear weapons were detonated along the Chinese southern border with Myanmar, Laos, and India. The damage . . . the damage is incalculable. Millions have perished and millions more will die from radiation poisoning which, of course, has no effect on the walkers.

"Our weather analysts are already predicting that the fallout will be blown south-southeast, reaching as far south as Indonesia and possibly far northern Australia, in coming weeks.

"Go to your families, if you can. Be with those you love, and pray for our survival. From all of us here at HealthWatch, good luck, and may God be with us all."

FORT DETRICK, MARYLAND

The gates that normally bar visitors to the US Army Medical Research Institute of Infectious Diseases (USAMRIID) were bent and twisted. One of the many trucks that had slammed through them was a flaming wreck just past the entrance.

The bodies of nearly a full platoon of soldiers are scattered nearby, some apparently torn apart by the mob that milled around the entrances to the buildings of the facility itself. Many wore religious symbols of every faith and creed, and carried signs proclaiming the end of days and the glory of the divine judgment sent to Earth by God's hand.

More than a few were covered in blood. Whether it was their own or someone else's was impossible to discern.

At first, none of the followers of the Church of the Divine Judgment noticed their members falling. They continued to shout and scream at the top of their lungs, demanding entry into the buildings that were, of course, locked up as tight as the prepared defenders can make them.

It was only when those crowding the biggest of the buildings finally heard the screams from the rear of the crowd that they noticed the walkers among them. The zombies had found a mobile feast. And they were hungry.

The church members didn't have long to worry. Another follower came roaring over the lawn in his over-sized Ford Excursion. Eyes red and hair uncombed, he was overwrought, but still focused on his target.

Ignoring the pleas of his brethren, he ran down walkers and humans alike who stood between him and his goal.

It was only when he crashed through the front door of the facility—foot never leaving the gas pedal—that the smarter followers realized that something wasn't right, and turned to run.

Even the fastest of them couldn't outpace the fireball that reached for them with violent speed. The would-be martyr had learned well from the lessons of Timothy McVeigh, and his ammonium nitrate-fueled truck bomb decimated everything within nearly a half-mile of the building.

The hot, stinking wind from the explosion threw parts of buildings, people and the truck outward, and the shrapnel tore through the flesh of the unfortunates standing nearby.

Broken, severed limbs from walkers caught in the blast rained in a ghastly downpour over those merely knocked off their feet, eardrums punctured by the blast.

Church members, walkers, and uninfected humans working hard on a cure were lost and gone forever in a moment of blazing light and incomparable sound.

ATLANTA, GEORGIA

Reverend Sebastian Wright's voice blared from the shortwave radios carried by his followers, many of whom were protesting and shouting outside the concrete and steel barriers of the Centers for Disease Control and Prevention. Several had already been shot trying to gain entrance. The soldiers guarding the gates and patrolling the grounds had itchy trigger fingers and weren't taking any chances.

"Brothers and sisters, now is the time to strike! Our cousins in Maryland, so close to the root of evil in Washington, have already struck a mortal blow for our cause! The enemy is reeling and they can see their defeat in the eyes of their conquerors! Strike now while the iron is hot, while we have evil cornered and on the run!"

A younger man moved through the crowd, loudly joining in the slogan-chanting, and earning more than a few friendly slaps on the back for his vehemence. He continued to move closer, his eyes bright and shining with the fire of belief.

As he neared the front of the crowd, one of the soldiers standing guard at the gate noticed him and moved a step closer. Then another. "Don't come any closer, kid. No one needs to get hurt—"

"You cannot hurt me, unbeliever," screamed the young man, throwing open his coat and revealing the C4 explosive and the ball bearings tightly wrapped in plastic bags. A thumb detonator was visible in one hand. "I am a servant of God and he has chosen me to cast down you sinners and make you pay for the evils you have wrought amongst us!"

As in Maryland, the more perceptive of the crowd began to move away from the kid and his too-bright eyes. These few had a better chance of survival as the sharp-eyed soldier slung his rifle and shot the poor youngster once, in the head.

As the youth crumpled to the ground, the bombs strapped to his chest began to beep, and the soldier had just enough time to realize what this meant. He turned to run as well, but only managed a few steps before being consumed in the blast.

"Rejoice, my brothers, for the end is nigh! I am the Reverend Sebastian Wright, and I say to you that the evils of this world can only be cleansed in the fire of retribution and justice. God be with all of you!"

This fireball wasn't as big as the one outside Washington, but it was accompanied by several others scattered around the property. Some fanatics had even managed to avoid the military patrols and slipped inside the gates and fences, right up to the walls. Their explosions were muffled, but it doesn't take much to knock out a building's power, if you know what you're looking for.

Primary and backup power units were destroyed, one by one. The soldiers could no longer hold back the swarm of people at the gates, and the Church's followers stormed the walls and the last holdouts of the one remaining place on the world's surface that could have stopped the prion plague.

The best biological researchers left on the surface—the last hope for those locked out of the bunkers—were hunted down, dragged from their laboratories, beaten, raped and tortured, then killed. The violence was all-consuming, a last shout into the void from a dying people.

Advanced bio-research laboratories were destroyed beyond repair, uncountable viruses and diseases releasing into the air or spilling across the floors of the basements and sub-basements. Those releasing the toxins died quick, horribly painful deaths.

The CDC had long been prepared for the possibility of an outbreak in any or all of its laboratories. Years before, they had instituted measures to avoid its dangerous inventory from being spread across the globe, should a catastrophic failure of their multiple containment systems occur.

It was doubtful that they had envisioned a zombie plague, but the end result was the same. When the advanced sensors in the air ducts detected the various viruses and bacteria, a series of valves opened, flooding the emergency system—and thus, the entire facility—with a liquid helium/oxygen mix, the same fuel that powered the space shuttles.

A few of the vandals noticed the warning sirens when they began to blare, but none left the facility, and when there was no one to turn off the automated countdown—or at least no one who *would*—the highly volatile propane crept into every nook and cranny of the facility, only awaiting a single spark to ignite.

A fuel-air explosive, or FAE, such as the one AEGIS had used during the Farmington incursion, is, quite simply, the largest and most deadly non-nuclear weapon currently fielded by first-world countries. It utilizes atmospheric oxygen in a chemical reaction to create a massive blast wave, far exceeding 'normal' weapons and explosives.

In a confined space, such as the CDC's undeground facilities, the effect of such an explosive is nothing short of annhiliation—hence the CDC's reliance on the thermobaric device to eradicate all trace of its escaping viruses and bacteria.

The few remaining on the surface were singing hymns and chanting in prayer circles when they heard what sounded like a rumble of thunder from far underground. Suddenly, they could no longer keep their feet and were thrown as the ground heaved and buckled beneath them, then dropped.

Where once was a pristine lawn, carefully tended, and clean buildings with learned scientists struggling to cure the world's ills, there was now a gigantic crater of smashed and broken earth.

Fire spurted from yawning rents in the earth, and the ground heaved as it settled. The CDC died not with a bang, but with a whimper, as it was consumed in all-cleansing fire.

FORT CARSON, COLORADO

I stood there on the airfield, looking over at the final loading of the C-17 that would take us to our new home under Mount Rainier. There was nothing I could do to help with the operation, and I'd been asked to get the hell out of the way and let the loadmaster and his crew do their jobs.

The smoke from burning buildings in Colorado Springs was thick in the distance, and I wondered how many people were alive down there.

Stop that. They're dead, or soon will be. And that's all you need to remember. Apparently, my inner voice hadn't gotten any nicer over the years.

The rest of 1st Team stood nearby, those of us who were left, anyway. Kim and Johnny were chatting with Maxwell and Dr. Adamsdóttir—*Dr. Maxwell, now, I guess*—as they walked up, the general's own C-17 apparently ready and loaded.

I saluted as he approached, and he returned it, letter-perfect as always. "So that's it, then, sir?" I asked.

He nodded. "Yeah. Everyone is gone except us. This place is a ghost town now. We're the last ones."

"How's it looking out there?" I asked, waving in the direction of Colorado Springs. Or what was left of it, anyway.

"It's all gone. You were right, son. When it happened, it happened fast." He shook his head. "It was only a matter of time, and once USAMRIID and the CDC went up, there wasn't much point in hanging around. Hard to believe two places could hold that much power over everything. We got all our people out, and the evacuations of the lottery winners went well. Last I heard they were at ninety-five percent or so."

"What about the government? The president."

Maxwell looked bleak. "I know the vice-president made it, but I heard a few minutes ago that the president's chopper went down in a storm as he was crossing into Pennsylvania."

"Pennsylvania, sir?"

"Bunker Five, under Mount Davis."

"Oh." We all turned to watch the C-17 finish loading the last of the Strykers. "And you, sir? Where are you and Mary off to?"

"We're headed to Bunker Seven, Wheeler Peak. It's near Taos, in New Mexico."

"Never been there, but it should be nice weather for you in your old age, sir."

Maxwell raised an eyebrow and laughed.

"Yeah, I suppose so. If I live long enough to see it once all this is over," he said, the laughter subsiding and turning to a sigh. "If it ever is."

He turned to Kim. "Well, Major, are you ready to take charge of Bunker One?"

She looked down for a moment and squeezed my hand, then stood tall, saluting the general one last time. "Ready and able, General, sir!"

Maxwell returned her salute slowly, then I saw something I'd never expected to see—never thought was possible. A tear fell from his eye, and another, and he grabbed her in a fierce bear hug.

Emotion. In General Maxwell. Who knew?

"You take care of yourself, you understand me?" he said, his words muffled as he crushed her to him. "You and David, you're our future."

She hugged him back just as hard. "I will, Dad. I will. And we'll talk. Radio, sat-comm . . . as often as we can. This isn't goodbye."

I took the opportunity to hug Dr. Adamsdóttir as Johnny Barnes and Maxwell said their final words in person to one another.

"Thanks for looking after me. I'm glad you and Kim found a way to bring me back."

She nodded and hugged me back. "She needs you, David," she whispered. "She might not ever say it, but she needs you as much as you need her. Never forget that."

I nodded and held out a hand to the general as Kim and Mary said their goodbyes. "It's been an honor, sir."

"Dammit, David, at this point I'm pretty sure you can call me George." He ignored my hand and brought me in for a bear hug as well.

Surprised by my own emotion, I hugged him back too. *It wasn't just Kim that had gained a father*, I realized.

"Thanks, George. For everything. And I'll take good care of her, I promise."

He laughed and stepped back, finally shaking my hand. "Care, nothing. You marry that girl the first chance you get, soldier. That's an order." He pointed at Johnny. "And you make sure it happens!"

Johnny nodded and we all chuckled. "Sir, happy to oblige, sir!"

A yell caught our attention, and I looked over at the C-17 loadmaster waving at us. I waved back and Kim and I watched as Maxwell said goodbye to each and every man in our team, just as he had with all the others.

A wave, and another couple of goodbyes, and we marched off to meet our future in the back of the huge planes headed in very different directions.

We clambered onboard and rolled down the runway before finally gaining enough speed to take off. As we made our lazy turn to head north-northwest, I looked down at what had been my home for several years.

Maxwell—*George*—was right. It was a virtual ghost town. I could see half-empty crates of supplies on the tarmac of the field, barracks doors left open and swinging in the wind, trash already blowing across the parade ground. Such a sad, lonely end to a place that had served us so well.

I looked over at Kim, and saw her looking past me at the base. I wondered if she thought the same thing I did, but she just smiled that smile of hers and kissed me on the cheek before glancing over at her brother strapped in across the way. Then she leaned back and closed her eyes.

"We're not going to be getting much sleep when we land, David," she said. "You might want to catch up now."

I snorted. "Already telling me what to do and you haven't even said yes, yet."

She cracked an eye. "Well, you haven't asked, either."

"Will you?"

"Seriously? *That's* your proposal?

"I was ordered to marry you, after all," I said, very obviously keeping the humor in my voice.

She sighed. "Well, I suppose, if you were *ordered* to do it . . ." Quick as lightning, she punched me in the side—lightly. "Of course I'll marry you, jackass. We're just going to have to think of a better story to tell our kids."

"Kids?"

There was no way I was getting to sleep now.

It wasn't so much the zombies that actually destroyed civilization as we know it. Sure, they were a component, but in the end, it wasn't the zombies that went crazy and started killing people just for *looking* infected. It wasn't a zombie that, in a fit of rage, threw a bomb through the window of a newspaper office in downtown Knoxville.

Zombies didn't trample each other to death trying to get away from the madman in the bomb-vest who decided that an evacuation center just outside Toledo, Ohio was the best place to demonstrate his love for Allah and the Prophet.

It wasn't just religious folks, either. Mobs of humanity formed, frightened and turning to the only people who showed any leadership of any kind. Packs of warring tribes fought each other in the streets of the once-proud cities, at least in those that weren't abandoned to the dead.

Militias rose and fell. So-called 'survivalists' took refuge in their hideouts only to find that one of their loved ones had been bitten, or that their entrances weren't as secure as they thought when other mobs tore them from the hinges and dragged their occupants out to be fed as offerings to the new gods, the walkers.

In the end, it was ordinary, average, everyday humans who panicked at the thought of everything they knew and loved coming to an end. The worst part was not knowing what came next.

When the end of all things is staring you in the face—literally, in many cases—you're forced to come to a decision: can I continue to live? Do I have it in me?

For many, the unfortunate answer to that question was "No."

They died by the hundreds to start with. Masses of people huddled together, praying or just hoping for a miracle, but providing a bloody feast for the walkers who found them.

For others, the instinct was to run—run far away. But where was "away"? Where was safety? Where was shelter?

"Where can we go?" they cried.

And the cold, cruel answer came back in the screams and moans of the dying and the dead.

Nowhere.

Cities burned and were left abandoned as their destroyers moved off in search of other prey. Countries collapsed into ruin, borders merely a memory on a map somewhere, safety the only concern now.

But they *had* to run, and to keep running. To never stop.

For almost everyone, there was nowhere to take shelter. For almost everyone, death was merely a question of when, not if.

Soon, the food would run out, or you wouldn't be able to bring yourself to put a bullet in your husband, your wife, your brother, or your daughter, and then it would be your turn.

Your death might be slow and painful or, if you got bit by a runner, would be quick and painful, and then you'd be more likely to kill everyone around you.

For most, death was a foregone conclusion.

But not for all.

OUTSIDE SEATTLE, WASHINGTON

"This is *so* gonna suck," said Gaines as he somehow pulled the straps tighter across his massive chest. He turned a little green as the plane dropped several hundred feet, then rose back up.

I saw him glance over at Martinez, who was, somehow, sound asleep. I could even see the drool. I looked over at Kim and saw that she was nervous, but controlling it. *Ever the consummate professional. I wish I was that good at not thinking about what was coming.*

"It'll be fine, big man," I said. "It's just a little turbulence."

"I still say we shoulda just landed at McChord anyway and taken our chances."

I snorted. "You saw the place, D. You saw what those crazy sons-of-bitches did to it. No way we can land there—no way."

"I've been in worse, Gunny," said Johnny, who had been saddled with the moniker of 'Junior,' for obvious reasons. "You should've seen some of our drops in Nigeria, coming in off the water . . . This is nothing, man."

Gaines just shook his head, tight-lipped and concentrating on not being sick. The loadmaster waved to Kim from off to the side in his own jumpseat, and I got each of us a helmet from the rack next to me so we could hear.

"Major, it appears that Swanson Field is clear. It's a bit short, but . . ." he shrugged.

"How short is 'a bit,' sergeant?" Kim asked.

"Three thousand feet, give or take, ma'am. About five hundred feet short of what this big bastard needs."

I shrugged at Kim's glance. "It doesn't have to take off again."

She looked thoughtful and nodded. "Tell them to land it anyway, Sergeant. And try not to kill us in the process."

The loadmaster grinned. "Yes, ma'am."

We listened to the sergeant passing along Kim's orders, and then to their back-and-forth chatter as we turned for our final approach. They seemed calm and collected. Not at all like the grunts in the back who were sweating bullets. I could feel us getting lower and lower, and for the first time in my life, I prayed.

In this case, the request was simple: *Please don't let us crash.*

"Don't worry, sirs," said the loadmaster. "We're only a couple thousand pounds over the limit." I realized that I had closed my eyes, and I opened them again, glaring at him, and he just laughed.

The landing was as rough as I could remember. We bounced once, and then I felt like I'd been slammed in the chest by a thousand-pound hammer as the pilots put on as much back-thrust as they could.

I glanced out the window and I saw trees as big around as Gaines and Junior snapping off like twigs as the huge wings of the Globemaster tore through them like so much kindling.

Not the best landing site, clearly.

Suddenly, the plane tilted forward, and I heard a massive clanging, ripping noise. We began to slide sideways and then dropped another few feet as the rear landing gear were sheared off. One of the wings must've clipped a somewhat sturdier tree—or a rock—because we were sent spinning.

Wouldn't it be a bitch to survive all of the walkers, only to die in a plane crash?

That's when the world went black.

"No time for naps now, sleepy-head," I heard an angel say.

I opened my eyes and saw Kim leaning over me, and smiled . . . right up until every bruise demanded its own individual bit of attention, and I groaned.

"I almost wish I'd died, instead," I said, struggling to get up. Kim put a shoulder under me on one side, her brother on the other, and together, we managed to get me on my feet. They held me there as the dizziness passed, and I looked around.

We were standing in the middle of the devastation left by the C-17's crash, and it was massive. At least four hundred feet long and twenty to thirty wide, the huge furrow in the earth was strewn with packaging and equipment. I winced as I saw a Stryker off to one side, an enormous dent in its side. The plane itself would never fly again, but I did a quick head count and everyone appeared to be in sight. Even the pilots.

I waved off Kim as she tried to help me walk, eliciting a snicker from Johnny, and made my way over to the two pilots, who were sitting on an upturned packing crate and being tended to by a medic. Other than cuts and bruises—and one arm in a sling—they seemed to have made it out intact.

"Thank you, gentlemen. I'm not sure anyone could have pulled that off without a hitch."

"Well, sir," said one of the men, "I think you're just about right. She's fucked, though. Pardon my French."

I laughed. "Not to worry. We weren't going anywhere in that thing ever again anyway."

"That's for damn sure."

Kim strode up and motioned for me to take a walk with her. "We didn't actually come out too bad," she said as we trudged down the gouge in the earth. "We lost some non-vital stuff, but all the important gear and equipment made it through okay."

"What about that Stryker?"

"Well, the driver says it'll work. Won't be pretty, but I told him we didn't need pretty, just functional."

"Damn right. The MTVs okay?"

"Yeah, they and the other Stryker are fine. We're almost ready to go, actually. You took kind of a nasty knock, so I wanted to let you sleep as long as I could."

"Roger that, I appreciate it."

"We took quite a bit of time off our trip by landing here. Swanson's *much* closer to the bunker. Should take us about a half day to get there."

"Excellent," I said. "Let's get to it, then."

"After you," she said, laughing. "Mary told me to let *you* take the lead occasionally."

I strode off to collect the men, grumbling as she continued to laugh behind me.

The trip to the bunker was uneventful. We didn't see any walkers, not that we'd been expecting them this far out from the city. The big doors in the mountainside rolled open for us, and the small convoy moved inside.

My first look at the bunker was a short one, as I stood next to the lead Stryker and watched the MTVs arrange themselves on the giant elevator that would take them lower into the facility. I was just losing count of their three-point turns when Kim grabbed me by the elbow.

"Let's go, soldier," she said, dragging me after her to the personnel elevator situated off to one side. I noticed Johnny following us with someone—*what's Janet Turner doing here?*—and gave him a questioning look as they entered the elevator with us.

He completely ignored me, staring straight ahead. Janet wasn't as successful. She kept darting quick glances my way and smirking fit to bust.

"Hey—" I started to say, but Kim squeezed my elbow in such a way as to make me wonder how she knew a move that caused so much pain.

One thing I remembered from every relationship I'd ever had was that there was a time to talk and a time to shut up, and this was definitely the latter. So I let her drag me down the hallway as we exited the elevator, and only started to balk when I noticed the sign next to the office she almost threw me into.

Bernard Delacroix.

Chaplain.

Junior was blocking the exit as I looked around, and if you've never seen a shit-eating grin on a big Arizona boy, it's not something to be missed.

"You knew about this, didn't you?" I whispered as I blocked out what Kim was saying to the poor surprised man behind the desk.

"Damn skippy, *bro*," Johnny said. "Orders are orders, after all."

Kim jerked my elbow again, and I faced forward.

Chaplain Delacroix was a portly gentleman, and the only living person I'd ever met who had an honest-to-goodness handlebar mustache. Even if it weren't for the name or the mustache, I would've picked him for a Louisiana boy the second he opened his mouth.

"This is highly irregular, Miss . . ."

"Barnes. Kimberly Barnes."

"Ms. Barnes. *Highly* irregular." I swear, he actually puffed out his cheeks. "That said, these ain't exactly 'regular' times, neither, so I reckon we better all make do with what we got, and move on from there." He turned to me and held out a Bible.

"We'll do this all proper like later, but the young miss here seems to be in a rather large hurry, young man. So if you'll put your hand on the good book there . . ."

I don't really remember the rest of the ceremony, if you can call it that. I know there was some speechifying, some swearing—the good kind, mostly—and more than a few tears.

Oh, and one more thing.

"I now pronounce you husband and wife. You may kiss the bride."

Boy, did I ever.

I looked at my new wife, marveling at how beautiful she was. "Hello, Mrs. Blake."

She smiled and shook her head, tears scattering. "Hello, Mr. Barnes."

We all laughed. "We'll have to talk about that, I guess," I said, laughing too. Then I sobered, and held her hands. "For Tom."

"And Rebecca. And Eric," she said, causing my heart to skip a beat or six.

"And Rachel," said Gaines softly as he put a hand on each of our shoulders.

"And for Gordon," said Janet Turner, and I caught the tear in her eye.

"For everyone," I said, smiling at her.

Even though we'd lost so very, very many, and more than a few that were close to us, when I looked into Kim's eyes, I knew that this was the hope for the future.

If we could still find some small bit of happiness, some small tiny bit of joy, despite all the misery and pain, then we would live on. We would continue, and eventually, come back.

I looked around at the others, and saw that they understood, too. That's when the rest of 1st Team broke into the poor chaplain's office and began congratulating us, causing the befuddled Southern gentleman to summarily dismiss us from his presence. In a nice way, of course.

That's ok. I looked at Kim. *I have everything I need right here.*

The next twenty years would be hard, but together we could get through them. We had to. For Tom, and Rachel and everyone else who hadn't made it. It was up to us now, and, as I looked at Kim, I could see the same determination in her eyes.

It wasn't over. Not by a long shot. As long as one of us lived, we would fight. Until every last one of them was dead, or we found a cure.

I drew Kim aside and held her close. "So, kids, huh?"

She smiled that megawatt smile at me. "Yeah."

"I think I can handle that."

"Good, Mr. Blake. Very, very good."

Epilogue

AEGIS BUNKER ONE

THE VIEW FROM THIS VANTAGE point always amazed me. This observation tower—built specifically to keep an eye on the surrounding area with access only to and from the bunker—was very, *very* high. Yet it still boggled the mind how much farther behind me the mountain—scratch that, the *volcano* —rose.

I turned to take in the vast western face of Mount Rainier, and marveled that AEGIS had been able to organize the preparation of such a massive facility in so short a time.

At this rarified height, I could see details I normally wouldn't be able to make out in the soft evening light without high-powered binoculars. Yet, still, a haze of smoke drifted across my view, and I turned back, sighing.

Tacoma was gone, destroyed in a blaze started not by the infected or those who had turned, but by those who merely *thought* that the infection had spread that far. What had been a few controlled blazes to destroy the dead and soon-to-be-undead were pushed together by unseasonable winds into a firestorm that consumed Tacoma and nearly took Seattle, too.

That the fire had been held back at all was a testament to the brave efforts of large groups of civilians and military. They had destroyed most of the roads, cut down or destroyed flammable objects in the fire's path and dumped load after load of chemicals and water onto the flames.

Their efforts had been successful, too. Successful enough to give those men and women time to die as the infection raging through

Seattle finally caught up to them. *Irony, you are a fickle bitch.* Only smoke remained of what had once been Seattle's principal suburb. Seattle, of course, was also destroyed, but in a very different fashion.

From here it almost looks normal. I guess distance really does provide a unique perspective.

The walkers had hit hardest in the Industrial District, arriving there in droves on commercial ships, cruise liners and a myriad of other boats. Those who saw signs of infection responded by crowding into the city's hospitals and care facilities—only making the problems worse, of course.

They never had a chance, not in a city like that.

I turned to Kimberly, who stood next to me, sharing what would most likely be our last view of the surface for quite some time. She shivered, and I saw a tear slip down her cheek as she turned to lean into me. I held her as we both watched the end of the world we had known. A low rumble vibrated through the tower and Kim looked up at me.

I pointed far, far below us and we could just make out the last of the giant bay doors slowly closing, the AEGIS logo clear and bright on its surface. No more hiding for us. The door's thick steel and concrete construction looked like tissue paper from this height, but it would withstand just about anything anyone could throw at it.

As I glanced down, I saw again the band-aid on the inside of my elbow. Gardner's final ploy—that I was a non-infectious carrier of the prion disease—still seemed ludicrous, but common sense had demanded that I do something about it. I'd contacted Mary Maxwell née Adamsdóttir at Bunker Seven in New Mexico, where all the blood samples had been taken.

She said that the results of her initial look were inconclusive, but, just in case, she wanted another sample. I wasn't sure which I hoped for more—the possibility of a cure or the relief that I wasn't going to be a scientific guinea pig for the next twenty years.

The light was almost gone now, as if the sun knew that we would soon be leaving. We few remnants of the six billion living, working, playing people that had once populated our world. We would continue to live and work and play, but we would do it underground, secure and safe in preparation for the day when we could return. A hundred thousand of us would survive, here in the US. Who knew how many elsewhere.

As the last few rays of sunlight dimmed and went out, I said once more the blessing I had learned so long ago, that had seen me through so much:

> *May the road rise up to meet you.*
> *May the wind be always at your back.*
> *May the sun shine warm upon your face*
> *and may the rains fall soft upon your fields.*
> *And until we meet again,*
> *may God hold you in the hollow of His hand.*

As I murmured these words once more, I heard my new wife repeating them with me. I took one last look at the world we had known, the world that was ending, then looked down and touched Kim's face as I looked into her eyes. She managed a sad smile, and we turned and strode into the elevator.

The sun had set on this chapter of the story that was humanity, but, one day, we would begin a new one.

We will see the sun dawn once more upon our world.

We will return.

Afterword*

THANKS ARE DUE TO A great many people for this, my first novel.

First and foremost, to my mother, father, and brother. They always believed that I was meant to write, and helped me see that, too—thank you so much for your support. And to my grandmother Margie, who was always my biggest fan.

Second, to the father of modern zombie myth and legend, Mr. George A. Romero, without whom this book—and many others—would hardly have been possible.

To my editor Hilary, without whom you would have all read a great many more typos, grammar errors and punctuation mistakes.

To all the friends who took their time to not only listen to all my crazy zombie ravings but also to critique, provide invaluable research assistance, and just be there when the writing got in the way of the story, and to those who, in their own way, inspired characters or other parts of the story.

In no particular order, thanks to Raissa, Scott W., Cindy, Kelly, Dennis, Todd, Kevin and Jennifer. Y'all have dibs on bunker space when it all goes to Hell.

To Max Brooks, whose 'novel' ideas about the writing of zombie fiction—namely *The Zombie Survival Guide* and *World War Z*—provided me with much help, organization of my ideas, and general inspiration.

To all those who provided much-needed technical assistance and vetting of the dialogue and terminology, especially that of the military units: thanks to Bart, Colin, Mike, Josh, Keegan, Tyson and Scott W.

To all my beta readers, both formal and not, because hardly anyone ever thanks them, and though I disagree with them occasionally, I still appreciate their work on my behalf.

To the cities of Georgetown, Colorado (inspiration for the fictional city of Fall Creek); Farmington, Maine; Houston, Texas; Tacoma and Seattle, Washington; Rawlins and Laramie, Wyoming and so many others. Also, to the real places in those cities that inspired my fictional locations.

To the men and women of the United States Armed Forces, for graciously lending me their personnel and facilities, though they didn't know it, and for valiantly protecting all the freedoms and liberties that so many of us take for granted.

— **Houston, 2011**

* THE THIRD EDITION

IT'S BEEN FOURTEEN YEARS NOW since I wrote the Afterword above. So much has changed for me, both professionally and personally. I've moved, found the love of my life, and importantly, become a *much* better writer.

So when it came time to revamp the covers for The Dying of the Light, it occurred to me that I could take all that I've learned about design and publishing in that time and give the interiors a good once-over as well. I mean, I did the original layouts in Word!

Little did I know . . .

The hardest part of laying out a new edition of this novel wasn't the minutiae of layouts like tracking or leading settings or horizontal scaling. No, the *hardest* part was actually re-reading the story as I went along and not editing the hell out of my younger self's work.

I've fixed typos and egregious errors, but the text is 99% the same as it was, and let me tell you, in some spots I was physically ill reading my own writing.

(This is what it's like to be a writer, and hey, you don't even have to wait fourteen years! It happens with Every. Single. Book.)

I'm still proud of the book, still happy I finished it, but I've come a long way, and I can't wait for you to read what I come up with next. Stick with me, folks. There's a lot more to come. Allons-y!

Interesting Links

Prion Disease:

About Prion Diseases. CDC. https://www.cdc.gov/prions/about/

Prion: http://en.wikipedia.org/wiki/Prion

BSE (Mad Cow disease): http://en.wikipedia.org/wiki/Transmissible_spongiform_encephalopathy

Prion disease can spread through air. MacKenzie, *New Scientist.* http://www.newscientist.com/article/dn19971-prion-disease-can-spread-through-air.html

Zombie Ants:

Zombie Ants Controlled by Fungus. http://www.livescience.com/5631-zombie-ants-controlled-fungus.html

Mind control by parasites. Christensen, *Live Science.* http://www.livescience.com/7019-mind-control-parasites.html

Zombie History:

Zombie: http://en.wikipedia.org/wiki/Zombie

Zombie Walks: http://en.wikipedia.org/wiki/Zombie_walk

About the Author

Jason Kristopher is the award-winning author terrifying readers with zombies in **The Dying of the Light**, thrilling them with 1940s noir in ***Loco Moco***, and harrowing them with boy-meets-gryphon-meets-robot adventure in ***When Iron Wakes***. With the love of his life and the dog that rescued him by his side, he plots his next traumatizing stories from Florida beaches.

Read more of Jason's work on Patreon or in his monthly newsletter. Patrons and newsletter readers receive lots of ongoing benefits, including in-progress snippets, exclusive news and announcements, free ebooks, Zoom AMAs, and more!

Connect with Jason

Patreon

patreon.com/TheFireinourHeads

The Fire in our Heads (newsletter)

https://BookHip.com/GTSBNNH

Facebook

facebook.com/Author.JasonKristopher

Web

jasonkristopher.com

MORE FROM JASON KRISTOPHER

books2read.com/dying2

Print | eBook | Audio

INTERVAL

The Dying of the Light #2

Becoming a zombie was much more painful than he had expected.

In a world devoured by chaos, survival hangs by a thread. Amidst the undead's onslaught, hope flickers dim. But beyond the horrors of the walkers lies an even graver threat.

Massive bunkers crumble under unyielding assault, plunging into monstrous darkness. Across icy wastes, stranded scientists fight starvation's cold grip.

Can David Blake and the remnants of AEGIS rescue the salvation-bearing scientist from the frigid grip of Antarctica, or will humanity succumb to the merciless jaws of extinction?

books2read.com/dying3

Print | eBook

BEGINNING

The Dying of the Light #3

He awoke and, for the first time in twenty-five years, remembered who he was.

Twenty years after Z-Day, humanity's remnants prepare to reclaim the surface from underground bunkers. But as survivors venture upward, they discover a chilling truth: the world above has changed in ways no one anticipated.

When a new threat emerges that could trigger a second Z-Day, Eden Blake and the remaining heroes of AEGIS must make their final stand. In this race against extinction, the greatest enemy may not be the undead after all.

books2read.com/dying4

eBook

THE WALKER CHRONICLES

Tales from The Dying of the Light

In a world where the dead hunger for the living, these classified tales reveal humanity's darkest hours and unexpected heroes. From remote wilderness to secret labs, follow the warriors who faced the walker threat before the world knew its name. Some stories should remain buried—but truth, like the dead, always rises.

The Walker Chronicles expands the universe of **The Dying of the Light** trilogy, uncovering the untold history of humanity's fight against the walking dead. These essential stories reveal the covert battles that raged for decades before Z-Day changed everything.

books2read.com/fancy

Print | eBook

A FANCY DINNER PARTY

Foreword by NYT Bestseller Jonathan Maberry

What's on the menu tonight? Something unexpected. Something forbidden.

Twelve deliciously disturbing tales await your consumption in this horror anthology where dinner becomes deadly and appetite turns sinister. From Victorian steam tunnels harboring unspeakable entities to futuristic alien feasts with humanity on the menu, these stories explore the darkest corners of hunger and desire.

Pull up a chair, but remember: at this table, you might find yourself on the wrong side of the menu.

More Tales to Sink Your Teeth Into

books2read.com/addleton

Print | eBook

Addleton Heights

With a name like Thorogood Kipsey, you might think I got into fights as a boy. You'd be right.

New Year's Eve 1901: Six hundred feet above the Atlantic Ocean, the platform city of Addleton Heights balances on massive, soot-covered stilts. A grisly double murder interrupts a party in the floating mansion of the city's most powerful man, and for reasons unknown, he coerces detective-for-hire T.H. Kipsey into taking the enigmatic case.

Join Kip as he races against time to unravel the clues that will thrust him across the city, up to the clouds, and into the depths beneath Addleton Heights.

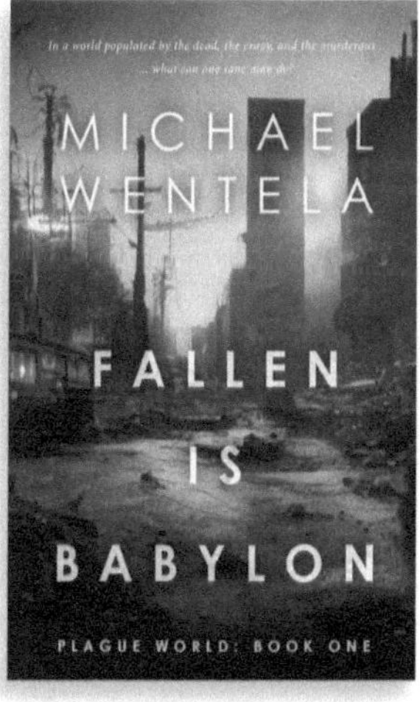

books2read.com/plague1

Print | eBook

Fallen is Babylon

The stench of death no longer permeated and fouled the air, but the city was still dead.

In the haunting aftermath of civilization's collapse, Vann Arnett stands alone—the last sane man in a world consumed by plague and stalked by the unhinged and murderous.

When mysterious outsiders shatter his carefully constructed survival routine, Vann must fight not just to stay alive, but to maintain his humanity in an apocalyptic nightmare where sanity is the ultimate weapon.

Grey Gecko Press

Thank you for purchasing this book from Grey Gecko Press, an independent publishing company that focuses on new and emerging authors, bringing readers the best in fiction and nonfiction at reasonable prices in all formats.

With books in nearly every genre of fiction and nonfiction (Aspergers to zombies!), there's something for everyone, and you can be sure that buying books from us leads directly to the support of independent authors.

Visit our website to purchase our titles, including special and autographed editions, and pre-order upcoming books at a discount.

Web: www.greygeckopress.com

Facebook: facebook.com/GreyGeckoPress

Support Indie Authors & Small Press

If you liked this book, please take a few moments to leave a review on your favorite website, even if it's only a line or two. Reviews make all the difference to indie authors and are one of the best ways you can help support our work. Reviews help us to earn more readers just like you and keep publishing great indie books!

Plus, get any other Grey Gecko ebook FREE with your review!

http://greygeckopress.com/free-books/